THE FAME GAME

CHARLES CASILLO

THE

a novel

Fame

GAME

alyson books
NEW YORK

Manufactured in THE UNITED STATES OF AMERICA.

Published by ALYSON BOOKS,
245 WEST 17TH STREET,
NEW YORK, NY 10011.

Distribution in the United Kingdom BY
TURNAROUND PUBLISHER SERVICES LTD.,
UNIT 3, OLYMPIA TRADING ESTATE, COBURG ROAD,
WOOD GREEN, LONDON N22 6TZ ENGLAND.

First trade paperback edition SEPTEMBER 2007
PREVIOUSLY PUBLISHED IN A HARDCOVER EDITION

06   07   08   09   10   a   10   9   8   7   6   5   4   3   2   1

ISBN 1-59350-043-2
ISBN-13 978-1-59350-043-6

LIBRARY OF CONGRESS CATALOGUING-IN-PUBLICATION DATA IS ON FILE.

Cover design by VICTOR MINGOVITS.
Book design by VICTOR MINGOVITS.
Author photograph by JEN MCDONALD.

For my parents, Gloria and Ralph

Prologue

DID YOU EVER love someone so much that you would kill for her? I did. With her there was a draw, a pull, a magnetic something I couldn't explain and couldn't resist. Was it because she was so incredibly beautiful that I found her so fascinating, I wonder? Would she have had the same hold on me if even just the promise of seeing her didn't color my mood for days? If the look in her eyes didn't melt me every single time? If I didn't get a hard-on each time I got a whiff of her magnificent hair?

You find her fascinating now—hypocrite—because she is famous. The model! The actress! But there was an anonymous period in her life, during the time that I knew her, when she was consumed with a longing to be noticed, to be known. And it was that longing that made her want to kill. And made me kill for her.

Now she is famous and a woman is dead. Carla Christaldi, the director's daughter, has been dead for nearly a year now, and you may think you know the story behind it, but you do not. Oh you've read about it in the papers, gossiped about the latest "revelations" in the tabloids, watched the highly rated *"E!" True Hollywood Story* about her life and death—but none of it is true.

The actress and I killed Carla.

And now I sit here in my seedy little room—where I have lived for more than ten years—determined to write down the entire story, wondering if it will change my life. Which is something that I have been trying to do for longer than I care to admit, or remember for that matter. And here I am, a man who has not made it, writing about a girl who has. A girl I knew and possibly loved. (Love? In truth I don't know if it really was love, not having anything to compare it to. Did I love her? Or did I want to *be* her, as some have suggested.) And in that way, by writing about her, I am using her. Like so many people are doing these days, right? But so what? She always wanted to be used. Still . . . still, I feel like a fucking leech. But I have to do it, man. The only thing I have to sell, all I have to offer you, is the truth. And I'm losing my looks and wondering what to do next. So I'm going to tell it—and I do want you to like me.

Lately I've been finding that the different hours of the night bring me different moods. It's early evening now, a time when it's still possible for me to feel hopeful. Usually a bit later, some time in the middle of the night, regrets fill up in me like rancid syrup—lost time, dying dreams—and I have to take something, a drink or a pill, to try and coax myself into sleep. Tonight I plan to be writing through it all. No pills. No booze. So by the time this night, which started out with hope, is turning into an angry, hopeless dawn, I will have told you our story. All of it. Exactly as it happened. And as I watch the morning sun pushing away the last remnants of darkness, as always, I will be holding my head in my hands in agony. Not for the woman I killed—for the woman I lost.

1.

THIS IS NOT a love story, as I would have you believe. It's a story about loneliness. And about what loneliness can do. And about where loneliness can lead.

I met Mikki Britten—the model, the actress—a few years back. (By now everyone knows the name is pronounced Mickie. There was a time some people called her Mikey, but she never corrected them. Her real name was Michelle, but she wanted to be called anything but that.)

There had been a resurgence of club parties; they were trying to make Manhattan feel like the old days, the days of sex, glamour, drugs, and Studio 54. The days before my time. Before everyone's time. No one seemed to care, though. There was nothing to compare it to except legend. These parties mixed celebrities, porn stars, crystal addicts, models, paroled murderers, transvestites, executives, and so on.

In gray, desolate areas you would see black stretch limos line up in front of some renovated building, in a neighborhood that a couple of years before had been a wasteland and now was prime real estate. Everything in Manhattan was turning into prime real estate; hell, even Harlem was on the rise.

It was at one of these parties that I, Mario DeMarco, met Mikki Britten. Let me state here and now at the beginning that we were never lovers; I never slept with her. I could have. I thought I wanted to. But I didn't—a decision that, to this day, baffles me. I can't understand why we never ended up in bed together. She gave the signal. But I let it pass. Maybe it was because my experiences before her had been with other men. Maybe because I sensed that she could really fall for me. I loved her. She deserved better.

I was a hustler, a working boy, a male prostitute. It wasn't one of my ambitions; I, too, wanted to be successful. And so, on certain nights, I hung out in elegant East Side bars hoping that an uptown aura would rub off on my downtown persona. What I did find were a lot of older gentleman willing to give me substantial sums of money for my . . . favors. Problem was, they rarely wanted to see me in the morning. Ah, life. The truth is I've never been ugly. I say this without guile, without conceit. I have a certain amount of beauty that I don't see in myself most of the time but others seem to recognize, which is no small gift, but really, not enough.

Most hustlers, I find, are not likable in the real world, as real people. Prostitution for them is not about money. It's about narcissism. Being paid to have sex nourishes their already enormous egos, making them feel they've accomplished something marvelous. It gives them a feeling of superiority, and they have an undeserved snobbishness just because youth gives them a temporary advantage over older men. Although to most men, they're really only slightly more valuable than a porno magazine and a box of tissues. I always say that it's not a compliment to be nothing more than a temporary receptacle for some horny guy's pent up hormones. But hustlers peacock around as if they've discovered the cure for cancer or created an undisputed masterpiece.

I don't want you to think of me this way. I hate what I do. I hate taking money. I never feel I'm worth it. And I want everyone to like me for me. So if it will make you like me more, let me tell you with total truthfulness: My looks have done nothing for me, have gotten me nowhere, and there are always many people far better looking, with better bodies than me at a party or a club. Physical beauty is not elusive in New York.

I do, however, have a certain talent that rarely fails me—I can make people want to go to bed with me. I can turn this quality on, as if by a switch that sets off some inner adjustment, and before I know it eyes are focused on my crotch. I can switch this quality off, too, if I choose not to use it. It's like some people can be funny, some imposing, some charming, some nurturing. I'm beddable. So I figured at an early age, with no education, no resources, and no rich daddy, that I had better use what I have.

"Get to the part about Mikki!" I can hear you screaming at me. You can't get enough info about her! Well, let me tell you something, you don't know her like I do. Most people know only the girl the newspapers and magazines and the blogs and entertainment television shows created and the image she herself built, capitalizing on everything said about her. The media is responsible for the Mikki Britten the world worships today. She's a fucking walking, talking press release. A few years ago, she wasn't even sure who she was herself.

See? She was happy to mold herself into what the general public wanted. Actually, I'm probably one of the few people who really knows the girl. There's a real person behind the sexual heroine—part little girl lost, part calculating slut. She always said I was the male version of her. But fame hasn't made her a different person, and that's what people don't understand. She's a human being, same as before. She eats. She sleeps. She shits. Just like the rest of us. What's with this "goddess" business? I don't know what her reasons are but, it hurts me now that she won't take my calls. Maybe she feels that by not dealing with me her past will fade away. Guess again, Mikki. That terrible thing we did—together—is an indelible part of our history!

You may wonder how I know so much about her. You must understand that we were great friends. We really were very much alike, and we often spoke many hours each week, detailing our progress, describing which parties we attended, who was there, what we were doing, who we were doing it with.

When Mikki was at her rope's end—betrayed, used, exhausted, and alone—it was me she turned to. I was the one person she could trust. It was me she asked to help plot the murder of Carla Christaldi.

So as you read this story don't distract yourself by saying to yourself, "How could he possibly know that? He wouldn't know what she was thinking. He's playing God!" Believe me, friend. I know. I know what she was thinking. She told me. She was in my pocket. She was in my ears. She was in my eyes.

And just in case there was anything left that I didn't know she gave me her most private thoughts. Just before she made it, Mikki entrusted all her diaries, letters, and notebooks to me. It was as if she knew something was going to happen. "If anything ever happens to me, do something with them," she said dramatically. "That way my name will live on." She saw herself as a modern-day Anne Frank. And if worse came to worst, she'd become famous after she was dead. Am I playing God? Buddy, when it comes to this story, I *am* fucking God.

But I wanted to tell you about the night we met. It was a while ago, can't remember the exact date—sometimes it seems like yesterday, sometimes a hundred years ago. It was at a club on Little West 12th Street, the Meatpacking District. A club that was the hot new spot had just opened. I remember that evening very well—a party was being thrown for Madonna. She had a new movie opening up, a lame comedy, which was getting plenty of hype and gleefully bad word of mouth, and the party was a big promotional kind of event designed to once again try to turn her from an aging pop legend to a full-fledged movie actress. Would she or wouldn't she show up?

I am not one of those faggots, or should I say I am not one of *all* the faggots, who worships at the Madonna altar. Guys who wait Breathless Mahoney for her next uneven album and then babble endlessly, "Brilliant! Controversial! Deep!"

I'm not saying this to be a judgmental dick, although I can, of course, be one. I'm only trying to explain . . . describe . . . illustrate how I never felt I belonged.

This was the kind of party that everyone wanted to attend, but very few obtained invitations to. People came by bridge, tunnel, and subway to line up outside the velvet ropes, hoping to be let in. Talk about degrading. There was a crowd of people out front; each person would have gladly donated several pints of blood to gain entrance.

How did I get in without an invitation? A little bit of luck. A little bit of flirting. A little bit of looking darkly exotic and intimidating in a magnificent ripped, red silk shirt I had bought at a thrift shop. It was flimsy and sexy and practically coming apart—held together by a few threads, which added to its appeal. I thought it would bring me luck. I thought it looked good.

"Who are you?" one of the doormen asked. I realized he thought I was some famous actor he simply couldn't place. That happens sometimes. I just looked at him enigmatically with a lopsided grin. (I was slightly drunk by then.) He whisked me past the crowd and lifted the velvet rope. Doormen make me laugh. They're so insecure and insignificant in their real lives that they compensate by trying to exert power at the entrance to a club. Failed St. Peters at the gate, they pick and choose who has the right to enter Paradise.

I walked through the entrance only to be bowled over by a tidal wave of buzzed hair and tattoos. I remember it as one of the loneliest nights of my life. I had never adopted the right attitude to fit in with this type of crowd and was lost in a maze of carefully styled fame leeches. All of them were on the same desperate hunt for publicity and notoriety as Mikki and myself.

Have you ever been to one of these New York success parties? Where everyone is so young and gorgeously put together—buffed, plucked, and spray-tanned—that you have to wonder where the time and money comes from for the upkeep? All those porcelain veneers! You can forget about meeting these people. They will not let you in. They will not acknowledge your existence. To them there are only two kinds of people, those who can further their careers and those who cannot. Being one who could not, I was ignored.

I recall so well wandering around the huge, multiroomed club, where waitresses dressed like mutant Madonnas served twenty-dollar drinks, and everyone gladly plunked down the money, thinking that being there made them a celebrity, while their ravenous, starved eyes sought out fame. Searching, searching, searching for a real celebrity, for someone real they could sink their veneers into.

Even though the party was supposedly private, there was another party, even more exclusive, being held in some VIP room. I stood at the doorway looking in. The burly guard at the entrance to this world would not allow me to enter. All the important doors were always closed to me. I was a part of the mediocrity set—the deceived, paying public. The people who could be easily fooled into believing the hype. The people whose stupidity financed the lavish lifestyle of the chosen few.

Still, I was hoping to catch some flashy creature's eye so that I'd have someone to share it all with. In spite of my loneliness, I was awed and excited. I wished I were there with someone. Someone I could separate from, then run into a little while later, to compare notes. It was scary being alone. But all of my efforts to talk to someone ran into a brick wall. *See them going out of their way to ignore me? See them blowing smoke in my face?*

People are so careful not to make too much eye contact, since they want to convey that they are better than you, more desirable than you. Even if one of them locked stares with me for a split second, checking me out, they quickly darted their attention back to whomever they were in conversation with, fearful that others might think that they found someone in my league attractive. They glanced at me and then flamboyantly ignored me. That was a time in my life when a "hello" would have meant so much. *If I ever become famous, God,* I said to God, *please don't let me become like that. Please let me always be able to recognize the humanity in others.*

But they judged me as a person with no fame, no money, no pull, and no connections. The name of the game is networking, my dears. In reality none of these fame leeches is important or happy or really much of anything. And they never will be. But they know how to pretend to be during the course of the party. Everyone with a camera is a photographer. Everyone with a headshot is an actor. Everyone with a keyboard is a writer. Everyone who has been photographed is a model. Everyone with an idea is a screenwriter. These are things that have taken me years to discover, and I share them now with you at no extra cost.

I was sitting in an out-of-the-way corner on a carpeted floor beneath a long staircase, each step lit up with colorful lights, making it look like the stairs leading to an alien spacecraft. If anyone noticed me sitting there, I was instantly dismissed with a look that said, "a nobody," so I receded into my own elaborate dream world. Suddenly I became aware of a pair of perfectly shaped female legs standing directly in front of me.

"Hmmm," she said. "Are you very disappointed with life?"

How the fuck did she know? "Sometimes," I said, looking up. She was wearing white. Mikki, I was to learn, often wore white.

"Me, too," she smiled. "But there's no use crying over it, buddy boy. No one will hear you. See? Look around. There's no red roses— no violins."

"Cut," I said impulsively, "end of scene." She was ironic and bitter and blasé. I liked her. "My name is Mario," I blurted. "And yours?"

"Mikki."

Her voice was lazy and low; it affected me like a long, warm embrace. I could tell she was also looking for someone to talk to.

"Did you ever walk around all day on the verge of tears?" she asked, sitting down next to me.

"Yes," I answered truthfully, "all the time." I had been on the verge of tears all that day, although now I couldn't remember the reason for it. I laughed, shit-faced by this time (all night I had been pushing my way up to the amazingly crowded bar, grabbing a handful of tips spread out over the bar top, ordering another drink, then tipping big with the bartender's own money).

I was surprised that she was drinking beer from the bottle. I liked the idea that she was presumptuous enough to sit down next to me without being asked. Later I discovered that that wasn't like her at all. We were just meant to meet: We were both ambitious and were working toward being something; we both talked to God; we were both ready to admit loneliness.

There was something about her—a "what will she do next?" quality. She was a little unsteady. A little out of control. As a result every move she made was different and exciting. She would look me straight in the eye, sure of her sexual magnetism, an expression that was half smile, half pout. But in the next sentence she would become vulnerable, clinging to me for approval, as if to ask if what she said was right. Her voice, too, was a provocative mixture of the little girl and the world-weary woman. Soft and girlish, but each sentence ending in a husky whisper. It made me wonder which was the act and which was the girl, or if she was real and didn't have an act yet.

Her hair was incredibly full, blonde, and wild. Sometimes she'd sweep it back with her hand, annoyed with it being in her face, and it would automatically fall into a new style, more lustrous and alive than before. Her lips were also full, almost too full, and beautifully shaped. But it was her eyes that really drew me into her. They were big and blue—but dark blue, like rare exotic stones that could change color with the surroundings. They hit you immediately because of the contrast with the paleness of her skin and hair. Under the club's lights I could sense the loneliness in those eyes. I think that she could recognize the isolation in my laughter. She saw that I was an outsider—and that drew me to her.

She asked me if I had met Madonna yet, and now we both laughed. Madonna! What an icon. Meeting *her* that night was as easy as flying to the moon without a rocket ship. I wondered what it was like to be Madonna. Fame. Once she had wanted it as badly as we did; once, many years ago, even she was tormented with the feeling that she might not make it.

"She knows what it is to sleep now," Mikki said, as if I had posed the question out loud (which I had not). "She doesn't wake up at three in the morning, crying, with her heart racing, unable to catch her breath."

Mikki and I both understood, without really saying it, that we both hoped to be in that very same position some day.

2.

ENTER GOD.

We are all pawns in life that other people will try to use, and maneuver, and capture, Mikki Britten had written in her diary earlier that evening.

Mikki began her frantic quest for fame as soon as she left her adoptive parents' house in Queens, New York, and moved into her own apartment, also in Queens but far enough away so that she wouldn't have to worry about running into them. "They're not my real parents," she would say to anyone who asked.

All she had going for her, all that might be her ticket to a new life, was her beauty—but it was significant, and if she worked quickly, there was still time for her to cash in on it. Her first plan, and it had been in the works for a long time, was to model by day and, with luck, be discovered at night in Manhattan's nightclub scene by an admiring casting agent or producer.

But she was having trouble breaking into the business. As the days ticked off the time left to her looks, she watched television and compared herself to models on runways or actresses in soap operas or, worst of all, girls with inflated boob-jobs who had mastered being a bitch or crying out a sob story on reality television shows.

Mikki was making her living mostly by doing what is known as promotional modeling. That means she spent many days promoting a new perfume in department stores by spraying cowering women. Or demonstrating a new hair removal device or hand moisturizer—any new product that a pretty girl might help legitimize. It was the very lowest form of modeling, filled with so-so girls with nothing going for them other than decent makeup and dreams.

Before the Madonna party, she had been on a modeling interview at the prestigious Payne Models agency. She had been recommended for the interview by another model, a real model, what is called a "supermodel"—the exotic Jana Janelow. Jana Janelow had a semi-crush on Mikki. Not really a crush, more of a fondness; she liked to play with Mikki the way someone might pick up a small furry animal in a pet store, coo over it for a few minutes, then put it back in its pen, clicking her tongue, hoping someone will eventually adopt it.

When shopping in high-end stores, Jana would always stop to talk to Mikki, who usually would mechanically be handing out some sort of sample promotion. Mikki was always giving Jana dozens of expensive skin lotions and eye creams for free, even though Jana could well afford her own products.

Models don't usually do favors for each other, particularly for women as extraordinary as Mikki Britten. There was always the chance that this newer model would climb up the ladder and become more successful. God forbid! Friends want their friends to do well, but *never* better than themselves. But Jana, in a generous mood, gave Mikki the name of her contact at Payne Models; it was actually the agency's owner, Laird Payne. Jana didn't feel threatened giving out a real and important contact, since there was no chance of Jana and Mikki ever being in competition—Jana was nearly six feet tall, Asian, with long black hair. Mikki was fair all over and petite, with blue eyes.

"Laird Payne is very particular about who he signs," Jana explained patiently, "but who knows? Maybe he'll see something in you."

"Oh, and by the way, baby," she added, "if things don't work out at Payne models, my ex-husband . . . you know, Justin Landis? . . . is starting up his own agency. It's not in the papers yet, but it's going to be big. Huge. He's calling it EYE Management. He's got the eyes for beauty. And yous got the beautiful eyes. I could get you an interview there, too."

Mikki could hardly believe it. New York. The modeling world.

Nobody gave a shit about anyone. And here Jana Janelow was offering two major contacts—one being her ex-husband. Justin Landis had been one of the hottest photographers in the business. Now she'd have a chance to meet with him at his brand-new agency in addition to interviewing with Payne Models.

"I'd switch over to EYE myself," Jana said, "but working with my ex again would be just um . . . um . . . "

"Too weird?" Mikki said, finishing her sentence.

"I love him. Don't get me wrong. But, baby, you have no idea. So see how it goes at Payne first. If it doesn't work out, I'll get you in to see Justin—he's sweet."

———

UNFORTUNATELY, THE OWNER of Payne Models, Laird Payne, a persnickety man in his late forties, was having a bad day when Mikki arrived at his office for their scheduled appointment in the late afternoon. (Laird's current lover, a seventeen-year-old wannabe male model, had recently dumped him after a big-time Hollywood movie producer had seen him at a party and snatched him up.)

"I really don't know why Jana sent you to me," Laird told Mikki as he flipped through her modeling portfolio.

"I thought . . . I think she thought . . . "

"Listen, I am a busy man and you are wasting my time. How old are you?"

"I'm nineteen," Mikki lied. "Jana thought that you might be interested in signing me."

Laird knew that the woman was beautiful and he saw her potential as a commodity. Yes, he did see something in her. But he specifically chose to ignore it. His boyfriend was on his way to Hawaii right now with one of the most powerful men in Hollywood and this girl was annoying him with her sculptured cheekbones, voluptuous lips, and remarkable eyes. Why didn't she stop staring at him? He despised beauty combined with complexity. Beauty, he thought, should be shallow, controllable.

"And you come to the interview dressed like that?" Laird snarled. "You look like a hooker."

Mikki was wounded. She had carefully chosen the little black skirt and calf-high boots, which were now being worn on the runways. It was a popular look. Perhaps he wanted to see the girls very "Plain Jane" so he could imagine what they would look like on different catwalks? Oh, why couldn't she get it right? She said nothing and hoped her silence conveyed the feeling of humility, that she was contrite for her fashion faux pas. She wanted him to know that he was the boss, that she was willing to agree with whatever he said. To do whatever he wanted—just for a chance.

He finished flipping through her book and snapped it shut with a slap. "Really, baby, I don't know why you think you could be a model," he told her, taking a sip from his bottled water. He picked up her headshot and stared at it contemptuously, without bothering to look at the resume attached to the back. "You're just a funny-looking girl with a character kind of face—and we don't use character models here. Maybe you should take some comedy acting classes and try to do some television commercials."

Mikki had taken acting classes but she was here for a modeling contract. Commercials would be great, but not as a "funny face"— for fashion and beauty. She felt the tears spring to her eyes. Nothing new there, she was often on the brink of tears—modeling and acting set you up for that—but this man was exceptionally cruel. If that was the way he truly felt about her, why couldn't he tell her in a way that conveyed more human kindness? She knew that not everyone in the world would find her beautiful. She could accept that. Why not just be nice about it?

For the record, Laird Payne was not a handsome man. His bugged eyes, hooked nose, high arched eyebrows, and jittery demeanor gave him the appearance of a particularly haughty owl in a perpetual state of surprise. He worked out regularly, as he was expected to in his profession, but he never seemed to be able to add brawn to his tall, skinny body, and he was little more than cartilage and bone.

Inside his office he ruled supreme. In everyday life he had no power. In Manhattan's trendy gay bars he was continuously ignored by the male beauties he desired—until, of course, they discovered that he was the owner of a top modeling agency. Then they were interested. But his looks, his personality, his love for opera and great literature meant nothing to anyone. That was frustrating. No one cared who he truly was. In the eyes of the physically beautiful, he was nothing but undesirable, and he knew that.

More often than not Laird ended up buying a young boy's favors for the night—and then, revealing his identity, he would hook them for a few months, dangling the hopes of a modeling contract in front of them like a tender scrap of filet mignon. He would never really share his contacts. He would never actually give the boy a modeling career. Ha! Why should he? The instant the kid's career was on the rise, Laird would be left eating dust. Not even a thank-you. So eventually the boy would grow tired of waiting and start looking for his career jump-start elsewhere, leaving Laird to start his frustrating hunt all over again.

But at Payne Models he was a king. He had the ability to make or break a person's career. To make a person feel elation or despair. How exquisite power felt! How delicious to be able to reject people who had more beauty, personality, and charisma than he could ever hope to possess.

Mikki was so injured by the meeting that she was on the verge of tears as she took the subway home and almost didn't make it to the party. *But,* she thought, *maybe this will be the night I meet someone who recognizes my value and will sweep me away from all of this.* So she pulled up just enough energy to redo her makeup, change her clothes, and take the subway back to Manhattan to the Madonna party.

She regretted it immediately.

As with most club parties, there were so many standouts that it was easy for her to be swallowed up by the crowd, to blend into the background of the glamorous freaks. Everyone wanted to be discovered by someone, and they all found things about themselves to exploit. High hair. A huge chest. Obscene clothes. *See me! See me!* their personalities screamed. *Bullshit! Bullshit!* she wanted to scream back. It was in her nature to be shy and self-conscious and unsure. Yet there were a good number of people checking her out. And then the quick head flick—which reassured her she was beautiful.

She had been walking around for an hour. *What a mistake to come out*, she thought, feeling bitter and blasé. *I should have stayed home and given myself a facial.*

Then she spotted me by the staircase. Separate. Unhappy. Searching for celebrity. She sensed that, like her, I was worthy of it, but without a single connection to help me through the door. No one had ever made a phone call on my behalf either. She approached me, sitting there alone.

"Are you very disappointed with life?" she asked.

We began talking. She could tell that I was enamored of her but not in a sexual way, really. I say that in retrospect. She suspected that I was fascinated with her in the way that some gay men are fascinated by Marilyn or Judy Garland or Madonna for goddsakes! Originally she thought that's why I was there. To see my living idol Madonna. But when she asked me if I was a Madonna fan I surprised her with the forcefulness of my "No!" When she asked me if I had met Madonna yet, I smiled and made a joke.

She thought I was beautiful, sardonic, charming—a lot like her. Mikki suspected that I was lonely. Certainly, I couldn't advance her career at all, but she liked me. I could be something she had so little of in her life, a friend.

She told me that she had been studying acting but that she usually didn't tell people she was an actress because every asshole in the city claimed to be an actor-model-singer-dancer-writer-producer, and she didn't want to put herself in that category. She told me that she grew up in Queens and was now living in another part of Queens. "From the frying pan to the fire," she said, and we both laughed again, knowing that people in Manhattan looked down at people on the other side of the bridges.

She told me she hoped to get work as a model and that her interview with Payne Modeling Agency earlier that day "did not go well at all," but she had an important interview with a new agency called EYE the following week. She told me that she wished she were taller, and that if she could go back five years she'd do things very differently. For once we admitted our true ages. Mikki was twenty-five. I was thirty.

She was intrigued by me because I lived on St. Marks Place, had lived there when it was still a slummy neighborhood, and I really struggled. I told her that I had no family and had started hustling as a child. She was honest with me; I felt the least I could do was return the favor.

"I have no family either," she said. "Maybe we can help each other."

Then I told her of my own ambitions. How I had always hoped to become a writer—as a way to escape the murderously grim life I had been born into. How, although I was uneducated, I had always loved to read and how that led me to writing. She sensed the creativity burning in me—different from the dreamy babble of stardom she heard in others—waiting to explode in some way, shape, or form. I loved to act more than anything else, I admitted, and hoped to someday write and star in my own movies. I loved acting for the same reason she did; I treasured the idea of becoming someone else.

"My dream," I told her, "is to become a sort of Woody Allen type of producer. I mean, I want to have a stable of actors, and write and direct and produce my own small films about life in Manhattan as I see it. Life in Manhattan is so mysterious. There's all these little . . . you know, secretive places, undiscovered people, private adventures that most people don't know about. Things I see and feel at firsthand. If only I could get it into a script!"

Mikki just stared at me, amazed, truly fascinated.

The evening unexpectedly became fun for us. Together we viewed people who before had seemed intimidating as merely affected.

A photographer stopped, took our picture, did a double take, and said, "Sorry, I thought you were somebody else." We weren't sure which one he was talking about, but it gave both of us hope.

The music became loud and disruptive, but there was no need for any further communication. The beat filled us up, and the repetitive lyrics said what we wanted to say, over and over again. Ah, this was a party. This was New York. This was life. There was a future. This was the way it was supposed to be.

3.

CARLA STOOD IN the corner of the club watching the action.

She had a plump, plain, pale face. Not pretty. But pleasant looking. "Pleasant looking" would not have got her into the party tonight; gorgeous was the order of the day. But she was not everyday people; she had been born famous. If she had been born beautiful—like everything else she had been born into—it would have been an added bonus. But certainly she didn't do anything to improve her looks. Wearing jeans and a wrinkled T-shirt with a coffee stain on the front, her face void of makeup, she had parted her dull brown hair in the middle without any style, and it hung lankly to her shoulders.

Her last name was Christaldi. The name explained it all—how such an average-looking creature got into one of the hottest parties of the year. Christaldi was one of the most recognizable names in Hollywood. Jonathan, Carla's father, was a force to reckon with. One of the biggies. You know him. You see his cocky face grinning at every Academy Award show, at which he usually is nominated for something. The kind of director who gets offered all the hot scripts first. All the big-name stars want to work with him. All the top-selling authors want him to buy the rights to their books. Whenever, wherever, whatever he wants to do in Hollywood, it's just a matter of putting it down on paper. A few years before, Carla herself was often in the papers, not so much for her accomplishments, but more for her tabloid appeal.

As a child she had often appeared in small roles in her father's films, but recently she had become one of those Hollywood kids always in and out of trouble. She was repeatedly in the papers. A chubby, foul-mouthed kid dressed in slutty adult clothes, talking trash to reporters. At twelve she was already a regular at many of the hot spots in New York and Los Angeles. A serious heroin problem at thirteen. A much-publicized stay at a drug and alcohol clinic at fifteen. Then she dropped out of sight.

Now she was back in New York trying to think of what to do with her life. She could call her father and get a job working in the movies—nothing creative, mind you. Her father realized at a very early age that Carla didn't have any talent. He never let her forget that. But certainly he could get her a high-paying job. All jobs are high-paying on a big-budgeted move. A production assistant. An assistant set decorator. A fuckingassistantsomething. She was Jonathan Christaldi's daughter, after all. The problem with Carla was that she didn't like movies, she wasn't interested in art, and she hated reading.

She walked around the club listlessly. She thought she'd stay for a while to say hello to Madonna, if Madonna ever showed up. Her father had directed one of her controversial videos, but when she tuned in she noticed they were playing music that wasn't really music—nothing more than a very steady, driving, pounding, pulsating beat manufactured in a studio by some half-assed producer. A sound that appeals to no one, except either the incredibly drugged or the imbecilic. Carla didn't like music.

Then there were the people walking around with cell phones pressed to their ears. That irked her. The music was so loud you couldn't hear a thing. *STAY HOME, her mind screamed, IF YOU WANT TO CHAT ON THE PHONE!*

What should she do? What should she do?

Everyone was so thin; she had to give them that. What did they do to keep their bodies so lean and fat free? Drugs, that's what! Even with her famous Dad supplying her with a substantial allowance, she had trouble keeping her weight down, and it bothered her. A blubbery ass was a prominent symbol of failure. From studying the other female bodies—observing the asses and stomachs—Carla could see that she easily needed to lose fifteen pounds to make the average good figure. Probably more like twenty to be perfect. And, of course, some exercise to tone up. She had youth on her side and could get into shape pretty quickly if she put her mind to it.

But Carla wasn't ready to start using drugs again, which would have speeded up the weight-loss process. She had spent too much time cleaning up and drying out. Sure, she did a little weed, a sip of vodka, an occasional glass of wine. But what did it matter? She had nothing to be sober for.

Stop being so negative, her horoscope had said that day, *and you will get what you want.* But what did she want?

Even the gossip columnists had stopped writing about her. Not that she cared that much, but seeing her name in print did make having an emotional breakdown seem more real, more worthwhile. She didn't care so much about meriting fame, but she did sort of like being famous. It got her into restaurants and parties like this one. Maybe she should shoplift? Talk about sexual abuse as a child? Say she had lived in her car for a period of time? Appear in a sex tape and release it to the media? Oh, it had all been done to death by celebrities far greater than herself. Would any of those stories get her more than a few measly seconds on *Access Hollywood*? "Probably not," she said aloud and continued on.

Carla noticed a bunch of guys checking her out. They weren't, of course, checking her out because she was hot. She was sure of that. They had recognized her as that famous director's kid—an object in a celebrity museum, only of passing interest. These were gay boys, all of them most likely trying to get into the movies. They took acting classes. All were writing unique scripts based on their magnificently exciting early twenty-something lives, involving their fascinatingly witty friends, high jinx, some broken love affairs, and lots of drugs.

They were all looking for the kind of ticket Carla represented. A one-way ticket to stardom. They all had fantasies of sleeping with her once, seducing her with their charm—and then she'd become their fag hag and introduce them to Daddy. No way! She'd been down that road before. She knew starfuckers like these guys back in Hollywood. Guys who are never satisfied with what they see in the mirror, so they add an earring, a goatee, a buzz cut, a tribal tattoo, cloning themselves into each other, working out intensely every single day. Carla didn't know what they saw when they looked in the mirror, but it wasn't what others saw in real life. Carla didn't like boys. She didn't care much for girls either—but boys she really didn't like. That was her problem.

When the boys started to approach, she did a head flick and walked away quickly. That's when she saw Mikki and me. She froze in her spot and stared. I remember her now, standing there watching. She recognized the aura around us that gave off a peculiar, intense passion. This is what it must have looked like to her: An old movie teaming two mismatched stars, say, Brigitte Bardot and James Dean. But there was a fiery chemistry between us she had to notice. We seemed like we didn't belong to anyone but each other. The music didn't bother us. We stared into each other's eyes, deep in discussion. Back and forth. How could we communicate over that music?

I didn't interest Carla as much—although she saw that I was also different. I didn't try to make myself into everyone else. At least not with the way I looked. My hair was not buzzed or shaved. It was dark and curly and slicked back. I had no tattoos. My face, although unshaven, didn't have a goatee or soul patch. And I wasn't wearing tight jeans and a T-shirt. I was wearing a frayed, silky, button-down shirt, which she thought looked like it had been plucked out of a garbage bin.

The blonde, though, was really something. To Carla, Mikki moved in slow motion while everything else played about her in real time. There was an other-worldliness about her, in her white satin slip and ivory pumps, a preternatural beauty, as if she were a high-flying angel who had crash-landed on Earth and was now bewildered to find herself trapped in an auditorium of denim-clad mortals showing their belly buttons.

Carla longed to join us. She thought we were models. She thought we fit in so easily. She thought we were beautiful. Oh, she was wrong on all accounts, but that's what she read into us. She didn't approach because she thought she'd be interrupting. A nuisance. She figured that we'd only be interested in her because her father was famous. Oh, if only she had come by and said hello. I would have recognized how very lost and afraid she was. I would have let her in. But she saw only a shell, a mask of beauty, and that gave Carla an idea. Maybe she could lose some weight. Maybe she should fix herself up a little. Maybe she could become a model.

4.

LATER THAT NIGHT, after Mikki had gone home, Madonna came out in formfitting black, long blonde hair, and heavy makeup, looking less like Madonna than the waitresses. Fading a little around the edges now but still with some juice left in her. I was on the dance floor. It was my luckiest break of the evening because I was up close to Madonna and up close she was absolutely glowing with fame and beauty and power. I absolutely fell in love with her. The most famous, in-demand object of the era was dancing, and I was dancing with it. Other guys surrounded her also, but for some reason she favored me. The closer I got the more stunning she became. Her eyes! Aw, shucks. I was madly in love with her now. A big part of her genius was for self-promotion and publicity. Her timing—impeccable. She came into vogue in an era when talent and originality took a backseat to vulgarity and scandal. She knew how to exploit that—along with her real talent. She became a role model for every fame monger who came after her, although most of them didn't come with the talent thrown in. Aw, the love. Aw, the darlin'.

I felt I should say something. I mean, who knew, maybe she'd fall in love with me, too, leave her husband, have another kid, and I'd become famous overnight? As I leaned in to talk to her, I saw her fiery eyes (still so filled with curiosity and passion) narrow in scrutiny, probably wondering what I wanted from her. Then she recognized the look in my eyes and she relaxed.

Because of all my talk about movies that night, I envisioned the scene as it might appear in one of my screenplays:

INT: DANCE FLOOR - NIGHT

                    MARIO
          (Screaming to MADONNA over music)
     Madonna! You are the most famous woman
     of my generation. Every time I turn
     around, someone is wanting to interview
     you, touch you, be you!

                    MADONNA
               (Leaning in closer)
     Be a good boy—some day maybe you'll
     have some of it, too.

5.

CARLA WANTED TO talk to her father about getting plastic surgery. Terrified of blood, the thought of being cut and sliced, she had for days weighed in her mind the pros and cons of reconstruction. She hated the idea of the knife but she realized it was absolutely necessary if she were to become a model, if she were to become famous in her own right; she would have to tack some beauty onto her notoriety. Her ultimate decision was to place herself in the hands of New York's best surgeon and take whatever extreme procedures the doctor recommended. She'd need her father to finance it, of course, and she was waiting for the right moment to bring up the subject. But the damn award ceremony kept getting in the way.

This was the New York Film Critics Circle Awards. It wasn't as glittery and glamorous as the Academy Awards or the Golden Globes, but it held a lot of prestige in the movie world. Basically it's a pretentious crock of shit—with the serious, joyless, passionless, politically correct films getting all the nods.

This year's big winner was by a white rap artist turned writer-director-star, Willie Boy, who wrote and starred in a film called *Urban War*. The movie slandered homosexuals, blacks, and women. In fact, it was so offensive and bigoted that it became politically correct because of the debates it sparked about the message of freedom of speech and art. The show-business world rallied around Willie and labeled him a genius for his cunning use of the word "faggot" and his superb satirical depictions of how gays should be gutted, bitches should be slapped around and raped, and niggers sent back to Africa. "Shocking!" "Disturbing!" "Cutting!" "Brilliant!"

Carla was her father's date for the evening. She was sure he'd rather be with any number of young models (even younger than her), or the thin, up-and-coming actresses he liked to date and create. But it was the sort of thing Jonathan Christaldi did from time to time to remind himself he had a daughter: He'd take her to some high-profile event. A great photo op for the photographers. And a great conscience-soother for himself.

Throughout the meal she had simply stared at her plate, not touching the sirloin or the sautéed vegetables. She regretted not sticking to her diet the week before. Carla wished she had lost fifteen pounds before seeing him again. He would have been proud of her then. She would have worn a short skirt, like his usual dates, rather than the plain black pantsuit she had chosen. Fifteen pounds. would have made a difference. She would have bothered to put on makeup. Have her hair highlighted. But why bother when you were carrying around extra weight? Everything she did would seem, to her father's trained eye, like she was simply trying to camouflage the excess baggage.

Jonathan Christaldi was a man you instinctively tried to please. His face had a similar look to Paul Newman's when he was in his forties. His eyes seemed wise and impenetrable. He had very thick and wavy silver hair, which he wore in a perfectly groomed and scented pompadour. Everything about him, his entire life, seemed perfectly groomed and scented. He had a robust, solid build, and carried himself as if he were the most attractive man in the room. In person he had an aura that combined intelligence, extreme confidence, and cocksure arrogance in massive doses. You simply could not help yourself. You found yourself trying to impress him.

So there they sat there, Jonathan basking in his celebrity and importance. Actors, producers, writers, and everyone else in the business kept stopping at his table with the secret ambition of working with him some day. At the same time, Carla was waiting for the right moment.

Jonathan had been nominated for his latest film, *Best Kept*

Secret, a subtle, well-acted film about family relations. He did not win any awards that evening. Nominated for everything, he rarely won anything. He was considered a master in the film world, and always received his fair share of excellent reviews, but a faction of the community saw him as an uncouth wop who managed to make it purely on his genius. Some resented that.

Where did his talent come from, people wanted to know. Jonathan was just a kid from Brooklyn who had dropped out of NYU film school to marry his nutty girlfriend, Babe, a dark, petite actress he had used in his school films. It seemed that it was in the cards for him to fade into nothingness. But shortly after their daughter Carla was born, Jonathan sold the family restaurant business to make his first feature film—this was back in the days when independent films were rare. It was a gamble that paid off. The film—about a small-time hood, a drug dealer from the Brooklyn slums—became the surprise hit of the year and was nominated for three Academy Awards, including best director.

From then on life in the Christaldi family changed.

Jonathan moved Babe and Carla with him to the upscale neighborhood of Brentwood, Los Angeles. He made an effort to balance family life with his Hollywood wheelings and dealings, but it was obvious where his heart was. He would disappear for days at a time. When he was home, it was to entertain entertainment execs and others who could help his career flourish.

With each step up the ladder that Jonathan took, his wife began behaving more and more strangely. Jonathan had tried to get Babe interested in reviving her acting career, but she had absolutely no desire to do so. Instead she withdrew. Chain-smoked. Lost weight. Along with growing uncommonly quiet, her behavior became flamboyant, bizarre. She burned her arms and lashed at them with razors. At the dinners and award ceremonies he took her to, Babe came across as a silent phantom. "Spooky," as one gossip rag described her.

Before she died, Jonathan began leaving his wife at home. Carla was lonely and confused. She wanted her old family life back.

Jonathan's solution was to use his daughter in any scene that required a young child in the current movie he was filming. He assumed that everyone shared his passion for being a part of the filmmaking process. He imagined that as Carla got older she would become an important actress. But there were problems with that scenario.

Some unattractive people produce very beautiful offspring. And sometimes the opposite happens. Unfortunately that was the case with Carla. She inherited her mother's enormous, deep-set, dark eyes, but on Carla—without the emotion behind them—they seemed doltish and blank. The strong Roman nose, which worked so well on her father, had not translated well to his daughter, making her look, as was often said behind her back, like "her father in drag."

Now was the time. All the awards had been given out and the dinner was almost over. The desserts lay untouched on plates before the guests. The second cup of decaf cappuccino was being poured. It was almost time to leave. He did not seem disappointed not to have won any awards. He appeared to Carla as he always did. Totally at ease. Completely self-assured.

"Dad . . . " she said. And then a half second into her sentence they were interrupted by Chase Bartholomew—the current darling of literary New York. Chase, who was seventeen, had recently written a novel called *Shit Floats*, about unhappy high school kids. Basically the book was a reworking of tawdry headlines from the papers (a girl who gives birth in the school ladies' room, smothers the baby, puts it in a plastic bag in her locker, and skips off to algebra, missing only one period). *Shit Floats* was on every bestseller list. Carla thought the book's title was either utterly oblivious to its irony or an insider's clever wink to the publicists.

Carla knew, as did her father, that Chase was the son of the editor-in-chief of a popular men's magazine and that his mother wrote trashy, glitz novels that got turned into miniseries every other year or so. His grandfather owned the publishing house that brought *Shit Floats* out and financed its expensive advertising campaign and yet the public lapped up Chase's novel. No one seemed to mind that he was a prepackaged celebrity before he wrote a single word.

Carla had read a few pages of the 190-page, thirty-five-dollar novel and put it out with the trash. "I wanted to flush it down the toilet, but I was afraid it wouldn't go down," she told a gossip columnist in the hopes of getting a mention in the column. (She did not.) Carla was angry at the world for exalting Chase. She was angry with Chase for successfully pulling off a publicity charade. And she started feeling sorry for herself, which only made her angrier. At least Chase had a plan.

Now Chase—with his carefully constructed grunge look—was talking to Jonathan about movie rights. She disdainfully took in his Armani tuxedo jacket, which he wore over a faded Beastie Boys T-shirt. His disheveled hair looked as if it had been set, combed through, and gently finger-tousled. From their conversation Carla could tell Chase wanted Jonathan to option *Shit Floats* as his next project. Chase handed Jonathan a card, mumbled something unintelligible, and slunk away.

"He didn't even write it. His father did," Carla couldn't resist saying when Chase was out of earshot.

"Hey, people are buying it."

"Yeah, it pays to have family in the business."

There was a silence. It was ironic because Carla felt the same mixture of anger, jealousy, and envy toward Chase that people felt for her when she had appeared in her father's movies as a child.

"I know, I know," Carla said. "Everything I do, no matter what I accomplish, people are going to say, 'Her father did it for her.' I really want to do something with my life." "I think that's great, Carla. Really. My ears are all yours at the moment. What is it? What is it that you want to do?"

"I was thinking of becoming a model."

She noted his skeptical look. She knew what he was thinking. So she quickly added that it was time she had some surgery. A nose job. Maybe some liposuction. Definitely a boob job.

"Funny," he said, sweeping imaginary crumbs off of the white linen tablecloth, looking around the room. "You were always so afraid of surgery."

It was true. He had suggested that she might, perhaps, want a nose job a few years back. Probably wanting the Hollywood daughter Hollywood felt he should have. Carla had said then what she felt now: She was terrified of the thought of blood. Blood brought back images of her mother.

"Your mother," Jonathan said, looking at her as if he had read her mind, "had her nose done when I first made money. But she didn't need it. She just felt it was the thing people in the movie business do."

Whenever the subject of her mother came up, either by another person or in her own mind, Carla felt as if she had been slapped. Suddenly the ghost of Carla's mother appeared screaming at her: *Do you want to see what your father did to me?* Carla blinked the image away and looked into her father's blue eyes.

"I'm not afraid anymore," Carla said.

"Well, look, if you really want to have some surgery done, I say why not?" Jonathan replied, relieved to be able to give his daughter something else other than her allowance and the expensive Fifth Avenue apartment in which she currently lived.

"A generation ago people had facials, bleached their hair, and took aerobics classes. Now we have elective surgery. But before you do anything, why don't you go see Justin Landis? He's opening a new modeling agency . . . EYE, I think the name of it is. Justin is a good friend. See what he has to say."

Carla agreed to make an appointment to see Justin Landis. She promised to mention that she was Jonathan Christaldi's daughter. She hated that she had to be part of the "who you know" food chain but life was hard enough. You had to use what it gave you. She wasn't given looks, so she'd use some of her father's contacts to get her through the door. And perhaps some of his money to buy her beauty . . . and, maybe, a real career of her own.

6.

MY LIFE IS not going well, Mikki thought as she sat in front of the mirror at her dressing table a couple of weeks after the party for Madonna. *I'm losing.*

She had nothing solid to grasp onto. No safety net. No man who loved her. No career. No money. The future held more of the same. She was desperate and weary.

The meeting at Payne Models had been a disaster, and that provided new motivation. She awoke at six to work out. She had starved herself for the past three days. She appraised her image in the mirror.

Looking closer, she saw a face, still beautiful, but one that could once party all night, stumble home after a horrific subway ride, and still look undeniably fresh. Now it was a face that definitely needed eight hours sleep to retain that fresh look. What next?

Laird Payne's insults about her appearance had stung her. Now she went for a look that was simple rather than sexy. She wore a man's white tank top, nice fitting jeans that showed her body, along with ten silver chains around her waist, worn as belts. Her bag was a Fendi. Mikki would often do that—mix something incredibly expensive with something very inexpensive and hope that it gave her an *unsoigné* appeal. An I-can-afford-nice-things-but-I-don't-give-a-damn attitude.

There was nothing more she could do except an expert makeup job. Her hands shook as she applied the colors.

Eye shadow. This was not her first interview with a modeling agency. There had been too many. It in fact terrified her that she had reached this age, twenty-five, and here she was doing the same thing she'd been doing for years. But a reputation was not preceding her. She would have to sell herself as if she were just starting out. And like all last chances this time was more terrifying than the others.

Her career, up to this point, had been unremarkable. *Almost* getting that great career-making assignment, *almost* signing with that top agency. Always just missing the big time. Her adoptive father's new wife used to tell her that she was pretty but had no luck. She would never be famous without it, luck. She was beautiful enough to get people interested, but her look, at the time, wasn't marketable. Or so they told her. Her lips were too full. Her face too exotic. They always seemed to have some new excuse as to why she would never make it.

Mascara: She had a feeling deep in her that she was something big, something special, and she was hoping some mentor would help her let it loose.

Oh, she recognized the mistakes she had made. Under her façade of beauty she was shy, meek, afraid. It was ridiculous, the way she handed herself over to men, expecting them to help her. Instead they used her. They saw how damaged she was. Vulnerable. Tender. Sensitive. That might mean trouble. So men fucked her and discarded her. Recently she had written in her diary: *Men have sniffed out the blood of my vulnerability like a wound I wear hidden under my blouse. NO MORE!*

Lipstick: But there was a buzz about this new agency, EYE Model Management, and she wanted desperately to sign with them. EYE was being opened by Justin Landis, a major player in the modeling world.

It was during this time that a remarkable change had occurred in her personality. Now she would manipulate her pain into a weapon. *Lure them in with the vulnerability—they come sniffing after it—but don't let them eat you up* she thought. *Chew them up and spit them out first. We are a society of liars*, she thought, *and to fit in, we ourselves must lie.*

In the past, men fell in love with her but not the right men—not men who could help her career. Her new decision was that no matter what Justin Landis looked like, no matter what kind of person he was, she was going to make him fall in love with her. *There is no destiny*, she said to herself, I must make my own. It was late, but not too late.

———————

"IT WAS FASCINATING," Justin Landis would tell a newspaper columnist a month later. "One minute she looked really tough and no-nonsense, and in the next glance she'd be about to fall apart—incredibly sensitive and vulnerable and wounded. A fascinating paradox. She was a phantom. A chameleon. She could be any woman. I saw it in her photographs and I saw it when she was sitting in front of me."

People are willing to believe anything about you if it fits the role they want you in, Mikki was thinking as she stood outside the door. She stared at the gold plaque on the door: EYE MODEL MANAGEMENT: Justin Landis, President. She wondered if her body could handle another rejection. It was not too late; she didn't have to go through with this. She could still go home . . . *Oh, fuck it!* She knocked and entered.

She was relieved to find that Justin Landis, the man she was about to seduce, was not hideous, but disappointed to discover that he was not seductive either. It was obvious that he had once been delicately handsome, but like many pretty boys, he had not aged well. When you looked at him you couldn't help thinking, *He must have looked great when he was twenty*. Now his fragile features seemed unmanly. You noticed every line because each seemed out of place around the boyish features. His light blonde hair was too thin, too limp. His blue eyes too watery. His mouth was serious but undramatic. His aura, too, was not the kind that drew her in. He had a sensitive air. A weakness. Mikki had heard somewhere that his parents had money; maybe he hadn't had to drop his sensitivity like so much unnecessary baggage.

Mikki had videotaped and studied the recent *A&E Biography*

done on Justin Landis. He had indeed come from wealth. He had been a broody, fussy, artistic little boy. His fashion became finding and documenting his own personal vision of beauty.

By the time he was a teenager his parents had come to an acceptance that their son was probably a homosexual. But Justin then surprised everyone, while studying fine arts at Harvard, by becoming engaged to a startlingly beautiful Chinese woman named Helen Woo. His passion, some would say "obsession" with Helen, was all consuming. He photographed her constantly, changed her name to Jana Janelow, moved her to New York, and navigated her career to the very top of the modeling world. Then he divorced her.

Since that marriage Justin had never been seriously romantically linked with anyone. But he himself had become the most successful fashion and celebrity photographer in the world—often shooting covers and layouts for *Vogue* and *Vanity Fair*.

His eye for the exceptional was truly amazing. He could look through a person's physical presence and see their essence. It didn't necessarily matter to him if the person's aura was "good." What had come to excite him was someone who was hiding something. His eye could see a person's concealed hurt, obsession, perversion. Looking at a portrait by Justin Landis was like looking at an X-ray of his subject's soul. Such was his art that no celebrity felt he was truly famous unless Justin Landis photographed him. Now he would be discovering beauty for his own agency and revealing it to the masses.

For Mikki, beauty wasn't necessary in a man, but she preferred striking men with outstanding characteristics, men who were bold and confident and pushy. The opposite of her. Somebody had to be the strong one. Even so, she immediately began to wonder what it would be like to be lovers with Justin and decided that it would be possible. *Great.* She felt a sense of relief. *I'm jumping the gun a bit, aren't I?* she said to herself, with a private half smile, which he noticed.

She started the interview by sort of interviewing him. "Congratulations," she said as she took a seat opposite him, noticing his concentrated stare. She placed her portfolio on his desk, her purse in her lap. "This is very impressive. Opening your own agency. It's a big step for you, isn't it?" She smiled. "But you've already accomplished so much as a photographer."

Justin, who for all his life had been considering beautiful girls every day, studied the striking, slightly disheveled blonde before him. She looked down and bit her lip. Biting her lips made them even fuller. It had become a subconscious habit.

By this time she was half drunk. That worked for her. She drank strictly for professional reasons. Later in her career she would move to drugs to get the blurred beauty, the fuzzy, sexy appeal that became part of her image as a supermodel. For this meeting she had carried a fifth of scotch in her black Fendi bag, and several minutes before the interview she sat in the agency's ladies' room in a stall and took two or three deep, quick gulps. It burned the sensitivity out of her. She hadn't had any lunch, so the scotch got straight to the point. She didn't get sloppy. She got oozy. A languid feeling—a slow sexiness, that of a lazy cat, pushed aside her nerves.

Now, sitting in his office, she hoped she hadn't overdone it. She hoped she wasn't too lethargic. Too slow. She was shivering with fear, but she concentrated on holding herself together. Her eyes were half-mast, her lips slightly parted. An erotic force field flowed out of her pores like steam. Justin could almost feel her heat from across his desk. He watched her, fascinated.

"It's been a longtime dream of mine," he said, answering her. She smiled again and slowly slid her sleek portfolio across his black lacquered desk. If she was exceptional in her photos, the photography was not. She had not had a chance yet to work with outstanding photographers. The tear sheets were from lesser known magazines and small-time catalogues. But someone in the know, someone with the right eye, would be able to look past the ordinariness of the photography to the artistry of the model. The way the poses conveyed just the right attitude for the clothes. The way her expressions were erotically inviting, yes, but also the way they made you want to know more about who the model was. Her secrets.

None of this was lost on Justin Landis, although many bookers before him had thought, "Inferior photos, inferior model." But, for once, Justin could not see the model's soul! What was it about her? What was she hiding?

"Tell me about yourself, Mikki," Justin said as he looked up from her book.

She was betting on the fact that Justin would recognize the real thing. She was betting on the fact that she *was* the real thing. And once and for all she'd know if she was kidding herself. It was like she was going through a metal detector at an airport. If she didn't have what it took, his buzzer would go off, as if she had a .44 caliber hidden in her garter. She would not waver. Mikki spilled her personality onto his desk, a beautiful mess, in a disorganized passion, she would let him pick through it and assess what was junk and what was valuable.

"I come from nowhere. I've been modeling for a while now. It's a tough business, as you know. I don't mean that the work is tough. That's the part I enjoy. That's why I'm in it. Meeting the right people—that's the hard part. See, only you yourself know what you've got inside of you. You can't let it loose though until you get yourself in the right hands. That's what I've been trying to do. But most of the people in higher positions . . . God only knows how they got there! They don't even know quality. Most of the time I've only had the opportunity to work with . . . " She let it go, although "assholes" is what came to her mind.

"How do you know it's the other people's fault?" he asked.

This made her feel that perhaps she had made a mistake in her presentation. Her heart started racing. His insinuation being that it was possibly her fault she hadn't gone further and that she was just a sniveling, whiny baby pushing her failures off on the establishment. Oh why, oh why, did she put herself through this? *Relax,* she said to herself, *he doesn't know who you are.*

"I'm still here," she said. She felt stiff and clogged. Then she imagined a camera rolling in front of her and the words flowed. "People come and go in this business. Disappearing forever when they don't make it overnight." The scotch urged her on. "I'm in it for the long haul." Her smile almost became a smirk. Then she added: "I've put my destiny in the hands of pricks with an attitude for too long; I have to take my life by the balls and steer it in the right direction—a psychic once told me that."

He threw his head back and laughed, as if he had dealt with one or two of the "prick species" in his lifetime. His laughter also urged her to go further. She waited for him to stop laughing.

"A lot of girls make it right away. But some of us don't. There's no guarantee. In the modeling world there's so many beautiful things. I don't mind competition if the playing field is level, if talent and looks are all that you're judged on. But it's so much networking and game playing and lying. I mean, you know, it's a matter of being at the right place at the right time. Getting recognized by the right person. One of the non-pricks. Like I said, it's about getting yourself in the right hands. That's always been my prayer, to get myself in the right hands."

His eyes narrowed in scrutiny.

"You have this quality," he said finally.

She looked at him uncertainly. Was she winning? She knew the quality he was talking about but could think of no answer, and so she smiled simply and let the silence be her response. At least now she knew how to finish playing out the scene.

"And why do you think you'd be an asset to EYE?" he asked her.

She paused and thought a moment, her fists involuntarily clenched, "I've got a lot in me, Mr. Landis. I'm burning. But I've never been given a chance. There's a certain torture in that. Maybe I've been fucked by the wrong people. Maybe I haven't fucked the right people. But I know what I'm capable of doing. For this agency and for myself."

"What do you think is your destiny?" he asked.

It was a serious question and Mikki wanted to give it the answer it deserved. But her scotch buzz was leaving her with a dull hangover headache and she was suddenly feeling very tired. She thought for a moment and then, as if to herself, very quietly said: "There is no destiny . . . only a system of doors that present themselves and ask us to choose."

He held her gaze, and she saw a look in his eyes that she had seen in many men's eyes before. A look of wanting. But sometimes there was an added kick. It wasn't really desire, but an admiration and recognition of beautiful things. Rare and beautiful and hard to know and possess. She was all these things. His eyes held hers, too, and in that moment she felt that she was in.

"Listen," she said, closing her eyes, which were filled with the emotions of the moment (and scotch), "I'm tired of living in Queens. I'm tired of taking the subways. I'm tired of being taken advantage of. I want a name for myself. You want to make a name for your agency," she opened her eyes and met his gaze unblinking, "Take a chance on me," she whispered. "Maybe we can help each other."

"How old are you," Justin asked.

"Nineteen," Mikki said. Justin thought she might be but probably wasn't.

"You're an interesting girl. I'll say that much for you, Ms. Britten."

"And I'm a nervous wreck. In an office setting, to boot."

"Oh? And what are you like in your natural habitat . . . or should I ask . . . what is your natural habitat?"

"At the moment the subway system—I wouldn't want you to see me there."

Justin laughed.

"How about dinner," Mikki asked, pushing everything she was feeling aside and letting the words flow out quickly.

Justin nodded. "I would like to have dinner with you," he said, "and talk about your possible future with EYE."

"I can't think of anything in the world I would rather do,"

she said.

"Your pictures are awful. Your composite card tells me you're at least two inches too short, and you're at least a couple of years older than girls I want to sign up." He handed her back her portfolio. "I'm willing to take a chance on you."

7.

THAT AFTERNOON I went to a gay bar I frequented on the Upper East Side called The Lion's Den. To lure an upscale clientele, this club was cleverly set up to look like a wealthy man's town house. There were dim lights, carpets on the floor, elaborately framed paintings of landscapes, expensive textured wallpaper, and fresh flowers, carefully arranged in enormous vases resting on ornate tables. Instead of stools or benches there were plush sofas, love seats, and comfy stuffed armchairs. It had the feel of an old boys club with a fair share of old boys hobnobbing and schmoozing with the younger ones, who were actually for sale. But the cruising was all done in a very covert, dignified way.

I walked over to the bar, with its polished brass border, ordered a scotch on the rocks, finished a third of it in one quick gulp, and looked around. Although it was mid-afternoon, there was a decent-size crowd. It was Friday, so men were starting the weekend early—a dozen suits, some button-down shirts, a scattering of very old men in cardigans. And, of course, the young hustlers leaning nonchalantly in corners, pretending to be preoccupied with mysterious, youthful thoughts.

Over on one of the love seats, I noticed the renowned modeling agent, Laird Payne, trying to pick up an eighteen-year-old hustler who I recognized as being one of the regulars. Like me. He was a short, beefy, good-looking kid wearing black jeans and a dark brown T-shirt. I don't think he had any idea he was talking to a powerful modeling tycoon, but the kid did have a smug air about him, as if he was aware that he had snared a live one, even at this unlikely hour of the day.

I recalled Mikki's story of how Laird Payne had not only rejected her but also humiliated her a few weeks earlier. I related to that. A few years earlier, I had interviewed with Laird myself, over at the Payne offices. In retrospect I had to hand it to him for being years ahead of his time when it came to having his eyebrows severely waxed and plucked into a feminine arch. He eyed me lustfully and then said, "You know, I think you're about a month too old." I was, I think, twenty-seven at the time. Not too old, really. He just wanted to hurt me in the same way he hurt Mikki. I wasn't so spectacular that there weren't twelve more of me, in various incarnations, waiting to see him later that afternoon.

At that time, I had taken a few half-hearted stabs at modeling—dropping by the bigger agencies, occasionally—but no one ever took me seriously. Usually I was greeted by a stiff receptionist, long accustomed to beauty and bored by the concept. She'd tell me to leave my portfolio (called a "book") overnight and pick it up the following day. I'd look around at the other guys there to drop off their books and suddenly feel inferior. *You think you're in THEIR league*, my mind taunted. I guess I was, but I could never feel it. And I never was able to get really good photos for my portfolio. I had done modeling for the men's porno magazines. Most of the time I'd have to shave my body (for me no small feat) and work out intensely for several months before. The pay was lousy, but so was my living situation most of the time. The resulting photos published in the magazines certainly weren't anything I could show to legit modeling agents—although, come to think of it, there's very little clothing separating a layout in *Torso* from a Calvin Klein ad.

Everyone has a sad sack tale involving his childhood, but mine has always done wonders for me. People liked me in the lost-boy role. My problem is, I've used it so many times as a selling tool it can come out sounding stale.

Sitting in a hustler bar, I didn't really want to remember my childhood but here it came, like a reminder in the mail. Stained. Everything was. Diseased and tainted. And stained.

"My mother was the typical drug-addicted prostitute," I once told a guy who was trying to pick me up.

"I read that on your Web site," he replied. I was surprised to be reminded that I actually put this sort of background information on an online site advertising myself sexually. As soon as I got home, I removed it. It wasn't necessary for men to come to me armed with this information—I needed something to talk about over the first drink or while I was hurriedly getting undressed.

It's true that my grandmother raised me. It is also true that my mother gave birth to me when she was fifteen. My father? Who knew? My grandmother had many men and many children. My mother had many men and many children. While I was growing up in that apartment, there were so many siblings of various ages running around I didn't know who were my aunts and uncles, or cousins, brothers, and sisters. It didn't matter.

We had a large, decaying apartment in the Bronx. Once it must have been considered grand, but all the time I lived there it was squalid. What I remember most is that the rooms were always filled with smoke. Cigarette smoke. Pot smoke. Smoke from cooking. Smoke from cooking drugs. I came to hate it. It disgusted me. Everything was stained yellow with thick layers of nicotine. Each object was covered with a layer of smut and cigarette dust. I'd open a drawer in the kitchen and find an ashtray filled with ancient butts. Grimy. Sooty. Dirty. Men continued to come and go. There was never a moment of privacy.

When I was an adolescent, my mother disappeared, as I always knew she would. She had been no different to me than one of my sisters. No closer than one of my aunts. They came. They went.

My grandmother was now my chief guardian. With her missing teeth, unkempt hair, and drooping body, I considered her a very old woman. Now I realize she was only in her early forties. Hideous men she met on telephone sex lines would come pick her up, and we'd rush to the window to see her disappear into the car with her "date." The car or van or truck would start rocking within minutes.

I didn't know the word "appalled" at the time, but that's what I felt. She contracted hepatitis C or AIDS or something. She was losing weight and leaving residue on the bathroom floor. It was time for me to go. I was sixteen.

My name was Mario. I kept it. That's all I knew. That's who I was. No other characteristics or traits.

I had nothing going for me except a hunger to improve. Little education outside of the education I got on the streets, which was considerable. But I never fit in. I started reading. I would go to the library or secondhand bookstores and browse, picking up things if the cover interested me. Many books I left unfinished, but if there was an author I liked, I tried to acquire his complete works. Then I'd go back and read the writers who influenced that author, and one book would lead to another. I began to love and respect talent. I came to love movies, too. All the classics. I wanted to be in the arts. I wanted to write and act and make films. I wanted to be a model. I wanted to be an actor.

I looked good. I started auditioning, but it was hard to get a foot in the door. I was coming from nowhere, and I knew no one. In the meantime I started making my living with the only thing I had that anyone ever put any value on. I'd walk around Times Square, just before those streets were improved and cleaned up. I met men. I'd get some money. Soon I was able to get a decent room. I got some decent clothes. I had no modern gadgets. No conveniences. Clothes, cologne, shoes. Upkeep. I met more men. I read. Occasionally I auditioned. I dreamed.

As time went on, people would say I became cynical; they would say I was moody or that my face looked sad. True, I had seen the unrelenting cruel face of life, but I don't like people who blame their childhoods for their later lives. Mine sucked, but so what? There are millions of people who had it worse than me. And yet, I became different from the people who grew up around me.

Now at The Lion's Den, I slouched on the couch across from the love seat Laird and his delicious young boy were sharing, so

I could eavesdrop better. I liked to watch the eighteen-year-old hustlers—over ten years younger than me and so in love with themselves. The sound of their voices. Their reflections in the mirror. They still eyed me with competition. With contempt. This one, for example, always watched me closely but refused to acknowledge me. He would not say hello. That made me feel a little sad while at the same time boosting my ego a bit. Still, my age worried me. Tick, tick, tick. I had started to see the eyes of potential customers go up and down, up and down my body, and then I could read in their eyes "too old" as they passed over me on to some lesser but younger commodity.

He was clever, this kid. He talked to Laird, not about modeling or acting or filmmaking, but construction companies he worked for and the ones he hoped to get work for. That's what Laird wanted to hear now. He didn't want a celebrity wannabe who would only fuck him. This was the kind of guy he wanted to bed: a simple, honest, hardworking, hot-bodied kid a little down on his luck.

"What would you do if you made a lot of money?" the older Laird asked the younger stud.

"If I made a lot of money?" the younger repeated, considering the question for a few seconds. "I guess I'd come out and get laid just for fun."

Good answer, I thought. I didn't have it. The gift for fake answers, phony charm. Most hustlers were excellent at it. A casual drop of an arm over the older guy's shoulder. And then, magically, the older's hand was on the younger's knee and everyone was happy. I couldn't do that. I didn't chew on straws. I didn't sit with my legs spread so wide they faced opposite continents. That was boy stuff.

That'll be the day I allow someone to paw me like that in public, I said to myself, watching Laird move in.

But then something happened that stunned me. Laird looked across the coffee table that separated the couch from the love seat and saw me languidly sipping the remainder of my drink. Our eyes met. For a moment I thought he recognized me from our ill-fated modeling meeting years before. But no. He was not looking at me with recognition. It was something resembling desire. I was more appropriate for whatever his taste was for that afternoon.

Quite suddenly, and not a little rudely, he excused himself from the kid and crossed over to sit next to me.

"Let's get out of here, Poet," he said. Obviously he had mistaken me for someone else. But what the hell? I'd played worse parts than a poet in my life, and we left the place hurriedly—Laird pawing me—without looking back at the kid, and immediately caught a cab on the street.

"What's your first name," Laird asked me, as I lay fully clothed on the bed in the hideously damp and reeking motel room he brought me to. Obviously he didn't think enough of me to bring me to a nice place, and his apartment was out of the question. He hadn't bothered to ask me my name before.

"Mario," I replied.

"Can I call you Master?"

I am hesitant to describe him, even though up to this point he had been a pretty hideous guy, not only to me but to Mikki and countless others.

Oh, he was truly grotesque in every way. Hustling is a funny business. It's all about make-believe. He makes believe no money will be exchanged; I make believe I'm not repulsed.

"Can I lick your feet?" he asked.

I nodded an affirmative. Before you could say "odor eaters" my socks were off and he was licking the souls of my tootsies.

"Can I suck your toes, Master?" Laird asked.

This wasn't my idea of a good time, but I let him go at it. His mouth, on my toes, was warm and wet and horrible.

"What do you want me to do for you, Master," he asked after several minutes of toe sucking.

I would have liked for him to leave the room but I knew I had to demand something that allowed him to stay. I tried it out: "Suck my nipples," I ordered. He became as eager and manic as a puppy dog.

"Yes, Master! Yes, Master!" he drooled. And before you knew it, my shirt was off and he was doing it.

He breathlessly babbled compliments throughout: "You're so hot looking. You're gorgeous. Oh baby, you're the best." I wished he would shut up. It was disconcerting and made it difficult for me to sustain a hard-on, which was unfortunate since that was his second-favorite thing to suck on. I tried to concentrate on a time my life would be different.

Afterward, as always, I was repulsed by myself, with a wad of my own cum on my stomach (Laird had spit it there). Selling myself, going home alone: no future, no prospects. And always, always, always the fear of dying. Of going too far. Of getting sick. I was longing for a way out. For a long time my dream of writing a film, making some money, and escaping hell seemed far-fetched and a long way off. Never more so than now. I started dressing.

Suddenly Laird's face, actually his posture and entire attitude, changed. "You really are pathetic, aren't you?" he said, as if he had read my thoughts.

I could have said that was the most extreme case of the pot calling the kettle black that I had ever heard of, but I wasn't in the mood for an argument.

I only had on my jeans. I was looking for a missing sock he had carelessly tossed somewhere. "It's not easy," I said in almost a whisper. He watched me scurrying around for a few more minutes with unfeigned hate in his eyes. This wasn't all that unusual. They turn sometimes.

Savagely he scooped up my sock from the side of the bed and handed it to me. I slipped it on, gathered up my sneakers and shirt and began to leave, figuring I would finish dressing out in the street. "Take care," I said and headed for the door. He had already paid me.

"Wait a minute," he ordered. I was curious. I stopped.

He asked me what I did outside of this. Actor? Model? "All of you *do* something," he said scornfully.

I was very tired. He meant nothing to me, but he had paid more than we agreed on.

"I'm a writer," I said. "I write."

"Ah, I was right. A poet!"

"No," I said with a little smile. "I want to make money at it some day."

"If you want to make money, honey," he said, "May I suggest you do something other than write. Like work in the post office. I mean, I do a little writing myself, on the side, and really, the publishing world is contemptible today, and it's doubtful, darling, very doubtful that you'll ever write anything that will even get read by anyone of importance, let alone get published."

I wasn't going to argue. He was probably right. Any short story I eagerly sent to *Playboy* or *Esquire* was returned with a standard form rejection. I didn't even dare try for *The New Yorker*. I didn't know anyone. How would I ever get a movie script read if I couldn't even get a story looked at? See the fucking power these assholes had over me? The thread of thought Laird had set in my mind? He had just paid me $300 for the pleasure of licking the cheese out of my toenails and yet he had *me* feeling like the loser.

I finished dressing silently. I didn't want an incident. I wanted out. He caught my eye coldly in the mirror.

"I have someone who might be interested in you," he said.

I needed the money. Whatever the plan was, I was game.

"Yes?" I said wearily.

"How old are you, Poet?" he demanded, suddenly.

I wasn't sure if he wanted me older or younger. One would assume he wanted me younger. I remembered the "month too old," line from four years before. But earlier he had ditched an 18-year-old for me. He waited for my answer, staring at me arrogantly and impatiently. There wasn't time to debate. I chose an age.

"Twenty-eight," I said.

He looked at me with suspicion. Did he think I was lying in favor or against? Oh, it was despicable, that I had to kiss up like this. "I'm twenty-eight," I repeated.

"That's a good age," he said. "Perfect. That's the exact age she likes them."

I assumed he was talking about a gay friend of his since these older aunties always referred to each other in the feminine tense. Or "Mary," as in "Mary likes them older."

"Who?" I asked.

"Do you like movies, Poet," he asked.

"Yes, I do," I replied. "Very much. Actually I hope to write them someday."

"Well, this isn't *that* kind of writing assignment. Do you know anything about nostalgia? Movie history?"

"Yes."

"Well, Victoria Sweetzer is a great friend of mine. Of course people have been after her for years to write her autobiography, but she was too busy living it. Now . . . now she feels the time is right. And she asked me to help her look for a ghostwriter."

I looked at him suspiciously. Why would a woman, a legend as powerful and well connected as Victoria Sweetzer, need a friend to find her a writer to work on her memoirs? And why would he choose to present her with a hustler whose writing he'd never even seen? A hustler he obviously loathed.

"Oh," he said, knowing what I was thinking, "Victoria wants an unknown. Plus, she likes to have young men around her. She'd open up more to someone that she felt was attractive and charming and you have a . . . a . . . ." He looked for a way of complimenting me without complimenting me. "You have a certain imitation poetic quality she might relate to. Shall I set up a meeting?"

I was beside myself with the thought of working with Victoria Sweetzer. As a kid I was abnormally passionate about movies—as much as I was about books—and for the same reason many people are abnormally passionate about movies: It was a way to escape pain and loneliness. Many nights I stayed up very late watching old films on commercial television . . . and then I'd become fixated on a certain star. I would spend the next few months reading up on him or her, and seeing all of the star's films. I went through a Jean Harlow phase. A Clark Gable period. Montgomery Clift. Marilyn, of course. And there was about a year or so that I could not get enough of Victoria Sweetzer.

I pressed a button on the computer in my brain and immediately called up everything I had on file for Victoria Sweetzer. She had been somewhat popular since she was a teenager in the mid-fifties but in that decade was overshadowed by Marilyn Monroe and Elizabeth Taylor, although she was ten or more years younger than the two of them.

In the late 1950s, like many actresses signed to a studio, Victoria made several films a year, many of which were crap, some of which are now classics—like *Dangerous Association* and *Lonely Town*. She was renowned for her perfect bone structure, fabulously voluptuous body, and her sexy, husky, low voice. Always impeccably groomed and photographed—the way stars were in those days—she had famous green cat eyes and usually wore her vanilla-blonde hair to her shoulders, sometimes with a wave over one eye in the style of an earlier star, Veronica Lake.

For a brief time, several years after Marilyn Monroe's death, Victoria had an approximate six-year reign as the undisputed queen of the entertainment industry, the biggest, most popular star in the world—earning the then-phenomenal salary of two million dollars per movie. Hollywood had been struggling to find and promote a new big female actress. Elizabeth Taylor was busy traipsing around the globe with Richard Burton, gaining weight, and appearing in expensive, pretentious, arty flops. The industry flirted with the idea of turning Ann-Margaret or Tuesday Weld into the next big female thing, but they never quite set the world on fire. It was during that period Victoria stepped in and made her most popular films, including the scatterbrain classic, *Don't Mess with Her*, and her cinematic masterpiece, *Helen of Troy*.

So, yes, there was a time, years after her greatest successes, that Victoria Sweetzer was one of the stars I became absolutely obsessed with: renting her movies, reading the frequent, premature biographies—but there was so much to write about, not only regarding her movies, but her private life. At first her legendary sexual encounters were with men who were many years older: Clark Gable, Gary Cooper, Cary Grant. In later years, men who were younger: Warren Beatty, Jack Nicholson, Robert De Niro.

Even after her movie career died, in the early seventies (when Barbra Streisand, Faye Dunaway, and Julie Andrews took over as female box-office attractions), the tabloid papers could never get enough of Victoria Sweetzer. Her many affairs and brief marriages. Her fabulous jewels. Her frequent stays at the Betty Ford Center and other clinics for various substance abuses. Her plastic surgeries. Her weight gains and losses. The coming and going and coming again of her substantial beauty. Oh, she was just absolutely too fantastic!

I didn't relay my excitement to Laird. I made my face a complete blank and my voice very business-like. "Sure. Of course. I'd very much like discussing a book with Ms. Sweetzer."

"Give me your number, Poet," he said. "And I'll be in touch."

8.

AFTER HER MEETING with Justin, Mikki rushed to the ladies' room, flushed and terrified. The meeting, although it seemed like it had been a success, had left her with a shaky, queasy feeling, as if she had just walked a tightrope in high heels. Did he believe her when she said she was nineteen? If so, that meant he was looking at girls who were almost a decade younger than herself.

She was just about to pour the remaining scotch down the drain (to show her appreciation to God) when she heard quiet sobs coming from one of the bathroom stalls, restrained crying followed by the sound of vomiting.

Mikki was always a shy person. Shy and private. The old Mikki would have dumped the bottle and tiptoed out, but this new Mikki was curious, and as Justin had noted, her two selves battled for dominance within her. Months later Mikki would wonder what course her life would have taken if the old timid Mikki won out and left that wretched girl to her crying.

"Excuse me . . . um . . . hey, are you okay?" she asked and tapped lightly on the stall door. "Do you need some help?"

The quiet sobbing, and all other sounds from the stall, completely stopped. Mikki stood by the door for several seconds, waiting. Nothing happened. She tilted her head to look under the stall and saw a pair of expensive-looking (female) cowboy boots firmly planted on the floor. She was just about to turn and leave when the door flung open and she found herself face to face with another young woman staring at her with disconcerting intensity. Mikki gasped, but she was uncertain why.

"Look at you!" Carla Christaldi said. "Shit! What a pretty face you have. It makes me feel comfortable."

"I was . . ." Mikki started to say and then stopped suddenly. Something about the girl made her take notice, too, " . . . wondering if I could do something for you?"

The young woman was not beautiful, but she exuded a quality of importance, as if she should be treated with more care than the average person. There was also something familiar about her. Distant but familiar, that feeling you get when you see a friend you haven't seen since grammar school on an early-morning subway and can't quite place the face. Although Mikki did not recognize Carla yet, Carla recognized Mikki as the girl who had captivated her at the club a week before, but she didn't mention it.

"No thanks. I'm okay, now" Carla said in a raspy voice. "Just a little nervous. I have an interview with Justin Landis in fifteen minutes."

Oh, a model wannabe, Mikki thought. Just having come from that particular boat, Mikki understood those feelings and she smiled reassuringly. "I know just how you feel. I just had an interview with the man, myself."

"Yeah, well, if I had a face like yours," the girl said, "I would never be nervous about anything."

Mikki stared at her with curiosity. What was it about her? She seemed normal enough. Her speech was clear and, well, educated-sounding but with a tough edge. Her expression was blank and practically immobile, but there was a frightened look in her eyes.

"Do I know you?" Mikki asked. "I'm Mikki Britten."

"Carla Christaldi," replied the woman, and, amused, she watched recognition dawn on Mikki.

Of course, of course! Carla Christaldi! Mikki remembered reading about her aspirations to model on Page Six of the *Post* a few days before, and it had struck her as incredible pretense. Anyone with a last name like Christaldi didn't have to go the normal route. One phone call from her father and she could sign with the most established of agencies.

Carla read her mind: "Look—yeah—I know I have connections up the asshole, but I want to do it on my own! That's why I'm so afraid. I want a career for myself, but I'm willing to earn it. Besides, my father is an asshole. I can't stand him and I don't want anything from him."

"Why?" Mikki found herself asking in spite of herself.

"Because his name is Christaldi, he's deluded himself into thinking he's either some direct descendent of Christ or Jesus Christ himself."

"I read you said that in an interview once."

"Yeah, well. I stand by my comment."

Mikki treated these opening moments of their conversation delicately. She realized that someone with Carla's background would be suspicious of people, so she asked no questions about her life. Instead she talked, her voice resonating through the white-tiled bathroom, about herself, her own intense ambition. How she hoped to use modeling as a conduit to acting. She talked about the meeting with Justin Landis that had just taken place and how he wanted to see her again. "At least I'll get a lobster dinner out of it," she deadpanned.

To give herself something to do as she spoke, Mikki fastidiously reapplied her makeup in the large mirror that hung above the row of sinks. Carla watched her, mesmerized. Mikki talked about her struggles the past few years, and she talked of how she had recently started to do some writing. She hoped to write a film for herself, she said, and raise the money, through modeling, to produce it independently. The thought occurred to her that perhaps to say this was a mistake. Carla might think that she was initiating the friendship because of her status in the film community, so Mikki quickly added: "I know what you mean about wanting to do it by yourself. I've been rejected so many times in these past few years I feel like I have something to prove, not only to myself, but to all the people that have passed me by." And then she started putting some makeup on Carla. As she did, Mikki talked about her insecurity and how it often caused her to be overlooked. Carla was amazed at how much better she looked with a few strokes of Mikki's handiwork.

Carla reached out and stroked Mikki's hair. "Oh my God, girl! If I had hair like that, I would never be unhappy," she said.

Mikki self-consciously ran a hand through it, brushing it out of her eyes. "You'd be surprised," she replied. "I was so nervous about meeting Justin Landis that I had to have a few drinks before I went in there."

"No shit?"

Mikki opened her purse and showed Carla the scotch bottle.

Carla burst into hysterics. "My kinda gal," she laughed, grabbing the bottle and guzzling down the remaining scotch in a few quick gulps. "Let's get out of here," she said in a scotch-heated gasp.

"What about your meeting with Justin Landis?"

"No, no, no! I'm not ready for that shit yet," Carla said loudly and smiled. "I have to work myself up to it. Right now I want to . . . I want to think of something else to do."

Mikki paused for a moment. "We can grab a bite," she suggested.

"Oh yes! Let me take you to lunch. I'd much rather have lunch. Wouldn't you?"

THE RESTAURANT ON Bond Street, which Carla chose for their lunch, was one that Mikki had only read about in the gossip columns. As they entered, she heard someone say, "There's the guy from the Calvin Klein advertisements," but Mikki didn't dare turn to look, lest she look like a nobody.

The tables were far apart and private. The meals looked like works of art, really. Color-coordinated vegetables, carved garnish, that sort of thing. But underneath the edible sculptures, there was surprisingly very little to eat. A sliver of chicken here, a sampling of mushroom there. The prices had made Mikki gag. The waiters looked like models, and probably were. The haughty way they performed the specials-of-the-day monologue suggested many a speech class. Actors, no doubt.

Carla insisted on taking a cab to the restaurant, even though the subway was nearby, and she paid the driver a handsome tip because she grew impatient as he fiddled around for the correct change from a fifty, and slammed the door, not waiting for a thank-you. The staff of the restaurant knew who she was and treated her with a celebrity's due. When the first bottle of wine was empty, Carla ordered another and it was instantly produced.

Carla revealed more of herself during lunch. It was thrilling for Mikki to hear stories that she had read about in the tabloids, told to her with behind-the-scene details. Her mother had died in a mental institution after a crackup. Carla said, "They committed her when she threw all her designer clothes out the bedroom window. Tons of originals, right from her window into the swimming pool." Her abusive father, brilliant but neglectful. "You have no idea what it's like living up to what that man expects. Yeah, he's fucking brilliant, but I mean, he was able to develop his brilliance at his own pace. Mine was expected from the time I was born."

In her lap Mikki nervously folded and unfolded her napkin. *We could be friends. We could help each other,* she thought. She wanted to believe that her heart went out to Carla, and she felt that falling into a friendship with her would bring her a sincere friend, a buddy to talk to and do all those girl things she never had anyone to do them with. But the visions in Mikki's head also danced with images of Hollywood—film sets and parties with A-list people.

After lunch Carla ordered double espressos. Anisette. Strawberries dipped in chocolate.

"I know I'm not beautiful," Carla stated bluntly. "But I've been through a lot and I think I can use that to create a compelling character."

Mikki frantically thought of what to say. "Everyone has a different opinion of what beauty is."

"I'm planning on buying my version of it. I may have character, but that's not enough. I'm having a total overhaul. As seen on television. An extreme makeover. Nose. Lipo. Breast implants."

Mikki simply stared. There seemed to be nothing that Carla Christaldi wouldn't reveal about herself. "You'd think, considering the fact I'm twenty pounds overweight, that I'd at least have big boobs," Carla continued. "But mine are awful. Small but flabby. Ugh! God figured he was giving me a famous last name, since he was going to skimp on the looks department."

They lingered over lunch for almost two hours, but not a single waiter gave them a dirty look. Afterward it was apparent that Carla and Mikki had hit it off beautifully. Each had a shield the other one wanted. Mikki had physical beauty. Carla had fame. Beauty is one kind of protection, but far too common in New York. What Carla had was a sturdier shield; fame was more elusive, more valuable.

"Thanks for lunch," Mikki said. "This was fun. Listen, I'm having dinner with Justin Landis this weekend. If you want, I could mention you to him. Hey, we may end up working for the same agency."

"I would love, love, love that!" Carla said. "But I think I'd rather wait till after my surgery. As luck would have it, I'm checking into Columbia Presbyterian. For my nose job this weekend—no flowers, please. It's probably better I flaked on him today—even though my dad made the appointment." Carla pressed her business card into Mikki's hand. "This was great, girl" she said. "You're good energy. I think we met for a reason. Stay in touch?"

Mikki became so excited her mouth went dry. "That'd be great," she replied. In one day, Mikki had gone further than she had in years of climbing.

9.

MIKKI CAME TO meet me at the corner of Fifty-third Street and Second Avenue, outside of The Lion's Den. Since the day we met, we had been seeing each other often, talking on the phone several times a day. I had told her I'd be at the bar. But after my meeting with Laird Payne, I couldn't stand the thought of going inside. The outside of the bar was just as cruisy as the inside. I myself had occasionally worked the corner, jumping into expensive-looking cars for quickies.

Mikki arrived just in time to save me from a fistfight with the rival eighteen-year-old hustler I'd taken Laird from.

Now the kid approached me and asked me for a cigarette.

"I don't smoke," I told him.

"Like hell," he yelled. "You fucking cheapskate, I saw you smoking around here last night."

"Not me, buddy," I said pleasantly.

I guessed that his anger toward me had very little to do with the fact that I didn't have a cigarette and very much to do with the fact that I took off earlier that afternoon with a guy he considered an easy and affluent score.

"Yes, *you*, asshole," he said, pointing in my face (I hate that) "I'm gonna break your fucking lyin' head."

There were a few other hustlers on the corner, and they stepped closer to see what he was gonna do to me. None of them were fans of mine because I was quiet and kept to myself and didn't really bother with them much. My fear of people did not come across as fear but as condescension. I must admit I was rather crestfallen that this very young stud was taking this attitude with me, since I had had a semi-crush on him for weeks and admired his puffed-up, confident swagger from afar. He was the short but strong, dark, and brooding type, very pumped up, and he always added a cocky spring to his step as if a jaunty walk would somehow make him taller. It certainly made him sexier. My admiration turned to fear, though, when he grabbed me by the shirt and pulled me toward him.

"You think who the fuck you are!" he screamed in my face. "I said hello to you before and you turned your head!"

I knew this wasn't true, and it made me angry because I'm not like that. I'm shy but I don't snub people. I said: "So many times in the past I've said hello to you and it was like saying hello to air. Forgive me if you were in the mood this afternoon for acknowledging me."

He looked like he was going to hit me.

"Buddy, buddy, buddy . . . " I said, changing my tone. He looked like he exercised a hell of a lot more than me. Frankly, I was terrified—chicken shit that I am.

"Don't 'buddy' me," he said.

Mikki's blessed voice came from halfway across the street, and we both turned to look at her. The streetlights, lighting her hair from behind, gave her a silvery halo. She was still slightly drunk and exhilarated from her lunch. "Sorry to bother you at work, darling. But I need to talk to you." She walked right up to the two of us and smiled at the stud at my side. He said nothing, but released me.

"No rough stuff, boys," she said.

"See ya," I said to the brute as Mikki and I walked toward Third.

"That's right," he said, "get the fuck out of here. And take your cunt with you."

It made me feel proud that he called Mikki my "cunt" in front of all those other boy whores. Of course they were all as queer as the day is long, but they always put on a butch act and talked about their "bitch" at home. And here Mikki was making me legitimate.

"Thanks," I said to Mikki, "you saved my life."

"You shouldn't let him point in your face like that."

I am a coward, no doubt about it, but I was in no mood for talking about it, especially with her.

"What's up?" I asked, changing the subject. "How did your meeting go?"

"I got it," she said.

"You signed with them!" I screamed. I was ecstatic for her; I knew this was something she really wanted. She had talked about nothing else.

"I haven't signed the contract yet, but I know I will soon. I'm having dinner with Justin Landis this Saturday to talk about it."

"Oh. It's that kind of a deal."

"It's not like that. I think he really likes me."

"Meaning what?"

"Meaning that it can't hurt to have the president of the agency lusting after you."

I decided not to tell her of the possibility of my doing a book with Victoria Sweetzer. In the past, I had shot off my mouth about promising possibilities, only to have them not come to pass, so I decided to wait to tell Mikki about my ghostwriting assignment until it was definite.

Instead, I invited her to my dump for Chinese food, but she wanted to go to the movies first. We talked more on the subway and on the way to the theater, with the sound of the beggars' cups rattling with coins all around us. Her dilemma, as she explained it to me, was that she felt she could make Justin fall for her. It would help her career. She was a weak person or so she said. She needed someone powerful behind her. On the other hand, she felt guilty using someone in this way. Yet in the next breath her face would drain of emotion and she would say, "I could make Justin Landis love me." She had this kind of discerning ability, you see.

On the subway Mikki wanted to sit down. She was exhausted and was wearing high heels. We were both holding on to a pole in the middle of a subway car and looking around for vacant seats. There were none, but a stout woman who sat nearby had a bag on either seat beside her, hogging up three seats. If she would remove her bags and scoot over, Mikki and I could sit next to each other. We both looked at her: Orange extensions in her hair, mean-looking, fat, proud. Of course we were both too intimidated to ask her to move her things, although we had paid the same fare.

I was surprised, as I always am, at people's audacity. I would never think of doing this myself. What if somebody wanted to sit down but was too timid to ask? It was rude to put someone in that position. She saw that we were standing. Why not just be nice? But there was no law about this sort of thing, and if there were, no one would enforce it. I tried, through mental telepathy and by staring at the seats, to get this woman to move her bags. Instead she pulled a foul-smelling cheeseburger from her pocketbook and started tearing at it with angry little bites.

Finally, smiling politely, I asked her if she would move her bags. She scowled as if I'd insulted her. Then, rather than putting her bags on her lap or on the floor, she took a sip of her Snapple drink, dusted off crumbs, sprayed a cloying aerosol on to her ample bosom, took out her Walkman, and finally, with great fanfare, pressed the bags closer to her side, thinking, I guess, that she was making room for us, but Twiggy herself would have been hard pressed to fit into the space she provided.

We remained standing in the center of the train holding on to the pole. Mikki was sweet. She'd slide her hand down the pole till it was touching mine. Then she'd rub her pinkie up and down the back of my hand. And her pinkie, let me tell you, was a generator of heat and electricity. I just closed my eyes and waited for the fireworks. At the next stop a shitload of people entered. Their bodies absorbed what little oxygen there was in the car. They smelled of body odor, breath, hairspray, sex.

Soon the subway car had become a giant mouth, hot and panting. Mikki moved in closer. We were going to have fun in this purgatory no matter what. She rubbed her pelvis up against mine, and we bumped together to the rhythm of the train. At each subway stop the train filled up with more and more people. If we'd gotten any closer, we would have procreated.

"Something else happened today," she said giddily, in a singsong voice.

"What?" I asked. Her breath smelled like Altoids. Cinnamon flavor.

"I met someone else. Even more influential and important than Justin Landis."

"Who?" I demanded. All this talk of influential men was making me jealous. I knew she wanted to make it in show business and I knew that would take a certain amount of whoring, but I had thought of nothing else but Mikki since I'd met her. It hurt to think that people might use her while I could do nothing but watch in the shadows.

"Carla Christaldi."

"Jonathan Christaldi's daughter?"

"She's in New York. She wants to model. She wants to sign with EYE. I talked to her in the ladies' room. Then we went for lunch"

I said, "With her name and her father's connections, if she wants to sign with EYE she'll sign with EYE."

"She's not what you would think," Mikki said. "I mean, she definitely got this tough girl thing going on—the stuff you read about in the papers—but she's actually very afraid. She was puking in the ladies' room a few feet away from me when I met her. She didn't even go into her interview. I told her I'd talk to Justin about her. But she's getting some surgery first."

"She needs it," I said.

"Be nice."

I wanted to tell her about the possibility of ghostwriting Victoria Sweetzer's autobiography, but again I held back, not wanting to jinx it. I continued to play the down-on-his-luck friend. "What about me?" I said, trying to amuse her. "I want a be a model, too. Do I have to throw up on your shoes to get some help here?"

She ignored my stab at flippancy. "Imagine what it would be like to help Jonathan Christaldi's daughter. Imagine what it would be like to be her friend."

I looked at Mikki carefully. I had thought she was so scared and helpless and vulnerable when I first met her. "I can hardly believe you. Who is this climber I see before me?"

"Something has to happen for me soon. Do you know what happens to a model after she turns twenty-five? They say she's over. They say she's tired. They say she's not a fresh face."

"But you're gorgeous," I said.

"The average eye can't see what they see."

And even in subway light, the most unflattering light known to mankind, she looked so beautiful and fragile that I knew that no matter what it took for her to become famous, it was worth it, and that I would do anything to help her.

———

THE MOVIE MIKKI had chosen to see was, of course, the Jonathan Christaldi film currently playing in theaters, *Best Kept Secret*. It was about a father obsessed with his son's fiancée—a simple plot, but filled with unexpected, powerful moments. In one scene, when the father spots the girl on a crowded, rainy, midtown street and chases after her in a sort of beautifully choreographed game of cat and mouse, finally catching up to her to silently hand her his umbrella, Mikki clutched my arm, digging her nails deep into me, and practically lifting herself out of the seat.

When I looked at her, I saw tears streaming down her cheeks. They were not tears brought on in the moment by the beauty of the scene. I knew what she was thinking. It was a movie she should have been in. A part she herself could have played. She could no longer enjoy the simplest things, like a movie with a friend, without feeling envy and anger. That's how badly she wanted to be acting and leaving her mark.

Afterward we ate a takeout Chinese dinner at my place, and

later we lay on the ratty rug in front of my broken-down TV set polishing off a bottle of cheap wine. At this late hour, the only stations I received on cable were showing infomercials. Mikki, lying behind me, was rubbing her hands in my hair, down my neck, to my shoulders and my back. Fuzzy gray dust balls dreamily floated around us like miniature tumbleweed.

I was wondering if we would sleep together. On the screen there was a fifty-five-year-old washed up television actress who didn't look a minute over thirty-five. She was selling a new and "incredibly different" skin care line. She enthusiastically pitched her super-duper, under-eye moisturizing, fine-line minimizing lotion. She gushed about her "miraculous" chin and neck-firming cream. Callers phoned in to sing the praises of how well her rejuvenating mask seemed to be working on them. She breathlessly revealed that the entire package was ONLY seventy dollars, and if you acted now, she'd throw in her "stupendous" exfoliating face buffer, just for the hell of it. She failed to mention her recent Botox treatments, face lift, collagen injections, and liposuction overhaul—all of which was, at the moment, being printed in the following week's issue of *The Star* magazine.

We were laughing, but then suddenly I felt romantic. I turned to face Mikki and was trying to think of something to say that wouldn't scare her by making her believe I wanted to take over her life, but rather conveyed that I was feeling warmly toward her. My mind went blank.

"I feel like I'm just at the beginning of my career," she said. Her career again.

"Fuck your career," I said and reached out and playfully bear-hugged her. "I've got you now."

"Justin Landis and Carla Christaldi both in one day. Carla gave me her number." She let her hand trail down my face to my chest, where she played with the hair there. "Imagine I get to meet Jonathan Christaldi . . . all those wonderful movies he's made . . . what did you think of *Best Kept Secret*?" she asked

"It was an excellent movie," I said.

"I wish I could work with a director like that. I'd kill for it," she said.

"Is that your idea of pillow talk?" I said. I reached down and stroked her ass, which was round and firm but with that extra nice spongy feeling that a girl's butt can have. I loved her ass. "This is my favorite part," I said. She looked away.

"I like to be sexual with you because I know you want me and it gives me confidence," she said in a whisper. "But I don't know if we should have sex."

I withdrew from her. "If you could be that honest with everyone else, you wouldn't have to worry about anything. If you could feel as comfortable with everyone as you are with me and just be yourself, they'd all feel the same way as I do. You wouldn't have to develop your personality as if it were a role."

"It *is* me. It's just a part of me I haven't let get out yet."

"The way you're talking, though . . . becoming friends with someone . . . making someone love you. Just to help your career. That's a lie."

"I do not lie," she said, "I embellish. I deceive. But I do not lie. Anyway, you would do the same."

"No, I wouldn't. I don't think I could."

"You do it for money."

I was stung. It was my means of survival she was slighting. "That's not love," I said. "That's not even friendship."

She sat up. "I am an evil, cold person now. And I don't care," she said. I thought she was only joking, but I detected a real anger there, the anger that comes over someone when they've been through too much and gotten nothing in return.

As if to confirm her new persona, she clenched her fist and said, "I curse anyone who gets in the way of my career now. I wish . . . death on their children! Death on them! A slow, painful death!" It seemed like a bit of melodrama, but I was a little afraid. I've always been semireligious and in a way she was spitting in the face of God.

"You shouldn't curse anybody," I said. "God will make it come back on you."

"I'm thinking about making a deal with the Devil," she replied sinisterly.

"Yeah, right," I said.

She went on: "I figure that's the way Jennifer Lopez did it. A contract. The Devil would give her twenty years of the greatest fame anyone could ever ask for, and she would do her best to rot and decay what's left of modern-day morals."

I said, "You have to admit she's doing her damnedest . . . and he's living up to his end of the bargain, too—she's got movies, CDs, perfumes, and a nice ass."

"That bitch's days are numbered," she said. And then: "The Bible even talks about women like her. The Whore of Babylon. I think it's in Revelations."

I knew what she was talking about. The Whore of Babylon would rise to power and lead many a nation astray with her poisonous pussy. I thought Mikki's J-Lo theory was far-fetched, but when I thought about it, it made sense. What else could be the reason for her incredible success? Madonna had probably made the same deal twenty years before.

"You're drinking too much," I said, as I downed what was left of my wine.

"Thank you, Daddy," she giggled. "I tried playing fair. I tried doing things the right way," she said. "Now I'm taking what I can get. So what if I'm not attracted to Justin Landis? So what if I fuck him for a contract? He's using me too, right? And so what if I'm using Carla? I'm making her feel better about herself, right?"

"So you're not really going to make a covenant with the Devil?" I asked. I wasn't sure if those things were possible, but the idea of Mikki spending eternity in hell filled me with dread. Although I must admit I sometimes thought of making the same deal.

"Let's just say we have a verbal agreement."

She reached for the wine bottle and poured the remaining drops into her cup, downed it, and lay beside me again, her face close to mine. The wine was making her drowsy, and now she grew serious again. Her eyes stared into mine sadly, without blinking. On my face I could feel her light, wine-laced panting.

"Truthfully," she asked, "is it wrong to use people to get ahead?" She couldn't seem to break away from the subject of what had happened to her that day.

I sighed. I didn't like the idea of her doing it, but I had to be truthful.

"No," I said wearily, "they would only use you if you gave them the chance."

We lay there looking at each other. Outside it had begun to thunder.

"You're the male version of me," she said. "An extension of myself."

"No," I said. "I think we're different."

"Then maybe we're exactly what we need from each other. I've decided to confide in you tonight, Mario. I've decided to trust in you. I don't know why. Maybe it's because I realize that, no matter what kind of monster I am inside, I still can't do it alone."

We wrapped our arms around each other again, my face buried in her shoulder, hers in mine. Ah, the smell of it! How lovely, I thought. How lovely not to be lonely. The time seemed right.

"How fucking lovely you are tonight," I said.

"Awfully fucking nice of you to say," she replied.

"I know you said maybe we shouldn't, but don't you think we should?" I asked. We both knew I was talking about sex. There was a pause.

"You care about me, don't you, Mario?" she asked. "I know it's soon—but there's a special bond between us. Do you feel it?"

I don't know how to express my emotions too well, and although I'm a bundle of feelings, I get strangled when trying to convey anything at all. She, however, let me off the hook and didn't even wait for an answer.

"I care about you, too," she said. "I don't want to spoil us. You're the first friend I've ever had. The only friend I've ever had. So if we do it, we have to make sure the time is absolutely right and brings us closer together. Not pulls us apart."

It could have happened. With the wine warming our blood and the rain beginning outside and the gloomy shadows from the TV set and the heat generating between us, I could have kissed her. She would not have resisted. But I didn't. I was afraid to. All my life I had used sex as a sort of weapon. A way of exercising power and control, even while feeling a victim. What would happen if I mixed in other emotions with it? I was a scientist experimenting with new, weird, highly dangerous chemicals. I guess I didn't want to combine too many feelings together, out of fear. And then what if I couldn't get a hard-on? When I thought about making love to Mikki I became rock hard, but could I actually have sex with her? Would I lose it midway? I didn't dare try.

"You'll get rich and famous and forget about me," I said.

"If I make it first," she said seriously, "you make it, too. Because I'll take you with me. And if you make it first, then you'll do the same. That's why our chances are better than most."

I couldn't think of anything appropriate to say. I thought that I wanted fame just as badly as her, but I think I was more terrified of spending my life alone than of not making it. She saw nothing else but making it. Nothing. "No one wants to work more than I do. No one wants to make it more than me," were two of her constant lines.

We lay there in silence for what seemed a very long, awkward time. What was she thinking? That, I guess, is a question we all ask ourselves when the person we love falls silent. Mystery plays such an important ingredient in desire. Outside, the sky rumbled its own dissatisfactions. I tightened my grip, concentrating on the perfect balance of firmness and softness that was her body. Just before she fell asleep, she said:

"After all the shit I've been through, I've decided I *deserve* to make it."

IN TODAY'S FAME market, unhappiness can be used to great advantage. Mikki had had to endure a lot, but she often imagined herself conveying her history on a television talk show, bravely yet tearily, to a sympathetic Oprah and her bizillions of viewers:

OPRAH (*Narration over photos of MIKKI as a child*): Perhaps it was a longing to belong to someone: Mikki began having sex with her stepbrother, Freddy, when she was twelve and he was eighteen.

CUT TO: MIKKI in OPRAH's studio opposite from OPRAH on a plush, tan sofa.

MIKKI: He didn't come to me like a white knight in a girlhood dream. He ran down the basement steps to my "suite" in a sweaty tank top, drinking a wine cooler. He said to me, "You're the hottest-looking girl around," putting his thin, muscular arm around me. "Better than any of the girls over at the high school." You know, it's funny, even to my adolescent ears those lines sounded lame and tired.

CUT TO: A middle-age woman in the studio audience looking pained.

MIKKI: He said he loved me. I knew he didn't, but it's something I spent my life wanting to hear. Freddy played basketball and was popular.

CUT TO: SNAPSHOT of a preteen MIKKI standing near a young man, Freddy, wearing a tank top. He has a thin, muscular body and sandy hair, but his face is blocked out in a blur to protect his identity.

MIKKI (*Extreme close-up*): Being close to Freddy felt so good—getting attention from him so uplifting—that I decided having sex couldn't be a wrong choice.

OPRAH (*Looking seriously sympathetic*): You were still a baby, really.

MIKKI: He . . . he couldn't get it all the way, but he pushed and pushed. It hurt.

OPRAH: (*Softly*) Did you know you were being raped?

MIKKI: Years later I would consider it rape. At the time it was like . . . a tearing of my body and soul. My periods had just started—you know? Just a light sprinkling of blood once a month. I didn't even have pubic hair yet . . .

CUT TO: A pretty, young blonde woman in the studio audience wiping away tears.

OPRAH (*NARRATION shown over snapshots of MIKKI's early years. All of her family members have their faces blocked out*): Mikki's stepbrother started making regular visits to her bedroom. It went on for months and months. "No Freddie! No!" she'd say. But she always relented. Because, even with all the pain, there was this feeling of being wanted, the comfort of someone's arms around her, the call of the possibility of love. It continued up until she was fourteen. Just before she started high school. Her stepmother came home unexpectedly and started banging on the locked basement door. When Freddy and Mikki emerged from the basement, flushed, disheveled, her stepmother realized exactly what was going on.

MIKKI: Later there was a terrible fight in the house. Things were twisted to make the story sound as if I had initiated everything. My father always believed whatever she said. First my stepmother beat me, slapping me in the kitchen, through the dining room, into the living room. Then she turned on Freddy. I remember her screaming at him "Don't you know you can go to jail, you moron?" After a lot of family discussion, they decided that Freddy should enlist in the Marines.

OPRAH'S NARRATION (*over photos of a teenage MIKKI*): Soon after, Mikki started high school. The whole idea of a new school terrified her; she truly was afraid that the other kids would recognize something different in her.

THE INCIDENTS MIKKI fantasized about in the Oprah interview were true. When she started high school, in many ways she was still a child. But because she felt dirty inside, she gave off a vibe of something unsavory—something mysterious and forbidden.

Her looks, which should have worked for her, worked against her. Beauty, mixed with her shyness, made her appear aloof and conceited. They said she was a whore. They started rumors that she was pregnant. They said she was insane. "She should change her name to MacDonald's—she's served over a billion."

She heard pieces of these dialogues before classes started, in the restrooms, traveling through the halls from class to class, and in the cafeteria where she eventually stopped going, except after lunch periods when it was quiet and she could sip her diet coke quietly.

As she got older, she imagined herself so famous that these people who rejected her would one day brag about being her friend.

10.

SHE LOOKED IN the hospital mirror and let out a scream.

There was nothing so unusual about Carla's postoperative face. After her nose job and the routine liposuction on her cheeks and neck, and the chin implant, her face was swollen and bruised in the normal way. But anything that had to do with harm to the body brought back memories.

Do you want to see what your father did to me!

She remembered everything about that night. About her mother. It came back to her so vividly. The swollen, red flesh. The peeling skin.

When Carla was nine, her parents gave a dinner party at their Brentwood home. Or, more to the point, her father gave a dinner party. The guest list consisted of big names in the movie industry, including Claire Wright, the eighteen-year-old actress who would star in Jonathan Christaldi's next film.

Carla sat on the steps looking through the living room to the dining room where the elaborate dinner was taking place. She was spying, not because she was curious about movie stars but because her parents were entertaining at their home, something they rarely did. And there had been extensive preparations all day: Extra servants bustling around, fresh-cut flowers, a caterer.

Throughout the first course Babe Christaldi had sat, heavily medicated, staring at her untouched plate of food, even as the others ate their creamed asparagus soup. She was thin. Hollow eyed, with dark, crinkly circles underneath. She was only thirty, but there were already lines forming around her eyes and mouth. Only the day before she had thrown most of her clothes from her bedroom window down to the swimming pool. Now, if anyone tried to involve her in the conversation, she made only the slightest attempt to acknowledge it. A vague nod or a private, faraway smile. Mostly she smoked.

But whenever Jonathan turned his attention to the ash-blonde Claire Wright, Babe seemed to snap to attention and watch them with a frightening intensity.

Carla could recall the smells of the different foods cooking in the kitchen that drifted toward her safe hiding place on the staircase landing, from where she watched the unfolding drama of the dinner party.

At one point Babe emerged from her stupor just as Jonathan was finishing whispering something in Claire's ear. "But it always seems that way," Babe heard Jonathan murmur and he touched Claire's hand for emphasis.

Without uttering a word, Babe stood from the table and headed for the kitchen like a zombie on a mission. Everyone fell silent. The next sound heard was one of the servants crying out, "No, Mrs. Christaldi! No!" Jonathan and several of the men ran to the kitchen.

Babe had stuck her head in a pot of boiling water.

"My God!" Jonathan shouted. "My God!"

Carla, in her nightgown, ran from the stairs, through the living room, past the stunned guests into the kitchen. Everyone was standing around staring, as if they were afraid of what Babe might do if they made a move. Near the stove her mother stood like a statue, her scalded face blazing red, swollen, and blistering. Babe met Carla's horrified stare.

"You see what he makes me do!" she screamed at Carla. And with that Babe picked up the boiling pot and poured it down her torso, letting out a wailing scream. Then she fell to the floor.

"Oh, it's not so bad, honey," the hospital nurse said to Carla, bringing her back to reality. To the present. There was no reason for her to spend the night at the hospital—she could have a friend pick her up after her procedures, but she wanted to be in a safe environment. She had her father pay for the night at the hospital.

"I was just surprised," Carla said. "It scared me."

"Oh, honey, I've seen much worse. You should see how some of them look after they get the works."

Carla had at first thought it seemed a fair trade to do great violence to her body for the sake of beauty, in the hopes of being more like Mikki Britten. But now the idea of anything else being done seemed impossible

"I think," Carla said turning from the mirror, "this is it for me. I can't see putting my body through anything else."

"Were you planning on having more?"

"I . . . well, I thought about getting some liposuction around my middle and a boob job."

"Both very popular items," the nurse laughed.

"But I think I'll just . . . " Carla started and turned back to the mirror. "Shit! I think I'll just exercise more and eat better."

11.

MIKKI DID NOT want to let her fantasies run wild. Justin Landis would be just another dinner date, another man dangling a key in front of her jail cell. Many women would be throwing themselves at him now. And she was just another woman.

She was meeting him at his apartment for a drink before dinner. And now she stood in his lobby on the East Side, United Nations Plaza in a building, she was later to learn, where Truman Capote, Johnny Carson, and Robert Kennedy once lived. There was a magnificent water fountain in front of it. There were many doormen, one of whom opened the door for her and greeted her cordially. There were uniformed men behind a desk, one of whom asked her what apartment she was visiting. He rang up Justin's apartment. "Mr. Landis, Ms. Britten is here for you," he said into the phone. *How wonderful it would be, she thought, to live in a world of politeness and respect and order, a world where she was addressed as Ms. Britten.*

People confidently breezed past the front desk. They had an air about them and a way of carrying themselves—casual and easy, yet privileged. They lived here! What paths did they take, she wondered, to lead them to this life? Did they all have head starts? Come from wealthy families? The contours of their faces told her they were around her age or only slightly older and she felt jealous.

"You may go up, Ms. Britten."

She held the elevator door for a man delivering a floral arrangement of exotic, brightly colored, long-stemmed blossoms wrapped in cellophane. "Thank you, Miss," he said. She hoped he thought she had an apartment in the building; those flowers could be for her! She made a silent vow that no matter what it took, someday—someday soon—she would live like this.

All week her imagination had been building upon what she remembered of Justin. She wanted to be filled up with his presence: sexy, confident, strong, passionate. Dressed flashily in an Italian-cut suit, hair slicked backed, with intoxicating cologne. These imaginary props helped her build sexual fantasies around him; something as simple as a delicious, masculine scent would sometimes help a borderline guy over the line for her.

But Justin was dressed simply in a pale blue cotton shirt and jeans. Unscented. The wispy, unkempt hair; lackluster, watery-blue eyes; pasty, flaccid skin were all more apparent than they had been the first time. He praised the way she looked in a whiny, childish voice that left her cold. However, in the instant that her nose took in the lack of cologne, her eyes focused on the breathtaking view of the bridge from his living room, the modern, expensive-looking bric-a-brac, the size of the foyer. *He's so kind to me*, she said to herself. Success was an aphrodisiac; perhaps his personality would be one, too. As they got in the cab, she hoped he'd turn out to be a modern-day Heathcliff Justin, brooding, complicated, strong, complex. The way he saw her. That might do it.

At the restaurant many of the waitresses were aspiring models. They recognized Justin, stood at attention, and side-glanced Mikki, trying to figure out the secret to what it was that singled her out in his eyes.

I must not let him go, she thought. *Protect me, God*, she said under her breath. *Help me to make the right moves.*

"What are you thinking about?" he asked.

She wondered how many other women had been in this very position. Sitting in front of Justin Landis, a lobster dinner in front of each of them. Knowing that he had the power to hand her a career with a couple of carefully thought out phone calls, wondering what to say to him, what self to present to captivate him, move him, reach him, make him fall in love with her. Each woman not really wanting him—wanting only what he could give. She ran through her repertoire of personalities, wondering which one to present. A strong woman, pushy and arrogant would exaggerate his own weakness. Someone too ambitious would instantly be crossed off the list; she would use him and then dismiss him. Overtly sexy would seem suspect. He was not a sexy man. By now he knew that if a woman threw herself at him, she'd have a hidden agenda.

Mikki had been hurt in her life, abandoned by her real parents, left alone when her adoptive mother died. Her pain was real. It stepped forward.

"Are you lonely?" Mikki asked Justin. She was looking for that thread, that magical string she could pull that would make him open up to her.

"No, I have lots of friends," he replied. As an afterthought: "Are you?"

She sipped her wine. Here was the opening she had been waiting for. She imagined she was playing a role in a very important movie. The scene would have gone something like this:

INT: RESTAURANT: NIGHT

                        MIKKI
                    (To JUSTIN)
        I guess because I was alone through most
        of my childhood, through my teen years,
        that being alone has become a part of me.
        I'm lonely but it's all I know, so it doesn't
        hurt as much.

            (Pushing hair out of her face)
        It's embarrassing in a way.

                        JUSTIN
        What is?

                    MIKKI
Admitting that you're lonely.

                    JUSTIN
          (Reaching across table to stroke
                MIKKI's cheek)
I always thought that a woman who looked
like you wouldn't know the meaning of the
word loneliness.

                    MIKKI
              (Whispering)
I know the meaning.

———

HER COSTUME WAS a strategically colored tank dress. The genius of the garment was that the beige silk was the exact tone of her flesh, which made it almost impossible to tell where the material ended and her skin began, forcing the human eye to decide what texture was the more luscious—with the silk losing out. She continued:

                    MIKKI
Of course, looks can always bring
something to you, at least for the moment.
So many nights, when I was lonely or
longing for something more in my life, I
was made to feel valuable and important
to someone. Yet after it was over—sex that
is—I realized the truth: I could have been
anybody. I may have been first choice, but
if I didn't respond, in this age of quick pick-
up sex, there was always second or third.

JUSTIN

But you have something else, Mikki. A
tenderness, a sensitivity that I find so rare
in women today. In anybody today.

MIKKI

You've known a lot of beautiful women in
your life, haven't you, Justin?

JUSTIN

Yes.

MIKKI

Do you really see something different
in me?

JUSTIN

That's why we're here.

MIKKI

I feel different, too. Ever since I was a little
girl I've had a hunger in me . . . a need. I
think other people sense this thing in me,
too, but it makes them step back, instead
of taking advantage of it and exploiting it
properly. I don't blame them—even I can't
describe exactly what it is.

JUSTIN

But if you did know what that special
quality was, if you recognized it, then the
impact of it wouldn't be so strong.

THE TRICK, OF course, was to not really expose a thing. She was merely acting on feelings that she had buried after years of humiliations. Knowing all along that he himself wanted to pass the night with her. But now she was determined to get something out of it. She was seducing a man for whom she had no physical desire. And because she did not desire him sexually, it somehow made her more desirable to him, for we all want what is unattainable.

"What was your childhood like?" Justin asked her.

Mikki didn't really want to think of her childhood, but there it was—like a saved message she thought she had deleted a long time ago.

"I was adopted. I don't know where I came from," she whispered.

"Did you . . . did you ever think of finding your real parents?"

It always seemed perfect, Mikki's story. A press agent couldn't have dreamed up anything better for her. The amazing thing is, she really did come from nowhere. She really had no roots. She was created for the public. For public consumption. Her adoptive father told her that her real parents were a teenage couple from the south. But since he was always lying to her, she didn't know what to believe.

She shook her head and tried to look at him with complexity. "No. I wouldn't know where to begin. The woman who adopted me died when I was ten. Then my father remarried—right away—some slut . . . the typical, wicked stepmother."

"Three mothers? By the time you were . . . how old?"

"Ten," she said, and lowered her eyes. It wasn't so exceptional. *It wasn't so horrible, really*, she said to herself. "Lots of girls had it worse than I did," she told Justin.

From a very early age she would stare at herself in the mirror for hours—playing the tragedy queen—sometimes making up her face with a variety of colors, sometimes just staring: "I belong to no one," she would say.

"I never knew where I belonged," she said.

"I knew there was something sad in you," Justin said softly.

She needed to show he was in control, so she allowed the seductress to emerge; she kicked off her heels. The hurt girl turned into a vampish slut. Leaning far back in her seat, she stretched out a leg and, placing her foot in Justin's lap, playfully jabbed at his crotch with her stockinged toes. Her eyes fixed steadily on him, with her cocky, crooked, model smile. She could feel, with her toes, that he was getting a hard-on.

"I'm not sad right now," she said.

Waiters seemed to be aware that something sexual was going on, and they circled the table like hornets. The combination of the lost baby and the erotic temptress who gave a great foot-job thrilled Justin.

"Mikki," he said, "I think you're just testing me."

"Testing you for what?"

"I don't know—but I hope I pass."

After the meal, over coffee (she had turned down dessert), he started talking about his plans for her career, and she willed her heart to stop beating so wildly.

"I want to break you in slowly," he said. "Get you a few small prestigious jobs and then, BAM, drop you like a bomb on the public."

"Does that mean I'm with EYE?" she asked.

"I didn't know there was any question of it."

SHE SAT IN the back seat of the cab holding Justin's hand. Their destination was Justin's apartment, and she knew what was expected.

He kissed her. His lips seemed to her too compliant, too loose—rubbery is the word that came to her mind. His mouth was too wet. Then his thumb circled the palm of her hand tenderly, and she reminded herself that not everyone in the world was her enemy. Not everyone wanted to use her. Some people would be pulling for her. He's not taking advantage, she told herself. He is a nice guy and he thinks this is mutual. She had given him every indication.

This is the one thing I have that is readily apparent and desirable, she said to herself. *This is the one thing I have that can empower me.*

MIKKI CHECKED HIS medicine cabinet for Xanax. None.

She came out of the bathroom and saw that he was already naked. Even in the half-light his body was fish-belly white and flaccid. *He's so sweet to me*, she thought. She began to undress. Lying down naked on his bed, she became an object, a peach, sweet and available and temporarily fulfilling.

"Do you mind if I give you a back rub?" he asked.

"No, not at all," she said.

Actually, she wouldn't mind a back rub. Maybe he was one of those people who got off while doing something other than fornication. Maybe she wouldn't have to sleep with him after all. She turned onto her stomach.

"It's cold at first," he said, a bit too late. He had already poured scented oil on her back and the sudden coldness of it sent a shiver down her spine. His hands started working on her. Even his back rub was inept, lacking in any finesse or force. Just hands rubbing in a helter-skelter fashion. An ass, a thigh, and oops, he slipped a finger under and into her vagina. Sneaky little devil. She allowed that, but when he tried to insert that same finger in her ass, her whole body tensed and he quickly drew it away.

"Do you mind if I switch that lamp off?" she asked.

He seemed disappointed. "Don't you like to see what's going on?"

"Actually I think it's more romantic with the lights off."

He switched the lamp off and went back to his work.

Her body, she was aware, was toned and firm thanks to constant visits to the gym and some recent boxing classes. His hands continued clumsily over her, and she tried to concentrate on what her flesh felt like to him. That didn't work. So to disassociate herself from the act she devised a sexual fantasy for herself:

Mikki Britten is a famous Hollywood actress. Because sexy comedies make the most money for her, she is internationally known as a sex symbol. A woman everyone talks about. A woman on the news, on the Internet, on the radio, in the magazines. Being in desperate need of a rest, she is vacationing on a cruise ship in the Caribbean. She has just finished three pictures in rapid succession and is on the verge of a breakdown. Rumors of an affair with her latest costar, Tom Cruise, are rampant. The tabloids have been reporting that he may ask her to marry him. Is it a cover-up? Is it a romance? "Are you Tom's latest beard?" one brazen journalist asked her as she left a swank New York eatery. "Is it true you went to his hotel room wearing a raincoat with nothing underneath?" another reporter asked her in a late-night phone call. "Leave me alone!" she screamed into the receiver (even though it was true), and the *Enquirer* printed the whole squalid story.

The reporters couldn't know that they never actually had sex, Mikki and Tom. They had an intense friendship. They filmed erotic love scenes by day. Shared cozy dinners together at night, discussing their lines for the following workday. Late in the evening he would come into her room and lie down next to her, perfectly naked. Never touching her. Never showing desire. She didn't dare move . . . and the two fell asleep that way.

Everyone wanted to know her next move—reporters, fans, producers, agents. The pressure of not being sexually desired was making her come undone. What could she do? How could she make him want her? Her doctors recommended a vacation. Her agent let out a press release: "Mikki Britten will be taking a short trip to relax after an emotionally draining period due to creative activity."

A CRUISE TO FLEE CRUISE, the headlines exclaimed.

Even an unsettling "affair," she had to admit, wasn't so bad when the entire world is interested in the outcome.

Now she is walking on deck, trying to get Tom out of her mind but unable to stop wondering why he hadn't touched her. "I'm walking around packing a lunch," she joked to her agent. Her body is inflamed. It is very late; she is wearing a nightgown of some kind of transparent white material and it billows behind her like an illusion. By chance she passes the kitchen, where she sees Antonio, a dishwasher. He looks up from a sink of greasy dishes. Doesn't say a word. His only reaction to her beauty is to let his cigarette drop from his lips into the sink, exhaling slowly, thick white smoke oozing from his lips. Their eyes meet and—Bing! Bang! Boom!— the reaction is like *that*. Instant. He has dark, Latin skin. Darker than any of the other guys she'd ever been attracted to before. He approaches her, his pecs rippling through an open white shirt. One of the things that turns her on is that he has a flashy, vulgar quality, sure of his sexual magnetism.

And she didn't have to impress or seduce him in any way. It was already there, sexuality stripped down to its simplest level, and there was a relief in this. He picks up a glass of ice water and lets an ice cube slide into his mouth. He's very close now. Eyes like spectacular green gems set in a dark velvet case. Wind whips against his thrilling black hair. Both their bodies are wet. They are alone. Anything could happen. She is in a position of power. Above him. Yet sexual desire brings everyone down to the same level. She wants to prove this theory wrong but is transfixed.

He takes the ice cube from his mouth and slides it down her cheek, her neck, over her breasts. She feels degraded but does not move. Then he places the ice back into his mouth and makes a movement as if to kiss her and, instead, passes the ice cube from his mouth to hers. The coldness is a violation to her mouth. She lets it linger there briefly, then spits it out contemptuously. Yet she wants him to degrade her, that's half the fun. He smiles, grabs her by the neck, and guides her face close to his with a gentle force. His skin is an exquisite rich brown, hers a flawless cream, and the sight of this contrast is a powerful turn-on. Her scents are mint, Chanel, and a hand lotion smelling vaguely of roses. His scents are beer, tobacco, sweat, and hair oil. Combined they are delicious.

In her a raging fire starts down below. And he opens his mouth, his breath pushing all the right buttons, and his lips encircle hers and sucks them. She relents and opens her mouth, and she kisses him hard and demanding, her hands roam his body, wanting more . . . it is thrilling to her to play out the scene simply to see what will happen next. Latin saxophones wail in her heart. When she places her hands under his shirt on his waist she finds the skin there taut and hard, an every-day-at-the-gym body. The kiss lasts a good long time; his tongue seems to want to know every centimeter of her mouth, even licking her teeth. This brings a thrill.

For the first time this is passion, and while living in the moment of it, she finds the feeling of passion so pure, so clear, so uncut by any other emotion, that she cannot remember there ever being anything else. Everything else that had happened, or would happen, was inconsequential to what was happening right now. And then they let loose on the floor. He sucks her. She sucks him. He fucks her. And it goes like that. She cannot stop herself from probing further, digging deeper, making the sex seem, to her, more degenerate and primitive. When he enters her—his body in motion is a machine switched on automatic, designed, built, and operated to give her pleasure. They start rocking in perfect rhythm, faster and faster.

Antonio, Antonio, Antonio, Mikki thought.

"Mikki! Mikki! Mikki!" Justin screamed.

It was over. Mission accomplished. A complete success. "I . . . it never was like that before," Justin said.

Yet.

After Justin came, she was repulsed, feeling all the more horrible about her repulsion because she liked him so much. But his cum was dripping down her thighs onto the mattress. The thought of him touching her now was equivalent to the thought of having sex with her father.

Don't cry now, fool, she said to herself. Smile, smile, and if there are tears in your eyes, don't explain them. Don't care what he thinks. He likes your mystery. Let him figure it out.

She smiled through her tears.

"What are you thinking about?" he asked.

"Nothing. I'm just enjoying being with you," she said. "Do you mind if I take a shower?" she added quickly. She didn't want him to detect her lie.

"Of course not."

I should ask him to join me, she thought as she headed for the bathroom, *but I just can't.* In the shower she regretted her decision to not have him join her. This night was too important to make any mistakes. The water blasted out as hot as she could stand it—she needed to cleanse and rejuvenate herself for the second act. There were no regrets, however, for sleeping with him. Sex was her calling card. She knew he'd call again.

After the shower she tried to repair any silent misunderstandings between them. Time for some spin control: She emerged from the bathroom with the towel draped as alluringly as possible. She let some wet hair hang on her face. The art of seduction.

Now came the time for more payoffs. When she had first walked into his apartment, its opulence had made her feel helpless. Now she felt secure in the fact that he wanted her sexually, and she felt her power creeping back—if only she could use it correctly. She placed her forefinger in her mouth and bit at a cuticle seductively, seemingly oblivious that he was watching. She had secured her position at EYE. But the fantasy for this meeting was not complete. After modeling there was the movies. A seed must be planted. And that's where Carla Christaldi came in. She wanted to help her. She wanted to be owed a favor by the daughter of the most powerful director in the world.

"I met a girl the other day who might interest you," Mikki said casually as she studied her manicure. The shower had succeeded in making her feel less dirty. It was easier for her to begin again.

"Oh?"

"Yes, I thought you might want to take a look at her for the agency. Carla Christaldi."

"That bitch? Ha. Her father made her an appointment. She didn't even show up."

"I know, but I talked to her. She did show up, but she was afraid to meet you. She's really determined, but she feels she's not good enough yet. Actually, she's in the hospital now. Recovering from some surgery."

"You think Carla Christaldi has potential as a model?"

"Truthfully, no, Justin. I don't think that she'd be a wonderful fashion model. But she's an interesting and complicated commodity . . . a fascinating object for the camera to explore. The publicity . . ."

"What about her substance abuse problems?"

" . . . the publicity that would generate for the agency could help establish it. She told me the drug thing is under control. She's ready to take charge of her life and claim her rightful position as a celebrity."

"Hmm," Justin said.

"She's in the news a lot—that would mean EYE would be in the news a lot." Mikki placed her wet forefinger on his lips and traced the outline of his mouth.

"True, but the whole idea of EYE is to bring the best and most beautiful models in the world to one agency. I'm not going for celebrity spokespeople."

"Justin, you said yourself that the standards of what makes a good model are changing. The public is obsessed with fame. That's the modern standard of beauty. And Carla has that." She placed her mouth on his nipple and casually sucked and lightly bit it, slowly, as if it were the most important and tasty object in the world. Justin moaned with pleasure.

"Okay, I'll see her. Tell her to call me and make an appointment. And tell her to show up this time."

Mikki lifted her head.

"It will be in a couple of weeks. After she heals a bit."

"Fine."

"But, Justin, tell her how good she looks. Make her feel good about herself. She has so little self-esteem—it would help her tremendously if she felt she had potential."

"So, you would want me to make it look like I'd be taking her on strictly for her potential as a model and not her celebrity status?"

"The art of seduction," Mikki said, ironically. " Feeling one way and making a person think you're feeling another. I've had a chance to get to know her. I think she's a really good person. She needs something to give her an identity. Make her think she's a model and let her name bring some prestige to the agency. It will be doing you both some good. Take her on, Justin. I have a feeling about her. She could only bring good things to us."

His eyes, Mikki noticed, registered something on the word "us." He drew Mikki closer, wrapping his arms around her. When she looked into his face, he was smiling. Her eyes, however, were black and far away, revealing nothing.

But it was not lost on him that she was already asking for favors.

12.

I STEPPED OUT of the freezing-cold shower. Looking down, I thought, if someone were to see my cock now, they'd think I was another "Princess Little Meat." I had read that some people had referred to Montgomery Clift that way. It was small and shriveled and looked pathetic. Luckily for me it was a grower. *A little stimulation, a few strokes, a look through a hot magazine, and I'd be back to normal,* I reassured myself.

I had been in the shower for a very long time, lost in thoughts of how to save money. Finances were, once again, getting to be a major concern. It had been so long since my cell phone rang, I was considering giving it up. The cell, I mean. I was getting most of my clients hanging out at bars late at night or from online chat rooms anyway. *Maybe I should give up my home phone and just keep the cell?* Either way I had to cut expenses. It was funny because just when I had decided the cell had become an unnecessary luxury, it rang. I grabbed a towel and ran for the phone.

"Hello, Poet," the voice said.

"Laird?" I asked. And then there was a frozen silence. A warning flashed in my brain—he had never told me his name. How would I know who he was? *Oh shit, oh shit, oh shit!* I hoped I hadn't screwed up the deal with Victoria Sweetzer.

"How do you know my name?" he asked icily.

"You're the only one who calls me Poet," I said.

"I never told you my name."

"Sure you did," I lied. "In the cab on the way to the hotel, don't you remember?"

There was another arctic pause, and then he said: "Victoria

Sweetzer wants to meet you. She likes to help struggling artists, and she thinks you might be the kind of ghostwriter she's looking for."

"Great. Excellent," I said. But I mean, huh? What kind of ghostwriter was she looking for? "When can I meet her."

"SHE'S NOT ON THE WEST COAST," he screamed into the phone. "SHE'S HERE IN NEW YORK!"

Was I going insane? I hadn't said anything about the West Coast. Maybe this guy was totally nuts and playing games with me, just to annoy me and make my life even more miserable. Obviously he had the upper hand.

"Okay, great. She's here in New York. Wow. Awesome. We don't have to spend the money on the plane fare."

There was another pause filled with undiluted loathing streaming at me across the airwaves. Then, with great effort, he completed the transaction: "Victoria has an assistant of many years. His name is Cooper. Call him at this number, the one I'm about to give you, and he will set up a meeting." He gave me the number and I wrote it on the palm of my hand. "Call him now." And then he hung up.

I was standing there in a towel, dripping into an ever-growing puddle, but before the moisture could erase the number from my palm (it had happened before), I immediately dialed Cooper's number.

"Yes?" (*Queeny, persnickety, bitch* my mind deduced from that one word.)

"Can I . . . I mean, um, may I speak to Cooper please?" (*Asshole, loser, retard* his mind deduced from my garbled sentence.)

"What's this in reference to?"

"I was, uh, recommended to call him regarding Victoria Sweetzer—about the ghostwriting position."

"Ghostwriting position?"

"Laird Payne recommended me." What the hell, I needed to use his name. It didn't matter at this point.

"Oh, oh! The *ghostwriting* position. Yes, that's right. Victoria is considering writing her memoirs and she's looking for the right . . . journalist."

"Yes, Laird told me."

He gave me a time and a Sutton Place address, but didn't ask a single question about my writing experience or *any* thing about myself. I knew something was up. But it was interesting. What would happen? At least I might get a chance to see Victoria Sweetzer in person. And, to me, that was something.

13.

"IT WAS A fucking nightmare," the voice said on the other end of the receiver.

"Hello?" Mikki said, in a hoarse voice. She had been sleeping. A deep, real, nourishing sleep, brought on without tranquilizers for a change. She had signed the contract with EYE model management two weeks before and was already starting to get booked into decent jobs.

"It's me. Carla. Christaldi! I just wanted to tell you I signed with EYE today. Justin Landis is fucking great! He said I have real potential. It's because of you I even had the guts to go, man. I owe you."

So, Justin had come through for her after all. "If you could see me right now, Carla," Mikki replied, "you'd see I'm smiling. But what are you talking about? What was a nightmare?"

"The plastic surgery, girl! I was black and blue and red all over for over a week. A mess."

"Really?"

"Grisly, baby."

"I thought you were going in for a nose job."

"A nose job and some other . . . face stuff. I guess it was a normal procedure, but I have this—thing—about bruising. It freaks me out."

"How does it look, by the way?"

"I'm a new person. Not so afraid anymore."

"I can't wait to see you . . . "

"Still, I was shitting a pill about meeting Justin. But I thought about you drinking scotch from your purse! How cute you were! And I said, 'Fuck, if Mikki can do it, I can too.'"

"Awww." Mikki said. "Really, I didn't do anything."

"Are you kidding me? You did everything. Talking to Justin about me. Setting up the appointment. Just talking to you gave me the confidence to go through with the fucking nose job."

"Well then, I'm happy I helped you out."

"I would have called you sooner, but I was having a celebration dinner with my father, asshole that he is. I'm a model now, so he's so proud of me. He said, 'God, Carla, you look wonderful. You're really becoming the woman you were meant to be.'"

Dinner? With Jonathan Christaldi? Mikki snapped to attention. "That is so great," Mikki said.

"I'm not going in for any body work though," Carla added. "No more surgery. I'm still gonna get a fab bod, like you, my dear, don't get me wrong. I'm just going to hire a trainer and work really hard."

"You're probably better off."

"I've already lost seven pounds . . . seeing my spectacular black and blues made me so sick, I couldn't even eat."

"Seven pounds? Without diet pills?" Mikki said. "Maybe I should have some surgery."

"As if anything on you could be improved," Carla replied. There was a silence. "Sorry to call so late," she added. "I just had to tell you. Did I wake you up?"

"No. Yes. It doesn't matter. I'm happy for you, Carla. Really happy." And Mikki was happy—here they were being chummy-chummy, girlie-girlie, in the middle of the night.

"I'm so fucking excited," Carla said. "It's the most amazing thing that's ever happened to me. We're both starting out. We're both at the same agency. We both have Justin taking care of us. And Mikki, only good things are gonna happen to us. Both of us."

She sat up in her bed, heart racing. The fact that Carla had just had dinner with her father added an extra charge to the emotions running through her. She climbed out of bed and took some clonazepam, a tranquilizer. It had been prescribed to her only months before when she complained to her doctor that she would wake up in the middle of the night in the throws of a panic attack, unable to breathe at the thought of growing older, her career going nowhere, and no possibilities in sight. Her career finally seemed to be on the right track, but she still needed the pills—no longer for unhappy torturous thoughts. Now her heart was pounding with an excitement for the promise of a better life. She took three and waited for the calm to embrace her. Drowsy and warm, she dialed my number, only to reach my voicemail. She left a drugged message.

When she slept that night, she dreamt of movie sets and Hollywood parties. The message I heard when I came in early that morning disturbed me. Mikki's recorded voice sounded odd and slurred, but she spoke with such force that I saved the message, and I have the cassette to this day: "Honey? Honey? This could be big, man. I met Carla Christaldi for a reason. Her father will become the love of my life. Creator of my life . . . 'night."

JUSTIN'S AGENCY EYE began to flourish, as everyone knew it would. He had snatched five supermodels from various top agencies, including his ex-wife Jana Janelow, who was now one of the hardest-working (and richest) models in the world. Justin also had a stable of ten up-and-coming girls, one of whom was Mikki Britten. He called in every favor that was owed to him and got write-ups in *Vanity Fair*, daily syndicated gossip columns, regular mentions on Page 6, and was the subject of a profile on *"E" True Hollywood Story*, a profile which was merely an excuse to interview a bunch of delectable top models. On the show Justin said of Mikki Britten, the newest model in his stable, "She catches sex in a photograph like no other model working today." And that little plug for the novice model made people ask about her.

Soon after their first night together, gifts came to Mikki from Justin—and cards and invitations to expensive dinners, opening nights of plays, fun parties. He began using the word "love" right away. He became irate and impatient when she didn't say "I love you." And so she began to say it—even though she did not feel it in the true sense. "I love my new pedicure, too," she would add in a way that conveyed that she was only joking about her love being on par with a terrific pedicure—but somehow this was also being honest. She was usually so vulnerable and needy; then this bitch would rear its furious head.

Her position at the agency was respected and secure because it was known that she was Justin's lover. He was aware of her ambition and sensed her restlessness. In those beginning months of the agency, he really didn't have much time to spend with her and that suited her fine. Justin knew his interest in Mikki made her important, and he realized that as long as he could further her he had a controlling power over her. For the most part, she pretended to adore him. He, in return, fooled himself into thinking she was in love with him. Was she taking advantage of him? She thought about it often. Yes! But no more than he allowed her to. And in many ways, they were taking advantage of each other. And when everything else, all the trimmings and drama are stripped away—that is what life in this city is all about.

———

I'M WILLING TO get ravaged in return for a few years of happiness, she wrote in her diary. If I make it big enough, they will be able to pick through the ruins and fix me up a bit.

Budding fame brought a new recklessness to Mikki. She was flown to Paris for an important shoot, almost missed her flight, and checked into the hotel. Arriving at the set, she found herself in the dressing room with Jana Janelow. They were changing clothes—being fawned over and desired. It was all she ever wanted.

She had dropped out of school and left home in her senior year of high school when she was almost eighteen.

"I want to be an actress," she had told her father.

Her stepmother voiced her two cents, about how Mikki did not know how to do anything, how she was afraid to simply go to the grocery store by herself. "You'll never get anywhere," she said. "You're not tough, like you need to be to make it as an actress. They'll use you up and spit you out. You're good at makeup. Better to go to beauty school."

The woman infuriated her. Not because she was cold and indifferent, but because she reminded Mikki of something ruined. Once she had been a beautiful woman; now, eaten by boredom and age, she resented Mikki because of the promise she showed.

"Believe in me, Dad," Mikki said, looking away from her stepmother to her father urgently. "Michelle," he replied, "you're a pretty girl. Do you think you're the only one in the world? Do you know what the odds are? Go back to school . . . "

"I'm an actress," she said, cutting her father short. "I'm going to make it." And she smiled with such luminosity that she silenced them. Mikki never stopped doubting herself, but that little something in her, that special feeling, pushed her forward. "And when I do make it," she concluded, "I won't forgive you."

An assistant was banging on the door. The sounds of a photographic shoot were going on around her and she hugged herself with delight.

"I'm never going to be able to get the hair right," someone said.

"Do we get to keep any of these clothes?" Mikki asked, reaching for the wine glass yet again.

Bang, bang, bang on the door. "Are you girls ready?"

"Out!" Jana announced. "Everybody out! Out! OUT! I want some time alone with Mikki before the next setup." A mob of hair and makeup and wardrobe people filed out. "Now, as for you, little girl," Jana said. She grabbed Mikki roughly, pulling her close and kissing her with a closed mouth—but pressing her lips forcefully against Mikki's, swaying her head back and forth, as if she were blending her lipstick in with Mikki's. Then she pressed her groin into Mikki's.

"So what is it like for *you*, fucking Justin?" Jana asked, pulling away.

"It's nice," Mikki said weakly. "It's good."

"Oh, come on, Boo. You're forgetting I was married to the guy. You can be honest with me."

"'Boo?' Where does that come from? Are we in the hood? What's going on?" Mikki did not want to answer Jana's question. She knew that whatever she said, even in a moment of intimacy, would be repeated at the next shoot or the next party or the next moment she wasn't present.

"He's very tender with me," Mikki added.

"Tender? Oh, I love that," Jana howled, throwing her head back with laughter. "You know, we got married when we were both nineteen. I didn't know shit about the world. I was brought up in the tradition, like . . . you don't ask questions. You accept. You marry someone—you take on their emotional baggage."

"I'm not saying Justin doesn't have some baggage," Mikki said carefully. "But we all do."

"On our wedding night," Jana whispered into Mikki's ear—a little girl with a secret—"I waited for Justin in bed. He photographed me there—could you believe it—waiting! His camera was his cock. I was wearing this little black peignoir, spicy perfume . . . the whole bit. God, I was ready. And he goes . . . 'It's too late for me to go to bed. I have an early appointment to show my portfolio. I won't be able to wake up.' I just laid there all night. Wearing the silvery lipstick *he* bought for me, by the way."

"Why did you stay with him?"

"I loved him, at the time, I guess. And he did make me a star. That was his obsession. He shot my portfolio, which was amazing. Changed my name. Brought me to New York. Got me into see all the important agencies. Got me in the papers. He had a knack for publicity. Believed in me when no one else did. I never would have made it without him."

"I wouldn't be here without him either."

"It would be so funny if he knew that . . . I really did love him. And the sad part is, after I made it—after he made me into a supermodel—he lost interest in me."

"Well," Mikki sighed, "at least he made you first. That's more than most lovers do."

"You know what the truth is, baby? He doesn't want to fuck us. Not really. The truth. The brutal truth. The cold hard, honest, up-your-ass truth, is that the motherfucker wants to *be* us."

"Oh, come on. He's very horny with me."

"Horny to *be* you, baby. There's a difference. Justin married me. He molded me. He dressed me. He made me. But he never really liked fucking me."

Mikki thought that over in her fuzzy mind. "It's funny, but I know what you mean. I have a friend like that. Mario. He thinks he's in love with me, but it's really just some . . . freakish fascination."

Jana moved in to kiss Mikki again. Mikki didn't feel any passion. But the desire in Jana turned her on. It was difficult for her to believe that only a few months before, Jana had been an untouchable goddess. Now she was touching her. She opened her mouth a crack, and Jana's tongue instantly slid in, full of force and fire, exploring every inch of Mikki's mouth.

"See?" Jana said quietly, pulling away. "You really didn't like that. But you went through with it because I'm where you want to be. In a way, you want to be me."

"Jana," Mikki said, her eyes still closed from the kiss.

"What?" Jana asked.

"You're at the very top. I do want to be there. Give me some advice. Please."

Jana paused. Placed her hand on Mikki's breast. Squeezed a little to check if they were real. They were. "My advice to you is always look as good as you do now. And never believe a word that is told to you."

Knock. Knock. BANG! "They're not getting dressed. They finished getting dressed. They're drinking wine."

Someone called into the room: "You girls shouldn't drink while you're working."

Jana picked up a nearly empty wine bottle from the makeup table and violently threw it at the door, shattering it in millions of pieces.

"Like the christening of a ship," Mikki said, monotone, the effects of pills and wine washing over her.

"What's going on in there?" someone shouted through the door.

"So much for all that anger-management therapy you've been through," Mikki whispered to Jana and giggling. And Jana, once again, passionately threw her arms around Mikki.

The door flew open. (Giggle. Giggle.) Jana and Mikki were locked in a mad embrace.

"How many more outfits do we have left to shoot?" Mikki asked nonchalantly, as a stream of hair and makeup people and stylists filed into the room.

"God, you girls look great, let's get you on the set."

"Oh, my God. We're going to be here all night."

"What?" Mikki gasped, loving it. "I have a plane to catch to New York early in the morning!"

Then she slouched to the floor drunkenly. Immediately hands lifted her from the floor and steered her steadily to the setup.

Her hair was being brushed out again. Her makeup reapplied. Outfit adjusted. This is the life she had always wanted. She could get as out of control as she wanted, and there would be a crew of people there to pick up the pieces, sweep up the mess, and see that she got through it. Finally she could do her high-wire act with a net underneath her. And Justin was the reason she was here.

The fashion crowd didn't care that Mikki was high; they just wanted her to hurry up. Sometimes they even preferred it. It seemed to unchain her. She flaunted her pill taking, her drinking to combat her sensitivity, her excessive food binging and purging and starvation diets. Her affair with the rich-and-powerful model management owner.

Later that night she would lay in Jana's arms, letting Jana's tongue roam over the delicacies of her body. It made her both queasy and excited. This was the modeling world. The big, bad world. The world of celebrity. This was the way people behaved. Mikki wanted to be the ultimate—the living, breathing, walking—example of extremity.

The people in the biz loved it! The industry had been dull for years. There were no new Gias, no new Naomi Campbells. Now there was Mikki Britten. She was like the Judy Garland of the modeling world! There was an excitement when she showed up. The more complicated her life became, the more pills and alcohol she swallowed, the better she performed, the more exciting she became.

Romantic, flirtatious, sensitive, vulgar, dreamy, moody, cruel—she was every woman wrapped in one magnificent package.

———

OFTEN WHEN SHE was in New York, late at night, after a day of shooting, Justin would call her. But the calls began to lose their potency; she found herself dozing as he talked to her. Usually she had to get up early to be photographed, which he well knew, and she felt he should let her get some sleep. His calls were feverish, drunken monologues that made her gasp in annoyance. Calls that were often an odd mixture of extreme insecurity and ridiculous bravado.

It's very hard for me to love someone, Mikki wrote in her diary, as he went on and on into the phone, *because of the things that I want even more than love. I wish I could give my ambition to somebody else. And if I have any talent, they can have that, too.*

"Why would someone like you want someone like me?" he would ask, although the answer to her seemed obvious.

"Because you're a special guy," she would say, wearily. This wasn't absolutely untrue. He was, after all, one of the first people to recognize her rare and singular star potential. She wanted to please him; she was aware of his importance in her life. "There's something dark in you," he would say. And she couldn't explain it, nor could she deny it.

Then, afraid to pursue the course of the conversation, he would ask, "Do you miss me?" in a whisper.

"What?" she would ask sleepily.

"Are you deaf?" he would snap, furious at her hesitation, "Or do you intend to act stupid all your life?" She took his insults stoically. No matter what, he had the upper hand. She wasn't famous enough to go out on her own. Not yet.

He continued to book her for the best go-sees, and if their telephone conversations turned ugly, it was Mikki who called him back twenty minutes later to apologize after they had angrily hung up.

———

BEFORE, SHE HAD made her living working in department stores. Standing as still as a statue, her heels spiking her to the marble floors.

Then, at night, at a current club trying to hook up. Into the early hours in some guy's bed thinking that, maybe, this will be the guy to make her a star. She became promiscuous; she lost track of the number of men she'd slept with.

After her long days in the city, her nights of casual sex, she always wearily crawled between the sheets in her own bed in Queens and cried quietly. It seemed better for the scene. It was easy to imagine recording her for a reality television show. Thinking of her past and present. How far off she was. How she wasn't aggressive enough to compete, how afraid she was of people, and how she often let them walk all over her. How afraid she was of everything. Fear became something to overcome when doing the most trivial things. She thought of how she had walked into a boutique in the West Village to look at a pair of white shorts and felt the sales girls were "looking at her," so she turned around and walked conspicuously out, embarrassed. Many things like that. In the videotape of life these were the scenes that would play back most during the nights.

She believed in God and turned to Him many times during these nights of despair, and she found comfort in knowing that He saw her and understood. She admitted to Him that everything was too complicated and problematic to handle by herself. She prayed; when she gave God her load to carry everything seemed to matter a little less: Empty-headed seventeen-year-old models making it. Her self getting older. Her own career going nowhere. Being alone. What good was worrying about it?

Instead she might lull herself to sleep by imagining herself lying at the foot of a golden throne while a kindly, colossal man looked down on her protectively. And she closed her eyes, and she told Him her secrets, and she felt safe and drowsy, and sometimes she could sleep. Sometimes.

On other nights, while she tossed about on tangled, sweat-damp sheets, Marlon Brando (the way he looked in 1950) would enter her bedroom, undressed, and slip into bed with her. They are lovers, an actor and an actress, both world famous.

This is not a black-and-white celluloid image from *A Streetcar Named Desire*. This is the real thing, hot flesh and blood. He puts his arms around her and she feels his muscles, hard and lumpy, but comforting. Their bodies meld together, a perfect fit.

Panting, touching, searching. There would never be a time when they were tired of being together. When they didn't crave each other. This is what she will bring to the screen in their movies together. Their chemistry in the love scenes will be the most electric ever, the most real. And Brando and Britten would be the greatest screen team in the history of movies.

And so her nights went, lying in darkness, at last falling asleep, resting assured that she was loved by Marlon Brando.

14.

AT LAST, I got a call back from Victoria Sweetzer's assistant, Cooper, and he said Victoria was interested in interviewing me "as a writer," and could I come up on Wednesday afternoon to meet with her? Could I? Yes! This was the most exciting thing that had ever happened to me.

I went up to the apartment in the East Fifties, trying desperately to remain cool, to look relaxed, and to stay dry. It was a very hot day in New York. By the time I got there, my shirt was sticking to my back. I walked into the lobby and, I must admit, was disappointed. First of all, there was no gust of air-conditioned air to greet me. This was the building where a legendary, one-time queen of American movies lived. Yet the foyer had a shabby opulence, like a palace that had been abandoned and fallen to ruin. The doorman's uniform looked like it needed to be dry-cleaned. He announced me. "Eleventh floor," he said, stifling a yawn. Victoria, I knew, had bought out the other three apartments on 11 and had turned the entire floor into her sprawling New York residence.

A sour-faced, Latina housekeeper opened the door. I walked into the apartment. Not only were all the windows shut, but heavy crimson velvet curtains covered them. There was no air conditioning. No air, period. Eventually Cooper (the persnickety, old queen I had imagined), came in, gave me a curt "hello," said "she's ready for you" and ushered me into her bedroom. There sat the queen of the movies, propped up in bed—and totally unrecognizable. She immediately held up her hand in a "STOP" motion, declaring, "I'm watching a soap opera; we can talk during the commercials but you can't talk to me while I'm watching my stories."

It was obvious that she had been drinking. A lot. She had a tall glass sitting there on her bed table that was—with lemon and straws and cubes—elaborately made to look like water, but I'm sure it was vodka. Languishing on the pillow next to her was a chihuahua who sprang to attention as I neared the bed and stared at me with undisguised hatred. At least it didn't start yelping.

The first and only time I had laid eyes on Victoria Sweetzer in person was several years before, at a tribute for the thirty-fifth anniversary of her greatest movie, *Helen of Troy*. I stood outside of Lincoln Center with the throngs of her still-adoring public. Though in her sixties at the time, she looked amazingly terrific, but you couldn't help get the feeling that she was pulled together by hours of work, held together by glue and staples, all well hidden under a complex coordination of makeup, eyelashes, wig, jewelry, and a silver beaded Valentino dress—with buttons down the front which were not rhinestones but real diamonds.

By that time, after years of fluctuating weight gain, she had already gone through many of her plastic surgery overhauls. Her liposuction reductions. Her breast implants to reinstall firmness, face lifts to reinstall smoothness, chin implants to reinstall a chin. She was reconstructed to a semblance of her former self and had begun doing carefully chosen television movies, and in her presence the evening of the gala you understood why she was Victoria Sweetzer and why she had endured as such an object of fascination for over forty years.

But now it seemed that in the five years or so since that event, she had not bothered with the upkeep and the surgeons' magic had worn off. What lay in the bed before me was a very old, worn, tired woman. The rest of her—whatever beauty remained—must have been spread out in jars and boxes throughout the room. I searched her face for tiny vestiges of what she had once been and, to my sorrow, could find none. She had about eighty hairs on her head, and the thin remainder was now dyed blonde and combed limply, with a side part, and straggled to her shoulders; you could see much more veined scalp than hair. Her eyes were small slits slanting downwards, surrounded by folds and wrinkles. Her mouth was kind of sockish—no lips, just a sunk-in crack surrounded by deep lines.

She was wearing a workout bra, with a bed-jacket hastily tossed over her shoulders, but it certainly didn't look like she had been doing much working out. She had gained weight again, the double chin a surgeon had so carefully sucked out years before had reincarnated weirdly, and her skin was soft, white, and wrinkled all over. You could easily surmise that set free from the restrictions of the black Lycra bra, her once glorified breasts, worshipped the world over, would hang loosely down to her stomach. Perhaps she had had the implants removed for health reasons? Her midsection was mercifully covered by a blanket (in that heat!). Taking in the entire image, I nearly gasped. I didn't want to see Victoria Sweetzer like this.

She had a little bed table set up. She was signing stock photographs of herself—but a very young Victoria Sweetzer, from one of her studio sittings in the sixties. Actually, she was rummaging through her mail—invitations and announcements, greeting cards—autographing pictures, and looking up at the television, all at the same time.

Finally a commercial interrupted the onscreen drama. She gestured for me to sit.

I pulled up a little chair to the side of her bed. The supposed reason for this interview was to ghostwrite her memoirs and for this reason, I suppose, she wanted to know more about the history of my writing, although she never stopped opening envelopes, signing photographs, and glancing up at the TV screen. I told her about my love of literature, my short stories, my hopes to write a screenplay. Even though she continued with her activities, she would occasionally stop and look into my eyes, hold them for a second, then go back to what she was doing. To my surprise she didn't ask if I'd been published. I asked her if she'd like to read some of my stuff, and she immediately said she wouldn't.

What I remember about sitting in her bedroom is looking around in-between commercials. Of all of the photographs she had around, none were of her children or grandchildren. They were all pictures of her dog. The chihuahua sitting next to her. Dozens of pictures of him. Every place. Maybe it was more than one dog—past dogs, parents and grandparents all with the same, evil, beady-eyed glare. No pictures of husbands or family. Nothing. It was like a shrine to her pets. I just thought it was extremely curious. In your bedroom you'd have pictures of your grandchildren at least.

And I was sitting there and the room was so hot. She didn't offer me any food or anything to drink, although I was longing for water. But she had this huge glass of iced vodka, which she was tossing back. I remember feeling so awkward. I was also thinking, how many people would trade places with me to be sitting three feet away from Victoria Sweetzer, having a chat with her on a humid afternoon?

Looking at her now this is what I could read into her: This was a lady who simply didn't give a shit. She had acted in masterpieces opposite some of the most exciting actors of her generation, slept with the most desirable men, been photographed by the most talented photographers, owned the most valuable jewels, wore the most expensive clothes by the most creative designers of her time, been to the most extravagant parties, conversed with the most interesting people, had heard it all, said it all, seen it all. She didn't give a shit. She had nothing to prove. She wanted to sit up in her bed, drink her vodka, watch her stories, and be entertained during the commercials. Period. End of subject.

She said she would pay me one thousand dollars a visit. I was to bring a notepad and a tape recorder, although she was not sure she'd allow me to take notes or record our conversations. Through years of dealing with loneliness, I got the idea, that basically she was a lonely person and wanted someone to talk to. This famous, wealthy, adored woman, who could pick up the phone and converse with anyone in the world!

Laird had been sent on a mission to find the perfect companion.

Not too young, not too old. Not too smart, not too dumb. Not too apathetic, not too ambitious. But on this last point Laird was mistaken.

I agreed to her requirements, she rang for Cooper, and as he ushered me out, he informed me he'd call me when Victoria was ready for our next session.

15.

ONCE THEY STARTED hanging out together, Carla and Mikki's friendship flourished. They had, it seemed, everything in common. The isolation in high school, the feeling of being different from their family members, the feeling that they had to prove themselves.

They wanted to bring back star power, controversy, fascination. Mikki often quoted Joan Crawford: "If the public wants the girl next door, let them go next door." Sometimes after a go-see or a modeling assignment, Mikki would stop off at Carla's apartment. She needed a confidante in the business, and she found herself telling Carla stories about how her association with Justin had changed her life in a very short time, building her confidence and self-esteem. Whenever Mikki brought up Justin or her friend Mario, Carla was filled with rage. Inexplicable, unexpressed, but rage nevertheless. Mikki was her friend. Mikki was hers!

If she told her about a modeling location she wanted to be there. *Why wasn't I there? Didn't she want me there? How could she possibly have fun without me?*

With Carla's name and Mikki's beauty, they got into all of the happening parties and all the popular clubs. Guys would send over drinks and flirt and be witty and take them out to breakfast. Then Carla and Mikki would take a cab back to Carla's apartment, alone, and they'd sleep, platonically, in her gigantic double bed.

———

FOR THE FIRST time in Carla's life, things were spur of the moment and fun. One weekend Carla flew Mikki out to Los Angeles for a party that was to announce the start of her father's next film. Because Jonathan Christaldi was on location in Europe and couldn't make the party himself, Carla was there to represent him. His next film would be a dramatization of *Shit Floats*, the novel by Chase Bartholomew. Although shooting wasn't set to start for months, this party was being held to get the attention of the press and the public.

The restaurant was wall to wall with international celebrities and supermodels who had crossed over into the show business world . . . so much so that neither Mikki nor Carla felt special. The scene had an otherworldliness about it. Every woman under sixty had a projectile boob job. Everyone, no matter what age, had porcelain, tile-white, veneered teeth. They all had perfected an attitude of utter indifference. They were thin. They were rich. Who gives a shit about anything else? Dawn-of-the-dead zombies with artful hairdos, swilling their drinks and talking on cells.

But when Carla looked at Mikki in her black little dress, she seemed so real, so exciting, so human! She was happy because she was with Mikki. This was a present she could give her. A door she could open. She was delighted when Mikki revealed that she was carrying a disposable camera in her purse. "I know it's tacky," Mikki said. "But I want to be prepared if an extraordinary moment presents itself."

The first thing Carla and Mikki did was head for the bar to prime themselves for the evening's events. Vodka rocks for Carla. Straight with a twist for Mikki. These were Carla's father's friends, and she was the one who had to work the room

Carla took an hors d'oeuvre from a passing tray, plopped it into her mouth and spit it into her hand. "Argh," she said, "it tastes like Ajax." Then she brought her hand to her forehead. "Oh, my God! That's him." And she pointed to Chase Bartholomew.

On seeing the disheveled teenage boy, Mikki recoiled slightly.

She couldn't explain this frightful, queasy feeling to herself. Was it because he was so young and had already reached the point where everyone of importance was labeling him "genius?" It was exactly the kind of thing that Hollywood wanted to believe, because Hollywood was always looking for someone or something new to worship.

As soon as the film was announced, Mikki had bought *Shit Floats* and read it in about an hour. Mostly to see if there was a part that she might play in the film—which there wasn't. The book dealt with teenage decadence; Mikki found it skimpy and heartless. But why the nauseous feeling on seeing the creator of it? There was nothing scary or imposing about him physically. Smiling and glassy-eyed, he was acting oblivious to the party. By now everyone was saying that his greatest talent was for self-promotion and that even the rumor that he hadn't written his own book was started by him. But what was it about him that affected her so?

"Gross, ain't he?" Carla asked.

"There's something about him . . . "

"Yeah, he's a pig."

"No, I mean, he's . . . not a good person, is he?"

"Baby, I can't tell you anything about him except he didn't write that piece of shit of his. It was ghostwritten. And he's a pig and he has the world fooled. Like mostly everyone in this room."

"Why is your father making his book into a movie, then."

"Because it's a hot property. Something my father can't resist. He thinks it will bring him to a younger audience. A bigger audience— another thing my father can't resist."

Mikki watched Chase wipe his nose on his sleeve. She didn't believe, really, in psychic moments, but something—and it certainly wasn't sexual—was drawing her to him. She had the urge to watch him all night, but just then Carla spotted someone she was required to say hello to.

Carla's first victim was Randy Magnussun—movie star Michelle Diamond's husband and the creator and producer of many hit television shows including *The Law Firm*. Diamond had starred in one of her father's biggest hits, and the couple were good friends with Jonathan Christaldi. So there was Randy Magnussun, standing by the buffet table with Diamond, who looked thin and gorgeous.

"I have to say hello to them," Carla told Mikki. But Mikki—all thoughts of Chase Bartholomew gone—stared transfixed at his wife.

Years before Mikki had read an article where Michelle Diamond was quoted as saying that she was the type of person who at parties looked for a place to hide and wait it out. This admission of vulnerability—coming from such a physically ravishing woman—endeared her to Mikki, and she identified with her for years, always thinking about her whenever she was hiding in a corner at a party. The fact that they both had the first name also endeared her to Mikki. It was one of the reasons she changed her name. "I'll change my name before I become a star," she'd say to herself. "There's only room for one Michelle in show business," but that was only one reason. Another reason, one she could never admit to herself, was that she was desperate to be someone else.

"I know it's stupid," Mikki told Carla, "but a photograph with her would justify me being in L.A.; it would mean I'm in the right circles, everyone back in New York would be so impressed."

"Relax," Carla said. "If I can attack all these Hollywood honchos, you can ask Michelle Diamond to take a picture with you."

"You've got guts, Carla. You don't hesitate at all when you dive into your schmoozing with these mega-executives."

"It's an act. I've known most of them all my life—my hands are shaking."

And then Mikki noticed that Carla was indeed trembling. "Here's the plan," Carla said. "I'm going to go over and say hello to them, and then you come over to me, like you're saying hello, and then I'll introduce you."

The party was a wakeup call for Mikki. Sure, maybe she had conquered a few avenues in Manhattan's modeling world, but Los Angeles, the movie industry, was still a foreign country, a different world to conquer. Being here, amongst these ruthless, rich, untouchables, knocked her down a few notches. And then there was Chase Bartholomew. He had conquered this world before he was twenty, and here he was wandering around like a recent lobotomy recipient, as if it meant nothing to him. *Part of his shtick*, Mikki said to herself.

Mikki watched Carla attack Randy Magnussun with gusto. She couldn't help but think that Carla truly was like a little girl without guidance, acting jaded. People recognized the immaturity in her. She was cramming peanuts in her mouth by the handful, from a little glass she had filled at the bar. Still slightly overweight, with uncombed hair and sloppy makeup, she was wearing a tight pink tank top with a daisy pin that lit up and blinked in the center, calling undue attention to her small, pudgy breasts. Mikki's eyes focused on the glow-in-the-dark pink nail polish on Carla's toes, which were on display through her pink wedgies. Her outfit showed how utterly clueless she was. If Carla had been less famous, Mikki would have been embarrassed to be seen with her. Everyone here looked at her with scorn; Mikki felt a pang of sorrow for her.

There was an awkward moment, a lull in Carla's conversation with Randy Magnussun and Michelle Diamond. So Mikki made her way over and said hello to Carla. Carla, relieved not to be alone with the dynamic couple, made the introductions.

Mikki turned her attention to Michelle. Older than the silver screen version, but still fresh and scrubbed and very lovely. Now Mikki was the one trembling. To Mikki she personified everything a star should be: talented, charismatic, and unnaturally beautiful. She brought to mind the Hollywood days of yesterday, when stars were stars, not people who look like someone sitting next to you on the subway. But more than that, she represented the very top of the show business ladder.

Luckily Mikki had just downed her vodka. While Carla stumbled through some small talk to Randy, Mikki leaned into Michelle Diamond and looked into her eyes, trying to call up all the pain and vulnerability her life of struggles could muster. "Would you do me a favor?" Mikki asked.

Michelle's whole body visibly froze. "What is it," she asked. There was no emotion in her eyes.

Mikki asked if they could take a photograph together.

"Oh, no," she said instantly, "I wouldn't do that." And it was clear and it was final.

It was no big thing for Michelle. She was used to it. But Mikki felt as if she'd been struck. There was nothing left to do but look down at her shoes. Michelle Diamond was wearing open toe sandals.

"I've read that she's very private, and the thing is, I understand her perfectly." Mikki told a furious Carla after they had awkwardly extracted themselves from the couple. "She's a human being, not a monument. It probably gets annoying always being asked, wherever she goes, for her autograph or a photo. In a way I feel guilty for asking. But why bother to be a movie star?"

"Don't worry about it, baby," Carla said. "You're better than that cunt."

It didn't help. Unwavering hurt, born of humiliation, spread through Mikki's body. She wasn't yet worthy to be photographed with the elite, it seemed. She could be a nutcase. She could be a stalker. She could be anybody.

"When I was a little girl, I used to dream of being at a Hollywood party," Mikki said, very low and very soft.

"You're taking it all the wrong way, baby. These people are like that. If you're going to play with them you've got to be a player."

"I know. Hey, listen, I know you have a lot of people you have to say hello to. Why don't we separate for a while and I'll meet you in a bit?" Carla frowned, nodded, and went off to circulate. Carla knew a lot of the people at the party, and now that she was a budding model and not just a celebrity's kid, she felt a part of the scene. She felt a little bit of the peacock, with something to talk about, something in her future—and she wasn't alone. She was here with Mikki Britten.

Mikki looked for a corner to hide in and found one behind a potted tree. She thought of Elvis, how famous he was and how he was supposed to have been so kind to people. The public gave him a lot, and he was grateful. Mikki also recalled an article she had memorized about Marilyn Monroe. Toward the end of her life, in an interview about people approaching her because of her fame, Monroe had said: "I don't mind. I realize some people want to see if you're real. The teenagers, the little kids, their faces light up—they say, 'gee,' and they can't wait to tell their friends. And old people come up and say, 'Wait till I tell my wife.' To me it's an honor. You've changed their whole day."

Mikki stood up and walked toward the bar. People would think she was indeed a wacko if she stayed hidden behind a potted palm. She headed for the bar, in need of a refill to ward off her encroaching despair. She wondered what it would be like to be so famous that people wanted to be photographed with her and if that would change her outlook at all.

"Mission accomplished," Carla said, when she bumped into Mikki at the bar. Carla had done all she could do at the party.

"What's wrong, girl?" Carla asked. "You drunk? Still down because of that unphotographic she-bitch?"

"No. No . . . I'm fine. This just isn't, you know, my town."

"Someday, sweetie," Carla said. "Someday."

Later that night Mikki lay in Carla's hotel room bed. At first sharing a bed with someone other than a lover had felt awkward and strange, but she had grown comfortable with it. Carla always took advantage of the situation, becoming the sister Mikki never had. She would encourage her calmly, cradle her.

By now Mikki knew the perfect combination of tranquilizer and sleeping pill; she timed it perfectly before crawling into bed and then allowed the luscious covers, with the help of modern medicine, to seduce her into slumber. Someday in her memoirs, Mikki thought, she might talk about her closeness with Carla Christaldi, the girlfriend with whom she was so comfortable that they sometimes shared the same bed. Everything she did, sometimes to her chagrin, was with one eye looking toward future fame.

Mikki had taken a large dose of tranquilizers and a powerful sleeping pill. Her encounter with Michelle Diamond had scared her, the sight of Chase Bartholomew, boy wonder, had jarred her. It was not a good night. Just before Mikki was about to go under Carla said: "I never met anyone like you, Mikki. You're so fucking special. What is it, Mikki? Tell me."

"Tell you what?"

"What is it you have? This ability to create an excitement around you, whatever it is you're doing. This charisma. This energy. Everyone notices it."

"Tell that to Michelle Diamond," Mikki said, still smarting from the rejection.

"Oh, Mikki, she saw it too; it wasn't so much that she was jealous, but she has to keep her protective walls up."

"It's so fucking insane," Mikki said, trying to remain in the conversation, although the medication was fuzzing her mind.

"I see them noticing it," Carla said. "They want to be a part of you . . . but they're afraid of you at the same time. It scares me too, sometimes. This thing . . . this thing in you. Is it ambition? Is it personality? Charisma? Something inherent?"

"What? What?"

"Are you so beautiful because you want people to perceive you that way?"

Mikki turned to look at her, blinking in the darkness. Her eyes were tired. "You're just saying that because you feel close to me. You really like me," she said, smiling drowsily. "But you don't have to be afraid of me."

In contrast, Carla was fully awake and alert. "Girl, I've known all the big stars of the past fucking twenty years. You can count on three fingers how many of them have *it* . . . and even they don't have it in as strong a dose as you do."

"Oh, yeah? Then why has it taken me so long to get people to recognize it?"

"Because you didn't know how to value yourself. You came from nowhere. You didn't have anyone to help you, like I did. People, I'm talking about the assholes with power. They couldn't define your beauty and so they rejected it. Listen to this: 'Mediocrity knows nothing higher than itself, but true talent instantly recognizes genius.'"

Mikki instantly liked that. From then on she would often quote it herself. "Who said that?" she asked.

"Arthur Conan Doyle. My father used to quote that to me when I was, like, three. It's taped above my computer. Some kids get the three little bears and stuffed giraffes. I got Sir Arthur Conan Doyle."

"At least your father read to you," Mikki said. "So you're true talent, huh? You recognize me?"

"You have a face. You have personality. You even have a body—that's real. I wish I had the nerve to get a boob job," Carla said miserably. "I don't even have the fucking guts to make myself beautiful."

"Oh Carla, you have your own qualities . . . " Mikki started to say.

"I want to be like you, Mikki. What do I do? What should I think about? What should I read? Who do I hang out with?"

"Just be yourself. Be true to you. Your own unique nature."

"But what is your secret?"

Mikki paused a moment. "Why are you looking for mystery in me," she asked. "There are no secrets in me. I'm more afraid than anybody." It was a line she was determined to say to the next person who brought up the subject of her mysteriousness.

"Then maybe that's your secret," Carla said, snuggling in closer. She reached out and stroked Mikki's hair, which was spread out over the pillow. "Man, you are so beautiful." Almost at once Mikki became aware of a heat. A heat that flowed out of Carla's body. This forceful heat contained a hunger that Mikki recognized, a longing for the nourishment of physical contact. Mikki knew this kind of ardor and had felt it from others and often felt it exuding from herself. But she didn't want it from Carla.

Suddenly sex was in the bed between them, a lascivious intruder. Mikki, horrified and confused, lay flat on her back, closed her eyes, and intentionally slurred her words. "My secret is drink champagne! Things matter less when you drink. You can be more charming when you drink. You are more sexy when you're drunk. At least I am." This was all an act on her part. She wasn't drunk. But Carla was behaving in a way that made her anxious, and she didn't want to deal with it, so by pretending she was drunk she could act vague and hide behind the liquor and pills.

Carla was unfazed by Mikki's abrupt non sequitur and continued stroking her, each touch becoming more intimate; occasionally she stopped the strokes to give Mikki's flesh a soft probing pinch.

"My booker at EYE says you're having an affair with Jana Janelow," Carla said.

"Affair? Please!" Mikki said. "We were shooting Civello's collection—very tough and androgynous. We were just fooling around. The chemistry we were generating was good for the pictures."

"She's not good enough for you," Carla said. "No one is. If only I was as beautiful as you, I would be the most powerful woman in New York by now . . . Hollywood, too. Totally." She brought her face close to Mikki's. "But together, Mikki, the whole world is ours."

In confusion Mikki opened her eyes. Should she go through with it? Another one she didn't want? Would a sexual fantasy get her through this? Where did her fantasies end? Where did her reality begin?

Mikki is on the set of her latest movie in the south of France. Her costar is Michelle Diamond. They are playing two women who had just killed Mikki's abusive husband, an unscrupulous lawyer who once drove Diamond's husband to suicide. Now, after the murder, they lay in bed together trembling and terrified. In the script their fear abruptly turns to desire. It is the big scene in the movie. A long, heated, sex scene, sure to be groundbreaking and to cause a lot of controversy, not to mention lots of media coverage: an erotic love scene between these frightened women, played by two of the most popular actresses in Hollywood.

Jonathan Christaldi is standing over the prop bed with the cameramen and lighting crew, directing every move. "Now slide your hand down her body." Mikki does so, over Michelle's taut torso. "Squeeze her ass. Kiss her hair!" And Mikki follows every direction because this is a big film for her. The movie will prove that she is more than a trendy kitten with big boobs. She is a serious actress, one to reckon with. She puts real passion into every kiss, every stroke. Anywhere Mikki pinched Michelle on her body—her stomach, her thigh—it is smooth and tight as the skin on a bongo drum. Mikki knew that her body felt the same. And there was a pleasure in this.

When Michelle's mouth probes her breasts, taking her nipple into her mouth, she throws her head back and closes her eyes and moans with an excitement that even the most trained ear wouldn't know was fake. Maybe it's not. Now Mikki slides her tongue down Michelle's rib cage, past her flat stomach. She buries her tongue between her legs. This will get me the Oscar, Mikki thinks. Michelle is making moaning sounds deep in her throat. "CUT! BRILLIANT!" Jonathan Christaldi screams.

Carla and Mikki lay panting in bed.

"Mikki . . . " Carla whispered finally. "I love you."

" I love you too, Carla . . . " Mikki sighed, "but . . . "

"But," Carla said, a panic in her voice that conveys she already knows the rejection is coming.

"I've had friends that I've been in love with but never touched," Mikki lied. "And I don't think we should do this again."

"Why? What? Fucking another woman?"

"Come on, Carla! You know it's not that. I'm talking about . . . about, sexualizing a friendship—that's not good. It will only throw a monkey wrench in the engine of our friendship. And . . . well . . . I'm with Justin."

"Uh-huh. I see. Right. And you're in love with Justin, right?"

Mikki didn't want to lose Carla at this point. But she didn't want to lose Justin either. Which was more important? Which one could further her career faster? Between the two she'd choose Justin. Mikki got up from the bed and took another tranquilizer from her purse. Maybe she'd overdose and be dead by morning. Problem solved. And a legend would be born. She sat on the edge of the bed, looking at Carla.

She decided to be honest with her.

"I need Justin at this point in my life," Mikki said.

"Do you enjoy sleeping with him?" Carla asked bluntly.

"Carla, this is just between you and me, okay. You can't tell anyone. Promise?"

"Can I have one of those tranquilizers," Carla asked.

"Of course." Mikki retrieved one from her purse and returned to the bed handing it to Carla with a glass of water. "A doll for the doll," she said, smiling. Then she began her confession. "Actually," Mikki said, "I don't enjoy sleeping with him. Well, I mean, I don't enjoy having sex with him. But he's good for me. And I'm good for him."

"How do you have sex with someone you don't desire?"

"Oh God," Mikki said, burying her hands in her face. "Don't make me say this, Carla."

"Come on! Tell me. How do you do it?"

"Well, the lights are out, for one thing."

"Yeah? So? That's enough to get you through it?"

"I fantasize. I use fantasies. It's the only way to get me through sex with Justin."

"You must have some imagination," Carla said. "Who do you think about?"

"Cab drivers, movie stars, old boyfriends . . . anyone . . . ."

"Anyone would have to be better than Justin." Carla said. Mikki thought of defending Justin but decided to let it go; why start a fight? Why jeopardize her relationship with Carla? Then Carla sat up and placed her hand on Mikki's cheek. "Do you ever think of me, Mikki?" she asked.

Again, Mikki chose not to answer the question. Instead she said: "I love you Carla, but I'm not *in* love with you. I hope . . . I hope that's enough."

Both of them lay down in silence; Mikki wondering if it was indeed Carla or Carla's name that she loved.

16.

I TRIED TO warn her.

During this period, while navigating her career, Mikki made one fatal mistake: She revealed too much of herself to Carla in the first months of their friendship. She was under the assumption that telling Carla her deep, dark secrets would bring them closer faster, believing that revealing herself to someone would endear her to that person. She wanted to be best friends, confidantes, from day one, and so she exposed every inner emotion to Carla—in late-night telephone conversations, at the frequent sleepovers at Carla's apartment that were, at about that time, just starting to become ritual. And I'm not being jealous, either—it was Carla who was jealous of me.

I'm not tooting my own horn in saying that I saw trouble coming. Maybe I'm just naturally distrustful, but I did warn Mikki about getting too close to Carla. It was early that fall and the weather was starting to turn cold. My apartment was freezing. Mikki had spent the night at my pad and was wearing a T-shirt of mine, which on her was oversized, but even that look on her seemed breathtakingly photographable. Without makeup she had a different kind of beauty that took a while to adjust to.

I remember her, fresh-faced and barefoot, sitting on my old-fashioned, hideously rusted, brown-splotched bathtub. (The thought of taking a bath in that tub to this day horrifies me as I think of the generations using it before me—what kind of person sat in that tub and what the hell did they do in it? I stick to showers.) She was watching me shave above an equally revolting, history-stained sink. The previous night she had attended some gala at the Guggenheim Museum. She was starting to become a successful model, and successful models are always in demand to dress up some charity event or the opening of a new wing in a museum.

Only months before, Mikki would often spend the night at my crumbling little place on Saint Marks Place after a day in the city rather than taking the late-night subway back to her Queens apartment. But now it was becoming rarer to see her sculpted, un-madeup face in the morning. She was spending a lot of time at Carla's place on Fifth Avenue. She was looking for an apartment of her own.

"I want to find the perfect place," she told me. "I'm taking my time looking. I don't want to be one of those people always moving around. When I get my apartment in the city I want it to be one I live in for a long time. Plus, I need a great deal. I'm not throwing everything I make away on rent. I have to save the money I make now for when I'm ready to produce my movie."

"Movie?"

"I didn't tell you about my movie?" she asked. "Well, you know modeling . . . I'm not a *real* model. I never had any ambition in that direction. It's a steppingstone. I'm an actress. And I'm working on a screenplay. I know, I know, who isn't? Everyone in this fucking world is a writer slash model slash actor.'"

"Let me raise my hand and join the club."

"I'm doing this as a vehicle for myself. Let's face it, no one's ever going to give me a part. Even if I do get called for the movies. What kind of roles do models get? Look at Cindy Crawford. They put her in garbage, and her career was over before it started."

"Well, she wasn't exactly an actress."

"I want a great role. I'll have to create it. I'll probably need some money to at least get it off the ground—when the time comes."

"I didn't even know you write."

"You don't know everything about me, baby," she said mysteriously. "Independent filmmaking. That's where it's at. My ambition is to make a cutting-edge, independent film."

I wiped the remaining shaving cream from my face and looked at her.

"I know," she said. "That's your ambition. Ever since we first met it's all I think about. You convinced me. So, I was wondering if maybe, we work together . . . write a kick-ass script together."

"Raise some money?"

"Yes! And do it ourselves. A part for me. A part for you. Some fresh-faced genius right out of film school to direct us. We get it into festivals, and we're the next big thing."

"Well," I said, considering her plan. "You're in a position now to make some contacts."

"I'm telling you about it now, Mario. You'll be a part of everything when the time is right. I'm still getting there myself."

"Great apartments at discount prices aren't that easy to come by in New York City, babe," I said, painfully aware of my own dump. I had never been ashamed of myself in front of her. Now I was starting to feel not good enough. It made me queasy to the point of almost being ill.

"Carla's helping me find one," she said. And once Mikki was on the subject of Carla, it wasn't easy to get her off of it. Carla. Carla. Carla. There she was in every crevice of Mikki's life. Under every bed. Behind every curtain. Under every rug. The funny thing was, Mikki didn't even particularly enjoy Carla's company. She just liked the idea she was there, like an ace up the sleeve.

"You shouldn't tell her personal things, Mikki," I said, when she told me that she had revealed to Carla that Justin left her cold sexually. This was one of Mikki's best-kept secrets at the time. She had Justin, and the public, completely fooled. It bothered her, though; it was a fly in the ointment of her rising success that she was deceiving him in this way. But she revealed her secret to Carla. "There's no reason to tell her things like that," I said.

Mikki's reaction was startling. Her eyes flashed at me in anger. "What do you mean by that?" she demanded.

"I'm just saying that you don't know her that well. You told her your real age. You talk to her about your sex life. How do you know you can trust . . . " She didn't let me finish.

"I never trusted anyone in my entire life," she said angrily (forgetting who it was she was talking to), "I'm tired of living my life that way!"

Her anger baffled me. I couldn't understand why she was reacting so strongly. I was only trying to give her advice that I genuinely believed in.

"What if you have a fight? She could use this information against you," I said, trying to reason with her. "You're on shaky foundation. And Justin Landis is the one who is truly trying to help you."

"We're not going to have a fight! Carla loves me. She worships me. She wants to be just like me!"

"Yeah, yeah. But you have to protect yourself from people at every turn," I warned her, from experience.

What Mikki did next shocked me. She grabbed the skin on my upper arm and twisted it in a pinch-like hold. It hurt like hell, and she didn't let go. Although we'd had our share of arguments in the past, she had never tried to physically hurt me before. She was screaming now.

"Ouch!" I yelled.

"Don't you see we're not normal, Mario! We can't go through life looking at everyone like they're out to hurt us!" Her face was red with rage.

I was enraged too now. "Get your hands off of me," I hissed. And I pushed her up against the wall.

She was discombobulated, but she continued. "It's holding us back! We have to stop looking at everybody in the world as an enemy."

What happened next is a jumble of feelings and memory. I was bewildered by her reaction to a bit of friendly advice. But I was mad as hell, too. We were screaming at each other, both at the same time. The radiator in the bathroom sporadically made angry hissing sounds, trying to cough out the compressed steam from its ancient lungs.

I remember her yelling: "You put this energy around yourself, this negative energy and people pick up on it!" And: "If you think of yourself as different, that's how people will see you, and you'll never get anywhere!"

And I yelled back: "You're so desperate to make her your best friend you're closing your eyes to reality." And: "You may think you're using people, but they're planning on doing the same thing to you!"

We may not have been educated enough to explain all the emotions we were feeling, but we knew what words to hurl to hurt. And we threw them at each other like sharp stones. Words like, "Cunt." "Faggot." "Phony." "Asshole." "User." Bottled-up hostilities escaped frantically like air from a popped balloon. We were hitting each other, too, I'm ashamed to admit.

"You just won't listen to anybody's advice," she said finally, when we were both empty of words and tired of swinging. Now she tried to rationalize. "I don't know what happened to us, but somewhere along the line we developed a 'me and you against the world' attitude, and it can't be that way because the world will win."

I knew at that moment there wasn't any "we." She was winning. I was losing. Big time.

"Get out of my sight," I said quietly. "I can't stand to look at you right now."

I remember the look of hurt on her face: She knew she had gone too far with me. I remember her dressing silently with slow, stoic calm. And I remember the words she said to me as she turned to leave: "Carla has no reason in the world to hurt me."

I DIDN'T TALK to Mikki for a couple of months. Each day that went by made it more difficult for either of us to pick up the phone. I had given up on talking to her or ever seeing her in person again.

It was a time of unemployment. There was no money. There were no jobs. Since my own employment consisted of me hanging out in bars late at night or surfing the Net or hanging out in escort chat rooms hoping someone would like my online photos and invite me over, I slept until early afternoon and stayed home all day, watching daytime television, ferociously flipping through the channels.

Every day some new crime, some new horror, some new atrocity cropped up and was presented by the media—flared white-hot to the masses—only to die down, the broken lives and the aftermath forgotten in the rubble. Perversion, hatred, torture, adultery, heartache, murder: These were the new entertainments, paraded daily in front of a ravenous, popcorn-munching public. Criminals who had committed the most horrendous crimes became celebrity headline grabbers. Female pedophiles were sweeping the country.

The public wanted to see people eat raw intestines, swing upside down from high buildings, or intermingle with other equally fame-obsessed hard bodies in long-term captivity. They wanted to see who someone would pick to marry or fuck, or who their friends or family would pick for them to marry or fuck. The new fame had nothing to do with dedication, hard work or talent. It was all about exhibitionism. All for the sake of art, my dears. All for the sake of money. It wasn't what you could accomplish—it was how much air time you could get.

I began to feel more and more helpless. More hopeless. How could I compete with all of this? I was only Mario DeMarco, a small voice screaming to be heard above the chaos, competing with all the madness around me. *Analyze me! Sympathize with me! Hear me! After all, I am a life!*

The only escape from this seemed to lie in becoming famous myself. It only would take one outlandish act; then a barrage of publicity would raise me up. Real money and fame, I thought, would lift me a notch above these freaks, roping me off into a world of sanity and order, or at the very least comfort and safety.

My life was dreary. At the same time Mikki's career began to take off, my own fortunes plummeted. The recession had made it nearly impossible to survive. A guy couldn't even eke out a decent living as a prostitute anymore. I wasn't taking this lightly. I was nervous and afraid, knowing full well that I couldn't pull off being a hustler for very much longer. There were always younger, sweeter boys showing up, well hung and valuable. Youth is the most desirable asset in that scene, even more so than a hairy chest . . . and my cock is not all that big.

The bright spot came when Cooper, Victoria Sweetzer's assistant, called me. "Victoria's ready for the first interview," Cooper informed me. Without waiting for a reply he added: "Be at the apartment at 2:00 P.M. this coming Thursday."

When I hung up the phone I felt happy. This was the big time. Maybe I was on the brink of some sort of a career after all; maybe Mikki wasn't so far ahead of me.

17.

IN HER EARLIER modeling days, before she met Justin Landis, Mikki would sometimes get a job for a circulation catalogue or in an ad in a lesser-quality small circulation magazine. She would package these magazines and send them to friends. "Thought you might have missed this," she would scrawl on the cover, since it was unlikely that anyone of them would have seen it. "Give me a call and let me know what you think of pages 134–138." She was merciless about what she saw. She criticized the photography, the other models in the shoot, the clothes, the makeup. Everything, she said, could have been done better.

Now she was working in the big time with the best in the business, but she did not lean back and let it all happen around her; she was still climbing, still fighting to be better, still a perfectionist about her image. She had an instinct for what was right for her and she courted friendships with those professionals who could best benefit her. But she never faulted any of the professionals who weren't right for her. She was known for being kind—even through her drug taking, her drinking, and her self-destructive behavior. The vulnerability she displayed at all the right moments made people want to please her. Her fragility made them want to help her.

She was getting her first taste of what it was like to be a star. She was coddled, pampered, catered to. A top booker at EYE was assigned to keep track of her comings and goings; she knew where Mikki hung out, where she could be tracked down. It was well known at EYE which days each month Mikki would be getting her period so that she wouldn't be booked looking bloated or tired.

She was given two expensive cell phones to carry at all times because she was always losing one in cabs or restaurants or at photo shoots. Her cell phone, which chimed to the tune of "New York, New York," rang almost nonstop. I read about all of this in tiny blurbs in the *New York Post* and the *Daily News*. Even if I had not read about this, I would still have known it.

All the while, Mikki's sex life with Justin remained the same. She could not escape the fact that he simply was not physically attractive to her. But after talking to Jana, she couldn't help wonder if perhaps they were both playing games. Did he really desire her or was he fucking her on Viagra? She couldn't figure it out.

Nevertheless, she was determined to keep up the charade of hot sex between them. Each night when Justin switched off the lights, it was Brad Pitt who made love to her. And Brad Pitt was so beautiful, so desirable, so utterly perfect that it almost did not seem possible that he could exist on this earth. He seemed to be a heavenly being that left a phosphorescent outline where his body lay—proof that he was heaven sent.

As a result, she became acutely aware of everything about him when he was on top of her. She studied each inch, each centimeter of his body, in utmost detail, with her senses of taste, smell, and sight. The ear, magnified, is magnificently structured. The sideburns perfectly groomed. The nape of the neck unblemished, divine. She must have it all. Every cell, every smell. Each look at his face breaks her heart. The eyes! The eyelashes! If her hand stroked his hair, she immediately brought her fingers to her nose—the smell of his hair oil was sublime. If her tongue touched his shoulder, she let it linger there, sampling the exquisite flavors of his flesh. If she gave him a blowjob and a pubic hair remained in her mouth, she carefully removed it and placed it on the night table to save it, a precious keepsake from a celestial god. Oh, she is at his mercy. He is a need. How amazing that someone can have such power over her.

And to think that out of all the women in Hollywood, in the entire world, it was she he loved. He'd given up his wife, his career, his money, his fame . . . just to hold Mikki. Oh, how perfect he was.

And it was Mikki he loved. It was Mikki he loved.

"Mikki. Mikki! I love you, Mikki . . . !"

Now, though, when the lights came on, to Mikki's surprise she started seeing Justin in a different light; discovering new feelings mixed in with the old. His face no longer seemed plain and uninteresting. She saw intelligence and understanding there.

Late one night he was lying with his back to her. Her arms were draped around his waist. Unlike the other men whose bed she had shared in the past, Mikki had begun to feel warm and loving toward Justin after sex. He was the first to actually do something to help her. Her lips touched the tip of his shoulder blade and the warmth surrounding his flesh smelled so very familiar and nice. There would never be real passion for him, but something else had begun to take over. She had been used so much in the past. Her wish had come true: Human kindness had become an aphrodisiac.

"I love you," she blurted out, for the first time in her life, and at that moment she really meant it.

"I know," he smiled. She had said it many times before because it was what he wanted to hear.

"No," she said, "I really love you."

He turned to look at her and immediately wrapped his arms around her and held her tight. Looking in her eyes he saw a look he hadn't seen before, and he concluded it was the truth.

"Aren't you afraid that this might complicate things?" he asked.

"Oh, Justin," she answered wearily, and to him her voice had never seemed so tired, so afraid, "it's not as if complications were anything new to me."

18.

"*ARE YOU FARTING?*" Victoria Sweetzer asked me.

"What? No!" I said emphatically. Mortified. Indignant. Although I am without a doubt a very gassy fellow and have been known to let one loose at the most inopportune times, I would have rather had my stomach explode than let one rip in the presence of this movie legend.

"Helen, get off of the bed now!" she scolded the tiny Chihuahua who was lying at the foot of the bed. I must admit I was relieved to be let off the hook, but still somewhat dazed at how I had come to be in this predicament.

I had no idea what to wear to a journalism interview, so I had gone all out and arrived at Victoria's apartment wearing my best suit, including silk tie and polished shoes. In contrast, I was carrying a filthy green knapsack, which contained a notebook, various pens, and a tape recorder.

Victoria was wearing a black workout outfit that judging from her loose white skin, looked as if it hadn't been used for working out lately. Again she had on no makeup and, as far as I could tell, hadn't done a single thing to make herself look more attractive.

Before I could say a word, she announced: "I want to do the interview lying down. I feel more relaxed and comfortable talking from my bed." With that she threw back the lush cream comforter and lay down.

I was confused, dismayed, stunned. What was I supposed to do? Pull up a chair and interview her from the side? Or perhaps she meant for me to sit on the corner of the bed and casually talk to her from that vantage point. I stood ridiculously in the middle of the room, frozen, blinking, and waiting for direction.

"Well," she said at last. "Don't just stand there. Join me."

Now what? Was I to strip to my boxer shorts and lie beside her? What did she mean? How should I behave? Without giving myself time to think, I took the tape recorder out of my knapsack and—without taking off my jacket, pants or shoes—lay down on the high, fluffy bed beside her.

Victoria did not protest. Instead, she grabbed the comforter and drew it around us so that we were both cocooned in its luxuriant softness. I let my hand, holding the tape recorder, pop out from under the covers.

"No," she said. "I don't want this to be recorded. It will inhibit me. You can take notes later."

Nodding, I reached over and placed the tape recorder on the nightstand next to the bed, discreetly pressing the record button while doing so. I was trembling. But I needed this recorded.

We lay there, only our heads peaking from under the covers, staring at each other for several seconds. Then the dog farted. Immediately she demanded that the demented pooch get off the bed. And that was my cue to do something.

I was still hoping this was legit. That I had indeed been brought in to ghostwrite her memoir. All week I had been thinking of something I might ask her that she hadn't been asked before. I had read all the biographies written about her thus far. I had seen all the taped interviews. Watched the *A&E Biography* of her life. It had all been covered over and over again. The only thing I could do was make a connection with her and hope to learn something new.

"Tell me," I said, "if there was anytime in your life when you loved someone you couldn't make want you."

I watched her very closely, for I was very close, and I saw, I'm sure, complete surprise come over her face. I guess she was expecting, "Where were you born?" Or "Which of your films is your favorite?" She seemed stunned.

"Mr. DeMarco," she replied at last. "This has started off as a good day; I don't want to talk about unhappy things."

I was terrified of her. But this was my first professional writing assignment and I wanted to talk about what I wanted to talk about not what she dictated, and something in me in that moment, some hidden confidence, made me be brazen—thinking, perhaps, that she would respect me more for it.

"But," I pressed on, "What about unrequited love? Do you know what that feels like?"

Her eyes scanned my face.

"You want to talk to me about love," she said, and her expression became hard and mysterious. "Let me tell you something. Something I witnessed last night. I was out to dinner, not as myself; I rarely go out as myself anymore because people would want to talk to *"her,"* Victoria Sweetzer, and *"she"* doesn't exist anymore. So I was out in my dark wig and glasses, as this new person I've become. I was alone, which is the way I prefer it these days. The tables were close together, and there was a very young couple a few feet away from me. Very young and very much in love. And in a moment of stunning clarity, the kind of clarity I did not want but can no longer stop from coming to me, I saw their entire relationship. I could hear their whispering. I could see the tender strokes under the table. Oh, at the moment—in the little restaurant—it was right and magic and *forever* for them. Forever only for that moment. But in a few months, or even less, there would come a time when he didn't call her when he claimed he would. And there would be nights when he intentionally wouldn't be home when she told him she'd call. When he didn't sign his emails with "love" but instead just his initial. A time when she had to make up something amusing to tell him over dinner to make her day sound more interesting than it was, in order to hold his interest, to make herself feel like a winner. And he wouldn't view her as the winner she once seemed. There would be signs that it wasn't all quite "right," that the magic was fading, that the end of *forever* was in sight. She'd overlook these things for a while, and then he would leave her for someone new and she would experience great pain.

Only to repair herself the best she could ... and then she'd start looking for *forever* again. But right then, in that moment, in that little Italian restaurant, with the wine buzz, the smell of her hair, the gaps of mystery in each other not yet filled in ... right then it was just right. That was forever. That, Mr. DeMarco, is love everlasting. And that's the way it's always been for me."

As she spoke, the years fell away from her, and she was like a young, young woman just beginning. When she was done reciting her speech, she was not weeping. I was. I knew what Victoria was telling me. That we all fall in love with an image and what lies beneath is the true test, the test that so many times we don't pass.

I guess men had always fallen in love with her persona. With what they had seen on the screen. The image she projected so perfectly. Once the real woman, filled with her own special brand of insecurities and bad habits and annoying attributes, started filtering through—then they became disillusioned. It was hardest for her because everyone had made her into an ideal, a person without inner flaws to be exposed.

She pulled back the covers, exposing us both. Then she stood up regally, letting me know that the interview session was over. She told me that her assistant would write me out a check, which he did, and that he would call me for a second interview, which he also would do later. But I knew in my gut that there was no real book, that all of this would lead to nothing, or very little. Victoria was a lonely woman who had run out of things and people to play with. I might be something to amuse her for a while, but she had no intention of having me write her authorized biography. In the long run, other than whatever money she paid me for my company, she'd do nothing to help me.

WALKING DOWN THE street from Victoria's apartment, my cell phone rang.

"Mario?" It was Mikki.

I was surprised and excited to hear from her. We hadn't spoken since our fight several months before. "Mikki! Hey stranger. How's my girl?"

I was relieved that she made the first move toward reconciliation. She was relieved that I responded in a friendly way.

"Darling," she said. "Baby. Just wanted to let you know you're on my mind. A lot." Her voice was teasing and playful, full of genuine affection. A voice, which in all the time I'd known her, I had only heard her use with me. In retrospect, God, I can't help but wonder if that affectionate voice was put on, as everything else with her turned out to be.

"I've been thinking about you, too."

"How's tricks?"

"Silly rabbit," I said feebly, "tricks are for kids."

"Listen: I wanted to invite you to the Civello fashion show. I'm in it you know."

"So I've read." The Civello show was being heralded by the media as the major event of the fashion season. "You, uh, mean I don't have to make an appointment through your agent?"

"Don't start giving me a hard time, Mario. This hasn't been all fun and games. It's work."

"Oh, don't be so cliché. Calling modeling 'hard work' is old hat. It's what you've wanted all your life."

"It's what *we* want. The Civello show, my boy, is the thing that could push me into the big time."

"SUPERMODEL!" I screamed into the receiver with that peculiar mixture of pride and jealously that sometimes takes us over when a close friend is doing well.

"Don't make fun. If I make it, *you* make it," she said.

I was feeling a bit crushed about the meeting I had just had with Victoria Sweetzer.

"I need a job. Right now," I told her seriously. "I'm desperate, Mikki." I had a thousand-dollar check in my pocket, but it was already spent in past-due bills.

"They'll be lots of important people there," she said. "We'll see what we can do." And she gave me the time and address and the other shit I needed to know.

THE AUDIENCE AT the Civello show was filled with the kind of people I had learned to hate. My hate stemmed from the fact that I wanted them to love me. And it stemmed from the feeling of being shut out by them. I looked very carefully into each face looking for something I could relate to, something to love. The women pulled, painted, and beaded. The men overweight, creased, and sprayed. And there was another set of people—aerobicized and tanned, looking fabulous but trying every trick in the book to look ten years younger, no matter what their age. Expensive clothes and jewels and scents were the order of the day. I'd probably be able to handle these people—to be friendly and get along with them on a one-to-one basis. Collectively, though, they seemed like the enemy. I wondered to myself how many betrayals and backstabbings it had taken to turn each one of them into stone. (And, oh, how I envied them. Stone does not feel.)

I was surprised and delighted to find my name printed on my seat. It was the first time I had ever been reserved. Kate Hudson was separated from me by only several seats. I looked around and saw a few other stars. Then, to my surprise, I saw Laird Payne sitting with Victoria Sweetzer. I wasn't sure if I should approach them; if I did, the fact that I had been scouted out by Laird to be paid company for Victoria might embarrass them both, and I might ruin my chances of further work with Victoria. On the other hand, I could simply say hello as if I were a passing acquaintance—an acquaintance important enough to be invited to the exclusive Civello show.

But when I started toward them, I saw them both spot me at the same time—it was like walking into a plate glass window—and their combined looks stopped me dead in my tracks; I felt myself bang up against their glares. I slunk back to my seat.

Ironically, Mikki had me seated next to Carla Christaldi who, to me, looked like a hooker—not a call girl, but a hooker. Her hair was newly dyed blonde and she was wearing way too much makeup. I had never seen Carla Christaldi as a blonde before. I recalled that when she was twelve, her hair had been blue, and a couple of years ago it had been shaved off completely. But never was she blonde. In our clumsy attempt at small talk, she took great pains to make sure I understood that she was also a model with EYE. She told me she was on a strict diet and said that Justin would book her into the next big show. It seemed very important to her that I was aware that she was important. At one point she said to me, "Mikki tells me you need a job. After the show I'll introduce you to some people. Do you know how to work a room?" she asked.

"No," I replied, "but I know how to let a room work me."

This response seemed to confuse her, but then lots of things about Carla confused me, too. For instance, she was wearing a black beaded jacket that I recognized as Mikki's, which was two sizes too small for Carla. Why a woman with Carla's money would wear a borrowed jacket from last season that did not fit properly, I could not for the life of me understand. That she did not have Mikki's sense for fashion in putting clothes together was embarrassingly obvious. She took a definite risk by wearing pink hose with red shoes. The poor thing just didn't know. I was risky myself, wearing a body-hugging Lycra T-shirt that fit like a snake's second skin. It was black with a beige cross (the color of my flesh) running from the neck to the stomach and across the chest. It looked like the cross had been cut out of the fabric in front of the shirt and my skin was showing through. I also had a black leather blazer, which I slung over my shoulder, as if I couldn't be bothered to put it on.

In truth I would have liked to be friends with Carla. Actually, all that day I had had brief snatches of fantasy about what a friendship with her would be like. But there was some silent barrier preventing this. I got the feeling that she wanted to be open with me, too, but that she felt the same separating force. We only managed a strained and artificial politeness.

We each had reasons for being wary of one another. To me, Carla represented Mikki's gleaming new life, ripe and juicy and waiting to be bitten. I, to Carla, was Mikki's anchor, someone who had been with her through her rough time, a piece of her past who could not be dismissed so easily. That we were jockeying for position in Mikki's life was unspoken, but this fact stood between us, a barrier as strong and separative as any brick wall.

19.

BACKSTAGE, HANDS REACHED out to Mikki. Hands all over her body. Fixing. Patting. Brushing. Adjusting. "This girl's got a beautiful body," somebody said about her, but they could have been talking about any one of the models. After her makeup job was complete, she fled to the ladies' room and sat in a stall away from the frenzy of backstage cameras and microphones and stylists and makeup artists and publicists. Away from the questions—"What do you think of the collection?" "How do you feel about the clothes?"

Alone and contained in the stall, Mikki sniffed heroin. She felt her body smile. *It's nice to smile for a change*, her mind told her body. *And the whole world smiles with you.* She giggled. Her eyes were droopy and her lips were parted. She remembered, even through her euphoria, to bite down hard on her lips. That always made them fuller, riper, more screaming to be kissed.

After the show started, she stood at the entrance leading to the catwalk, which ran straight down the middle of the audience, separating it in half. Mikki watched the girls who were on before her strut confidently down the runway. She looked out over the audience. She was shy and afraid to face these people who from the safety of their seats would be judging her on a strictly physical level.

In the audience Carla and I nervously waited for Mikki's first appearance. We watched an endless parade of the gorgeous. Civello's show consisted of lots of body-conscious clothing, gowns with transparent areas, only the sex organs covered by swatches of material or beads. Dozens of girls breezed past with their long legs, full lips, translucent eyes, and fat-free bodies. So much beauty that in a strange way, it was no longer beautiful. The average watcher began to long for a nose with a bump or a bit of rippling flesh. It was like *The Twilight Zone* episode where the truly beautiful people were considered ugly and the freaks were the real beauties.

Everything that could be interesting has already been done on the runway, was the thought cutting through Mikki's mind as she braced herself for her entrance. *What can I possibly do to make an impression?*

Suddenly she was propelled by unseen hands onto the runway.

Some people have power. A power to affect people, to change opinions. A power to manipulate. A power to seduce. Mikki Britten possessed this in huge doses, but her power had been lying dormant, waiting for a chance to be freed, like a leopard poised on a tree. A chance presented itself on the runway that night.

I hadn't seen her in a while and I noticed she was even thinner. Her hair was fuller than I had ever seen it before, lion-lush, and spilling down her back. She was wearing a transparent black gown of a filmy material that seemed to be nothing more than a smoky illusion covering a black beaded bra (barely covering her nipples) and a tiny V of panties.

She came out tough. The thoughts that motivated her first moments in front of the audience were about her wasted years, her years of struggle, and the younger girls—fifteen, sixteen—who were already getting a chance and who were in the show with her, and she became angry. But Justin Landis, the man with the best eye in the business, the man who had booked many models for this show, had chosen her as his lover.

Mikki walked with an arrogant stride, the way she'd seen the girls from her old Queens neighborhood do on the streets. She flung her hair around, and it cut through the air like a switchblade, as if she were angry. It landed in her eyes and mouth. The attitude she conveyed toward the clothes she was wearing was that she didn't give two shits about the gown. It was the woman inside of it who demanded the attention.

Halfway down the runway she stopped. Her hands flew to her face, her body language changed. Relaxed. Was that a tear falling down her face? Her hands slowly slid down her body with a feline grace until they rested, palms forward, at her side. It seemed as if she was silently pleading for the audience to like her. Accept her. Love her. Up to this point she had been hard as nails. Wild. A predatory animal. This was a new vulnerability.

The jaded audience was speechless. There was an electric hush in the air. Flashbulbs! Popping! Popping! My mouth went dry. Mikki, *my* Mikki! Here she was, making it before my very eyes. I had noticed her first! I wanted to stand up and shout, "She's mine! I recognized her when you rejected her!" I was jealous beyond belief. Not just because I thought of her as my own, but mostly because I wanted what was happening to her, right this very minute, for myself. A star, a glorious star, was being born.

I was beside myself, and when I looked away, I noticed someone more overcome with admiration and jealousy than myself. Carla's eyes seemed to be on the verge of popping out of their sockets. Her face was flushed scarlet. At her sides her fists were clenched in rage.

"It's only a matter of time," she said.

"What?" I asked, my eyes back on Mikki.

"I have things going on for me, too," Carla said, as if in a trance. "And it's only a matter of time before I'm more successful than Mikki."

20.

AT THE PARTY following the fashion show I came to the realization that I had grown tired of being a man. Tired of things having to be hard all the time, pumping, pumping. How nice it would be, I thought, to just lie back and have someone else do all the work for a change. And I watched from the sidelines the attention the women were getting, Mikki in particular, fawned over and adored, catered to, and protected, simply for being beautiful. And I was tired of masculinity, of having to be the aggressor, having to be strong, having to make decisions all the time. I wanted someone to do things for me for a change.

The party was being held in a tiny, new, chic club in Hell's Kitchen. I'd tell you the address but it doesn't matter; it's closed now. The name of the drug that was in vogue that year? Who cares? Every year it's something different. But it's all the same. My feelings of isolation intensified. The more I tried to become like the partygoers there, the more I stayed the same.

I felt as if I were in a glass box, caged away from these people who all seemed like the real thing, while I was a mere facsimile. They all appeared so sure, so successful, so confident. I envied them. They roamed around the club with attitude, drinks in hand, deep in shadow and mystery. They looked at me, then exaggeratedly ignored me

Mikki was busy being a star, wearing a short red dress of a flimsy, shiny material. Usually she preferred slip dresses in black or white or beige. Although it often looked like she was wearing little more than scanty underwear, a beautiful body like Mikki's never appeared cheap or vulgar. Because she rarely wore color, whenever she showed up in red, like tonight, to look at her was like staring into the center of a fire. You could not look away. Justin whisked her from person to person, introducing her and showing her off like some goddamn precious jewel he'd unearthed. Carla followed behind them, covering up her jealousy with a manic hyperactive quality—Bette Midler on uppers.

Most of all, I watched Carla with a keen interest. Now it hit me! Shockingly, she seemed to be creating a third-rate version of Mikki in herself. I noticed this clearly now that I saw them together; it was spooky. Her expensively dyed, combed, and highlighted hair was a feeble imitation of Mikki's wild mane. It didn't have the same liveliness and looked like a wig. She was wearing Mikki's beaded jacket, and when she remembered to slow herself down, her movements seemed to be patterned on Mikki's feline gracefulness (although on Carla this seemed more clumsy than anything else). I was struck with the absurd notion that I had walked into an updated version of *All About Eve*. I tried to push that thought away. Carla's behavior didn't seem threatening or conniving; it just seemed pathetic.

Still, though, it seemed silly for a woman who was born with all that Carla was born with, a woman who had everything at her fingertips, to be jealous of Mikki. I reminded myself that imitation was the sincerest form of flattery and decided to join the party. I downed my drink and, with a wobbly determination, left my corner and headed for the action, circling the crowded room, courting a situation. First I'd have to spot an interesting person that I'd like to talk to—no small feat in this life.

I was very drunk.

The booze was free, and I was downing scotch at an alarming rate. So alarming that I was not even aware when I passed that wonderful high feeling brought on by the first few drinks, which is paradise, and into that queasy, shaky place, where one is not in control, which is hell. Almost at once I was invited to join in several conversations, although I felt as if the real Mario had invisibly floated up to the ceiling, while my automaton double was sent out to wonder amongst the action. He fit in better.

I noticed and registered many things. It was a hip party, man. There were many more young people at the club who had not been at the fashion show itself. For the most part the people who treated me with a condescending attitude were the ones who were not important. Also, people always asked, "How old are you?" terrified that someone younger might be making it before them.

I learned that it was easy to appear unafraid. All it took was to get them talking about themselves, their current projects, and I could come across as totally normal for minutes at a time by simply staring intently and occasionally nodding. I did okay for a while, keeping my balance, until my witty, party conversation ran out, and I was entombed in my own special cave of loneliness.

Finally I ran off to a corner looking for a place to hide. I was feeling sick, so I switched to light beer and I stood there sipping it, carefully watching people who hadn't seen each other in a long time grope one another with theatrical yelps of pleasure, and I was thinking: *This is human contact, but is the affection real?*

Before long I found myself talking to one of the male models who had a shadowy bit part in the fashion show. He looked very charming because his outfit was a study in fun contrasts. The top half was a very expensive suit jacket, with a silk shirt and tie. But his pants were cut off at the knee, and he was wearing white sweat socks with big clunky sneakers. Cute. His face was very handsome; he had ice-blue eyes and pouty pink lips. But most remarkable about him was his hair. He had the most incredible blond hair with sun streaks, slicked back but thick and beautiful, as if the nutrients in his body were so healthy and supreme that the foliage from his head sprung out wonderfully lush and full.

"I like your shirt," he said, eyeing my Lycra top with the beige cross on the front.

"I like your look," I replied. "I was just thinking, 'I'm gonna copy that.' And I don't like to copy anyone else's look."

He seemed pleased. "Is that shirt you're wearing Versace?" he asked.

I was stumped. I had bought the shirt at a thrift shop. I knew it was cool and in good condition, but the tag had been cut out. "Um . . . er . . . " I said.

"You don't have to be embarrassed if it's Versace."

"I wouldn't be. I swear."

To change the subject I asked him his name. His name, I kid you not, was Fountain. Whether or not this was his real name given to him by idiotic parents or some ridiculous pretense on his part, I cannot tell you.

"I'm only a model because I was forced into it," Fountain told me. The idea of anyone being forced into modeling struck me as incredibly weird and stupid. There are so many people willing, begging, dying to do it. Why would anyone have to be forced, as if physical beauty was hard to come by? But that was one of the tricks I had learned by now in the fame world. Always make believe it was something you didn't want. Make believe your career was a series of accidents. You were discovered on a corner buying a pack of cigarettes. Or an agent spotted you in a sleazy pizza dive. It was a cliché and a dumb idea; I challenged it.

"Who forced you?" I asked.

"Oh, you know, photographers who wanted to work with me. I only finally relented because I, uh, got a chance to work with some top photographers who let me express my creativity. We create the photos, you know, together." And here he mentioned the name of three very well known photographers.

"Hmm," said I. The translation of his startling speech was that prominent photographers found Fountain so irresistible that they were willing to give him control over their photographs just to have him pose for them. Unlikely, in my opinion, but who am I to say?

Fountain continued gushing: "I would never, you know, um, consent to being a model if it, you know, got in the way of my art.

I'm, uh, not one of these models who just stand around and look good in clothes while I, you know, get my picture taken."

"Oh, are you an artist, too?" I asked.

"I'm an actor," he said impatiently. "Acting is my art."

This I should have guessed, for he mumbled and stumbled and fumbled in a pseudo-Brando, pseudo-Dean, pseudo-Clift kind of a way. My built-in extrasensory equipment for assholes was going wild. Actually, underneath all of this pretense, Fountain seemed to be a nice guy; he was just dealing with the business in his own way, with his own masks, his own protective devices.

He asked me if I was a model. I told him I would like to be, but at the moment I was a hustler. "Hustling is my art," I announced with a shit-faced smile. If I hadn't been drunk, I probably wouldn't have said that. It wasn't something I was particularly proud of or told everybody on a first meeting. Actually the only other person I ever did tell was Mikki. But I figured that he was a bit of a hustler himself. I had noticed more than a few of that species at this club/party. And anyway, I had been feeling lost and what I was trying to do with Fountain was give him a thread of truth that we could possibly follow to a real conversation, perhaps cutting through this patent leather bullshit talk. It seemed to be nothing more than extended rehearsal chat for when he was on the talk show circuit. This was something I tried to do with everyone, but Fountain, like mostly everyone else, responded with total incomprehension.

Fountain's disgusted stare (through a James Dean furrowed brow) told me I needed to explain. I stupidly tried for more honesty: "I have such low self-esteem that if people didn't find me desirable, I don't know how I would have made it this far," I said.

"Gotta go get a refill," Fountain muttered, looking down at his beer as he took off.

Well, so much for trying out my vulnerability on Fountain. I didn't particularly like him, but there I stood, hiding, knowing that our brief encounter had been unsuccessful. I thought it might have been nice to spend the night just holding someone—but it's not like that in real life. There's very little tenderness. It's not something modern civilization can relate to.

I wondered what I could have done differently. I concluded that I should have played the game, saying that I was a model, too, but I found the profession degrading and was only doing it to work my way through law school. Damn, that's what's expected! Surely I could've been a model. I even, in a vague way, resembled a darker version of Fountain's look—straight nose, prominent cheekbones, full lips, and a five o'clock shadow.

Certainly I could've done what he had done in the show—glide down the runway with a grave expression carrying a bouquet of weeds and wild flowers. Why did I think so little of myself? My damn honesty blew it for me yet again, and what might have been a warm and friendly sexual encounter to help pass the chill evening had turned into a humiliating embarrassment.

Mercifully, Mikki found her way to me. Mercifully, she was alone. She had been drinking, too.

"Hi," she said tipsily.

"Hi," I said back, drunkenly.

She handed me a pill, which I promptly swallowed without asking. "I see you met Fountain. Did you notice him in the show? You have lots in common," she said. "He's a part-time prostitute too—and he wants to be an actor!" I simply smiled at the ironies of life while I drank in her new image.

Even in this inebriated condition I realized my feelings for her already had changed. I felt an uncomfortableness with her now, brought on by her new success. From the very beginning of our relationship, I had always felt very easy and relaxed with Mikki. Now I felt like I had to compete for her attention. Surely, my mind thought, there were people more fascinating than me whom she could be talking to at this moment. People more interesting, more successful. Surely she was just giving me a token five minutes of attention for old times' sake?

Still, it was she who wanted to impress me.

"You'll start seeing me on the covers of the better magazines now," she said. "Not just on the inside."

"Once you're in that league, everyone will see it in you," I said. "And we'll take off."

"Or you will," I said.

"I just want to model long enough to raise some money to independently produce my movie. I've been writing it, Mario. Just making some notes really. But I think it can be good."

"I don't doubt it." I noticed she called it "my" movie.

"It's called *Fame, Trains and Other Sexual Fantasies*."

"That about sums it up," I said after a pause. "My life, that is." I thought that today, people fantasize about becoming famous the way they used to fantasize about sex. The words were slow in coming out of my mouth, and I knew I sounded sarcastic and bitter but I was simply plastered. Then again, maybe I was sarcastic and bitter.

"It's a sweet little tale," she said. "With a Manhattan backdrop. About all the little mysteries the city has to offer. The secret little adventures that start on street corners and at newsstands, and develop into something extreme and spectacular."

I let silence do the talking for me. I was thinking about the conversation I had with her the first night we met. How she later said I had inspired her, how she had promised to help me and hadn't as of yet lifted a finger to introduce me to anyone at all tonight. She had more or less ignored me most of the evening and it hurt me. I wouldn't have done the same to her.

Because there were a lot of distractions at the party, this feeling of hurt took up only a small part of my thinking. Writing a movie about New York experiences had been my idea. I told her about it the first night we met. Now she was doing it, and the way her life was going, she'd probably get it produced—and forget about me.

"I want you to work on the script with me, Mario. It's a movie for both of us to act in, remember?"

I said nothing.

"You could start off modeling, too, Mario," she said. "I could help you now."

"At my age?" To my shock and horror I started to cry. It's not that drinking depresses me and makes me cry; it's just that alcohol brings up to the surface all the horrible buried feelings already there. My facial expression didn't change, but the waterworks opened; the tears silently rolled down my cheeks. The more I tried to stop crying, the faster the tears sprang from my eyes. I felt humiliated, which seemed to be an ongoing emotion for me that particular night. Mikki put her arms around me and licked a tear rolling down my cheek.

"There's a part in my movie for you, too, which I want you to develop with your own ideas," she whispered. "I didn't forget about you. This is happening to both of us."

This movie of ours seemed far away and unlikely at the moment, and I needed something to change my life right away.

"I'm exhausted," I said, and placed my head on her shoulder.

"You think I'm not?" she gasped incredulously. "Does it ever end, I wonder. This selling, this climbing, this clawing. Does it, Mario?"

I lifted my head and looked at her but said nothing. To me she seemed to have everything she had been working for, but I realized it would never be enough for her. Every time she reached a plateau she would become dissatisfied and start looking toward the next, higher mountain.

"I only want a few good years," she said, looking directly at me. "Five would be enough, and then I could die peacefully."

AFTER OUR CHAT Mikki started bringing people over for me to meet, perhaps to show off a bit. Mostly she brought over models she had worked with in the show, and I was awed beyond words to be chatting with these goddesses I recognized from magazine covers and TV commercials and practically everywhere else I looked. When you are in their presence, you understand why they won't get out of bed for less than forty thousand dollars a day. There's something about them, a quality, an aura, that separates them from mere mortals. Yet each one's quality was distinct. Even Jana Janelow, who to me is not conventionally beautiful, was weirdly stunning. These were the real stars. Actresses were just plain people with a good hair highlighting, a boob job, and lots of exercise. Models were out of the mainstream. Superstars.

Eventually Mikki brought Justin over for me to meet. Our eyes met only for one second.

After years of dealing with men of all species, I have an excellent intuition for character, almost as if I can look through people's masks, straight into their soul. My gaydar is unparalleled. My brain started transmitting the information on Justin at an alarming rate. Justin was a homosexual. He had never been to bed with a man and had not yet, in fact, admitted to himself that he was gay nor had he entertained a homoerotic thought for more than a few moments at a time. He had convinced himself he loved women sexually, when he merely loved women. He sort of enjoyed banging women because it was the only kind of sex he knew. And as the saying goes, sex is like pizza—even when it's not excellent, it's still pretty damn good anyway. Eventually, two or three years down the line, he'd meet a man on a plane sitting next to him or on line in front of him in an upscale deli. They'd strike up a conversation, exchange business cards and, later that night, have a torrid sexual encounter in a hotel room. Justin would think that for the first time in his life, he was madly, totally, and completely in love—but the man would never call him after that first encounter. Justin would feel emotional pain in a way he'd never experienced before. He would then, tentatively at first, start going to gay bars, wanting to experience once again the exquisite enjoyment of real, passionate sex. Sometimes, late at night, just before closing, he'd pick up someone he found acceptable to bring home. Justin would be a bottom. After years of fucking rather unsatisfactorily, he would want to lie there, spread out, and be pumped into unrelentingly. In time, he'd meet and buy a series of young men . . . all of whom he'd fall in love with after the first night of being fucked silly. All of these young men would zero in on Justin's vulnerability and extract wildly expensive gifts from him—wristwatches, cars, plastic surgeries, trips, educations. He'd pay their rent. He'd pay for their acting classes. He'd pay for their drug addiction recovery. All of these lovers would simply be looking for someone to give them a free ride while they pursued their life of working out and doing drugs and "working" on a screenplay. Justin's friends would lecture him about the quality of boys he chose. Justin would respond with, "Yes, he has drug problems and can get a bit rough, but basically he's a good kid and he has a good heart. He just needs a little help." Eventually, after spending many thousands of dollars on the rehabilitation of these boys who would never get rehabilitated, he'd grow weary of them and start looking for someone who truly loved him. By then he would be in his late fifties and it would be very difficult for him to find true love. He would acquiesce to a life of being very wealthy and able to buy a boy's affections for temporary enjoyment, but always feeling sudden stabs of sadness because of having never experienced true man-to-man love.

Our eyes met only for one moment. But as if looking into a crystal ball, I could see all of his concealed feelings, hidden longings, and excruciating pain . . . all within a fraction of a second of our first connection. He looked away.

But if Justin would do for me what he had done for Mikki, I would have blown him myself and saved him a lot of time and energy and heartache. I could have pulled him aside and explained to him, very gently, the facts of his life. But he was not ready to hear such truths. As a result, I scared him to death.

"Hi, Bubbie," he said to me. I think that's how you would spell it: like "Bubbles" with an "ie." "Hi, Bubbie" were his exact words. I took them as derogatory.

I smiled wanly. I was tired of feigning politeness. I was tired of feigning anything.

"Mario is a model," Mikki told Justin matter of factly.

"Yes?" Justin said, scrutinizing me through narrowed eyes in a way that made me extremely uncomfortable. He was, after all, very used to dealing with beauty and I was afraid of how I'd stack up. "You have a certain look," he said. "A type of look that is coming in now."

I dared not ask what that was.

"Yes," Mikki added, joining in on his appraisal of me. "Dark and mysterious."

"Scowling and broody," Justin added.

"Weak and vulnerable and very beautiful," Mikki said, smiling.

"The kind of man who waits for other men in dark alleys," said Carla Christaldi coming up from behind, not about to miss out on any conversation involving Mikki—or the chance for a dig at me! Yes, I was insulted but I had to admit, the bitch had hit the nail directly on the head. They all laughed at my expense.

Justin handed me a business card. "I'm thinking of concentrating on a men's division at EYE next year. How old are you?"

"Twenty-five," Mikki jumped in. I was closer to thirty-two than I had ever been in my life but as good a liar as she.

"Give me a call," Justin said. "I'll sign you on." I took the card and stuffed it in my pants pocket, but I knew there was no way on earth he would ever help me. And he knew I knew.

I WALKED THROUGH the city tired and alone, finally away from the phonies at the party, but no less lonely for that. Fifth Avenue in the Fifties, past the Fendi shop, Ciro, other designer shops, all filled with clothes I couldn't afford to wear (*if I had the money I would have worn that silk jacket tonight*, I thought), past the church—not Saint Patrick's, the other one. Smoking sewers added a surreal splendor to everything. I was on a movie set. There was an address blazing proudly in red lights, 666.

The streets were empty. This part of the city is so formal and clean and erect and orderly. The buildings so new and straight, adorned with the magnificence of modern architecture. Polished chrome and marble, streakless glass with leather shoes and belts displayed in an organized fashion. And then I passed St. Patrick's. I longed to go in, but I knew it would be closed to me. Even religion was closed to me on this night. When I had to throw up, which was on almost every street corner, I was careful to go to the curb and aim for the sewer. I didn't want to mar the area's perfection. This was the city I was never at home in. This was the city I could never belong to.

It was so cold. My nose started to bleed, probably not from stress and unhappiness, as I would like to report for dramatic purposes, but more from the extreme cold weather and my sinuses. Still, it seemed dramatic at the time.

I needed the subway. I needed the subway! And finally I found the F train which, I had some vague memory, would take me somewhere near my neighborhood in the East Village. I waited forever for the train to come and by the time it did, my drunkenness was passing and an excruciating hangover was taking over. Headache, nausea—the pain involved in all of this was at times so bad that I was sure I had a mild case of alcohol poisoning, at the very least.

The subway car was filled with the usual late-night deviants. This particular car reeked of stale cigarette smoke, cheap wine, and the stench of a various assortment of human filth. One man, lying across a row of empty seats, put out the cigarette he had been dragging on, sat up proudly, and began smoking crack. This is something I have never seen on the subway before and it scared me. The crack-smoking man stared at me menacingly.

The criminal, the remorseless, the dangerous always seemed to be in my car. This was a topic Mikki and I had often discussed in the past. Our contempt for the subways was another link we had in common while we had been struggling. Now she was above subways. *Down jealousy*, I said to myself. *Down, boy*. It was a fairly long trip to my neighborhood. Trying to forget about the torture going on in my body, I picked up a newspaper from the floor and tried to become absorbed in it, anything to keep my mind off myself.

My nose was buried in that newspaper when I became aware that someone sitting across from me was speaking to me. I looked up. He seemed to be a homeless man, about fifty-five years old. He had a full head of matted, sand-colored hair combed in bangs and a dirty parka jacket—forest green and covered with stains. His pants were also dirty, with a slit in one knee exposing the pink flesh underneath. He was mumbling something to me. I noticed his eyes were very blue. After asking him to repeat what he was saying several times, I thought I understood what he was asking.

"I'm looking for a room to share in the Village."

I repeated this back to him to be sure I had heard right. "You're looking for a room to share in the Village?" I asked.

He nodded. "Do you know of any?"

I told him I didn't and immediately went back to my newspaper, but something about him haunted me. He did not seem to be dangerous or evil. What had led him to this point in his life on this cold night, friendless and homeless? I looked up at him again and he was still staring at me. He mumbled something, which I didn't understand, and with great embarrassment he showed me his left hand, which he had been hiding under his coat sleeve. It was a dead hand, limp and unable to move, and at the end of each lifeless finger there was a nail as long as a whore's. Maybe he was trying to explain to me why he was destitute. His useless hand was his excuse, I guess, and my heart was momentarily choked with pity. Could I take him to live with me? It was a notion I seriously considered for about one minute; I had only a limited supply of sympathy left in me and I had to save every ounce of it for myself. At my stop, I stepped off the train and broodingly looked at the man still sitting there.

"Bye," he said through the open door.

I waved and said, "Bye."

"Thank you," he said as the doors closed.

———

IN UNSETTLING DREAMS that night, expressionless models whirled passed me, unspeaking but mocking. And there were voice-overs in the dreams . . . the homeless man asking me for a room . . . Carla, with her obviously dyed hair, whispering to me that she would soon be more successful than Mikki . . . and Mikki saying about Carla: "She loves me. She worships me. She wants to be just like me."

The next morning, sick in bed with alcohol poisoning, I went over these scenes from my dreams and wondered why they returned to me and how they would be pertinent to my life.

21.

MIKKI BEGAN TO grow wary of Carla's friendship. The novelty of being a celebrity's friend had begun to fade, and besides she was a minor celebrity herself now. She saw other qualities in Carla that she hadn't noticed before. Laziness—the fact that she constantly talked about wanting to be famous in her own right, but was unwilling to make the slightest sacrifice for it (like taking dance lessons which Mikki had suggested to her and which would have improved her runway performance; Carla had only shrugged). She expected instant success.

Jealousy—Mikki saw that Carla kept all of her best connections to herself and was crafty about keeping Mikki from meeting any of her contacts who could have really helped her get into the movies, which was the number-one place Mikki wanted to be. Especially now that she was working on a screenplay she hoped to star in. But when Mikki mentioned her script, Carla acted uninterested and noncommittal.

Mikki was annoyed that Carla had not introduced her to her father. She began to see two distinct personalities in Carla. One was the worshipping, adoring friend, who listened to Mikki complain about her current problems with Justin or about a lesser-quality model who got a job Mikki felt she deserved. Carla would listen attentively and give good advice as long it was some kind of problem, and she never seemed to grow bored, no matter how many times Mikki repeated herself. But if Mikki called her to talk about her latest appearance between the pages of *Vogue Italia*, Carla would grow stony and silent. "I'll call you back," she'd say abruptly. Mikki noticed all of these things.

The truth is, Carla had become alarmed at how quickly Mikki was advancing since the first day they had met in the agency's ladies' room. As she saw Mikki's importance grow, she saw her own value diminish in Mikki's eyes. Carla realized, without ever really admitting it to herself, that once Mikki got everything out of the friendship, like a meeting with her father (whom Carla had no doubt would be charmed by the exciting temptress), she would be dropped like a hot tamale.

For Mikki, it was the age-old story of competition between friends. You want then to be happy. You want them to do well—but not better than you're doing.

THAT SEASON CARLA was starting to be seen as a model. It was easy to get publicity for her. *20/20* featured her in a piece about celebrity children. Mikki originally thought that Carla would object to this kind of build-up, but Carla never said a word about it. It was, after all, national exposure. The segment, entitled "In the Jeans," featured Carla posing for a new denim ad.

Carla was no beauty, but her looks improved during this period. At first, it was just her nose settling into its new, daintier shape. The swelling from the lipo around her cheeks and chin had subsided, giving her a more sculpted look. And her hair had changed from dark brown to ash blonde. But more changes came. There was gossip that she had checked into a weight-loss clinic for the rich and famous, where she was put on a no-carb diet and a strict regimen of exercise. The Carla Christaldi who emerged from the clinic was toned and waif thin.

"All of a sudden she's improving her makeup and taking more time and care with her clothes," a booker at EYE told the *New York Post*. Before meeting Mikki, Carla had had no sense of style. Now she was molding it on Mikki's. She began to pick up on subtle things at first—an expression on Mikki's face, a figure of speech she used. Soon other traits became apparent: Her hair, her clothes, her attitude in photos—that peculiar mixture of toughness and vulnerability. Jonathan Christaldi seemed pleased at his daughter's blossoming career; she was something to be proud of rather than explained.

It would be Carla's only season on the planet as a model.

Aside from the weight loss, another thing about Carla's body changed dramatically around that time: her tits. All of a sudden they were high and full. The funny thing was that even when she was overweight, Carla had been flat chested. Now thinner, her boobs jutted out.

A columnist humorously brought this up, under the clever headline, MOUNTAINS FROM MOLEHILLS; a before and after photo accompanied the article. How could Mikki, famous for her naturally voluptuous proportions, help but notice?

Mikki complained bitterly about Carla's new "boob job." "At least I'm real," she groused.

Mikki also started to notice that quotes and anecdotes she had told Carla were now appearing in Carla's interviews. One example, one that Mikki always went back to when complaining to me about Carla (a new development in our relationship), was the "fame" issue.

At the beginning of their friendship, Carla had been fascinated by Mikki's obsession with fame.

"Why do you want to be famous?" Carla would ask. "Why is it so important to you?"

Sometimes, Mikki's answers would be simple: "Because I need it to survive. The more successful I become, the more I'm able to assert my true self."

Sometimes her answers were curious and touching: "Because I've never been an anybody. There are certain writers and actors and other famous people in this world who I want to meet and know. At this point if I met them, they'd want to fuck me. When I'm famous, they'll want to know me."

You can imagine Mikki's shock when, reading a brief article about Carla in the Sunday *Times* Style section, Carla was quoted as saying: "I'm a survivor! I want to become a success in my own right to discover my true self, and to feel comfortable when asserting it, you know what I mean? Right now, there are many famous people in the world I want to know. And, because of my father, they might want to meet me; because of my looks they want to (expletive) me. But when I'm successful, they'll want to *know* me."

Carla was now cultivating the mixture of arrogance and vulnerability that had been Mikki's alone. Could it be Carla didn't realize she was stealing an identity?

I, by now an expert on Mikki Britten, caught a clip on TV of Carla doing a runway walk, and it was an out-and-out imitation of Mikki's at the Civello show. She didn't do it as well as Mikki, but people had heard of Carla, watched her grow up, read about her, seen her on the TV, so they watched her more carefully. Plus, publicity had taken over; the public was told over and over and over again that Carla was fascinating, beautiful, and talented; as a result, people believed she was.

Mikki and Carla were no longer good friends. They rarely called each other, and the fact that they were now going up for the same jobs only made it worse. A television studio announced that it was developing a new variety show on the modeling business, and both Mikki Britten and Carla Christaldi were being considered to host it. Something had to give.

It was Carla who acted first.

22.

THE PHONE RANG, and the caller ID said "private." I was greeted by Cooper, Victoria Sweetzer's hanger-on, who said that Victoria was ready to see me again.

"When?" I asked.

"Tuesday."

"Does she have any idea what she's going to want to talk about?" I said, trying to keep up some semblance of the charade that these meetings were actually about writing a book.

"Listen, kid, I think by now you know the truth. If you don't, allow me to enlighten you. Victoria, or 'The Mattress' as Laird Payne refers to her, is a lonely woman. And a very sexual one. Her sex drive, and I'm sure you've read about it, has not waned one bit through the years. She's taken a shine to you for whatever reason. From now on, when she calls you, feel free to bring your little note pad and pen to keep up the fiction—for both your sakes—that you're working on a biography. But the cold hard truth, baby, is that she's going to want to start having some hot play."

"I ... uh ... I ... " I said.

"That's the truth, kid. That's why she's called 'The Mattress'. Every once in a while she wants some young hunk o' meat to flop down on her. Get it? Tag. You're it."

"Cooper—I don't mind spending time with Victoria. She's a fascinating woman but I ... "

"You don't sleep with women?"

I let a long moment go by, hoping he'd fill it for me. He didn't. "No," I said at last. "My clients have always been men. But, I mean, what did Laird expect? He met me in a queer bar!"

"Well then, my dear boy, I suggest you get a hold of some Viagra. I'm sure you have it in stock. In your, uh, *occupation*, it's part of the on-the-job tools, right? Take some Viagra, watch some porn, devise a fantasy, and climb aboard the ol' Mattress. Tuesday, 2:00 P.M."

And then he hung up.

23.

THE THOUGHT CAME to Carla that she would some day die a suicide. Her body couldn't put up with much more of life's cruel practical jokes, its heartless punch lines. Mikki had been the first person in years she had opened up to, and now Mikki was pulling away, distancing herself.

The plan didn't come to Carla in a flash of inspiration. It had developed inside her for weeks, but the seed had been planted in her late-night conversations with Mikki at the beginning of their relationship.

Lately when she went on necessary photo op excursions with Mikki and Justin, Carla—the eternal third wheel—would sit in the back seat listening to Justin rhapsodize about Mikki. "You look so beautiful today," he would whisper across the seat.

If only he knew the truth about her, Carla would think sarcastically to herself. It was annoying to listen to other people's sweet talk while she was alone. How horrible Carla felt, sitting back there, awkward and alone! No one told her she was beautiful.

Not being able to have Mikki for herself, Carla longed for anything Mikki had. And the fact that Mikki was sleeping with Justin but didn't even desire him made Carla burn with a sexual jealousy that was almost too much to bear. So the idea came to her to put an end to it.

One night, while sitting home alone over a Chinese takeout dinner, she read a blurb in the papers about Mikki and Justin being seen at a trendy restaurant. Surely her father had also read it. Why couldn't it be her sitting in a restaurant, looking radiant beside an important man? Why did others deserve recognition? Why did things seem to come so easy to everybody else, while she was denied the tiniest bones of happiness?

A realization will alter your life, her horoscope read. *There are answers available, even if you don't want to look for them. Don't be afraid to ask for what you need, even if it seems like too much. You can't always be giving of yourself, unless you're getting things in return.*

The following day, she was supposed to have brunch with Mikki and Justin—a farewell meal between the three friends, since Mikki was leaving that weekend for three weeks of work in Rome.

Why was she crying? They probably didn't really want her to come along. She missed Mikki—she had to admit it—although lately Mikki had been cold and distant. So she tried to convince herself she hated Mikki. *The bitch. Now that she's making, it she doesn't need my fucking connections anymore*, Carla thought. She dialed Justin's number.

"Hello," Justin said.

"Justin . . . it's Carla. Is Mikki there?" Her voice was small and flat.

"Carla, where are you?"

"I'm still at home."

"Are you drunk? Are you okay?"

"Is Mikki there?"

"She's asleep."

"I wanted to know . . . if we're still on for tomorrow afternoon. For brunch." A pause on the other end of the line. "Are we?" Pause. "Yes or no?"

"No."

Carefully, cheerfully, Carla said: "Okay, I had a feeling. Okay, bye."

Justin: "Give us a call sometime soon."

Why should the fact that they didn't want to see her matter so much? But it did. It did. The pain obliterated her sense of right and wrong; she was able to carry out her plan with methodical calm.

IT WAS A gamble. She knew it. But if it failed, what did she lose? Carla knew that Mikki would be having dinner with Jana Janelow on this particular night, whenever she woke up from her fucking nap at Justin's place, and that she would be leaving the following morning. To execute her plan, Carla had to go to Mikki's apartment, use Mikki's computer, sign in under her screen name, and send an email. All of which was fairly easy. She had a key to Mikki's Queens apartment. And Mikki was always signed on to her computer under her screen name. See the things you learn when you become close with a trusted friend? Carla set out from Fifth Avenue in Manhattan to Elmhurst, Queens—a neighborhood that was almost always quiet at night. Mikki checked into her apartment maybe once a week, using it as a sort of office. A rest stop from her new and glorious life.

"So what if you're a disappointment to your father?" the cab driver said, opening up the conversation on their drive to Queens, not bothering to turn to look at her. And the flat-out statement was so sudden and so unexpected that tears sprung immediately to Carla's eyes. The cabbie was drunk. Even from the back seat she could smell the alcoholic fumes in the air between them.

"Excuse me," Carla said, stung, trying to catch his eyes in the rearview mirror.

"We all disappoint each other," he said, "in a million different ways."

She looked at her reflection in the mirror, her hair tucked under a baseball cap, big round glasses covering half her face. This man certainly hadn't recognized who she was and knew nothing about her life. He obviously had his own disappointments to ponder and was looking for another soul to communicate his emotions to. But he was right; she was a disappointment to her father. She was no model. Once again it was simply her father's name that had gotten her through the door. Everything she did, from her look to her poses, was a fake, a mere imitation of Mikki. And everyone knew it. But Mikki had looks. And talent. And the ability to make people love her. *Oh, Mikki, Mikki,* her mind screamed out in despair, *why can't you love me?*

She was filled with a sickening mixture of jealousy and guilt and, strangely, satisfaction. She was about to betray the only two people who had ever done anything to really help her. But she needed to be famous, really famous in her own right, and Mikki, who had started as her inspiration, was now an obstacle. With Justin behind Mikki, Carla knew she would always be a second-string Britten. A Jayne Mansfield to Marilyn Monroe. She felt Mikki had been a piece of shit to abandon her when Carla needed her most. Like everyone else had abandoned her. *I wish her all the unhappiness in the world,* she said to herself.

Carla needed to be the best. The number one. She needed that for her father. Last month she had awkwardly danced with him at a Hollywood party. During the dance she could think of nothing to say to him. They were strangers. She knew that he knew she was no model and again was making a living from his name. Oh, why couldn't she just stop trying to live up to his expectations? Why didn't she just move away, change her name, get married, raise a family . . . some place where she wouldn't have to live up to any expectations?

She blamed herself for her mother's death, too. She didn't really want to bring up her childhood, but there it was, like a bad rerun. She was only a little girl, and her mother seemed to be reaching out to her. Looking for validation. Looking for someone to unite with in hatred of Jonathan Christaldi. The day after Babe had scalded her face and body with boiling water at the dinner party, Carla was brought in to see her. For some reason everyone decided it would be best to leave mother and daughter alone for a few moments.

"Mommy," Carla said tentatively. Her mother looked so scary. Her face was scarlet and raw and blistered. Her eyes swollen to slits. Yet she was calm, almost catatonic, from the heavy doses of morphine given to her. "Mommy," Carla said again.

Suddenly Babe snapped to attention. "Do you want to see what your father did to me?" she screamed, while flinging the blanket off of the bed. She quickly lifted her hospital gown and exposed her red, swollen vagina. She pinched a piece of the raw flesh of her labia and pulled at them; the lips were not fully attached to her vagina.

Do you want to see what your father did to me! Babe screamed at her daughter. Then Carla herself screamed and ran from the room and never told a soul what she had witnessed there.

But a couple of weeks later, upon Babe's release from the hospital, it was Carla who came upon her mother's dead body, hanging from her spacious walk-in closet. Other than the corpse, the closet was almost empty because Babe had thrown all of her clothes from the window into the swimming pool weeks before.

Carla had dealt with this in therapy for years. Why did it still haunt her? Why was she not able to get on with things, get past it, grow up!

"What have I done with my life?" Carla whispered to herself. She whipped off her glasses and again looked at herself in the rearview mirror, and her eyes locked momentarily with the driver's in miserable camaraderie.

She made him stop one block away from Mikki's apartment. She hesitated a moment and then stepped out of the cab.

Mikki would not know that Carla had been in her apartment, that Carla had listened to her absence. How her absence screamed at her. She would never see the image of Carla nosing around her place . . . looking for something, some reason to not go through with her plan. She found new clothes, boots, handbags piled all over the tiny apartment in complete confusion. Prada. Gucci. Chanel. Versace. Open suitcases with clothes crammed in them. The belongings needed for her three weeks of work in Italy.

She saw pages from recent magazines tacked up all over the place. In them Mikki was dressed in high fashion, modeling the latest makeup colors. On her computer desk there was a snapshot of Justin and Mikki at some New York function, Mikki smiling radiantly into the camera. Justin, who was slightly out of focus, had his eyes closed. If only there had been a shot of Carla and Mikki somewhere around. Where were all the stuffed animals Carla had given her? Oh, there was one: the Siamese cat with jeweled eyes, casually tossed in the corner of the room, under a pair of belted jeans, next to a single stiletto heel. Carla had spent a day looking for the adorable beast and dropped a small fortune on it. She had imagined Mikki holding it tenderly on nights she felt lonely.

Carla sat at Mikki's computer, the computer Mikki used to attend to her correspondence. She read Mikki's email. Dozens of letters from adoring fans. Invitations from men. Marriage proposals. An email from Jana Janelow, which read, "Been busy lately, but how about we squirrel away to a late dinner before you leave?" Why did it enrage her so much that Mikki had a life outside of her? There was also an email from Carla; if Mikki had read it, she would have known that Carla was feeling very low and needed a friend and would Mikki please call her. The status of the email said "unread." *That's the fucking status of my life: unread*, Carla thought.

Carla started an email addressed to Justin Landis. It read as follows:

> Justin, this is very hard for me to say, and I could never say it to you face to face. But it's something I need to say to you before I leave for Europe. It's something that I need to get out in the open between us because I can no longer play this game. I can no longer live this lie. Let me say first that I am very fond of you. I appreciate all you have done for me, although in my heart I know I could have done it without you. I would have found a way. You just happened along and I took advantage of the opportunity—yet I don't want you to think I'm not eternally grateful. I am. But Justin, I feel our sexual relationship has to end, as it is a lie. The truth is, Justin,

that I have never desired you sexually. Truthfully, I just did whatever I felt was necessary at the time to sign with EYE. I know that that was wrong, but I know that you understand that I HAD to do it. I'm sure you must have suspected this. There were signals I gave off.

Remember that first night you told me you liked to make love with the lights on and I said I prefer them off. The truth is that I needed them off to get through it. I am not saying this to hurt your feelings. Understand me. I need to get this out in the open. It was sexual fantasies, and sexual fantasies only, that have gotten me through our entire sexual relationship. Fantasies involving waiters, dreams involving actors, old boyfriends . . . but it was never you in bed with me. You deserve better Justin and so do I, so let's just end it now, without talking about it, while we can still, hopefully, salvage a working relationship. If, however, you want to continue with this sexual charade, I will, but you have to know that it is only because I feel I owe it to you. There are so many things I lied to you about Justin. Almost everything I've ever said was a lie. Even things like my age. I am not twenty but twenty-five. I suppose, now that I am a success, things like that don't matter much anymore. I'm on my way up, and I know you recognize my worth as a model and won't let me down. I know that we will continue to work together long after our romantic relationship stops. I'm sending this now because I'm going to be out of the country and it will give you time to digest all of this. But I beg you never to mention this email to me. I will never mention it to you. I could NOT bear talking about it with you. And if you ever do bring it up . . . I will deny it.

With respect and admiration,
Mikki

CARLA REREAD THE email. She looked at Justin's email address. The curser was poised on "send." Carla's heart was racing. *What bad karma, what evil spell, what unstoppable destruction will this bring on me?* she thought. Then she clicked and the email disappeared. Message sent.

It's done, she said to herself. *It's over. I sent it. He'll receive it, and I'll never think about it again. I disassociate myself from this incident completely. Whatever happens, happens. Ignorance will be my talisman.*

She called for another cab and headed back to Manhattan.

24.

IT'S ONLY SPIT, I said to myself, as I lay on Victoria Sweetzer's bed, my mouth glued to hers. But she seemed to want to give me more and more of hers. I tried to force some of mine into her mouth to keep her satisfied. Oh, I was going to gag. It was all so fucking yuck.

Instead of gagging I took a deep sniff of the little bottle of amyl nitrate, also called Rush, also called poppers, also called on by me in an emergency when I needed to get as horny as possible in the shortest amount of time.

I was so nervous that I wouldn't be able to perform that just before arriving at her apartment, I took the Viagra a fellow hustler sold me, plus some Horny Goat Weed, the natural Viagra I bought in a health food store; a Xanax; and many, many martinis.

Doctors warn against taking Viagra and then drinking alcohol, snorting poppers, or mixing in any other pills. And here I was doing all of that. I was pulling in the heavy artillery.

When I arrived, Victoria was lying in bed, waiting for me. Again I was wearing a suit. The same one I wore to our first meeting actually—only the tie was different. As she lay there, I took out the notebook and pen, in the hopes that she had changed her mind, that she had decided that I really did have the intuitive nature to write a magnificent book about her life.

"Take off your clothes," she said. I can't say it was really a demand. A request? No. It was just a statement. I had heard it many times. Never did it sound so strange. I had a lot of substances in my body. It was as if I were in a dream. I lay down naked beside her. "Don't look to love anyone," she said softly. "Love only in that moment—in that restaurant—when it's right and magic and forever. Only in that moment."

The next thing I remember, she was blowing me, sometimes using her hand to rub me along, as if she were milking me, but then when it was gooey enough, she would begin deep-throating. Obviously it was my cum she was after. She didn't realize that when she grazed against my shaft with her dentures, it didn't feel delightful. It hurt. She was hurting me. Scratching me. Now, listen, I'm used to a rough blowjob now and again, and I've had a few that left me sore for several days, but this was really painful. She took my groans as moans of pleasure. I was thrashing about, but that only made her more determined. I thought of asking her to stop but then I decided to just wait it out, though I'd probably end up in shreds.

This was grossness in the most high. I started to lose my hard-on. I couldn't let that happen. It might insult her. Hurt her. I started thinking about her in *Helen of Troy*, in all her near-naked splendor. My hard-on status continued to dwindle. I wanted to make her happy. Her films, specific moments from her films, had made me so happy so many times in my life. Sometimes almost to the point of keeping me alive. This was so little to ask. I wanted to give it to her so desperately that it only inhibited me more. There was too much history here to have sex.

She began milking and rubbing more frantically. I grabbed my poppers from the bedside and inhaled for several seconds—then waited for the fireworks. I decided it was Colin Farrell blowing me. We had just come back after a night on the town, downing beers, chain-smoking, sitting happily through a few lap dances. He was feeling slightly out of it and wanted to come back to the hotel, babeless. As soon as we walked through the door he decided to start a make-believe boxing match and hit me a soft one to the chin, which hurt nevertheless. We took off our shirts and assessed each other. Then our pants came off. We stood there in briefs, like boxers in the ring. I hit him with a left hook, and before you knew it, he had me in a headlock. From my vantage point I could see the bulge in his briefs. I pulled down the underwear, and with his arm holding my head, I took his sweet Irish meat, with its European cut, or opposite of cut, into my mouth and started sucking. Oh, he is such a gorgeous, little, tough pretty boy. Oh, the darlin'. Yum! After a while he decided to return the favor, and now I lay on the bed and as in everything else, he's rough. He's rough. He's hot. He's a fucking god. When he lifted my head and made a move to kiss me on my mouth . . .

I felt myself exploding in Victoria's mouth and, man, gurgle, gurgle, she swallowed every last drop and gave me a few extra squeezes to make sure I was empty. I was quivering. She kept sucking long after the explosive orgasm, as if the cells in the juice of my semen contained a rejuvenating youth serum or some answer to the mysteries of life.

It was obvious, by her mental telepathy, that she wanted me out of there fast. Not faster than I wanted to get out. I dressed hurriedly, said goodbye. She didn't say anything, but I didn't want her to think that she disgusted me or that I had any ill will for her. "Thank you," I said and stumbled out into the hallway, where I found Cooper waiting for me with an ugly smirk.

"So?" he said. "Did you manage to sleep on 'The Mattress?'"

I was disheveled. My eyes were watery. I was on the verge of vomiting—throwing up the spit and the poppers and the Viagra and martinis and the entire episode. "It's cool," I said and didn't add anything else.

His smirk did not change. He handed me the check, which he had already filled out. I found my way out of the apartment, wretched and disoriented, and walked into the night, which was very black— the way I wanted it.

25.

"HELLO MOON," MIKKI said, and cried and cried and cried. It was 6:00 A.M. and she was waiting for sleep to take over. So exhausted that she couldn't even put a coherent thought together, yet she also couldn't sleep. But definitely no more sleeping pills. The last dose had left her dizzy and shaky but not at all drowsy. She watched from her bed as the sky changed from black to that familiar ashy gray. A color that for her had become synonymous with her darkest depression hours—the end of night—the time when the things that were bothering her most danced through her head. In years past it had been images of her career moving too slow, not doing enough, growing older, being alone. But tonight it was Justin. Some inner alarm had told her that their relationship was irretrievably over.

Even Carla could not have guessed how perfectly her plan would work. Justin received her email and never for an instant suspected that Mikki did not write it. He could not express, even to himself, how hurt and bewildered he felt learning that his entire sex life with Mikki, now in its eighth month, was a fraud. Oh, he had his suspicions that her feelings weren't as strong as his own, but he never thought she could be so cunning, so utterly devoid of feeling. The ironic part is that Mikki was really beginning to feel something special in the sex she and Justin had together. If it wasn't real passion, it was tenderness, a feeling of being with someone who appreciated what she was giving him. A gentle feeling. A safe feeling.

Justin, humiliated beyond belief, stopped calling Mikki. She would come back to her hotel in Italy and check her messages. *Nothing from Justin!* her mind exclaimed. *How can that be*? After three days of not hearing from him, she called him. Voicemail. She left a message. It was not returned. A panic started setting in. Had he met someone else? When things were going peachy, she thought of him maybe once or twice a day. His many messages on her cell phone were a pleasing confirmation of his devotion. Now that there was no confirmation, she could think of nothing else. Nothing.

When she returned from Italy, he called her rarely, and only then if it had something to do with her work—modeling jobs or interviews that were being set up for her. Mikki, in return, was angry and bewildered at his abrupt change toward her. More and more, she began to feel his absence. She realized how much she had grown to enjoy being seen at the best restaurants with him and the fanfare that went with that. But she also missed the quiet nights they spent together in his apartment, where he always gave her his full attention. It was obvious that he was truly in love with her. And she realized how much she cared for him, even if she did not love him. But what had happened? Had he grown tired of her? Was he simply busy? What had she done wrong?

WAITING FOR A phone call from Justin became a torture. She couldn't concentrate on reading or watching TV; the silence of the phone was too much of a distraction. If it did ring and it was somebody other than Justin, her voice on the phone sounded hollow and diminished. When he was calling her every night, she had taken his calls for granted. Now she missed them. It's nice to be wanted. It's nice to be loved. Even if the sex was bad, the emotions were real. Now she wondered if it was all an act on his part. (Was he faking his love for her as much as she was faking the sex?) *He wants to be you,* she heard Jana Janelow's voice repeat in her head. Was that true? How could a man be so in love with her one day, then completely ignore her the next? She felt upset, betrayed, lied to—awful feelings that went back to Year One.

Meantime, as the moon faded, pictures of Justin and her together forced their way into her head as if to tell her: *See, you had a shot at being happy. You let him get away. You screwed up. Ha, ha, ha, foolish little girl! Fickle little girl!*

Several weeks passed before Mikki discovered what she thought was the reason for the distance between her and Justin. It was late one Tuesday night. She had completed a long, laborious sitting for Naked perfume. Although she did not know it at the time, this would be the last major modeling job of her career. Right around the corner from the studio where she had been shooting was Bar Nothing, a popular hangout for the modeling set. She was exhausted and in a bad temper, but she decided to stop in, more out of a need to pee than to socialize. It was a busy night and everyone was in an up mood. There was a piano player singing Sinatra classics in a voice and style that was very close to the original.

There was, she knew, something wrong with her career. She noticed it in the attitudes of the bookers at EYE, the impatience they showed when dealing with her. A delicate change in the balance of power had occurred among the top girls at the agency—and she was slipping. Or was it her imagination? She was taking diet pills, starving herself, sniffing heroin occasionally, taking tranquilizers to sleep. Perhaps all this was simply making her paranoid.

Mikki rushed past the jovial patrons toward the ladies' room without looking into anyone's eyes. She sat on the toilet and took out a small silver envelope of heroin. Sniff, sniff. From the stall she could hear the piano player singing, "She gets too hungry for dinner at eight . . ." *One drink and I'm out of here*, she promised herself.

As she stepped out of the ladies' room, though, to her surprise the first person she saw was Justin. He was standing at the bar talking to a blonde whose back was turned to Mikki. Thrown off her guard, Mikki made an about-face and stepped back into the bathroom. She closed herself into a stall, aware of her heart beating in frantic little palpitations. What should she do? He hadn't seen her yet; perhaps she should try to sneak out and pretend she hadn't seen him? Or should she confront him? Cause a scene? Now at last she had a chance to get answers, yet instinct warned her not to pursue them. She wanted to call her real mother in Heaven. She wanted to visit Mario and go to sleep in his arms.

Baby, she said to herself scornfully, *grow up*.

She took out her compact and powered her face. She applied a fresh coat of lipstick. She combed out her fast-becoming legendary hair. She decided to bury the rage that was bubbling up in her and face him. Shaking out her tresses to a carefree wild mane, she stepped out of the ladies' room and walked toward Justin with a stoic calm.

" . . . that's why the lady is a tramp," the piano man sang.

When she looked his way, the first thing she noticed was the back of the blonde. The chick was in Spandex. It was backless and it was open on one side, held together with little strategically placed straps. Tacky. The woman was leaning toward Justin, talking to him intimately.

As Mikki approached he saw her and his eyebrows lifted in surprise. Mikki tilted her head, cocked an eyebrow and gave him a quick little wave. Smilingly, she stood beside the woman, who still hadn't noticed Mikki. The blonde stopped mid-sentence and at the same time the two women faced each other. And the fact that the blonde was Carla Christaldi hit Mikki with the same breath-snatching impact as a good swift kick to the stomach. Her smile, though, only quivered slightly.

"Hey, you two," Mikki said, in what can only be described as a brilliant recovery, "long time no see." She could not bring herself to look at Carla again, but in the brief instant that she had seen her, she noticed how much thinner she had become since they last hung out. Suddenly pieces fell into place. Carla had not been calling Mikki lately either. *Imagine*, Mikki thought, *him wanting Carla over me*.

Justin seemed awkward. Even though he was still furious with Mikki, he was gentleman enough to tread cautiously at this sensitive moment.

"Did you get my message?" he asked.

This was a lie and Mikki knew it. There was no message, and there hadn't been one for nearly two weeks. Why give him the fucking satisfaction of playing his stupid game? If she said she didn't get the message, he would say, "Gee, I left you a message. Is your voicemail working?" Fuck that.

"Yes," she said.

"You . . . um . . . got my message?" he asked, confused.

"Yes. I got your message, Justin." And now he knew she knew he was lying. She didn't know if he would ever want her again, but if he did, this exchange canceled out any chance of him ever having her again.

The bartender set down a Cosmopolitan in front of Mikki, a drink she had not ordered but which the server knew she favored.

"So what have you been up to?" Carla asked. Mikki and Justin continued staring at each other.

"Not much. I just finished shooting the Naked campaign and I'm exhausted. Andres is a great photographer, but he works you like a horse."

"I know," Carla said. "I shot 'Them There Eyes' with him on Monday."

POW! Another sucker punch to the gut! Now Mikki turned to Carla. She tried not to keel over. As everyone knew—everyone *in the business* knew—Mikki had been up for the "Them There Eyes" campaign, which Revlon was launching. It entailed print ads, TV commercials, billboards; the works. Maximum visibility and big-time bucks. That Carla had gotten this important job, signed and shot it, without Mikki even hearing about it, was the first real sign that her status at EYE was diminishing.

Oh, the pain was spreading through Mikki like blood on a band-aid. *I must get out of here with a semblance of dignity*, Mikki said to herself, *before it gets any worse*.

"It was great to see you both," she said suddenly, her drink untouched.

"Stay a while," Justin offered.

"I have to go home," Mikki said, her voice a shade hoarser than she would have liked. "I'm very tired."

Carla started to say something, but Mikki didn't stay to hear it. She blindly stumbled toward the door. Some of the other models drinking at the bar turned to look at her. "Mikki Britten, stoned again," one of them said, and a general burst of laughter followed her into the night. Mikki, numb by now, didn't feel that final blow.

The night air was cold.

Keep my mind distracted, God, she said to the Person she always turned to in distress, *help me to get home.*

Justin and Carla. She couldn't bear the thought of them together, and she walked down the streets like a zombie. Passing headlights momentarily illuminated her ghostly face. One arm was raised trying to wave a cab over. A ghostly sight. As usual they zoomed past her. She took extremely shallow breaths; if she tried for anything deeper, she'd either cry or vomit. Dry-heaving was yet another option. Shallow breaths won out.

Pace your steps briskly, she told herself as she walked toward the subway, *and don't cry.*

The subway was the last thing she needed in her state of mind. It represented longings, ambitions, failures. Her career was disappearing before her eyes, like a particularly provocative dream in the first moments of waking. Without Justin pulling for her at the agency, her days of cabs and limos might well be over—soon she might end up back on the trains.

The subways were so different at night. There was none of that franticness of the daytime, that rushing around to get to a place on time. And there was always that damn feeling of menace.

The train roared into the station. *He won't miss me,* she thought to herself. *Sex can be sweet with anyone. She was back at square one. At this age! If she was going to survive, she would have to start all over. Stop it! Stop it! Keep these ideas away from yourself,* she warned herself, *or you'll never make it home.*

She took her seat and, looking for a distraction, studied the middle-age man opposite her. His face, clearly handsome at one time, was now worn and tired. An air of permanent disappointment hung around him like the cheap aftershave she was sure he was wearing. To Mikki he represented the set of people who never quite make it—the people who spend their days hanging around offices on the fringes of success, accepting the fact of a life on the margins. She imagined his wife, too, at home drying dishes, a worn woman who had also settled for less, never being able to catch the man she really loved and so instead making do with one who would have her.

What did it feel like living in this world of the defeated (which she felt herself fast approaching)? The land of no turning back? Of having to make do? Of two-weeks vacation a year? Of scrimping and saving? Of some late-night TV, a drink, and bed?

Mikki's sympathy for this lonely loser pierced her, as well as the agonizing fear of ending up like him. She stared at him openly in the hopes that he would start up a conversation. She wanted him to prove her wrong. She wanted to find a cheerful man, bragging about his grandchildren and his upcoming trip to Disneyland. And in return she would flirt with him so he would receive an extra dose of encouragement from a desirable girl on a subway train. She would send him to his wife recharged and invigorated.

Instead of any of this happening, though, he spread his polyester-covered legs wide and placed his hand over his crotch. His eyes held hers with a look of defiance, shame, and sex. One of those shocking, late-night subway things was about to happen, and she felt the beginning waves of a nervous energy that always took her over in these situations. Now his eyes asked, *What are you going to do about it?* Mikki, in confusion, looked around the car. A snoozing black woman in a soiled nurse's uniform, a Puerto Rican man absorbed in the *Post*, a homeless man lying across a row of seats, his face covered by a filthy sweater—his stench drifting heavily through the car.

Mikki looked back at the man's hand on his crotch. Now he was making a circular rubbing motion. How could she, one hour ago a rising model on her way from an important shoot, be in this type of situation yet again? *I am probably worth nothing*, she thought. *Prove it. Let him have you.* She looked away from him but placed her hand on her own inner thigh and let it slide up her skirt. With a startling jerking movement he shot up from his seat and sat beside her. He did indeed smell of cheap aftershave, and the smell of it intoxicated her, cutting through the foul odors of the subway, agitating her senses beyond belief with a mixture of erotic energy—desire and disgust. It seemed every part of her body was shaking with repulsion and longing. The two of them sat awkwardly beside each other for several moments as he continued rubbing his crotch in a circular pattern.

This was harmless stuff. She was longing for him to touch her, to put his hand on her leg and slide it up her panties. However, he continued masturbating.. He was still looking at her, hoping for some reaction. She showed none. Instead she grabbed him by the sides of his face and kissed him, closed mouthed at first, then she let her tongue slide into his mouth. His lips felt crusty. She put her hands on his arms and they were surprisingly solid and muscular. They separated from the kiss and continued with their separate activities. His circular jerk-off session through his polyester pants, her hand running up and down her own inner thigh. She took his hand and guided it up her skirt to her panties. His hand greedily explored the small patch of hair. He tentatively ran a finger down her vagina. An involuntary moan escaped her lips.

She would invite him home, she thought. He was a harmless, run-of-the-mill pervert, the kind that rubs up against girls in the rush-hour crowds. She was a worthless piece of shit. The sex between them would be quick and frantic, and then she would kick him out. That was her plan.

But on New York subways, especially late at night, the unexpected often happens. Shockingly, the man reached into his suit jacket and pulled out a lacy bra, bright red in color. Without warning she had become a character in a nightmare. The beautiful girl and the subway creep. Of course she was startled, but she tried not to show it. To show strong emotion was to exclude yourself from this exclusive dark world and to bring yourself back to reality.

"Do you mind that I have a bra," he asked in a voice that was perfectly calm and normal, almost like the voice of a late-night radio DJ—which only made him more sinister and perverted.

"No," she replied, devoid of inflection. Of course she did mind that this creature had a scarlet bra tucked away under his cheap suit, but she was now glued to the scene as if she were a spectator with her nose pressed to the window of an old-time freak show.

The shiny, lurid bra contrasted harshly with his muted gray suit. Mikki watched, repelled and fascinated, as he began to rub the bra between his legs. *What is he going to do now?* Mikki asked herself, thrilling with fear. And her biggest fear was that she would never wake up.

"I have to wear a bra," he said, "because my tits are too big."

The remark frightened her. She imagined what he looked like under the cheap suit, a deformed monstrosity, half man, half woman, with grotesque tits harnessed into a flimsy red bra. All remaining erotic feelings fled from her at once. She stood up.

"I have to go now," she said, heading for the door that led to a connecting car.

He wasn't angry at all. He carefully folded the bra and returned it to his inside pocket, where presumably it would await its next adventure. "Good-bye," he called after her as she stepped into the next car. She collapsed in a new seat and buried her face in her hands.

———

A HALF HOUR later, she stormed into her apartment, tears streaming down her face. She took off her jacket and threw it over the picture of herself on a magazine cover, an achievement she had been proud of earlier, but now she couldn't stand staring at herself.

"How dare he! How dare he treat me like this!" she screamed, thinking of Justin.

She took off the rest of her clothes and stood naked in the middle of the room. What should she do? Dial Justin's number? Confront him. Find out what the hell was going on. He'd be home by now. Compulsively, she dialed his cell. Voicemail! Voicemail! He always answered his cell! How could he not pick up? Did he see her number on caller ID! Oh, God! Did she make it clear to him when they were together how much he meant to her? How much she wanted him. Did she do something subconsciously to drive the relationship to an end? Oh, God! If Justin and Carla were together, she knew her modeling days would be over. Her body slumped to the floor.

Get through this lonely night and you'll be a stronger person, she reasoned with herself.

To soothe herself and her ego she thought about some of the better conversations she'd had with Justin. She thought of how she had introduced him to the music of Billie Holiday. How he, drunk on brandy, had sat enthralled as she read poetry to him, her voice bringing the poems to life. She thought of ways she looked when they went out, the care and preparation she put into creating just the right image—exactly what he was looking for. She decided that she would never call him. *Let him go out with others*, her mind screamed out. *I'll overcome this fucking shit! Whatever you want to throw at me, God! I'll withstand the competition! I will prevail!*

And although it took her many months, the plotting of a murder, and a violent rape, she was right.

26.

I HAD RECENTLY added new nude photos to my escort Web site, so my cell phone had been ringing more than usual. I never checked caller ID before answering because I usually didn't recognize the number anyway. But I was surprised when I heard Cooper's voice on the other end of the receiver. I thought after my last encounter with Victoria, I'd never hear from anyone in that camp again.

"Honey," Cooper said, as usual, his voice dripping with conde-scension, "you made the tabloids."

"What are you talking about? What tabloids?"

"Well, so far it's in the *Star* AND the *Globe*, but I wouldn't be surprised if the *Enquirer* elaborates in the next issue."

"Elaborates on what, Cooper?"

Me? In the tabloids? Were there photos? Was Victoria claiming I raped her? These were but a few of the thoughts racing through my mind while I tried to keep a coherent conversation going.

"Just go up to the corner newsstand and read all about it. The phone here's been ringing all day. Victoria's having her PR people handle it. She has no comment, of course."

"Is my name in it?" I asked instinctively.

"Oh, honey, just go read it for yourself—you'll recognize the situation."

And then the phone went dead.

I ran to the corner candy/newspaper/everything store, where they had a huge magazine rack covering the entire back wall. Floor to ceiling magazines and newspapers. I knew where the tabloid papers were stashed—eye level, in the middle of everything else.

From many feet away I could see the cover of one of the tabloids. It was a paparazzi shot of Victoria, probably taken several years before; she seemed to be in the middle of a scream, but in reality it was probably just snapped mid-sneeze.

I felt temporary vertigo when I was close enough to read the headline: VICTORIA SWEETZER IN CALL-BOY SCANDAL. And then the subhead, HOTTIE HUSTLER CLAIMS HE USED VIAGRA TO GET THROUGH STEAMY SESSIONS WITH FADED STAR.

Still dizzy, I found the double-page spread, and raced through the rest of the article. It was contemptible beyond words. Not to me! My name wasn't even mentioned. I was referred to as a "hirsute boy-toy" and a "handsome hustler." It was so vile and ugly toward Victoria, making her sound like a desperate old nymphomaniac, even going so far as to say, "the fading goddess friends now refer to as 'the old mattress.'"

I looked at the other tabloid and it was more of the same. It was lavishly illustrated with photos of Victoria's career and her many husbands and lovers. They had a picture of a male model, shirtless, with his face X'd out, I suppose representing me. The copy called me the "Viagra-fueled stud." Mostly I was depicted as a money-hungry piece of trash. The way the articles were worded made it sound like I was the source of the story, which I was not.

I felt sick. Other than myself, the only people who knew about my encounters with Victoria were Cooper and Laird Payne. There was the Hispanic housekeeper, but she wouldn't know the details. I couldn't imagine any reason Laird Payne had for revealing anything to the press. So it must have been Cooper. For what? A lousy ten or fifteen grand? Oh, it was all so horrible, because Victoria, I'm sure, would believe it was me who sold the stories and said those hideous things about her.

There wasn't even any way I could call and warn her about Cooper because he was the only way I had to contact her. He probably read all of her mail, too.

It was incredibly weird reading about myself in a paper with a circulation of several million, yet knowing that my identity was hidden. It was a relief, but I still felt helpless. I wanted to explain to every single person reading those tabloids—on checkout lines, on subway cars, on toilet bowls—the truth of the situation. How I had been tricked to going to Victoria's bedroom, lured by my ambition to be a writer. I wasn't a money-grubbing user. Victoria wasn't a desperate old slut—she was a lonely, elderly legend. But there was nothing I could do. I couldn't even call the papers myself and offer my side of the story. My identity, I was sure, would somehow come out. They have spies and detectives and expert snoops to find out everything. And I didn't want to go down in history as the person who defiled Victoria Sweetzer in her final years.

I put the papers back on the rack and left the store. Next week, I reasoned, there would be something else on the cover. Some other person slandered and accused. Probably all this "Victoria and hustler" business would all be forgotten.

Besides, I wasn't the only one making the papers that week . . . and at least I remained anonymous.

27.

THIS TOWN'S NOT BIG ENOUGH FOR THE TWO OF THEM (Coast to Coast): For the past several months it has looked like Mikki Britten would soon be elevated to supermodel status. We certainly used up plenty of tissues after, uh, "looking" at her pictures. After several high-profile ads, a much-publicized affair with EYE Models president Justin Landis and a runway charisma that keeps 'em on the edge of their seat, her place at the top of modeldom seemed assured. But after the announcement of VH1's choice for host of their new weekly fashion reality show, Cutting Edges, it looks like Britten's once red-hot career is now officially ice cold. Everyone thought that Britten was a shoe-in for the sure-to-be-hit show, but it was announced late last week that Carla Christaldi would be taking the high-profile hosting honors.

Now comes word that FAST-Forward, the active-wear company that has used Britten's face and body everywhere, from colorful magazine ads to a Times Square billboard, has dumped her for Christaldi. "Losing FAST-Forward is a tremendous blow to Mikki's career," said one fashion insider. "It is a very prestigious campaign."

Britten has inspired a wave of vulnerable, tough-girl models sporting wild-mane hair and teary eyes. But how long did she think she could pull that act off? Now it's Carla, also blonde and sullen-eyed, and the daughter of movie maverick Jonathan Christaldi—who is being touted as the next big thing on the fashion scene. As for Britten, she'll probably be crawling back under that rock she slithered out from.

AFTER THE NIGHT that Mikki ran into Justin and Carla at Bar Nothing, her career just ... well ... fizzled. It's as simple as that. Important jobs she had been seriously considered for fell through. Auditions and go-sees led to nothing. It became apparent that Justin had no plans for her future modeling career, and without him she felt helpless.

People never asked her what had happened between her and the modeling tycoon but they knew they were no longer together and she felt a definite change in their attitude. Within a month of the Bar Nothing incident, it was announced in tiny items in the press that Mikki Britten had left EYE Model Management. There were no explanations from Justin for his sudden change toward her and she never confronted him.

So she said good-bye to comfort. To security. To love. To the safe place Justin had made for her. It was difficult to let go of something that had given her hope. But at least she could be grateful to Justin for having given her a glimpse of the happiness she had always sought.

More than the loss of love, she mourned the loss of promise. The promise of a great career. The protection of money. The shield of fame. How unbearable it was to go back to being a nothing! Where would she get the strength to start over? With the tic, tic, tic of the clock never allowing her a moment's peace.

After she left EYE, the press turned the tables on her. She was no longer the darling of the fashion world. She was made into a joke because that was a good story for the tabloids. The press found out her real age; once the rumor had been confirmed, reporters flocked to her neighborhood in Queens and gathered up every old classmate, every person who had known her or said they had known her.

Once the media started laughing, it was hard to let a good joke die. She wasn't a big enough name to be a really hot story—many people didn't even know her by name—but she made for amusing items, and the columnists looked for more things about Mikki to ridicule. One item started: "Lest we forget Mikki Britten is a drunken whore . . ." and went on to detail her falling off a bar stool in a trendy Tribeca bar. Another column voted her, "the most annoying model on the planet (and that's saying a lot)."

Now it was Mikki Britten who was viewed as an imitation Carla Christaldi. Each new article she read felt like a stone hurled at her from another direction. She couldn't stop reading them, though. It was like picking at a wound. Every day she'd do an Internet search using her and Carla's names as search words, and there'd be some new item ridiculing her.

She had lost the competition between the two rising blonde models, and it created a stigma around her. No agency would touch her, though she could have pushed for it. A lesser agency would pick up her contract, perhaps, but she was too tired and too old to start over again from the bottom. There would be more hurdles to overcome, more people to befriend, more beds to lie in.

From her bigger campaigns Mikki had saved some money. But she was perilously close to total despair—the kind that renders you completely helpless. The pills she took now were to knock her out for long hours. She knew she had to do something fast or be finished.

28.

I WAS READING the "Coast to Coast" gossip column, as I did every day, and I read that Victoria Sweetzer was coming out with her "sensational" authorized biography, written by modeling tycoon Laird Payne. A book that promised to "reveal all."

I took a few moments to digest this startling information. I felt somehow involved with these two people. Then I figured it out. It was Victoria Sweetzer and Laird Payne who had been using me all along. The whole Victoria-caught-with-anonymous-hustler story had been staged for publicity. As difficult as it was to believe, that's what it came to.

This was only a few months after I had met with her about becoming her biographer. They couldn't have possibly written a book, even with the help of another ghostwriter, in that stretch of time.

My gut instinct was that Victoria and Laird's book had been written and ready for publication for quite some time. I had been brought into the whole book deal as a way of grabbing some headlines a short time before publication. To whet the hungry public's appetite with a few tantalizing tidbits. For the sake of money, for the sake of a best seller, even Victoria Sweetzer was willing to sell a few lascivious tidbits about her life.

For my few meetings with Victoria, I was paid a grand total of three thousand dollars. That was a small price to pay for the amount of publicity it created. Now everyone in world was eager to read about her life again. I had been used as part of the bait. The latest escapades of a woman people thought they already knew everything about. It was brilliant marketing, I had to admit. But I can't say it didn't hurt me. I can't say it didn't make me feel more defenseless and weak and used than I ever had been before. And that's saying a lot.

Suddenly the biography was everywhere. If I saw something about it in the papers, I immediately passed over it. If some television show was talking about it, I intentionally (and quickly) changed the channels. I didn't care if my anonymous part of her later life was mentioned or not. I didn't care what they had to say about Victoria Sweetzer, her biography, or anything else. But I did catch glimpses of Laird and Victoria on this or that show talking about the project—Larry King had them on for an hour. Victoria was always pulled, glued, and painted together to look rather attractive. Funny how she never bothered to make the least bit effort for me.

There were times, however, that I felt like going up to Victoria's apartment and confronting her. I could arrive at her apartment unannounced and push past Cooper and confront her as she sat propped up in bed drinking vodka and watching her soap stories. Maybe I could make her—for one last time—relate to another human being as a real soul, rather than something that intersected with her career.

But I never got up the nerve to do it. And, unbeknownst to me, there wasn't much time. Victoria would die in the same terrible season as Carla.

29.

MIKKI DECIDED SHE would live on her savings while she worked on her screenplay. Modeling, after all, had only been her intended stepping-stone to films. Of course she had hoped to have more money saved before she gave up modeling to finish her script, but her career had ended abruptly and Queens would have to do for now. The great success she craved would have to come as an actress, when she starred in a movie.

She knew the part that would propel her to stardom would be great; she would create it herself. And so her days were spent working on the script, possessed by the images and fantasies that haunted her. She often felt as if she were on fire, yet it was a great relief to have something to distract her from her pain.

But during her nights, which were empty, she was overcome with the horrible thought that all this might be for nothing. She might end up nowhere—a waitress or a salesgirl spraying people with perfume in Manhattan department stores. Her heart would start racing, and she would need to take Valium and a drink and flee into the night. But the dark feelings followed her. All the dreaming and the planning and the hoping and the clawing and the struggle might lead to nothing. Nothing. Nothing.

———

DESPERATE, MIKKI TURNED to the one person she knew loved her unconditionally. She called me and asked me to meet her at Marco's, an inexpensive Italian restaurant where the waiters let you linger. We sat across from each other over Caesar salads, and if our lives were going to change, we were going to have to do it together. As a team, perhaps, we would have the strength to survive.

"I'm twenty-seven years old, and life has already sapped most of my energy. My will to live. I can't do this alone, Mario. I need you. We need each other. Together we can make it work."

"What do you want me to do?"

"Write a script with me."

"Just like that?"

"Yes! Just like that! What? People haven't done it before? You talk about writing all the time! Take your experiences. Write it down. Your life. What's going on. We're already two interesting characters with fascinating private lives—we'll document our adventures, our experiences."

"But that's not a plot. Everyone in New York, and I guess in Los Angeles, with an idea, says that they're writing a 'screenplay.'"

"Don't you dare, Mario! Don't you dare put us in that category! I know you're a writer. I've read some of your stuff. We'll take our experiences and manipulate them into a plot. We'll take the two main characters, telling separate stories, then bring them together. We'll come up with some sort of dramatic meeting, a climactic ending."

"You mean a character-driven kind of film. Something that can get attention at festivals?"

"Yes! It happens all the time now. Ten years ago it would have been impossible. But with the technology of today, we can make a film on a very low budget."

Her excitement was contagious. "This can work! This can work!" I gushed.

"Of course it can! I'm not talking about fucking *Star Wars Episode IV*. This is a festival, arty, Sundance kind of a thing. It will give us a start. It will give us a name."

"So we start now with our experiences, right?"

"Yes, but we have to . . . have to . . . *have to*, Mario, be brutally honest. We have to put our souls into this. We're not going to have the money for big stars or extravagant special effects. All we really have to make us stand out is our own real stories."

"Then after a few months we get together and start interweaving the stories."

"And inventing the glue to hold the story together."

"This could work, this could work!" I said again.

"But remember, Mario. You have to be honest. You have to go in your writing where you might be afraid to go in your own mind. It has to be real."

30.

WOULD YOU BELIEVE me if I told you that I hate this?
Mikki wrote in her diary. *That I hate sleeping with someone that I don't
love . . . or know . . . or even like. Would you believe that I'd give anything
to change, to be free of this . . . I don't know what . . . sadness? . . . that
makes me do the things I do. Would you believe I can't control it?*

After Mikki left EYE it was like the floodgates came open and
her life overflowed with . . . sex. There was a certain amount of self-
hatred involved in her relationships with the men she started having
sex with, as if she were punishing herself. She began sleeping with
men who treated her badly, men who were geeks and losers—the
ugliest and weirdest men she could find.

IT WAS THE motion that was making me ill, she sat there
thinking on the quickly moving subway, coked beyond repair,
demurely sipping a diet Coke through a straw. Actually the nausea
and sickness had passed and she felt, temporarily, good. Her
destination was uncertain. The train rocked back and forth, and the
motion soothed her. It was just a matter of waiting for something
to happen.

She had been working all day—writing, structuring, editing,
trying to whip her screenplay into shape so she could start sending
it out. And after being cooped up all day she needed to be with
people. She found herself on a subway bound for Manhattan.

At a club she met a guy named Rob, an obese, Wall Street–broker
type, while Wayne, another guy she had been flirting with, left

for the men's room. Rob and Mikki began flirting. Why flirting? Because he was unattractive; because it's what she felt she deserved.

And he! He couldn't believe his good fortune. A beautiful girl like that, giving him the eye. Their conversation flowed marvelously. Turned out that Rob wasn't a Wall Streeter after all. Something to do with sales. From out of town.

"I'm working on a screenplay about my adventures in New York," she told Rob, to dazzle him even more. He didn't need dazzling. He was obscenely fat—well over 300 hundred pounds and a couple of inches shorter than her. His huge face was a moon in full bloom. His eyes were tiny slits on the moon. He was bald on top, with gray hair on the sides, which he slicked down and wore long in the back. His one attempt at being hip, which backfired.

"Would you like to do some cocaine?" Rob asked.

Mikki had to crack up. An old guy like this. He looked squarer than square. And he was partying. *What an incredible turn-on*, she thought. She would have preferred heroin but she shouldn't complain. *This guy probably hasn't been fucked right in years.*

They went to the club's downstairs bathroom because it was a one-room toilet. Privacy, you see. He locked the door. Because of his girth they were squished in like a couple of sardines in a can. She sat on the sink. He held a tiny spoon up to her nose. She sniffed hard. Then he blew some into her mouth. Then he took a snort. Then she snorted some more. Her head and mouth and body went numb. And his kiss on her numb tongue was just . . . just . . . just . . . exquisite! *How gross he is, she thought. I am the queen of obscene.*

Knock, knock.

Someone was at the door. They didn't care. Kiss! Kiss! Coke! Feel! Feel! He was so fat and gushy. She explored his body as if it were a foreign planet. How she would love to disappear in his mounds of flesh. Disappear forever. No one would ever find her. Everything was wonderful. She was the prize possession of this monster's life. I'm your girl, Rob.

Now back to the club. Embarrassment when the two came out

of the bathroom designed for one. More embarrassment when she passed Wayne. Even more embarrassment when Wayne and the rest of the bar's patrons saw that Mikki was now with Rob. But so what? This was her world. She was different.

"Hey, you want to go back to my hotel for a beer?" Rob asks. *How deliciously perverted*, she thinks. *I want to experience EVERYTHING!*

He had a rental car. The universe was conspiring with her. And away they went.

Back in his room, he offered her a beer. She didn't really want it, for fear of calories, but it is the supposed reason for being there so she accepts. She sits with him on the hotel room bed. Then she reaches out for him touching his rotund belly: "Going right for the girth," he says merrily. "They always do."

That really sets her on fire—*it means other girls find him sexy, too!* As you may know, sex mixed with cocaine is just like a little piece of heaven dropped in your lap. They undress hurriedly and fall to the bed. He doesn't have a condom. "I'm negative," he says. "I've just been tested. You?" She'd been tested, too. Negative. She knew that she was telling the truth. What about him? She was high. *Fuck it, fuck it, fuck it*, she said to herself. If she died, she wouldn't be missing much. That's not how she feels all of the time, but hey, the moment is now.

"I'm not too heavy for you am I?" he said, rolling onto her in a frenzy. He was, of course, crushing her, but that's what she wanted. To be crushed. To dissolve into this disgusting mountain of flesh.

His dick was laughably small on someone so large; he slipped into her easily, and it felt magnificent. If he was crazy with desire, so was she. What they were doing mattered so much to her right now. Immediate problems faded away. Of course, somewhere in the back of her mind, she was aware of what could happen as a result of this. The health risks. The price she might pay. But the present should count for something, shouldn't it? She wanted to live a long time, yes. She wanted to star in her movie and become a successful actress. But she had to do things that were fantastically pleasurable for her right now, too, didn't she? Not fair. Not fair that she might have to die for this. *OH, GOD*, she yelled in her mind, *THIS IS SO GOOD. YOU CAN'T JUDGE ME FOR THIS! YOU WOULDN'T PUNISH ME FOR THIS!* It's better not to talk to God at the moment, she reasoned. She concentrated on the sex. And after sex there is more coke and more talk and, oh, what an evening!

So they talked, and even though his tale was interesting, all about how his first sexual encounter was with his uncle, she couldn't wait for him to finish his story so she could tell him the plot of her screenplay. And they lay on his bed and talked and talked and did more coke and talked some more and the night wore on.

And then, in the middle of one of his monologues, nausea welled up inside of her quite unexpectedly. Damn! She'd done too much coke. Now she saw him for what he was. A quivering mound of grotesque, aged lard. Mountains and mountains of it. God! her mind yelled out suddenly, *how could you let this happen to me?*

Suddenly she was very sick and afraid. Shaking all over, her tongue and throat were numb, in an unpleasant way, and she could not swallow. *People do die from plain cocaine overdoses, don't they? I mean, I know John Belushi died of cocaine mixed with heroin, but what about straight cocaine?* Was she choking? Should she stop his story to tell him she was dying? No, no, that would be of no use. If she was dying, Rob would be no help, she reasoned. She waited it out. He went on with his story. She wasn't actually listening anymore, just nodding every now and again, but he didn't seem to mind. But still she wanted to leave. Although she'd felt something for him in the beginning, it was all gone now. She was sickened. Even so, he was very nice and she had enjoyed their time together. She couldn't deny that. She felt warmly toward him and hoped he had a happy life with his wife, wretched creature that she probably was. Then he received a phone call that destroyed any delusions she had of Rob being a nice, fat, happy, jolly man, whom for just one night she had made a lot happier and jollier.

"Hi Rob," the voice on the other line said, loud and clear. From where Mikki was laying she could hear every single word. The voice on the phone continued: "I'm sorry I missed you at Stingers. That's why I'm calling to apologize. I slept straight through our date."

Mikki was aware that Stingers was a bar that was a popular call-girl hangout. It was a couple of blocks away from the bar where she had met Rob. She knew that the woman on the other end of the line was a high-class hooker. There was something about her voice that was so consistent with all the other whores she had ever heard speak: Cheery and raspy and full of confidence.

"These things happen," said Rob, keeping his voice low and neutral.

"Would you want to get together tomorrow?" the voice purred.

"Maybe," Rob said abruptly.

"I'll call you tomorrow. Late afternoon?"

"Yes, yes. Do that," Rob said quickly. Quietly.

He hung up the phone. Mikki's body, starting at the toes and working its way up, turned to stone. Rob jumped up and disappeared into the bathroom. He was aware that Mikki had heard every word.

Mikki had thought of him as a family man and she wanted to reward him for being content with his normal mundane life. She was his prize. Part of her passion was about that. And all night she had presented him with her very best self. In fact, she had just been a replacement for a dumb hooker. She could have been anybody—any willing hole who happened to trot along.

Rob returned from the bathroom with a wet towel, and he slapped it between her thighs in (she supposed) an effort to be nice and clean her up. But the washcloth hit hard between her legs, and the sudden coldness sent an explosive shock wave throughout her body. *WHAT DO YOU THINK MY BODY IS*, her mind screamed, *A MACHINE?* He cleaned and rubbed her as if she were an object. Once finished, he tried to kiss her again. But now she was repulsed for a million different reasons, one being that he frequented prostitutes. Another that he was repulsive. And now what were her chances of having HIV or hepatitis C or some other horrible, irreversible disease? Ninety percent greater than before Rob, probably. The sex didn't seem worth it now.

Disgusted, disgusted with everything, she got out of bed, signaling the end of their encounter. Being a gentleman, he walked her to the subway (not even cab fare? the bastard!), buying her a diet Coke along the way.

Now she sat on the slowly moving train experiencing a myriad of feelings. Remorse replaced by elation, elation replaced by nausea. She sat drinking her soda with slow steady sips. The train rocked back and forth like a cradle. Rock, rock, rock. Sip, sip, sip. Sipping the soda didn't make her feel less dry, but it gave her something to do.

And without any warning the train stopped in the middle of nowhere. And her feelings changed again: trapped, stuck, claustrophobic. *For your information WE'RE NOT MOVING! Help. Help! HELP! I'm dying on this train! Oh, stop overacting, she says to herself, just sit back and wait it out, dear.*

"Ladies and gentleman," said the conductor's monotonous voice, "we apologize for this delay. We shall be proceeding shortly."

NOT GOOD ENOUGH, her mind raged, DON'T WE DESERVE AN EXPLANATION?

Silence was her reply.

And after a very long time, the train started moving again. Goody, goody. Where was she going? She didn't know yet. She was feeling too awful to go out but too good to go home. She pressed her eyes closed with indecision, trying to force an answer up to the inner screen. The subway crawled into the next stop. Her eyes opened.

A gorgeous guy got on and sat across from her. Where else? He looked like a TV soap star, only he was for real and therefore more beautiful—the exact opposite of the monster she had just been with. The world is filled with spectacular men, tempting her with their beauty. She pulled out a notebook from her purse and took notes for her screenplay:

This fucking guy that is sitting across from me—tempting me—looks like he stepped out of some damn porno magazine. *Playgirl.* You cannot believe the levels of handsomeness his face reaches. You simply would have to climb right into the pages of this book to see for yourself how truly delectable he is. He has tons and tons of unyieldingly thick, chocolate-brown hair, cut short on the sides, long in front, with a few wisps pulled down over his forehead. His eyes (from here, across the aisle) are gray-blue. The structure of his face, my dear, is perfection from any angle that he turns to, and he is turning every which way and looking at me, too!

A dollar has fallen out of my pocket onto the seat next to me, and he signals to get my attention. It's a little embarrassing to appear so careless about money but nice to know he's nice enough to care. He smiles as I stuff the dollar back into my pocket. I could lose myself forever in this guy. Gray sweatshirt with a hood. Matching tight gray sweatpants. Duffel bag. He's been working out, you see. Serious face, carved by Michelangelo. He's got a cleft in his chin. Is there anything else in life other than cleft chins? The type of guy I could love for always. Never get tired of. Never stop finding things in him that I would find interesting or desirable. He wants me, too, but probably just to use for the night. But that hair. Those eyes. What lucky girl has had him? Has he loved? Is he a nice person, I wonder. He seems to be. If we had an affair, would he disappoint, or would he love me and take care of me and rescue me? He probably wants to get lucky tonight. I've already had sex once with a freak. But this one is different. If I sleep with this one, maybe it will obliterate sleeping with the other one. And I will be beautiful again.

31.

AS FOR ME, I finished my part of the script very quickly. I used my life as a hustler, knowing that that was the part that people would find most interesting. Besides, that's what made up most of my life. What I had wasn't really a screenplay. It was seven very interesting scenes dealing with my experiences with an older, famous actress (who I changed to an heiress), ghastly men, and other hustlers. It wasn't a complete script, but when I read through the material, as I often did, making a change here or an addition there, I viewed it as a series of fascinating scenes that could be shaped into a whole. I could hardly believe that on paper at least, I made a very "actable" character. It needed a storyline, of course, but there was very little I could do until I saw Mikki's part of the story. I didn't want her to feel rushed, so I didn't tell her I was ready to begin. I simply waited. I knew with all my heart that she was pouring everything she had into it.

DURING THIS PERIOD of time I didn't see Mikki all that much. We knew we were both working, though, and often one of us would call the other for encouragement.

Occasionally, she'd climb three flights of stairs to my walk-up, and there she'd be, her big black eyes blinking rapidly, filled with tears.

"Mario, I need to talk to you," she would say.

Often desperate, she'd talk for what seemed like hours, her baby-whore voice edged with hysteria, about her most recent experiences—about degrading sexual encounters. About men using her. About how she felt depressed all the time, how it was such a struggle to fight off her feelings of hopelessness. About how no one believed in her. About how important it was for her to become a "somebody," to prove herself. "Help me, help me," she'd cry, putting her head in my lap. "You're the male me," she would say.

We'd go out and order Chinese food to bring back to my apartment, and we'd stop off at the deli to buy ice cream and cake and cookies, and we'd rent a movie, eating all the goodies as we chatted throughout the film. This kind of indulgence was obscene to both of us, but it was something we wanted to do. She'd stuff all of this food down with incredible anger, just gorging, unmindful of the calories. I'm sure she forced herself to throw it all up later, since she'd disappear into the bathroom for long stretches of time.

Then she'd be gone. She never stayed the night, sometimes to my relief. She would leave and I would go on with my night. Bars, clubs. I had finally put up a decent Web site, complete with moody nude photos of me, and I had clients calling me at all hours.

Or I would go to my favorite hustler bar in the East Fifties, where I could still be a hot property. I'd score some money for the night with an older out-of-towner. I'd write about what happened or talk about the experience into my tape recorder—so I could transcribe it and use it later. But in the mornings, lying in a hotel bed with a stranger, I'd think about Mikki.

Certainly my life was ugly, but I felt I had a reign on it. I knew beyond a doubt that Mikki's life was out of control.

Like so many beautiful women I have known in the past, Mikki had little self-esteem. She was filled with self-doubt and saw herself as worthless, and so she sought out acceptance from men as a way of finding respect for herself. She felt the only thing of value she had to offer a man was her face and body. Men found these attributes very valuable indeed. But only for a short while.

"Do you think you're getting yourself into these sex situations to get back at Justin?" I asked her one night. "Are you angry with him?"

"I'm doing it for myself," she said. "I don't blame Justin for anything."

"He just dumped you without any explanation. After supposedly being in love with you . . ."

"He doesn't owe me an explanation," Mikki replied. "He presented me with a fairy tale. I fell for it."

"But you were never this way before. Not until after you broke up with him."

"I'm doing this for me. It's a side of me I have to explore and then I'll walk away from it. It's great material for my script . . . how are you doing on your end?" she said.

I didn't answer. "It just seems like a dangerous game to me. Exposing yourself to that kind of life just to build up material for your script."

"It's our script," she said. "And enough about me. How is your part coming along?"

"I'm finished," I replied, unable to conceal a smile.

"What?" she exclaimed. "And you didn't show it to me?"

"I figured I'd wait till we're both done and then we'll swap."

"What's it like?" she asked. "What's your story like?"

I smiled again. "You already know it."

"Is your character good?"

"Fine," I said. "Fine. Blanche DuBois crossed with *City of Night* crossed with *American Gigolo*."

32.

WALKING AROUND HER bedroom, tall glass of vodka in hand, all was not well with Victoria Sweetzer. She took four tranquilizers, trying to numb the mounting agony.

Well, at least she was back in the news, but it didn't give her the rush of old times. Her well-planned comeback was a success. Her photo was on magazine covers, she was an in-demand guest on TV shows, her book was number one, and some decent television movie offers were coming in. But it was nothing like the spectacular adoration she felt years ago when *Helen of Troy* had been released and she was at the height of her beauty. Tonight she felt nothing but despair.

She had done too much. Seen too much. Spoken too much. She was tired. Exhausted really. It was all the same bullshit—hours spent pulling herself together, giving her best in front of the camera for an hour and then coming back to her bedroom, taking herself apart, and propping herself in bed. Alone.

Her doctor had prescribed her the latest antidepressant, which she had been taking for several days. A week, perhaps. She recalled him explaining that it worked on this and that nerve ending in the brain, had fewer side effects, started working more quickly. What he didn't tell her was that there might be a "hump" period. A few days before the drug actually started working when she might feel a bit worse. Queasy. Edgy. Anguished. That's exactly what she was feeling. The depression had formed a lump of pain that was somewhere in her chest, a cement block weighing her down. She had felt this way before, knew it would pass eventually, but she was tired of the pattern.

She tried to read an interesting article about the murder of a beautiful young actress in the latest issue of *Vanity Fair* but could not get past two sentences. The television was showing the same garbage: three girls and one guy in a hot tub, drunk, flaunting themselves, laughing like idiots. There was no one to call. There was no one in the world she felt like talking to.

Oh, she could call some friend and say she was "down." The person would listen and pass on some words of encouragement they'd recently read on a calendar with daily quotes of inspiration. They'd end the conversation by advising, "Cheer up!" Then they would hang up and go on with their lives and might deliver the gossip to another friend that "Victoria is being a diva again."

Maybe she should have invested more time into making real friends? She thought of that young man. That Mario. Of course, he was just another hustler. Out to use and discard. She and Laird showed him. Their little plan had grabbed them plenty of salacious headlines and helped stir up amazing interest in her biography. But there was a moment—or maybe she had imagined it—when the boy had seemed genuine. Real. Caring. Lost. A possible friend? Oh, hell. She was only imagining it. There is no such thing. No real person ever felt such things. She used him before he used her, plain and simple. She'd been around too long. No one pulls any shit on Victoria Sweetzer.

With the four tranquilizers mixing in with the vodka, she was starting to feel woozy. But not woozy enough. Coherent thoughts were still cutting through. She took four more. She'd have to act fast. Once her mind was made up, she acted with amazing discipline. She knew exactly what to do.

She thought of the possibility of "deathbed photos," and sat at her dressing table. She couldn't make herself up too much, or they would speculate it had been intentional. She wanted it to look like an accident. Pills! It had been done to death. They will compare her to Marilyn. They will compare her to Judy.

She did her more natural-looking makeup. Her "day" face.

Makeup that she would have been wearing earlier in the day running errands, if she had any errands to run. Thousands of artists had made up her face in the past fifty years. A photo of her in any makeup artist's portfolio would be the crowning achievement. Now, for the last time, she would do it herself. After her lips and eyes were made up lightly, her face delicately powdered, she took four more tranquilizers. How many would it take with her high resistance to pills? She certainly felt dizzy, but she was sure that twelve wouldn't be enough to kill her.

A wig would have been too suspicious. She wouldn't be relaxing in her bedroom wearing her wig, so she did what she could to fluff her thinning hair. She picked an emerald green satin nightgown, simple yet elegant. After she put it on, she was definitely stumbling. The cement block of despair in her chest was a terrible thing to live with. How wonderful that she was smashing an ax through it— she would never have to deal with it again! Without counting she poured a handful of tranquilizers into her hand and swallowed them down with a big gulp of her remaining vodka.

Ready for slumber. She had always loved to sleep. How she looked forward to it.

Repose! Repose! I'll wear it like my clothes, she thought drowsily and smiled to herself. She had always wanted to dabble in writing poetry. Then a warm, very welcoming blackness embraced her. "Hello, stranger," she whispered.

33.

MIKKI. FIFTY-FIRST and Second. Late night again. Walking the streets. Needing something, some kind of inspiration.

A car passes and slows down to look at her. She smiles to herself. It's dark. He looks handsome and distinguished and maybe a little noble, like an aristocrat. After he circles the block for the third time, it is obvious he thinks that she is a prostitute. He stops at the corner. She'd be passing there in a minute. What should she do? A prostitute? The thought hadn't crossed her mind. What do those girls feel like? Should she experiment? Strictly from an actress's standpoint, of course. She's passing the car. She peers in the window. He unlocks the passenger door. Quickly now. She decides to get in. In the brief flash of harsh light when the car door opens, she can see that he is not really handsome. And older than he appeared at first. Yet she cannot stop herself. Now she's getting into a car with an old goat who thinks that she is a prostitute. Why is she doing this?

She isn't sure if she should bring up money before or after the act. How do these girls bring up payment? What is the proper etiquette for prostitution? She thinks about this as they pull away from the curb.

"It's hot in here," he says and unzips his fly.

The air in the car is warm and heavy—as well it should be, she thinks. *This is the way the scene should be played.* She can see his monstrous penis, which is only semi-erect, through his gray underpants. People this old are not supposed to have dicks this big, are they? He strokes it. It grows bigger still. All around them Saturday-night traffic zooms by. He takes her hand and places it on his penis, and she feels it with curiosity through his damp underpants. It is stiff and throbbing, destroying another myth: Old men have trouble sustaining a hard-on. She slips her hand under his underwear; she wants to touch skin.

Even in the dark she can make out several warts on his chin, and he is much uglier and older than first suspected. The obscenity of the scene repulses and fascinates her, and that she is a player in it astonishes her even more. What would Carla think if she witnessed this? Carla, whom she hadn't talked to in weeks but at one time had told everything to, would never know about this part of her life. This corner of her existence is only for her. Not for friends or boyfriends or anyone. It belongs to her and her alone.

"Feel my ass," the man croaks hoarsely while lifting himself off the seat.

She does and finds the skin there cold and flabby. The skin on his legs is the same. She has a sudden strong urge to fling herself out of the car and make a run for it. It's not too late to do this. She hasn't done anything yet. Not really.

He puts a hand on her knee. "No!" she snaps, brushing it away as if a tiny rodent had jumped on her lap. No touching allowed. Curiosity killed the cat. He pulls out a condom and tries with one hand to cover his dick. He is fumbling with it. She continues stroking him. Her mind drifts. What should she do? There is no real passion for this creepy monster, and what the hell does she care if he thinks that she's crazy? Tell him to stop the car. Tell him you're sick. Tell him . . . suddenly her hand is squirted with that familiar milky substance, only his was not warm, it felt cold and hideous. Disgustedly she wipes it on the car seat. *He is disgusting and now I am disgusting*, she thinks. The car pulls over to the curb and he yanks his pants up, his signal for her to get out. He doesn't offer her any money—but the scene would make it into the final screenplay.

> MIKKI
>
> Aren't you even going to help me out?

> MAN IN CAR
> (Smirking)
> I don't have any money.

> MIKKI
>
> Are you kidding me?

> MAN IN CAR
> I didn't know you were a hooker.

> MIKKI
> (Incredulous)
> What did you think? That I was attracted
> to you?

No response. She gives up. She is angry and humiliated, but she has asked for it. It is best to just write it off as a bad experience and get home quick. He waits for her to get out of the car.

> "At least take me back to my subway stop
> on Fifty-third," she snaps, feeling defeated.
> He testily pulls away from the curb, semen
> glistening on his jerk-off hand. Then he
> gives her the last line for the scene.

> MAN IN CAR
>
> Got a rag?

34.

I HEARD ABOUT the death of Victoria Sweetzer while cruising the Internet with no destination, listening to a jazz station that was playing a tribute to Louis Armstrong. During a break in the music they announced that Victoria Sweetzer had been found dead in bed, apparently after an accidental overdose. Since this was a music station, they didn't give any more details. Besides, I wasn't in a rush to hear any more of the particulars. They started playing the music again, and I sat at my desk and listened, trying not to think of Victoria.

I love Louis Armstrong. I can't help but smile every time I hear him sing. During the time that he was alive, he probably had the same perversions and inconsistencies in his personality as we all do. But when he sings I forget that. He's one of the pleasures of my life.

But then they played Louis singing "Hello, Dolly!" and I remembered that Victoria had chosen a revival of that play as her one-and-only shot at Broadway. The show was a success, not because she could sing or dance, but because celebrity-hungry audiences flocked to see how she looked, how she aged, how she moved in person.

The accidental death of Victoria Sweetzer caused the usual three-day media storm. There were specials, magazine tributes, long news items, and talk shows devoted to her memory, involving costars and longtime friends. But she had not died in her heyday, so the hubbub did not last long. And since her death came directly after her publicity junket for her biography, the public had already pretty much had their fill of her—although the fact that she died probably added a hundred thousand sales to her book. So she joined the immortal ghosts who would live forever on passing channels. I locked what I knew away in one of the many locked places in my mind, and remembered Victoria only when I happened upon her glorious face on some late-night movie or on a postcard in a shop that specializes in nostalgia. To me she had been a legend, a goddess, an untouchable.

———

"I'M FINISHED," MIKKI said to me when I opened the door to my apartment the following day. Her face looked feverish, but she was beaming and she seemed ecstatic. "I bet you thought it was all talk. I bet you never thought you'd live to see the day that I handed my part of the script over to you."

She handed the script over to me and I let her in. It was a computer disk. I glanced down at the cover. It certainly looked official and legitimate. *FAME, TRAINS AND OTHER SEXUAL FANTASIES:* by Mario DeMarco and Mikki Britten. I noticed she put my name first. That had always been the title. She came up with it, I liked, and we never considered anything else. Ironically, we had a title before we had a script.

"Wow," I said, impressed.

"It's very important that you're honest with me."

"And you with me," I said, going to fish out my part of the screenplay for her to read.

"Mario," she said. "Don't be angry with me, but I don't want to read your part. It will confuse me. I trust you completely. You're the real writer here. I'm giving you my fair share . . . and I know you've done your own homework. Now it's up to you to shape it and give it a story. I trust you. But I'd rather wait till it's complete."

"Are you sure?" I asked.

"Yes," she replied. "I'm one-hundred percent sure—I trust you."

She stayed for a while, of course; she had traveled a long way from Queens to hand-deliver the script. I made tea and offered chitchat, but all the while I couldn't wait for her to leave. I was slightly pissed at her, and myself. I was the one who had told her I was going to write a script about my experiences in New York. But she was the one who had pushed me into it, and I could only admire her for being so ambitious. "What's the matter with you?" she asked, interrupting my thoughts.

"What do you mean?"

"You look a million miles away."

"Nothing," I said. "I'm just a little tired."

I was dying to read her part of the screenplay. Dying. As soon as she was gone, I grabbed a bag of pretzels and a beer and climbed into bed to read Mikki's writing. I read for a couple of hours without stopping once.

Obviously extremely autobiographical, it wasn't really a screenplay or even a piece of a screenplay. It consisted of notes, snatches of dialogue, diary entries, and descriptions. Her brief stint as a successful model, her decline into promiscuity. There were parts about jumping into cars with strangers. One scene told of shooting up heroin with a man in a bar toilet—only to be thrown out by a burly bouncer when she was discovered giving the guy a blow job in a stall. Page after page told of her desperation. Her degradation. Her damnation.

These were the ravings of a lunatic; this was documentation of a mind out of control. It was brilliant. I was speechless. I was dazzled. I was on fire.

I started working at once. I downloaded her notes onto my computer and began blending them in with my scenes and putting it all into proper screenplay format. Perhaps because Mikki's passionate autobiographical sketches had inspired me, I wrote like I had never written before. It was almost as if I wasn't actually writing; it was as if someone were writing through me. I worked through the night and, when I was finished, looked over at the clock. It was 11:00 A.M.

Fame, Trains and Other Sexual Fantasies very explicitly told the story of a haunted woman (whom I called Marisa) abnormally obsessed with becoming a famous model—fame being the only means she knows of to escape her troubled existence. Tormented by memories of the sexual abuse she had suffered years before at the hands of her sadistic stepfather, as well as the fear that she was going mad, Marisa fantasizes about stabbing a brutish modeling agent whom she had interviewed with earlier that day. In her imagination the agent shows up at her home after the disastrous interview to offer her a contract, but only if she agrees to shit on his face. Instead, in her fantasy, she stabs him and cuts up the body with a kitchen knife. Haunted by this vision, Marisa flees her claustrophobic apartment.

This disturbed woman wanders through the New York subway, tortured by the heat and the swarming crowds. Here her unsettled mind goes wild, imagining disturbing sexual encounters with fellow passengers, movie stars, and past lovers. Unable now to distinguish fantasy from reality, she has various encounters with New York's most grotesque inhabitants. A gang of teenage girls surrounds her, mocks her, and steals her diamond earrings.

Then I wrote myself a grand entrance. On a subway platform she meets up with a sensitive male prostitute (Anthony). There is an instant attraction. An amazing connection. He admits to her that he gets his clients through the Internet and by meeting them at upscale clubs. He offers her tranquilizing drugs and, at one point, stops her from throwing herself in front of an oncoming train. Anthony recommends she go down to the Hudson River piers—a place where he often finds peace when he needs to be alone to reinvent his life.

The script then goes on to show my own desperate life. Anthony sleeps with a few nameless, faceless men and is having an affair, of sorts, with an aging heiress. Increasingly dependent on drugs, he is terrified what his life will become when he becomes too old to hustle (in about five minutes). In one scene I have the heiress give a long speech about love only lasting for the moment it first presents itself—immediately following that moment, it begins disintegrating. Anthony sits silently listening, tears streaming down his face.

Meanwhile, Marisa spends the night on a subway bench, where her fantasies of fame intermingling with sex continue to plague her.

Eventually she takes a cab to the piers where she dances along the concrete slabs taking the pills Anthony gave her, which she has been carrying in her purse.

Marisa is saved once again by Anthony, who has come down to the piers himself, perhaps to commit suicide. He is taken aback by Marisa's wretched, pathetic state. Instead of taking her to an emergency room at Bellevue (where she clearly belongs), he takes her to her apartment where they discover that the murder was real. The place is covered in blood and there is a butchered corpse— Marisa had indeed killed the modeling agent. But the hustler, by now obsessed with Marisa, brings her back to his own apartment, where it becomes apparent that these two disturbed characters will lock themselves away from the rest of the world and live out a bizarre fantasy life together.

I FELT ABSOLUTELY ecstatic about the script when I first read through it after typing "Fade to Black." Reminiscent of Roman Polanski's 1960s thriller *Repulsion*, each scene was wrought with a compelling sense of menace as the girl and the hustler interact with a steady stream of threatening characters and slowly drift further and further into madness. The setting and situations were gritty, but the dialogue was both genuine and poetic. Once again I couldn't help but admire Mikki and her determination. I used a lot of the actual dialogue from her notes. And from my own. Together we had managed to pull off what most people only talk about doing. We had completed a screenplay. And a damn near-genius one at that.

I emailed the finished script to Mikki immediately and phoned her. She was somewhat taken aback that there was already a completed script waiting on her computer. She said she would print it out and read it immediately. We hung up and I waited by the phone.

"It's fucking brilliant," she gushed when she called me a couple of hours later. "We did it!"

THE NEXT STEP proved to be more difficult. Yes, Mikki and I had an interesting script, but now what could we do with it? At first we were enthusiastic and rushed out query letters and a five-page synopsis of the script to the few film contacts Mikki had made during her time as a model. But now, no longer the subject of a media blitz, she quickly discovered that she was not viewed as a woman with a unique and incandescent presence. She was just an attractive girl living in Queens who had co-written a screenplay. So what? Big deal. Who hadn't?

Mikki and I realized that everyone in New York has a screenplay or is working on a screenplay or has an idea for a screenplay, and would be more than happy to talk about it over a cocktail at your favorite bar or club. Everyone has a deal with HBO. Everyone has a property being considered by Spielberg. So no one really took the idea of two nonwriters writing a screenplay seriously. Not one person we sent the treatment of the story to asked to see the actual script. Polite, terse rejections started arriving regularly in the mail: "Interesting, but it's not what we are looking for at the moment." "I am so incredibly busy with current projects that I simply do not have the time to take on another, but I do wish you luck . . ."

I was anxious, but Mikki was desperate. Her savings were dwindling.

WE MADE MORE phone calls. We sent out more letters. Days turned to weeks and there were so many days of nothing. *Do I exist?* Mikki absentmindedly doodled on a napkin as we sat in a pizza joint. She was always willing to go the extra mile. She was always willing to meet people who were interested in film. A friend who had a cousin who was a filmmaker. A neighbor who had a friend who produced music videos. She made phone calls. She met with them. She took them to lunch. She talked to them about her project over drinks. Mediocre, all of them! Nothing ever came of her efforts; scripts she gave out were not returned. Phone calls were ignored. Meetings were not followed up. There are dedicated people scouting for talent in New York, but she never found them. She met the fakes. To produce something—even a small low-budget film—takes a tremendous commitment. The people she met were content with talking big plans and dreaming.

I tried to raise money to get the project off the ground. For the first time in my illustrious career, I started hitting up some of my johns for big-time money to invest in the film. To no avail. It is not all that unusual for a hustler, at least once in his life, to make a big score. To meet an extremely wealthy john who becomes smitten with him and finances his schooling or his apartment or his acting lessons or some other such expense. I, however, am not good at asking people for anything, and as obnoxious, confident, pushy people are the only ones who get what they want, I was a hopeless case. I have no self-esteem and I have always given myself away for far too little, while others of lesser value, but with all the confidence in the world, got more, simply because they felt they deserved it.

Our situation was maddening. We knew that she had a potentially hot Hollywood property, but it was doing no good collecting dust on our desks. Like any other fresh, original, exciting new work, it needed to get seen by the right people. In the past Mikki had been right about having what it takes to be an exceptional model and only needing to be seen by the right person, and when she was seen by Justin Landis, her career did indeed take off. Now she knew she needed to get our script into the right hands in order to get the movie off the ground. And every instinct in her body told her that Jonathan Christaldi's hands were the right ones.

———

LOOKING BACK NOW, I wish that Mikki had never thought of calling Carla. I wish she had realized that Carla was a closed chapter. That the friendship was dead. If I had talked her out of it, Carla would have never entered our lives again. Her career, I am totally confident, would have fizzled. The public, as gullible as they are, were already catching on to the fact that she simply was not interesting, talented, or beautiful . . . and they even stopped believing the publicity that told them that she was.

Sooner or later she would have left modeling. She might have asked her father for money and opened a restaurant. Perhaps she would have left New York, settled in Chicago, married an advertising exec, and raised a half-dozen kids. Maybe she would have gone back to drugs and booze, hit rock bottom, and written yet another tell-all book, which she would publicize on the talk show circuit. Certainly Carla Christaldi's life could have taken any number of courses. Except we ended it.

But I wanted the movie made. I WANTED THE MOVIE MADE! The time was right. I felt it. And I knew that a genius like Jonathan Christaldi would be able to recognize the brilliance of the script, and he, more than anyone else I could think of, had the power to get it made. But he was one of those unreachable people, protected by the maximum-security systems of fame. Systems specifically put up to keep losers like us, Mikki and me, out. If Mikki simply mailed the script to his studio office, it would have been received (along with the hundred or so other scripts sent to him that particular week) by a secretary, passed on to an assistant, tossed on a slush pile of unread screenplays, and maybe after a year, sent back to her with a form rejection slip. There was one definite way, however, to get to him.

"Call her," I urged Mikki when she mentioned to me that she was thinking of doing just that, "What have you got to lose?"

35.

MIKKI REACHED CARLA at the VH1 studios.

And why not? After the anger of seemingly being dumped by Justin had faded, it did not seem to Mikki that Carla had done anything that awful to her. So Carla copied her look and style—big fucking deal, models were doing that all the time to each other. So Carla dated Justin for a while. It wasn't as if, as far as she knew, she had anything to do with their breakup. Besides, Mikki's anger had subsided a bit when she read that they were no longer dating. Why not use Carla Christaldi to get to her father? It would be stupid to let a contact like that go to waste, she reasoned.

Carla was called to the phone and walked off the set where she was taping segments for her show called *Cutting Edges*. The show that had initially been developed with Mikki Britten in mind.

"She's fucking awful," the assistant director said when Carla was a safe distance away.

"You'd think by now she'd be able to get out two lines without fucking up," said cameraman number one.

"Long live nepotism," said cameraman number two.

"Somebody call Mikki Britten," the director said and there was a general burst of laughter. It seems like they were always laughing at Carla Christaldi. She was a joke. The woman could not master the most fundamental techniques of a television personality. She read her lines in a zombie-like monotone. She couldn't improvise or ad-lib even the most mundane small talk. She couldn't read the monitors. Her eyes would wander off vacantly in search of cue cards, which had been specifically created for her, in the middle of an introduction. Her interviews with famous models and competing designers and photographers were the joke of the business. Even though the questions to every model, designer, and photographer she interviewed were specifically written for her and given to her in advance, she would always invariable ask: "So tell us about this great new project?" It was the only off-the-cuff question she knew, and she continuously asked it in the same monotonous drone. When she wasn't around, someone would invariably say, "So tell us about this great new father." And everyone would laugh knowing that it was her name, her father's name, that had gotten her the job.

The show was a moderate hit due to fancy editing, lots of coaching, voice-over dubbing, and big-name guests, but the producers began to wonder if Carla was worth the expense and the trouble.

⸻

"CARLA? . . . IT'S MIKKI," the familiar voice piped over the telephone.

Carla's heart took a giant leap, stopped for several seconds, and then beat rapidly to make up for lost time. Her first instinct was to hang up. Had Mikki discovered the deception? The fake email? No, no. Impossible. Carla had covered her tracks.

It was not that she hadn't been missing Mikki—she had—but she wanted to have something to say to explain why she had started dating Justin. She wasn't prepared. There was no excuse. And she couldn't admit, even to herself, that the only reason she wanted him in the first place was because Mikki had him.

Carla decided, instead, to let Mikki do the talking. She bit her bottom lip. She tapped an unlit cigarette on the Formica tabletop. She listened to Mikki rattle off a disoriented (carefully edited) account of her life for the past months. She had not been working at all; she hadn't even been looking for work. She hadn't been going out much, which was why they hadn't run into each other. She'd been obsessed with her writing. She and Mario had been working on a screenplay night and day.

At the word "screenplay" Carla's ears perked up.

"And we finally finished," Mikki explained.

Carla remained silent. She knew what was coming.

"And I was wondering if you would read it. We'd really be interested in your opinion."

Carla lit her cigarette and exhaled slowly. So Mikki needed something from her and had come crawling back. Oh, God! Why did life have to be so fucking predictable? For once she didn't feel inferior to Mikki; she felt like an old-time movie vixen who had just been dealt the trump card.

"I'd love to have a look at it," Carla said at last, her voice unreadable. "Why don't you drop it off at my apartment tonight. I'll be home around eleven."

THE TWO WOMEN sat across from each other in Carla's clean, spacious apartment. The modern furniture, which at one time had been completely familiar to her, now snubbed Mikki and made her feel like an intruder. Carla, who chain-smoked, was slightly heavier than Mikki remembered her but somehow looked less healthy. Mikki knew that she was having problems with her TV show; she had read about animosity on the set of *Cutting Edges* on Page Six. Perhaps as a result of the pressure she was under, all the health seemed to be drained out of Carla's skin, which was sallow and drawn. She wore some makeup, but it only made her seem artificially colored, like bright, translucent paint hastily applied over a gray surface.

If she was unhappy with the show she didn't mention it. They were both extremely uncomfortable, and each felt the other's suspicion. They had a long conversation, filled with unfinished sentences and strained pauses, about what had happened in their lives since they'd last seen each other. They drank, wine though, which eventually brought down their defenses some.

"I thought you hated me after that night you saw me with Justin," Carla said.

"I was angry for a while, but then I realized it wasn't really your fault," Mikki said.

"Do you hate Justin?" Carla asked, fiddling with her cigarette.

Mikki looked thoughtful for a moment but then answered with a statement she had said many times in the past in regards to her relationship with Justin: "Life isn't a fairy tale and when you fall for one—that's when you get into trouble."

Mikki was getting over a cold and was still slightly congested; as a result the smoke from Carla's cigarettes irritated her sore throat and added to her discomfort. "What about you?" Mikki said. "You were with him for a while?"

Carla did not tell Mikki the truth. She did not say that she and Justin never really dated, that he simply hung around with her for several months, trying to get over the pain of Mikki's rejection, hoping that Carla would reveal some insight into Mikki's character. Carla's relationship with Justin was a series of harrowing nights of restaurants, theaters, and popular bars. Both of them would drink a lot, but neither could get drunk. Evenings of averting eye contact and awful silences, which usually ended with Carla lingering in doorways with hooded eyes and drowsy gestures, waiting for Justin to make a move. And Justin probing, asking subtle questions about Mikki, but Carla revealing nothing. Knowing nothing. Carla allowed these humiliating encounters to go on because she knew the photos of them together and the gossip they created would reach Mikki—and hurt her.

Why? Carla asked herself now. *Why?* Why was it so important for you to hurt her?

"We found out that we weren't the right person for each other," was all that Carla said and let out a tense little sigh. Mikki simply nodded.

There was a long silence, and to break it, Mikki started talking about the script. It was a speak-now-or-forever-hold-it moment.

"It's a psychological character study," Mikki began. "I know that sounds like a boring art-house thing but it's not." By now she was an expert in telling the plot and did so quite compellingly. As she spoke, she recognized an expression that slowly took over Carla's face feature by feature. It was a mask that Carla used to cover up her raging jealousies at anyone who had an original, clever idea. This mask of hers was supposed to represent indifference, but instead it was an expression that conveyed anger and fear. For a moment Mikki's intuition kicked in, warning her that it would be best not to hand over the script to Carla at all.

She probably won't even show it to her father. She's terrified I might make something out of myself, she thought. But it was too late to bail out now. She could think of no logical excuse for not giving her the script; it was her reason for being there. And besides, people weren't knocking down her door to take an option on it. If nothing else, Carla represented a shot at the big time. She was better than nothing. And nothing was looming.

"So the thing is," Mikki concluded, "if you think the script is good, I was . . . um, wondering if you could show it to your father."

Carla swept imaginary crumbs from the table. And laid down her four aces.

"Well, I'm willing to read it, but truthfully it may take me a while. I'm extremely busy."

"That's okay. Whenever you get a chance."

"The thing is, I'm in the middle of production for my show. And then I'm shooting this big Revlon campaign."

Cunt, Mikki thought and tried with all her might not to wince. "I understand that, Carla," Mikki said, smiling. "I'm willing to wait. See, I don't know the right people—neither does Mario—and it's been getting into the wrong hands. I know it's good, and I think your father will recognize that."

Carla managed to squeeze out a weak half smile. "Sure," she said, "let me take a look at it. Maybe I'll pass it on to him. But you have to understand one thing, Mikki. I'm not making any promises."

———

THE WAIT WAS not an easy one, but we tried to get on with our normal lives. For Mikki that had become sitting around in her robe and slippers waiting for her life to begin, watching soap operas in the afternoons, comparing her age to the female soap stars'—sometimes not even bothering to get dressed until the evening, when she would go out.

36.

"I THOUGHT YOU couldn't stand my fucking guts," Chase Bartholomew said to Carla as he entered her apartment.

"I can't," Carla said. She could not. She was in no mood for sweet-talk bullshit. She had long ago passed that point in her life.

He was a fake and she knew it. Her father, however, was in the middle of filming the adaptation of "his" novel *Shit Floats*, and more than ever, he was being touted as the boy genius of the literary world. She hated him, not because he was a fake, but because he had managed to somehow rise above his lack of talent, to parley it into real celebrity, real success.

She could smell, right off the bat, that the guy hadn't taken a shower in at least several days. Stale cigarette smoke, beer, sweat, greasy hair.

"Then why am I here?"

"My father's in the middle of filming your book."

"Yeah?"

"Let me ask you a question, Chase."

He scratched his greasy hair. "Yeah?"

"How much of *Shit Floats* did you actually write?"

"What the fuck?" he said.

"Tell me. Really. You don't have to hide anything from me," she said. "Baby, baby, I'm a bigger fake than you are."

He scratched his head again and looked at his nails to see what funky things he had collected there. "I wrote enough of it to get my name on the cover."

"So you can actually put a sentence together?"

"Fuck you, cunt," he said.

"Listen, Chase. I don't care if you like me or not. I already told you I can't stomach you. But I have a career opportunity for you—too good to pass up."

She handed him the script of *Fame, Trains and Other Sexual Fantasies*. The title page with the names "Mario DeMarco" and "Mikki Britten" had been removed.

"Read this. Tell me what you think."

"Did you write this?"

"Just read it."

"Sure. Okay. Fine." He gathered up the manuscript and started to leave.

"No. Here. *Now*."

"What the fuck?"

"Now," she said. "Make your self comfortable. Drink?"

"Black on the rocks" he said. He sat down with the script on her dining room table.

She handed him the drink and sat on the couch watching him read. He smoked cigarette after cigarette, blowing smoke onto the pages as he read. He had finished half a bottle of Johnny Walker by the time he had finished.

He flipped over the last page. "Who wrote this?" he asked.

"Two friends of mine."

"Famous?"

"Nobodies. A wannabe model and a hustler."

"You mean the characters in the story?"

"Sort of."

"Do they have any money?"

"Not a dime."

"Who knows them? Who do they know?"

"No one."

"Honey," he said.

"Yes?"

"This is my next project," Chase said. "My next script."

"No way," Carla said. "It's ours. We collaborated on it."

"A collaboration with Jonathan Christaldi's daughter?"

"Yep. You and me, motherfucker."

"That might work."

"One small problem. The title page said it was copyrighted."

"Don't worry about that."

"What do you mean? Why not?"

"Copyright. Big fucking deal. You can't copyright an idea."

"Can you do it, Chase? Can you make it ours?"

"Ha. Leave it to me. Shit. Making things my own is what I do best. It's ours. It's fucking brilliant. And now I got a follow-up."

37.

I WAS READING during the subway ride home. My cell phone had finally been cut off for lack of payment—I owed them several million dollars, and it seemed I was always rushing home to check my email or to make a call.

So I sat on the train, simply scanning a copy of *People* magazine that someone had by chance left on the seat, when the name Carla Christaldi hit my eyes. I read the short article and afterward experienced a moment of temporary vertigo so severe that I almost fell off my seat. I was in shock. I stood up shakily. I knew I should wait to get home, but I could not. This news would not wait. I jumped off the train at the next stop to find a pay phone on which to call Mikki. I ran up the stairs into the Manhattan streets.

There are no pay phones in New York anymore. Even fucking homeless people have cells. I ran block after block, stopping in stores, buildings, bars . . . anywhere.

Finally, the first one I found was at the entrance to a subway station. It was dead; someone had pulled out the wire that connects the receiver to the phone. I paid another fare and ran to the next phone at the other end of the platform. Breathlessly I dropped a quarter into the slot, and it went directly through the phone into the change-release tray. I tried again, this time putting a spin on the quarter. The same thing happened. The damn phone refused to accept my money. It was like stepping into a frantic dream I often had where I needed to make a life-saving phone call and could not, because of numerous obstacles, dial the correct number.

I followed the exit and ran up the stairs back into the night, which of course meant I'd have to pay yet another subway fare to get home, but it did not matter. I had to get to a phone. Each one I came to, like in my dream, was either unavailable or broken. I ran and searched for several blocks until I finally found one that worked outside of a tiny Italian pizzeria run by Indians.

"Mikki, you're not going to believe it," I said nearly hysterical, as soon as she picked up.

"What is it?" her voice was alarmed.

"It's bad, Mikki." It was almost a wail.

"Mario, what's the matter? Are you okay?"

"She fucked us," I blurted out.

"Who did, Mario? What's happened?"

"It's Carla Christaldi. Listen to this." I read her a portion of the article from *People*:

Talent really does run in some families. He's one of the top movie directors in Hollywood. She's a hot young model. She also happens to be his daughter. Carla Christaldi, one of the top models at EYE Model Management and currently starring in the magazine-format cable show *Cutting Edges* is following in the footsteps of her famous daddy, filmmaker Jonathan Christaldi. With bad-boy writer Chase Bartholomew, Carla has penned a screenplay tentatively titled *Mind Trips*, which she describes as a psychological character study. "But a commercial one."

"It deals with the struggles and fantasies of an aspiring actress and her encounters with various people in New York," said the twenty-one-year-old Carla, who was genetically preordained for movie stardom. "Especially with a male prostitute who has an eye-opening array of clients." Carla will also be playing the lead in the movie, which has just been optioned by Clockwork Films and is generating excellent word-of-mouth. "Writing with Chase Bartholomew was just incredible. He really is a genius, and we just bounced ideas off of each other like we've been working together for years."

Carla's father, who is currently filming the version of Bartholomew's best-seller *Shit Floats*, is also set to direct his daughter's collaboration. Christaldi says, "It's the most exciting script I've read in years."

"I think this is going to be the project that really brings us closer together," says Carla. "I've always been a little in awe of my father, but on this movie we'll be working together as partners."

EVEN FROM THAT brief description of the screenplay it was obvious to both of us, as it would be to anybody, that Carla and Chase Bartholomew had stolen our script. But of course it was Carla who was behind it. And all this time we had been waiting, in good faith, to hear from her.

"No, no, no," Mikki gasped on the other end of the line. "It can't be. She couldn't do this to us."

Her anguished voice sounded like a grief-stricken mother's who had just seen the first mound of dirt shoveled on the coffin of her child. And it made me start wailing. Loudly. Uncontrollably. In utter, utter despair. People stopped to look, and I cried louder and louder.

"Mario, Mario, Mario . . . " Mikki kept repeating. And she kept repeating it until my tears and wails stopped just as suddenly as they had begun. Then Mikki spoke again.

"Please, Mario. Is this a joke? Are you kidding me?"

"Oh, my God, Mikki," I said. "What are we going to do?"

There was a long pause during which I could hear her shallow breathing. "Meet me at your place," she said finally. "I'll be right over."

SHE ARRIVED CLUTCHING a copy of *People*. "Do you believe that fucking cunt?" she asked. She didn't appear to be as upset as I imagined she would be. Obviously she had had a chance to grow used to the idea of Carla's betrayal during her long train ride to the city or perhaps she was just used to being betrayed in general. But when I walked her into the kitchen, with its merciless naked light, I saw how pale she was and how dead her eyes were.

We went to my computer and did a general search using her name and found a few other items in various different publications about Carla's script. *Variety* wrote that Chase Bartholomew, "the current hot young genius of the moment," had found working with Carla Christaldi an "inspiration."

"Well, I mean, they can't get away with it, can they? We copyrighted the script," I said.

"It would be hard to prove. They may have changed it around. I mean, we have to prove that they did steal it from us. I just handed it to her. There's no paper trail that she actually read it. We'd have to prove it."

"Which means a lawsuit."

"Which means lawyers."

"Which means . . . ?"

"A lot of money. Which we don't have."

"Call her. See what she has to say for herself," I said.

"Mario," Mikki flared. "What the fuck do you think she's going to say?"

"What other choice do we have?" I kept repeating. Eventually she calmed down and agreed to call.

My only advice to Mikki was to not lose her cool. If she became angry and Carla hung up, we would lose contact with her. Carla was a very powerful girl with lots of powerful contacts. And money. We had to get her side of the story first. If we were going to declare war, we could only win, I thought, with an intelligent, well-thought-out plan. Information was power.

Mikki asked me to hold her hand while she made the call, which I did throughout, silently trying to send what little positive energy I had left from my body to her body.

"I know what you're going to think, Mikki. But believe me, my screenplay is totally different from yours," Carla said over the phone. "Chase and I have been working on a script for a long time. I just didn't tell you about it."

Mikki said, "I'm trying very hard to stay calm and be rational about this, Carla, but how do you expect me to feel? I give you a script Mario and I wrote, and I don't hear from you for over a month."

"That's not my fault. You didn't call."

"I didn't call? Carla, I was waiting for you to call me. You told me you were busy! I just assumed you gave it to your father and you were waiting to hear from him."

Carla paused and said, "Well, what do you want me to say? To tell you the truth I don't think your script is good enough to show him. In all honesty I didn't even finish it. The first few pages have a lot of promise, Mikki, but it needs structure. It needs polish. The characters are cartoons. It's certainly not ready to be produced."

"Oh, and yours is polished and ready to be produced? Chase Bartholomew is a writer? Give me a fucking break, Carla. I mean, not for nothing, but it's really ridiculous. The plot is the same as the one I wrote with Mario." Her voice was getting shrill, and I waved for her to bring it down.

"How would you know? You haven't even read our script," Carla said.

"No, but you read ours. Since when do you even write? It's a little bit sick. Do you have to do everything I do?"

"I write, Mikki. I write. I have always been a fucking writer! If you would listen to someone talk other than yourself for a change . . ."

"I don't care if you write, but did you have to write the same script as me?"

"It's a completely different story. *US* magazine totally edited my synopsis of it so it just seems similar to yours."

Mikki's face was damp. It was the first and only time I ever saw Mikki sweating. "Listen, Carla, I can't talk to you about this on the phone," she said, her composed voice betraying the turmoil within. "Could we meet?"

38.

"CAN I GET a picture of you two together?" asked a photographer who had been lunching at a nearby table. They did not answer, but they both looked at the camera blankly. When he snapped the picture, neither one was smiling.

The photographer, happy to get a picture of the two ex-rival models sharing a midday meal together, gloatingly sat back down with his lunch date. Carla patiently waited for him to be out of hearing distance, lowered her voice a decibel, and resumed the conversation with Mikki.

"It's stupid of you to think that there's any similarities in our scripts, Mikki. Your screenplay was rejected all over the fucking place," Carla said. "Mine has gotten major studio backing. I could actually get a movie made while your script sits on a shelf."

Mikki stared at her with disbelief. "*You* can get a movie made?" she said. "Stop kidding yourself . . ."

"I know what you're going to say," Carla interrupted. "But my father's name can only get me so far. No one's going to put up that kind of money if my script is garbage. My talent, mine and Chase's, is what's getting *Mind Trips* made."

"You're forgetting one small detail, Carla," Mikki said lowering her voice to a frosty calm. But her hand, as she reached for her wineglass, was trembling. "It's my screenplay. Mario's and mine. You stole every single thing in that script from us."

"Maybe we got some background flavor from your script. A teeny amount of inspiration. We're artists—we all get our inspirations from somewhere."

"That's true. That's true, Carla. I watched dozens of movies for

251

ideas. But the backbone of the story is Mario's. And that's what you took."

"Wrong," Carla said. "On the whole the story and structure was my idea."

"Idea? You never had an idea in your life."

"I don't want to hurt your feelings, Mikki, but I've said this before to other people—your screenplay has some good scenes but it's far from acceptable. Mario should stick to hustling. You should stick to . . . whatever it is you do. You need to learn a lot about structure and about what makes a good film. Keep working on it, though."

"You robbed us and you know it. Let's talk about that. Let's talk about the fact that I can take you to court."

"You're the one who gave me the fucking script to read."

"So you're saying it's my script that you showed your father?"

Carla gasped in exasperation and intentionally made her voice a mocking singsong. "No. No. No. I'm not saying that at all, not at all. It's my script, co-written with Chase Bartholomew."

"We'll let a jury decide that."

Carla's tone was even and unconcerned. "You're going to take me to court? Ha, Mikki. Ha, ha. Let's just see what happens when you put your lawyer against my lawyers. I have a whole fucking studio's TEAM of lawyers behind me. And Chase Bartholomew is the hottest writer in the world right now. He's got a TEAM of lawyers. He's a fucking genius. Who would believe you and a hustler wrote that story? Come out with that one. It's good for a laugh. We'll see what happens then. You'll come across as being exactly what you are: a stupid, jealous, little bitch."

Mikki clutched her drink tightly so she wouldn't throw it in Carla's face. *Stop, stop,* she scolded herself. That kind of Brooklyn-Queens behavior would get her nowhere. She let go of her wine glass and tried to control the violent shaking that seemed to be going on throughout every single limb in her body. She willed herself to relax, but when she spoke, her voice was near tears.

"Maybe we can work something out where we both work on a

new draft together," Mikki said. "We can build up another part for you . . . "

"Why should I do that when I'm playing the lead in *this* version?"

"Carla, look . . . listen to me . . . we were friends. Or maybe we weren't. I don't know what we were to each other. But we're both human beings. And you know that what you're doing is wrong . . . I mean you have to know that in your heart. But it doesn't have to be that way. Do what's right, Carla. Give my script back to me. And then, maybe, in some way, we can help each other."

Mikki could feel the tears pressing heavily in her eyes, begging for release. She tried not to let them go. It was painful. "Don't," she said out loud, but she was talking to herself. However, it was too late. A real tear escaped her eye and rolled down her cheek. Then there were more.

"It's my script," Carla asserted. "I don't need your help." And then, seeing Mikki's tears she added gently: "Don't worry, something else will come along for you, Mikki. It always does."

"Don't you dare feel sorry for me," Mikki said, crying fully now. They held each other's gaze, and Mikki used that moment to build composure. But her voice, through tears, was strong and calm and rising, and people at neighboring tables stopped talking and leaned in to listen. "I'm poor. I'm weak. I have no power. But as long as I live . . . " her voice cracked. She stopped momentarily, her self-control slipping. " . . . as long as I live I'm going to fight to do something to make you pay for this."

Carla stood up to leave. So did Mikki.

"I'm not afraid of you, slut" Carla hissed. "You'll stay exactly where you are. You came from *nowhere*, and that's where you'll fucking die."

Impulsively Mikki reached for her wine glass and threw its contents in Carla's face. Suddenly it seemed that everything in the restaurant stopped, every sound, every movement. Time itself. The two women stood facing each other, Carla with wine dripping down her face, down her blouse. The photographer raised his camera to snap a photo. He got only one shot before a passing waiter stopped him, but that one shot was a doozy. Carla abruptly turned and headed for the ladies' room. All eyes were on Mikki. Should she stay? Should she leave? No! This was her last chance to resolve this. She had passed the point of no return. She followed Carla into the ladies' room.

Carla was already at the sink, dabbing at her face with a paper towel while examining the damage to her makeup in the mirror. When in the mirror's reflection she saw Mikki enter, she raised her eyes to the heavens and sighed.

"I see I'm going to have to get a restraining order to keep you the fuck away from me," Carla said with pretend annoyance.

"I'm going to talk to your father. I'll explain to him what you did. How I gave you the script to give to him."

"Like he's gonna believe you? He's in the middle of shooting *Shit Floats*, another story by Chase."

"Justice will win out, Carla. After all the work Mario and I put into that script, do you think you can just walk away with it, as simple as that?"

"Oh, why don't you just cut the melodramatic bullshit? There's no cameras turning on you now. It's not your script. The story is totally different from yours."

"Then let me read it."

Carla laughed. "And have you steal it from me? I don't think so, Mikki. You can pay ten bucks and see the movie when it comes out."

The thought of Mikki seeing her own movie, starring someone else in her role, was a terrible reality. It seemed that her whole life was a train speeding toward this moment, all her climbing, hoping, working, planning, hurting, conniving, all had led up to this place in time, the ladies' room of an expensive restaurant, with her last hope snatched away. Carla seemed to be the embodiment of everything and everyone who had held her back.

Unchained, Mikki let loose everything she felt about Carla, everything she felt from the first day they met. "You want everything handed to you, don't you—you skanky little bitch? Everything ready-made. So you're not pretty? So you're not talented? Why can't you just get off your fat ass and try to work for something yourself? Make it on your own!"

Carla cut her off again. "I know it's hard for you to see other people making it. You think you're the only one in the world who's ambitious. You think that you want things more than other people, that you're more fucking special, more talented. That you work harder. It's what you want to hear, so people tell it to you. Even I fell into that trap for a while. Face the truth, baby, if you really had what it takes, you would have made it—you're just a no-talent, narcissistic, wannabe."

Unfortunately for Carla, at that moment Mikki realized that the beige silk blouse Carla was wearing was hers. She had probably left it at Carla's place during a friendly sleepover months before. Seeing her blouse on Carla's body, and filled out rather nicely thanks to Carla's alleged boob job, was more than Mikki could take at this particular moment. She lunged at Carla and, her nails bared with tiger-like ferocity, ripped the blouse off of her in one fell swoop. Carla reacted instantly, grabbing two fistfuls of Mikki's hair.

With all her might Mikki pushed Carla, and Carla flew across the bathroom into a row of sinks, landing directly in one, her fat ass knocking it loose from the wall. Water started to spring out of some broken pipe.

Carla got her balance and lunged at Mikki, giving her a solid right hook to the jaw worthy of Tyson. Mikki recovered, and now she was a rabid animal caught in a trap. She started swinging, scratching, pulling, and kicking at any part of Carla she could get at.

A society woman walked into the bathroom, screamed shrilly, and ran for cover. Torrents of water were pouring out of the wall, and in a matter of minutes, the two models were fighting ankle deep in it.

Bloodied, Carla tried to get away from the animal that Mikki had become by closing herself in a stall, while Mikki continued clawing at her, not feeling any form of retaliation Carla tried on her (which consisted of an occasional kick, a swat of her hand, or a yelping yap). Carla got the stall door closed, but there was no door on earth that could shut Mikki out. In a white-hot, blind rage she flattened herself on her stomach, and through the rising water, she began to crawl under the stall door, while Carla stamped on her hands and arms, trying desperately to keep her out.

"What are you doing, you crazy, fucking cunt?" Carla screamed.

"I'm gonna kill you, you hideous monster!" Mikki raged back. "What the fuck do you think I'm doing?"

In spite of the violent opposition of Carla's stomping, Mikki managed to crawl through the water, under the stall door, into the stall where Carla stood shrieking. Once in there Mikki struggled to her feet and grabbed a fistful of Carla's hair at the back of her head, and with the superhuman strength of a mother whose child is trapped under a car, she forced the screaming, flailing thing's head into the toilet.

"Drown you worthless hunk of shit!" Mikki shouted triumphantly.

"What the hell is going on in here!" a snooty restaurant host screamed, as he entered the bathroom, now eight inches deep in water. Mikki released Carla's head, and she sprung up like a demented jack-in-the-box. She flung open the stall door and escaped into the raging river that was now the ladies' room.

"The bitch is psychotic!" Carla gasped standing there in her bra and wet snaggled hair. "She's trying to kill me!"

The harried host looked on blinking—then bolted out for help.

Mikki emerged from the stall like Lazarus from the tomb. She stared at Carla contemptuously for a second or two, gasping for breath.

"Did Daddy buy those tits for you, too?" Mikki asked finally, grabbing at Carla's bra with one quick hand movement. Instantly the bra snapped open and Carla's breasts came off in Mikki's hand. Suddenly, to Mikki's shocked amazement, it became apparent that EYE's number-one model's tits were nothing more than foam rubber filling. Both of the women were momentarily dazed. Carla, mortified, stood with her arms folded across her tiny chest. Mikki stared, first at Carla and then at the two foam rubber cups in her hand.

"Unfortunately for you, baby," Mikki said, "there's certain things in this life you just can't steal."

That accomplished, Mikki regally marched out of the bathroom, past the by-now-inevitable crowd of curious diners, carrying Carla's artificial boobs with her. When she emerged into the dining area, every person who remained at a table had his or her eyes on her. Mikki looked like a waterlogged Tippi Hedren after the birds attacked her. Her face was bloodied and tear streaked. Her wet hair was all over the place. Her drenched clothes were in tatters. Yet she held her head high and walked straight over to the photographer's table; this vulture-like paparazzo was too shocked to even lift his camera when Mikki appeared.

The photographer had, like everyone else in the joint, stopped what he was doing to look at her, his mouth agape. Mikki smiled dazzlingly at his luncheon companion, then at him. She plopped the fake breasts on the table directly in front of him.

"I just thought," Mikki said, her voice composed and strong, "that you might want to get a picture of Carla Christaldi's tits."

39.

WHEN I THINK of Carla now, I think of the blood and how it must have felt as she lay dying in Mikki's arms. It is the strongest image of my life, man. Watching someone die. It develops instantly inside my mind's eye at weird moments—when I'm in bed with strangers, on the phone with a new interest, waiting in line for a movie. Whenever I'm not looking. FLASH! A videotape playback of a young girl thrashing about on a leather couch, blood streaming down between two cushions . . .

It was Mikki who first thought of killing Carla, and she talked me into it. I'd be lying if I said she didn't. It seemed a spur of the moment decision. And yet now, God help me, I can't help but wonder—was it always her plan? Did she come to me knowing she could make me do it? Who knows? Time has passed. All I know is she is where she is today. And I am still stuck where I am.

We had been talking about Carla's betrayal for three days straight. Talking in circles. I was tired of talking about it. Not just about what Carla did. I was tired of talking about all the problems. Every injustice that was done to us. Talk, talk, talk. And life goes on. And the Marios and the Mikkis of the world lay ourselves down and let everybody walk all over us. *Wipe your feet, dears*, we say, *I am your doormat*. I was tired of being a vulnerable asshole. I wanted to do something. Not just for Mikki. For me, too.

"I could kill her," Mikki said that night for the millionth time. I had become hypnotized from hearing the litany of the sufferings and betrayals of her life culminating in Carla's theft of our screenplay, always ending with: "I could really kill her."

This time, as an instant reaction, like when a psychiatrist holds up an inkblot and asks, "What do you think?" I said, "Let's do it."

Mikki was sitting at my kitchen table with a mug of tea heavily laced with scotch in front of her. I had inherited the wood table from the previous tenants. A horrible, splintering hunk of grayish wood that resembled an abandoned picnic table. Once in a burst of optimism, I had painted it white, shellacked it, and bought Deco place mats. It looked good, but instead of cheering me up, it only made me feel more miserable. Like every other nice thing that I ever brought into this apartment, it seemed to scream at me with vehemence, "Get me out of here!"

"Do what?" she asked, her fingers circling the mug.

"Kill her. Waste the bitch."

She looked at me very carefully for a long time. I could tell she had entertained that thought, too, but I thought that like me, she considered it only a whimsical Grimm's fantasy. Maybe as a way to lull her to sleep at night, she planned different ways to do it. It was just too delicious a thought for real life. Now that she found someone who was thinking along the same lines, she was trying to see just how serious I was.

"Do you mean that?" she asked. Film noirish. An eyebrow arched.

"Mean what?" Now I was the one playing games, stalling, feeling her out.

"Kill her. Do you think we could?"

The determined seriousness in her face startled me. I thought for a moment and then replied: "This is real life, Mikki, not a movie."

"Shit," she said, "this is real life, you're right. And we're wasting ours. How much longer do you think we've got left to be beautiful? And you make your living from it!" She knew this was hitting me below the belt—where I lived. But she was on a roll and she wanted me to get on it. She was dead serious and needed to make me understand her feelings. "We bet everything on the fact that we're beautiful. We thought that was enough to help us rise above this. That didn't work, so we pooled our talent. Well, now all our chips are on that number, and the wheel has one last spin!"

I started seriously entertaining the thought of murder. I figured maybe if we did something to show fucking life that we weren't going to take everything lying down, it would stop kicking us in the ass.

I was just about to answer her when she said: "You think it's hard to make it now. Wait till the lines start, baby. Then you tell me how hard it is to make it."

"I'm doing everything I can to help us, Mikki. You know I am."

It unsettled me terribly to think that all of her beauty might go to waste, unappreciated by the masses. I'm not talking about the people during the course of everyday life—on the subways, in the stores. I thought her face should be syndicated for the masses, all around the world. The thought of her beauty being wasted made me unbearably angry.

"Do you think I'm the only girl in the world who ever wanted to make it? In the Sixties and Seventies girls flocked to New York and Hollywood thinking they'd be the next Marilyn Monroe. In the Eighties it was Madonna. Now everyone comes thinking they're gonna be Britney Spears. And ten, fifteen years go by, and what happens to them? Aging. Trying to look younger. Always having to compete with the younger girls just coming up. They become a joke; living off the little glories the business allowed them—an underarm commercial, two lines on a *CSI* episode—and their lives are wasted. What makes you think—I'm talking about in real life, not in your fantasies—what makes you think I'm gonna be any different? And you," she added scornfully, "sucking the dicks of men you despise. Don't you think I've done the same? Losers who use you. What do you think life has in store for you seven years down the line. What makes you think you're gonna be able to get out?"

I didn't answer; I just looked at her, stricken. Mikki knew she was getting to me, so she continued, "Do you think it's because you want it more than anyone else does? Is that it? Do you think that you want it more?"

"No," I whispered, close to tears now.

"Because it's not true. It's not true, Mario. You don't want it more.

Maybe you want it just as much. But not more."

I buried my face in my hands for quite a long time, but didn't make a sound. Damn, I wanted out of my life. I wanted some small success. I wanted to have to stop worrying about the rent next month or the tooth that needed to be capped or the line that's starting to get prominent on my forehead. Finally I looked up at her and she stared at me, looking tired and wan.

"All right, Mikki," I said. "You're right. We're no different from millions of others right now. We do have to be more resourceful. More daring. More creative . . ."

" . . . but we did all that with our screenplay," she said, exasperated.

"And the screenplay was stolen from us," I reminded her.

"That's why we have to do something now," she said, her voice rasped with agony and frustration. "Something drastic."

"But what good will killing Carla do now? It won't get our screenplay back. Everyone already believes she wrote it. Even with her dead, we'll still be exactly where we are."

"But it will be doing something radical! Life hasn't given us justice. We'll make our own. After it's over, it'll be like nothing can stand in our way. Our aura, our karma, will go up. Look, you've always said that one of the reasons you have so much trouble getting ahead is because you're not aggressive enough. You don't have the iron balls needed. Well, here's your chance to grow a pair. What Carla did to me—to us—is a terrible, terrible thing. She stole our careers." She paused deliberately, to let me absorb some of this.

Mikki had moved restlessly from the table and was now sitting on my filthy brown plaid couch, a couch from generations ago that someone had thrown out and which I had picked up on the street, sprayed with two cans of Raid (a smell which mixed in with the smell of mildew and which never entirely faded), and dragged back to my place. Seeing her on that piece of junk only made me angrier. I looked around the apartment. The ancient gray walls, peeling and cracked, the grime on the sink, the dust on the dirt-stained wood floor, and the cobwebs hanging from the ceiling and from the naked light bulb gave the impression of a prison cell in a Third World country. I had never done anything wrong. Not really. Why did some people deserve more than others?

"You know," I said at last, "I think that people like us, people who come from nowhere, we're lucky if we get one real chance to make it presented to us. We may have had our chance with the script. Let's face it, though. The story comes directly from our lives. It's very strong, but I know I felt drained after writing it. I'm not going to be able to write another one as good for a very long time. Do you think you have it in you to write another one?"

"I know I don't," she replied.

I was speaking much too fast, but I couldn't stop the words; I was on her wavelength now. "So our one chance was destroyed. And it's unlikely we'll get another one. We're not babies—and every single day we're a day older, the odds are less and less in our favor. That's what she robbed from us. Success in our youth."

"Exactly," Mikki said, excited that she was getting through to me. "She deserves to die . . . we could do it, Mario. We could really do it."

My heart was beating, and I could hardly catch up with my breath. It was a mini-panic attack turning into a major one. I looked for a reaction in her, but she was looking down at the floor. It was only when she looked up that I saw she was crying.

"The thing that really bothers me," Mikki said, "is that she didn't need to do this to us. Her life was mapped out for her. Her father would never have really made her struggle. Even if she never made it as an actress or a writer or a model, he would have set her up. She would have always been successful in one way or another. But I've already given as much as I can. I've gone as far as I can go. There's no fight left in me."

I got up and went into the bathroom to get a towel for her to wipe her face, but when I came back to her she no longer needed it. Her face was dry and her eyes were clear.

"Let's do it," I said.

ONCE, ON TELEVISION, I saw a documentary about teens who kill. One segment was about a homely, nerdy, seventeen-year-old boy who became obsessed with a pretty cheerleader who at one time had been kind to him. Day after day this popular girl invaded more and more areas of his mind, spreading through his senses like a disease. His eyes couldn't see anything but her: the expressions on her face, the shape of her legs. He couldn't hear anything but her voice. He couldn't taste food. He couldn't feel. He said that he couldn't go on living with the thought of this girl alive in the world. He had to kill her to survive.

That's what happened to Mikki when she became obsessed with the idea of killing Carla. I probably would have let the idea go. It was absurd. I had vented my anger by talking of a fantasy of murder. I would have erased it and moved on. But Mikki—she couldn't forget.

Mikki was not, I think, a cruel person. She was not a heartless person. Not really. I remember sometimes when she was reading the newspaper, she would weep when reading about a particularly horrendous crime. She often wondered aloud how we could exist in a world of such cruelty, where murder is nothing more than a hot item to be exploited on the evening news shows. Now she had been reduced to that.

Mikki's idea was to make the murder look like a suicide. The tragic Carla—so addled with drugs, so screwed up, so deep with family history. She was high-strung, anyway—everybody knew that. She was always calling people in the middle of the night ,babbling about how desperate she was. She'd tell anyone who would listen about how some boyfriend or girlfriend had dumped her, how unloved she was, how her father hated her. Like all people with this disorder, her friends had long stopped paying attention. She was nuts. She flaunted her suicidal tendencies on talk shows, in tell-all interviews, in one-on-one, late-night phone calls. No one would really question the fact if one night she carried out something she'd been threatening to do for years.

How to do it was the next question. It had to be painless. Quick and easy, no mess, no fuss—like a self-cleaning oven. We didn't want it to hurt, of course, but we couldn't force pills down her throat. I kind of liked the idea of locking her in a garage with a car running, but where would we get a garage, not to mention a car? Then Mikki saw an old movie called *A Kiss Before Dying* in which a murder was made to look like a suicide by putting a gun to the victims head, pulling the trigger, and then placing the gun in his hand (yes, yes—that's exactly where the idea came from). I knew of plenty of places to get a gun. Mikki wanted everything to be believable and wanted to be sure nobody was suspicious in the least.

I hate to admit this, but I have to tell the truth, damn it, so here goes: I was the one who talked Mikki into letting me do it. Pull the trigger, that is. I mean, there was absolutely no way to link me with Carla. I'd only met her a few times, and no one would even think to question me. Here's the plan we cooked up.

Mikki always saved important messages from her voicemail. Eventually she would tape them onto a cassette, and when the tape was full, she'd date it and put it in the drawer where she kept her diaries. It was sort of her way of keeping records, dates, addresses, etc. Now she was sure—actually she knew—that she had some really distraught messages from Carla.

Her idea was to call a friend (we decided on Justin) and play one of Carla's depressed messages into his home voicemail that night so it would look like she was desperately dialing acquaintances in a fit of anxiety. To make sure Justin was out, Mikki would ask him to meet her for a drink, under one pretense or another. While they were meeting, I would call his home number from a public phone, play Carla's message into the receiver, rush over to Carla's, shoot her in the head, put the gun in her hand, if possible type out a suicide message on her word processor, and high-tail it out of there.

It may seem a bit farfetched; it did to us too in the beginning. But the more we talked about it, the more real it became. Easy as Easy-off.

ON THE NIGHT of the murder, I asked myself, *What are you doing, Mario, have you gone mad?* I was on the subway heading toward Carla's apartment with the intent to kill her. Knowing that Justin was out meeting Mikki, I had already called his number from a pay phone and left the tape-recorded message of Carla's distraught voice saying she was depressed and to please call back. I didn't use my cell phone, which I recently had turned back on (my finances continued to zigzag), because I didn't want anything to be traceable to me. In the pocket of my leather jacket was a gun bought from a rough-trade black hustler I knew and liked—he never asked questions.

Every day I take a New York subway, and every day I suffer the worst torture. Tonight there was a long delay, and I stood on the platform sweating. Waiting. Waiting. And there was no explanation, as if the people didn't matter, were nothing. As a result of the delay, when the train finally did come, the car was packed. The air conditioner was turned on, but low, really just a daddy kiss of air. *Turn it on high, assholes! We paid our fare!*

On my left was a fat, suffering, wheezing, sneezing, snorting white woman, breathing with a whistle up her nose. Her smeared, lipsticked face in mine, she searched for a handkerchief in her purse, snorting all the way. Then she sneezed, letting loose a bazillion sickness-carrying droplets, one of which landed on the back of my hand and which I quickly wiped on my pants leg. I turned my face to the other side.

On my right was some kind of man from a foreign land. He was wearing a swami head wrap and a hairnet on his beard. He smelled heavily of stewed onions. I promptly started looking for an out, but the crowd was so thick, it would have taken a miracle on par with the parting of the Red Sea to get through them. And I'm no Moses. On the other hand, the thin Jamaican woman heading toward me might have been his twin. The people separated, making her a narrow path as she regally walked through the car babbling a steady stream of religious consciousness in a slight island accent.

"Mothers don't give up on your sons. Your daughters: They are in jail. They're out standing on the street corners. They sell dopes. They push cracks. Pray, and God will hear. He can save your children. Fathers don't give up on your children. God is looking down on you. In our mother's womb we were conceived in sin. You're gonna need the Word. You may not need it now, but you you're gonna need Him later. Yes! You're gonna need Him. God is God and He always will be God. God will not pass judgment without first sending a warning. You may say, 'Yes, I know God.' The Devil knows him, too! God destroyed Sodom and Gomorrah. It was a rich city. They had fame. They had riches. God said, 'I will destroy Sodom and Gomorrah.' But God will not destroy virtue. No matter what you are going through, take up Jesus as your personal savior. Don't try to fight it on your own! You can fool me, but you can't fool God. Be encouraged. God is with you . . ."

She kept right on going with that rapid-fire delivery. Where did this woman get her energy? In this heat I barely had the strength to breathe and had to keep reminding myself to do so. She, however, kept on spewing and kept on walking as if in a trance. Actually, to my extreme discomfort, it looked like she was staring directly at me. Her eyes were burning into mine.

"Brother? Brother? Brother? What do you have to say for yourself?" She was talking to me. The hot, sweaty, annoyed people all turned to look at me to see what my reaction would be to this wacko zealot. I half expected a chorus of angels to fly through the window and carry me off to Paradise. I half hoped for it.

"Nice try," I said to her.

40.

ON THE NIGHT of the murder, Mikki chose to wear white, as if wearing that color held magic purifying powers. Her hair hung very blonde at this time. Her skin, as always, was pale and unblemished. She was wearing a white silk suit, the skirt coming just above the knee. Under the jacket she wore a camisole of ivory lace. Blonde hair, white skin, white silk. She was white on white on white.

She made her way through the crowded bar toward Justin's table in the back and as she passed, it was as if the very air motes around her were charged with crackling electricity. Men stopped in mid-conversation with their new dates to watch her. Bartenders paused in the middle of mixing drinks. Even the women turned and stared at this ethereal-looking apparition.

Of course, she was aware of the attention she was getting. She fed on it. But you would never know from looking at her. Her eyes stayed glued to the back table where Justin sat waiting for her. To look as if she were aware of her sex appeal would destroy it. But she knew it was there. Everything in her was geared toward getting this reaction. To be famous was to do this on a bigger scale. She was capable of getting this kind of reaction from a room full of strangers, so if you put her image on a screen and showed it to billions of strangers around the world, the reaction would be the same, right?

Yet it didn't make sense. In all the books she had read in her life, the heroine, if beautiful, always ended up getting exactly what she wanted. People were always telling Mikki she was beautiful, yet she was still on the outside looking in.

I had power over her and I exercised it, Justin reasoned to himself as he watched her approach him. There was no reason to feel guilty. The bitch used him! *But she is magnificent. What a waste.*

After receiving that email from her, Justin made sure her career dwindled. How could he stand to be around her after that humiliation? How could he stand to watch her climb to an even higher, more powerful level than himself? The true hurt stemmed from the fact that she had had him utterly fooled. He thought she was different. He thought she was genuine. As it turned out, she was simply a better actress and a more skilled and ruthless manipulator than he had ever come in contact with. Well, he had showed her.

As she made her way to his table, she smiled and waved to show him she was there.

Her job was simple. She just had to keep Justin out long enough for me to call and leave Carla's distressed message on his machine. Of course it was awkward for Mikki. She hadn't spoken to Justin in months, since he dumped her, so she planned on using this meeting as an excuse to get to the bottom of it.

"I'm surprised you wanted to see me," Justin said as she sat down. He was already drinking; she noticed half a glass of some vodka concoction in front of him.

Mikki was thinking: *I'll never be drunk enough to get through this. Mario is on his way to kill Carla. It is because of me. But is it? He wants to do it just as badly as I want him to. Will he go through with it? Will it change us? Will it change our destiny?*

She said, "There's a lot of things that were never cleared up, about us, that have been on my mind. I've been too, I don't know what . . . confused? . . . to confront you with this after we first stopped seeing each other. But now I'd really like to know."

Her mind was reasoning: *I could stop this. I could get up from this table. I could run over to her apartment. I could keep Carla alive.*

"Know what, Mikki?"

It's wrong to kill someone. No matter what she did. It's wrong. It's wrong. It's wrong.

"Why it happened. Why you just dropped me like that. Without any explanation. I mean, I'm a big girl, Justin. If you were more interested in (she mustn't say her name) someone else, fine. But to just dump me like that? You became so aloof, so distant to me. I don't know, I just don't understand it. If nothing else, I thought we were better friends than that."

Justin looked at her with disbelief. "Wait. Wait. Wait. Wait a minute, Mikki! What are you talking about? Did you ever stop to think that maybe that email had something to do with us splitting up?"

Her father never gave her the love she needed. We all need. I certainly understand that. She's been hurt; I understand that, too. But that is no excuse. I would never do what she's doing to me. But, oh my God, would she do to me what I'm doing to her?

"I don't know what you're talking about, Justin. What email?"

The waitress appeared. Mikki ordered Dewars on the rocks with three lemons, and make it a double, please.

"Wow, powerful medicine," Justin said.

"I have a toothache," Mikki replied.

"The email, Mikki. The email you wrote me saying that you couldn't . . ." He looked down. "I'm embarrassed to even talk about this." He stared at his drink as if contemplating it and then brought it to his lips taking a deep swallow. "Saying that you just couldn't get excited about me. In bed. How that's the reason you always insisted on the lights being out when I wanted them on. How you used to fantasize about waiters and actors while we were making love . . . how you thought we were better off as friends. I'm sorry, Mikki, if I hurt your feelings by becoming aloof. I just thought that, maybe, I had some justification in being a little hurt myself."

Justin, her mind screamed, *I never wrote such an email! You were kind to me. You're one of the few people who ever believed in me. I would never do anything to hurt you. There's only one person in the world I told all those things to. Carla! Carla had to have written that email. Don't you see? She ruined it for me. Shit, Justin, she ruined it for us. I should have been the one with the TV show. I should be the one making a film with Jonathan Christaldi. I should be the one!*

Of course she couldn't say any of that now. Saying that would give her a motive. For murder. So she had to take the rap for that obnoxious email that Carla wrote. Carla once again had put her on the spot.

Is it possible for anyone to be so conniving, so heartless, so cruel? That bitch. That bitch! THAT INCREDIBLE BITCH!

But that was being taken care of right now, wasn't it? She took a sip of her drink. She looked deep into Justin's eyes and saw real hurt there.

"Justin," she said, "I wasn't myself when I wrote that email. I was under a lot of stress. I was probably drinking. Taking pills. I didn't mean those things. I just . . . when I'm suffering inside, I want the people who are closest to me to suffer as well. And maybe that's one of the reasons I wrote it. I didn't mean any of those things. To tell you the truth, I totally forget I even wrote it."

I offered her friendship. And yet Carla did everything in her power to destroy anything that was good in my life.

Justin did not answer; he just sat there with a look that made her want to go home and put on the *Lady Sings the Blues* soundtrack album. But in a way his wishy-washy attitude was also to blame for Carla's triumph. Of course Mikki didn't write the email, but Justin didn't know that. So why didn't he call her, confront her, scream and yell, tell her off? His passivity was what Carla had been counting on and he didn't disappoint. But because of his vulnerability Mikki felt tender toward him rather than angry.

"Deep down inside, Justin, I never felt good enough for you. And that's the truth. I felt as if I was unworthy of all the attention you were giving me. I guess that's another reason why I did it. I'm a little crazy, Justin. You know that. And Justin . . ." she grabbed his hand, "I loved making love to you." It was a lie, but a lie that would somehow make him feel easier. Better about himself. And a lie was all she had to offer him at the moment. His hand squeezed hers. In a small way maybe she had undone some of Carla's damage. And only God knows what other things she had done. What other horrible deeds that we would never even know about?

As long as I live, Mikki thought sadly, as she held Justin's hand tightly, I will never understand someone like Carla. Oh Carla, Carla, Carla. Who are you? Why did you do this? You could have had everything. We could have been friends. But you never revealed yourself to me. And I know now you never would.

Let her die, then, and take her mysteries with her.

41.

"WHAT ARE YOU doing here?" Carla said. I didn't answer her, but she stepped back so I could come in. I did, and closed the door behind me. I was surprised that she did not ask me how I got into the building. Carla's did not have a doorman. It was one of those New York apartment houses with a locked front door and doorbells to ring for each apartment. You had to be buzzed up. I pressed every apartment number except Carla's. Somebody has to be expecting a delivery, I reasoned. Sure enough the buzzer instantly rang, allowing me entry.

Oddly enough, I didn't feel guilty when I thought about killing her. I felt strangely alive, as if all my senses were heightened, more sensitive, like in the moments before an orgasm.

"I've come to kill you, Carla," I said.

"Oh, yes?" she said calmly, giving me the once over.

I guessed my voice was too casual for her to take me seriously.

"I decided it's best for you."

She walked into the living area of the apartment. I followed. She sat down on a black leather couch and leaned back languidly. I remained standing.

"What made you decide that," she asked finally, when she was comfortable enough to acknowledge me.

"I decided you can't make your own decisions. I decided you need me to tell you what to do. I decided that you're too unhappy to live."

She thought that was funny. I took the gun out of my jacket pocket to show her I meant business. Her eyes went directly to it but she didn't stop laughing right away. I waited for her to stop.

"Don't scream," I said. "'Cause the second the sound comes out of your mouth, I'm putting a bullet in you."

"I have no intention of screaming, Mario," she replied and started biting her pinkie nail with a relaxed demeanor that threw me. If she was acting, she was a damn better actor then I would have given her credit for. Although I wasn't so bad myself. My heart felt as if it had caught on fire and was beating out of control, trying to put itself out, but I acted like I was soaking in a hot tub, tranquil and ready.

"Only a truly unhappy person would do what you're doing to Mikki and me. If you had any faith in yourself at all, any pride, you wouldn't have to do it."

"Fuck you, hustler," she snapped. "Who the fuck are you to preach about pride?"

She was wearing a nightgown. Not a sexy one. Rather, a long T-shirt with a faded picture of Snoopy sitting at a desk. It said, *Here I am still looking for the answers.*

"Oh, Carla," I said in a pitying tone, "you really are pathetic. I *do* feel sorry for you."

"Oh? You do?" she asked with a bitchy and sarcastic edge to her voice. She was starting to get on my nerves, which was gonna make my job a lot easier anyway.

"You think this movie that you STOLE is gonna make you into a real person?"

She said, "I'm really not in the mood for explaining this again. Especially to you, but let's get something straight: I didn't steal her screenplay. I wrote it."

"Come on, Carla. Give me a break. It's the same plot. The same story."

"Maybe she inspired it, but you can't copyright an idea. I put a lot of my own ideas into the character I'm going to be playing."

"You know you can't even act. I mean, that's gotta be keeping you up nights. What do you think? You're gonna fake your way out of it?"

"My father is directing it. He'll make me be good." From the way she said this I could tell it was something she'd been giving a lot of thought to.

"You'll be a laughingstock," I said. "And you know you didn't write it, so you can't write another one. People will start to know that you didn't write it anyway; they'll say Daddy paid Chase Bartholomew to write the whole thing. You'll be an embarrassment to your father and to yourself. You'll never get another part. How will you ever live with yourself knowing that you robbed two other people's one chance and fucked up your own?" I was making this up as I went along, but she was buying it. "You'll be a bigger failure than ever." She had no response to that. I guess she never did think of it.

I noticed a fish tank on an end table to the far left of the couch. It was a large tank, but she had it filled with only about four inches of water. On the bottom was one monstrous goldfish tilted in an awkward position, trying to keep his whole self covered with the murky water, but a tiny portion of him was actually out in the air. His fins were flapping rapidly but he could not swim at all, and one vacant eye stared at me and somehow seemed menacing.

"Hey, Carla," I said, "why don't you give that thing some water?"

She didn't answer me. She just stared ahead with a look as blank as the fish's.

"Carla," I said again, "that poor thing is suffering. Why do you have the fish with no water like that?"

"A friend of mine is coming to pick it up. I don't want it anymore," she said listlessly without even looking at it.

I panicked. What if she had a friend dropping over tonight? Shit. Shit! SHIT! I hadn't even thought of something as simple and as likely as that.

"When?" I asked as nonchalantly as I could.

"I don't know, Mario," she said, annoyed. "Whenever."

"Well, I'm putting water in it."

"I told you, a friend is going to take it."

"So when he comes, he can take some of the water out, stupid bitch," I said, not in a nasty way, more or less conversationally. I can't stand to see anything suffer.

I put the gun back in my pocket and went into her white-tiled, antiseptic-looking kitchen. Don't ask me how, but I just knew she wouldn't do anything. It was as if this scene had been scripted long before, and we both had to play it out just to see what would happen next. I filled a pot with water from the tap. "Just leave it alone," Carla said from the living room, but she didn't make a move.

I poured the water into the tank and it stirred up layers of neglected filth, turning the water a swirling opaque. When it settled a bit, I could see the startled orange fish darting to and fro with crazy helter-skelter movements. It scared me a little, seeing something moments before so dead, now violently alive. The deranged thing was probably half mad from being constricted in four inches of water for so long. I took the gun out again.

"I'm afraid," Carla whispered suddenly. But her comment wasn't directed at me or what was going on in her apartment at the moment. It was spooky the way she said it. In an empty, hollow kind of way.

I leaned beside her on the couch so that one of my knees was resting on it. I kept my other foot on the floor for balance. To my surprise I found myself answering her. "So am I," I said, "every day."

She looked at me, interested. "And what do you do about it?"

"I keep on fighting. Keep on trying to lift myself to the next plateau where, maybe, I'll be safe."

She shook her head solemnly, like some wise old school principal, passing along years of acquired knowledge. "I've been to the next level," she said. "It's not safe. It's the same thing."

I noticed that on the modern glass coffee table in front of us was a Diet Pepsi and a half-eaten Lean Cuisine. These useless details made me feel warmly toward her, damn it. I, too, had to watch my calories.

"I don't believe you'll do it," she said, with a slight head motion toward the gun. It was a challenge from her.

I put the gun to her temple. She didn't move.

She looked so sad and helpless sitting there in her nightgown. *I shouldn't be here*, I said to myself. *This is wrong. I shouldn't be doing this.* My face was very close to hers. I noticed she had a tiny mole above her right eyebrow and a lot of other beauty marks on her face and going down her neck. I also noticed the dark hairs on her arms. She really was too dark to be a blonde.

Poor Carla, I thought. She was never really beautiful. She had no talent to speak of. No wit. No charm. She really was marginal in every way. How terrible it must have been for her growing up with that brilliant father of hers. Everyone expecting so much from her. Everyone trying to get next to her with the hopes of meeting her dad. Never knowing what anyone's true feelings for her were. All her evilness probably came from that—the fact that she wanted what we all want. She wanted to be loved for who she was.

And at that moment the love I felt for her was so strong, so overpowering, that I had to close my eyes and catch my breath. I wanted to do something for her. To help her. *I don't care who your father is*, I wanted to say. I wanted to hold her face tenderly with both hands and kiss her. I wanted to run away with her so we could look for happiness together. But you know what? My second thought was *Wow. What a score it would be to run away with Jonathan Christaldi's daughter. To have him as my father-in-law.* So, I guess that makes me just as bad as everybody else.

In my mind's image of death—murder—I saw people tied up, begging, trembling, scared of what would happen. Carla wasn't like that. She was serene and expectant.

"Do it," she whispered. "Do it!" She made a motion as if she were reaching for the gun herself. Before she had a chance I said.

"I love you, Carla." Then I pulled the trigger.

MY CELL PHONE rang once. I knew it was Mikki. That was her code. I picked up.

"Mario?"

"Yes."

"Did you do it?"

"Where are you?"

"I'm still at the bar. Justin just left. Did you do it?"

"Yeah, I did. But she's still breathing."

"What? Is that possible? With a bullet in her head?"

"Obviously. It's only a matter of time I would imagine."

"Wait there. I'll be right over."

"No!" I said, but she already had hung up.

I raced through the back compartments of my mind trying to think if I ever heard of anyone living with a bullet through the brain. Mrs. Buttafucco, shot years before by the Long Island Lolita, came to mind. The Lolita was now out of jail and had written a book and was doing talk shows and Mr. and Mrs. Buttafucco have since divorced. Life does go on, doesn't it? When you're alive. I remembered some guy who was with Ronald Reagan when he was shot, who took a bullet in the head. And he was still living, I think. But was he all there? Or did he become a vegetable? I couldn't remember. I was so pathetic when it came to important world events. Unless they had to do with show business.

Carla lay on the couch, her soul slowly escaping her earthly body like a stream of steam from a kettle, rising to the ceiling, through the ceiling, floating past the upper apartments, out into the night sky, and hopefully for Carla's sake, straight up to Paradise.

"Soon you'll know all the mysteries, Carla," I whispered. After I shot her, I wiped the gun with my trusty handkerchief and placed it in her hand letting her arm drop where it might. The gun fell from her hand and landed on the floor next to the couch. And there it would remain. As long as there was a clear set of her fingerprints on it, I guessed it would be okay. If there were things about the scene that were unexplainable, well then let them remain unexplained. There are always some unanswered questions at a death scene—and these questions would give tabloid books and television shows years of fodder for conspiracy theories.

"I CAN'T BELIEVE you really did it," Mikki said in queasy wonderment when she saw Carla lying on the couch, her dark-red blood glistening as it flowed in a steady stream down the crack between two cushions.

That frightened me. Mikki's comment and her lack of concern for me—how *I was feeling, how* I was coping.

"What do you mean you can't believe it?" I said. "We planned this thing together for weeks. Of course I did it! Do you think I was playing with you?"

Suddenly I imagined her going on tabloid talk shows concocting a sensational story about me, minimizing her participation. Painting me as some deranged villain. It dawned on me that there were only two people in the world who knew the true story. And I was the only one (of the two) I could trust.

Mikki said, "I'm not blaming you . . . you came up with the idea, but we both . . ."

"Blaming me?" I asked in disbelief. Even the word "blame" made me freak. And what the fuck was she talking about, *you came up with the idea?*

"Accusing you, pushing it off on you. I know we both did it. I'm not freaking out. It's just that, God, it's not every day you see something like this."

She had dressed up for Justin, but now she took off her cream suit jacket and stood in the gloom in what looked like a flimsy white slip. Her growing panic made her seem all the more beautiful and vulnerable to me. She hugged herself tightly and ran her hands up and down opposite forearms. *Oh*, I thought, *if only I could've been a satin glove on those hands that I might touch those forearms.*

"I'm just as guilty as you," she added.

"And she's just as guilty as us."

"That's right," Mikki said. "We shouldn't even use that word. 'Guilt.' This is just something that we had to do."

"You look perfectly gorgeous," I said.

Mikki moved closer to the couch. She felt for Carla's pulse, first on her neck. She didn't feel anything. She picked up a wrist.

"Is she . . .?" I asked.

"Almost," Mikki said.

Oh, why wouldn't she just die already! Couldn't she do anything right? We moved away from Carla's body to give her time to expire. We sat at her dining room table, and perhaps to make ourselves feel better about the murder, we started talking about all the hard knocks life had dealt us. About the years of struggle we both went through. I haven't talked much about this, but I think it's important for people to know that Mikki and I went through years of trying to take the normal route to success. Yet we were lost in the shuffle and remained invisible.

We talked about this as Carla lay dying on her couch, as if our failures somehow justified our actions.

And we also talked about nepotism and show business today. I'm afraid that my voice may come out bitter in these pages and then everything will backfire. But I have to be truthful and admit that part of our hostility toward Carla stemmed from the fact that she had a ready-made career and had no talent to back it up, while we felt we did and couldn't get noticed.

Mikki had knelt down in front of the couch. I watched from a few feet away with my fist in my mouth, as she, crying, stroked Carla's face and hair. Then she put her arms around her.

"Don't touch her," I snapped crossly. "You're gonna get blood all over yourself!"

"Oh, shut up," she shot back, just as harshly. "We're human beings, too!" She regretted that instantly and said in a softer tone, "Stop being so paranoid."

"It's just that you still have to leave here, and don't you think people are gonna question the fact that you're covered with blood?"

"You're in New York, dude. What's a few blood stains between train passengers?" she said with a choked laugh as she wiped away tears.

"How can you joke about it? This isn't a game."

"Don't worry, I'm being careful. I don't have any blood on me."

"And you've been touching everything since you walked in the door."

She smiled fully. "Don't be stupid. I've been in this apartment dozens of times. My fingerprints are all over the place. Would you stop going crazy? There are no suspects. This is a suicide, nothing more. They won't even be looking."

It was true. This was all so incredibly easy. Too easy. That, I suppose, is the way most murders are. TV and movies have us conditioned into thinking that a resourceful detective will sprinkle some magic powder on a death scene and, TADA!, a criminal is exposed. In truth no one would be dusting for fingerprints or snooping for clues.

Mikki walked over and put her arms around me, and I pulled her very close. She tightened her grip and I buried my face in her hair. She was wearing a perfume that by now was familiar to me.

This will bind us together, I was thinking. Now we are more One than if we were lovers or married or created a child together. We had taken a life, and nobody has the right to do that. Our souls would somehow merge; we would always be together.

———

THAT NIGHT, AFTER Carla was at last dead and I left Mikki, I could not face my apartment alone, so I went to one of my old haunts, The Lion's Den, on the east side. I wasn't working. I'm not that heartless. I just wanted a drink. Something quick and fast-acting. I had half expected that Mikki and I would spend the night together comforting and reassuring each other, but she unexpectedly said, "It's better if we're not seen together tonight." But why? We were always seen together. Perhaps she simply wanted to be alone. I went to the end of the bar and ordered Dewars on the rocks.

At night, this was a strictly upscale joint. Most of the prostitutes wore jackets. Most of the johns wore suits. I was known here. While I was waiting, I noticed this old guy started scoping me out. My drink came and I stared down at it. Everything in my demeanor said I didn't want to talk to him, but I could feel his stare. I started to concentrate: *Don't talk to me, don't talk to me, don't talk to me . . .*

"I'm the only one in this place with a history in the theater," he said. I was thinking, *Look, mister, I've already killed tonight*, but rather than say that I just smiled a little.

He had the kind of voice you can only get after smoking fifty million cigarettes. He had thick white hair, which was his, but his face looked like life had thrown him on the ground and walked all over him with heavy boots. He wore a shirt of deepest red, hoping no doubt that the bright color would reflect on his face and make him look alive. Without prompting on my part (I tried to look as disinterested as possible), he started telling me his life story.

I kept thinking, *I killed Carla. I killed Carla. I killed Carla.* I thought if I kept repeating it to myself it would become real to me. It seemed weird, sitting in a bar, having a drink, ignoring a queen, doing things I've done thousands of times before, and yet I had just done something so obscene, so shockingly sinister, that it had to somehow change me into somebody else, and at least that was a positive thought.

" . . . then in 1969 I had my nervous breakdown," the old man was saying, and he gasped and clasped a hand over his mouth in mock horror. "I'm not supposed to talk about that! I'll let you read about it in my memoirs. I'm working on them now. I'm just getting it all together."

This was said to impress me. Memoirs. Ha! His book, I would imagine, was filled with tales of how he'd been close friends with Tallulah Bankhead and Ethel Merman. Who's to know? There's no one around to discredit him now. I wondered how many people in this lousy city were also working on their memoirs on this night. I wanted to say, *Listen, friend, I just killed Jonathan Christaldi's daughter.* Instead I gave him a vague smile and pretended I was drunk. He ordered me another drink. I promptly downed it.

He asked me if I wanted to have dinner but I wasn't hustling. "I'm going to a late movie with a friend," I said, and I gave him the name of a movie I had been reading about while Carla lay dying and I was waiting for Mikki to arrive at her apartment.

"You'll love it," he said.

How did he know what I would love? Because he read it in the reviews? He mentioned that he himself hadn't seen the movie yet, and I grew impatient with the conversation. I really wanted to be alone. Yet I knew he was just trying to be nice. Just trying to make conversation. Just trying to get into my pants. There was no need for me to be angry with him. And I wasn't. I was just wondering if I would end up with nothing in my life, too. Perhaps if he had done something drastic when he was younger, perhaps if he hadn't let people shit all over him, he wouldn't be in a prostitute bar looking to buy a boy for a night's companionship while selling his dreams.

All of a sudden I felt sorry for him. He had messed up his one chance, and it was too late to do anything about it. So I kept smiling and was pleasant because I knew that was important to him. And I stayed with him a long time, talking till he almost had no voice, but I kept staring intently, even though I wasn't listening anymore, and I had to press down tightly with my eyes to stop the tears from coming. He grabbed my hand and squeezed.

I have killed, I thought.

"I'm so glad I met you," he croaked. "You have real sensitivity. It's so rare you meet someone who's really sensitive." And I said good-night and got up and left him sitting there bewildered. Once again he had made a wrong choice and would be going home alone.

Later, in my apartment, I could not sleep. My bed, or actually my entire bedroom, seemed frightening to me, partly, I thought, because my phone was in there and I was terrified of it ringing. I knew it was ridiculous. No one was going to suspect me, or anybody. Nevertheless I took three sleeping pills and moved to my secondhand couch and, as a distraction, tried to imagine the lives of the people who owned it before me. I wanted to invent happy families eating Cheez Doodles from a big bowl and watching Walt Disney movies on it, but for some reason I kept on fantasizing it had once belonged to a man whom I had read about in the paper years before, a lawyer who abused his wife and beat his adopted daughter to death.

I imagined the poor little girl cowering on my couch in a previous life. It was an atrocious thought, but at least it was a distraction so I allowed it. If only I could have helped her, the little girl. I would have, if I had known about it. I imagined holding the child in my arms and whispering to her that I loved her—not in a sexual way, damn you! I am not sick—but in a tender, fatherly way and maybe even adopting the kid myself.

This fantasy led me to other fantasies of going throughout recent history and saving vulnerable female victims. I was with Marilyn Monroe the lonely night she died—I gently held her hand and told her how loved she was and how no one would ever forget her. I knew that would make her happy.

I walked in on Sylvia Plath, whose poetry Mikki had introduced me to, with her head in the oven and turned off the gas just in the nick of time to convince her she was a genius and her life was worth living.

I was at Sharon Tate's estate, and I smuggled her, pregnant and slow, out of the house before the Manson clan arrived. We crouched in the bushes as the knife-wielding killers passed by us. "You saved my life," Sharon said—they all said. Of course I knew this was wacky but it did keep my mind occupied. Eventually I drifted into an uncomfortable, half sleep.

The next morning my eyes sprung open snapping me out of sleep and for a moment I thought that the entire night before had been a dream, that killing Carla was simply part of my fantasies of helping women in distress. Then I remembered. I called Mikki first thing. "How do you feel?" I asked her.

"My voice is very breathy today," she replied. And I knew exactly how she felt. I, too, was finding it hard to speak. "It's not online yet," she continued. "I already checked."

"I guess they didn't find her yet."

"They will soon. Justin has gotten the message off of his machine by now, that's for sure. I'm sure he's trying to reach her."

"But do you think he'll go over there?"

"Oh, definitely," Mikki said. "He told me last night that there was never anything serious between them. But if nothing else, Justin is a caring person . . . and she does still work for him. He'll go there."

AND THAT'S EXACTLY what happened. Mikki and I heard about Carla's death, not in the papers, but on a cable news channel. It was the lead-in story, actually the only story they had on that night. With everything that was going on in the world, they dedicated round-the-clock coverage to Carla's suicide, and through interviews with policeman, voice-over narration, clips from Carla's cable show, modeling photos from her career, paparazzi shots of her stoned, a press statement from Justin Landis, and various psychiatrists and analysts giving opinions, they reconstructed the story of what they thought happened the night she died.

Carla did not show up on the set of her cable show that next day, and a production assistant reached Justin at EYE. Justin was concerned. He had gotten Carla's message, which I left on his machine, when he returned from his meeting with Mikki. He tried to call her several times but finally gave up. Nutty, depressed messages were nothing new from Carla, so he finally went to bed. But when the call came to him from the set late in the morning informing him that she had not shown up, he was alarmed. He called several people who knew her, but none of them had heard from the flaky star. And then he went to her apartment and found her as we left her.

Of course during the next few days it was all over the papers, snatching away the speculation, gossip, and headlines surrounding the recent suicide of Victoria Sweetzer. Carla Christaldi was more up to the minute, more current. Her sordid, scandal-filled past was in our favor—the media dredged up every bit of dirt they could find. We devoured all the papers, watched every TV show, did every Internet search.

It seemed strange to us that we were responsible for all of these stories and yet there was no mention of either of us. To our amazement and utter relief there wasn't even a hint of foul play. On the contrary, everything about her life that the media focused on pointed to suicide: Carla the teenage alcoholic who checked into the Betty Ford Clinic. Carla the difficult model. Her friends talked about her depressions and wild mood swings.

The Post ran a five-day series on her life story called "The Sad and Tragic Life of a Hollywood Child," but the picture they used to illustrate the first installment was of a chubby, fifteen-year-old Carla, eyes half closed and stoned looking, cigarette dangling from her dark lips, clutching a beer in one hand, giving the photographer the finger with the other.

It was on day four of that series that they ran the photo taken of Mikki and Carla during their last meeting in the restaurant several weeks before Carla's death. Mikki had not been aware of the picture's existence. In the picture Mikki had just thrown a glass of wine in Carla's face. Carla's expression was startled, eyes closed, and it looked like one hand was in the process of wiping off her face. Mikki is looking at her with a stricken expression. In the lower right-hand corner you can just make out the shocked look of a snobbish-looking woman, with a huge bun in her hair, staring aghast at Carla from a nearby table. It was quite amusing, but neither Mikki nor I saw the humor in the photo at that time.

But Mikki had no problem dealing with being a murderess. She had distractions. Jonathan Christaldi had entered her life.

42.

MOST PEOPLE WOULD have advised Mikki not to attend the Carla Christaldi memorial service. But her philosophy was that she would have attended if it really had been a suicide, so she acted accordingly. Probably she was aware that the memorial service would be well stocked with celebrities and important movie-type execs.

She thought Jonathan Christaldi was the most beautiful man she had ever seen. It was the first time she was actually seeing him in person, and he possessed a charisma that no camera in the world could capture. It wasn't the kind of physical beauty that the male models she had worked with possessed—the kind of beauty that had to do with flawless skin, perfect features, well-worked-out bodies, and youth. Jonathan Christaldi's beauty had to do with a mixture of mature handsomeness, assured genius, unlimited money, and power beyond fantasies.

The more Mikki looked at him, the more beautiful and desirable he became. Everything else that in others, like a hairy arm, would seem normal, became on him a valuable treasure she longed to own. Mikki didn't realize it at the time, but she was drawn to him because he had all the qualities she so lacked herself.

At a very early age Jonathan Christaldi had known what he wanted and had meticulously mapped out his goals and reached them. Here was a man who wasn't afraid. A man who had made it. A man who was able to surround himself with wealth and lots of pretty things. But during the service he seemed to notice no one; he sat quietly in the first pew, his head respectfully bowed.

After the service, Carla's friends were invited to her father's New

York apartment, a huge, sweeping place on Central Park West. When Mikki arrived there, she noticed a definite change in the attitude of the guests. Unlike the artificially somber atmosphere at the church, it seemed to her here she had more or less stepped into a lively cocktail party. She said hello to Justin Landis, one of the few people who seemed truly upset. *Luckily you were born with money, Justin, honey. Otherwise you would have been crushed like the rest of us vulnerable lot.*

She chatted briefly with models she knew from her brief moments of glory, but her eyes were on the lookout for Jonathan. She spotted him deeply engrossed in conversation with Jana Janelow, who was studiously ignoring her. Jana looked absolutely ravishing, even with little makeup and a simple black dress. Mikki wondered if she was trying to get into the movies. *She's got a better chance than me*, Mikki thought. *She's such an icon.*

Jonathan was smoking a cigar in a macho way—always a tremendous turn-on for Mikki.

Eventually he noticed her noticing him. *Thank you, God*, she silently said. She knew he wanted her. He excused himself from Jana, hastily put down his cigar in a crystal ashtray, and headed toward Mikki.

"Speaking of gorgeous . . ." he said to Mikki with exaggerated charm.

Mikki smiled back with exaggerated charm. "Were you?"

"Was I what?" He was chewing gum now, jaunty and mischievous.

"Speaking of gorgeous?"

"Yes," he said. "I was talking about 'gorgeous' with an expert over there, Miss Janelow, and then I saw you, and I just had to ask you . . ."

"Yes?" Mikki asked, cocking an eyebrow, her voice very soft and very low.

"I have to ask you where you get your gorgeous looks from?"

"My mother was beautiful," she said very quickly, and at once she was sad. It hit her suddenly that her biological mother might truly have been beautiful—even on the inside. Mikki might have inherited her beauty from the unknown woman but wasted it.

"Gorgeous," he repeated. "And yet you seem so sad." It didn't occur to him that, well, maybe she should seem sad. She had, after all, just attended the memorial service of a friend—his only child. She instantly perked up; she didn't want him to think she was a downer.

"No," she said, "that's just the kind of face I have."

She had been drinking and through her glittery haze she knew that he found her face beautiful, and so she stared at him with complete confidence—even while knowing that he had stared into the most beautiful female faces of his generation. But she also presented her best package with the ensuing conversation. Here was the Mikki Britten who could hold her own with any woman on any level. A woman who was sharp and intelligent and who gave opinions with wit and charm. A woman who knew how to make a man want her.

They talked about the current film scene, authors that they both liked, current novels that would make good movies. He was amazed at her insight and instincts. Throughout he either stared at her intensely or allowed his eyes to wander the room. She took his cue and did the same—all the better to not seem too eager. At times he grew pensive. His silences disconcerted her. *I must not try too hard*, she thought. *Whatever happens, happens.*

What could she possibly say, do, convey, that would penetrate him? He'd already met the most interesting people in the world. The most talented men. The most beautiful women. Of which she was just another.

"You were a friend of my daughter's, weren't you?" he said abruptly.

It was a cold, hard blast of reality. She was a murderess. The secret she had more or less been able to keep buried deep down under, hidden by banter and liquor and strands of blonde hair in her face, now sprung out of her like a horde of demons out of Pandora's Box. She tried to stuff it back inside. No matter what other feelings were involved, she had killed this man's daughter.

"We were very good friends," Mikki said carefully, "at one point."

There was an awkward silence as Carla's phantom stood between them, staring them down, demanding her due. More should be said, this they both knew. An involuntary chill ran up Mikki's spine. "Did she speak of me?" Mikki asked finally.

"Yes. Very often, actually—Mikki Britten. Mikki Britten! She thought the world of you," he said. "She idolized you."

Mikki wanted to tell him that Carla had felt the same way about him, but she thought he might recognize it as the lie it would be. It occurred to her that she should say something about the photograph of Carla with Mikki's drink in her face. In all likelihood he had seen it, and she did not want to come across as if she were hiding something.

"We were very good friends," Mikki said carefully, "but sometimes with me she had a difficult personality. We did fight sometimes."

Jonathan looked serious then winked—a naughty little boy. "I loved her, too. But there were times when even I wanted to throw a drink in her face."

How the hell did he know she was thinking about that photograph, she wanted to ask. But her desire for the subject to be changed was much stronger. She felt drained suddenly. The energy she had put into presenting all that beauty and charm she had displayed earlier was taking its toll. She cast her eyes downward. She wanted to go look in the mirror. Maybe powder her face. She was tired and drunk and in need of lipstick. Again it seemed like he read her mind.

"Oh, my dear," he said, tilting her face up to his, and the subject was changed. "You really are exquisitely beautiful."

"I'm not as beautiful as I look," she said, looking away from him.

———

HE WANTED TO go to bed with her, that much was clear.

She promised herself she would not fall in love with Jonathan Christaldi. Not that she didn't want to. Not that it wouldn't be easy. But it would be futile. And it would strip her of her power. Have a good time with him. Make connections. Get cast in Carla's movie, which was really *her* movie. These were but a few of her goals with Jonathan. They seemed far-fetched, but here she was spending time with him; a couple of months ago that in itself would have seemed far-fetched, impossible!

Then they were alone in his apartment. After such a long spell of sleeping with losers, her body would accept him so readily. They didn't start off kissing softly as she anticipated. They started rough and hungry, and she knew (even before she admitted to herself) that she would not keep her promise to herself. She would fall in love with him. The taste and feel and smell of him inflamed her, and she squeezed her arms around him, melding his body into hers. In return his hands roamed up and down her body as if he were trying to locate some flaw . . . and not finding any, allowed his passion to become inflamed to the point of treating her more roughly. His kisses seemed to be an attempt to bite off her lips. Her hands wandered over him, too, up and down his thick, hard body. They rolled around on his bed, this way and that way, and when he entered her, the noises they made were involuntary. And it lasted and lasted, and she hoped it would never end.

"I could get used to this," he said when it ended. But he held her all night.

QUITE SUDDENLY, WITHOUT much preparation or discussion, they were a couple. She had never met a man who was more sexual than Jonathan Christaldi. After he had an orgasm, his thick, fireplug penis was hard and ready to go again. Mikki had never experienced anything like him. They'd be watching a movie in his screening room, and before she knew what was happening, his face would be between her legs.

He wanted to have sex before they went out to dinner and then he was ready immediately after they returned.

Is he this way with everyone? she asked herself. *Or does he truly find something magical about me?*

Yet, when she sat beside him at a private movie screening, she didn't accept it as her due; instead she viewed it as a glorious gift that she must savor and be thankful for. Sometimes in the middle of the film, she'd remember God and his possible role in her good fortune. *Thank you, God,* she'd silently say, *for giving me Jonathan and this wonderful opportunity.* Then she'd once again get absorbed in the movie, imagining what it would be like for her to be on the big screen, giving her all, dazzling and awing.

As much as she enjoyed sex with Jonathan—and she did more than she ever had with any other man—she began to wonder if she'd be able to keep up. If she could go on having sex as many times a day as Jonathan's appetite demanded. Already she was faking it sometimes—something she thought she'd never have to do with him. But it also made her feel strong. As long as he desired her so much, she had a power. She didn't underestimate it. She didn't play games. She always made sure he was getting her at her very best.

BUT HE WAS busy. He was important. He was in demand. He never let her forget that. If they were in the middle of a discussion, no matter how animated or serious, if his cell rang, he'd hold up a hand and say, "Excuse me just a minute." And sometimes he'd obliviously leave her sitting there, silently sometimes, for forty-five minutes or more. If the call were business related, he'd tell Mikki who it was and what it had been about when the call ended. Other times, however, he'd set up a business meeting or dinner, and when he hung up, turning his attention back to Mikki at last, there were no explanations, no acknowledgment at all that he'd even been on the phone.

But hope didn't leave her. He threw her just enough crumbs . . . compliments . . . words, that would make her think that he could love her. Maybe she could break down some of his protective layers. What she couldn't see is that those layers took him years to put up and were the very layers that helped him become the success he was. He wasn't about to tear them down. Certainly not for a girl.

She became obsessed with him because he was one of the few men she really wanted and couldn't break. She knew subconsciously that she could work on a man and she could eventually make him love her. She left her mark on so many men. Jonathan was different. Her never let her personality penetrate him. He was very fond of her and seemed to be enjoying her company, but at the same time he was able to keep his distance.

—————

"HOW CAN PEOPLE be so cruel?" Mikki quietly asked, looking down at the table. And as an afterthought she said to herself, "But there's so much cruelty in the world that we don't even know about."

Jonathan had just ordered a lamb dish for both of them and explained to her how this restaurant acquired their lamb. The meat here had a reputation for being exceptionally tender. It seemed that they bought baby lambs that had been forced to stand completely still in total darkness in cramped cubicles.

And in some terrible connection, her mind recalled an image from a documentary she had watched that very evening while getting ready for this date. In the film footage, baby seals had been slit and torn open, their insides spread and steaming in the snow. She thought of these pathetic creatures—given life, only to experience nothing but pain. These thoughts made her want to take all baby seals and lambs and calves to live with her in her apartment in Queens. She wondered if baby seals and lambs have spirits that go up to Heaven. If so, she looked forward to being together with them there. An absurd thought, she knew, but that is what she was thinking about.

"Jonathan," she said as they waited for their meal, "I read in the papers yesterday that you're still planning on directing Carla's film."

"It's what she would have wanted."

"Yes," Mikki said. "*Mind Trips* really is a terrific script, isn't it?"

"Oh," Jonathan replied thoughtfully, "I wasn't aware that Carla gave it to you to read. But, yes, you're right. It is terrific."

"Jonathan," Mikki said and the uncontrollable trembling started, "I, uh, I have something I want to tell you."

"Yes?"

"Well, it was very important to Carla to make you proud of her. I'm sure you know that. And, um, she was always so damn insecure when it came to dealing with you. We all felt that. Very, very insecure when it came to you."

"What are you trying to tell me, Mikki?"

"I'm trying to tell you that I helped Carla write that script."

Jonathan reached for his drink and took a deep, long swallow, but he never took his eyes off of Mikki. The ice cubes in his glass rattled noisily. "Are you saying you co-wrote the screenplay with my daughter?"

"She came to me and said she needed help. She was trying to write, but it didn't come easy to her. I had already written a screenplay—with a friend of mine—which we had abandoned a few months before . . ."

She stopped and tried to read his thoughts. As always he was inscrutable. "And?" he asked.

". . . and I gave it to her. My screenplay. I told her she could adapt it as freely as she wanted to. Then, I guess, she invited Chase to help her rework it. I knew how much you meant to her, Jonathan, and I wanted to help her any way I could." She felt her own fingers encircle her glass, but she didn't dare lift it for fear of exposing her shaking hands. "I would never be telling you this if she were alive," she added.

"So why are you telling me now?"

"Because I should play that role, Jonathan. I should star in *Mind*

Trips; only the real title—my title—was *Fame, Trains and Other Sexual Fantasies.*"

"Good title."

"That's what it was originally."

"You and your friend handed your work over to Carla and were willing to let her take full credit for it?"

"No, I mean, yes. My friend and me were . . . you have to understand what kind of pain Carla was in, Jonathan. Was always in. We weren't getting anywhere with the script, anyway. My friend and I tried to send it out, but nothing came of it. So I told her she could use whatever she wanted from it. I knew I could never get the movie made on my own, so why shouldn't she use it? At least she had a shot at getting it produced. But I never thought that she would . . ."

"Would what, Mikki? Would what?"

"I never thought that she would want to act in it, too."

"You thought that she would have suggested you for the lead?"

Mikki nodded. "That would have been the payback."

"Mikki, I think . . . ," Jonathan began, but the white-sleeved waitress serving their dinners interrupted them. They both fell silent. A plate of steaming hot lamb and vegetables was placed before each of them, the smell of which immediately made Mikki sick to her stomach. How she would get it down, she did not know.

"Mikki," Jonathan continued after the waitress exited, "did this have something to do with that fight you had with my daughter. When you threw that drink in her face?"

The way he said, "my daughter," made Mikki feel as if she might faint. She leaned back in her seat and clutched the end of the table with both hands. "No. Jon. No! It had nothing to do with that. Nothing. I loved Carla. And she loved me."

"I know for a fact she did," he replied.

Her senses slowly came back to her. "That fight—in the restaurant—the day I threw the drink at her, that stupid argument was about Justin Landis! Justin Landis. We both dated him at one point. Did you know that? And it was a jealous, stupid, catty argument. Nothing more."

Jonathan allowed a faint smile to pass across his lips. "Girls will be girls," he said and picked up his knife and fork, carefully cutting into the lamb in front of him. Mikki watched in a state of complete repulsion and anxiety.

"What are you thinking about?" she asked finally.

"Actually, I knew," he said. "I knew that the screenplay was a little too good for Carla to have written on her own, God bless her. And Chase Bartholomew . . . well, let's just say I had to hire a lot of writers to make his novel filmable."

"Why is that?"

"He was having, shall we say, trouble, working in the screenplay format."

"Is it true he didn't write the book?" Mikki asked. As was the way with Jonathan sometimes, he simply ignored the question.

"You're a much more talented girl than I gave you credit for, Ms. Britten," he said instead.

"People are always underestimating me," she replied in spite of herself.

"It's a mature piece of writing. I have to admit—I did wonder about it."

Mikki sighed audibly. "I don't want any credit for the screenplay, Jonathan. That's not what this is about. Let her have her writer's credit for it, posthumously. I'll never even mention it again."

"What about your friend?"

"He won't either. He wants what's best for me."

"Really? Odd. Is this guy in love with you?"

"No," she said, "He's in love with the idea of me."

"What do you want then, Ms. Britten?" Jonathan said, smiling fully now, lightening the mood, or trying to. It was obvious that his daughter—her life and her death—was not among his favorite subjects. And Mikki wondered if Carla, as a topic of conversation, was too painful or too boring for him to consider.

"But I've already told you. I want to play the lead. I want the part of Marisa."

"Only, the character's name is Amanda now," Jonathan corrected.

Mikki returned his smile. "Then I want to play Amanda."

"No, no," Jonathan said, "I like the name 'Marisa' better for the part. Hmm. Well, Mikki, I'll tell you this: I'll test you in the role. I can see you in the role. Definitely. But the money people are going to have some say. I can recommend you—I can submit you—but ultimately you have to prove yourself. I wouldn't work with anyone just because they were my friend, you know."

Mikki did not outwardly wince at the word 'friend.' "I can deliver," she said.

"Well, let me talk to the studio," he said. "I can offer you a test, with me directing." He winked. "And that's no small accomplishment for an actress to achieve. But the rest is up to you."

"Oh, but Jonathan," Mikki said, picking up her knife and fork, "that's all I ask for. I wouldn't even consider asking for more. All I want is a chance." And then she enthusiastically cut into the lamb.

———

LATER THAT NIGHT, breathing heavily, he rolled off her after his third climax. "I have to go back to Los Angeles to reshoot the final scene of *Shit Floats*," he said. "We have a new ending."

He was leaving her! Panic gripped Mikki for a moment. But before she could really slip into a tizzy he added, "I'd like you to fly out and meet me there. We're having the wrap party on Friday night. You should be there."

Mikki closed her eyes with relief. "Of course," she said.

———

LATER THAT WEEK, Mikki flew to Los Angeles to attend the wrap party of *Shit Floats*. She arrived the day before and was put up at the Mandarin Oriental hotel. There were flowers waiting for her when she arrived. The suite was more lavish than anything she could imagine. But she was there alone. Jonathan was busy with some post-production, last-minute movie business, so he was staying at his Hollywood Hills home. She wouldn't see him until the wrap party, which was being held at the Penthouse at Chateau Marmont, a hotel with a legendary past she had long been aware of. It would be her introduction to his Hollywood world. He was Caesar. She would be his Cleopatra, triumphantly sweeping into Rome. The dress she chose for this occasion was a flesh-colored body stocking with silver beads advantageously interspersed. Mikki planned to look like she was naked, covered simply by an early morning dew.

She specifically didn't want to walk in to the party with him. That had been prearranged. He'd be busy meeting and greeting, being bowed to and saluted, and she'd be left standing there—everyone giving a little nod in her direction—like an idiotic trinket. She hadn't accomplished anything. Yet. No one needed her approval.

The party started at 9:00 P.M. If she got there after all the schmoozing was over, people would be in party mode and she'd be able to make a magnificent entrance to a crowd hungry for a new arrival.

So she pulled up in a cab at the Chateau Marmont at 10:15 and was surprised to see a long line of people still waiting along Sunset Boulevard to get into the party. Shimmering and splendid—she couldn't imagine any woman looking better—she stepped out of the cab. Obviously these people had read about the party in the papers and wanted to crash. They couldn't *all* be on the list.

Mikki walked to the front of the line to where the—doorman? security guards? hotel staff? list checkers? henchmen?—were standing but didn't seem to be checking any list or bothering to let anyone in at all. They just stood around looking smug and aloof. It felt foolish to Mikki, in all her glamour, walking to the front of the line to inquire about entry but, after all, she was the date of

Jonathan Christaldi—the man who was throwing the party.

As she waited to be acknowledged by one of the list-checking henchmen, she noticed in detail the gathered crowd. How young they all seemed. Young Hollywood. We're talking babies, seventeen to twenty-three. Hair was the order of the day. Big, full, lustrous hair. Carefully styled to look casual and tousled. If a man wasn't blessed with a thick head of hair, it was grown out long and combed and slightly teased in such a way that suggested volume. Women simply added extensions.

She stood there awkwardly, waiting to be noticed. *This is just like New York*, she thought. *They still refuse to admit that I exist. What is it about me?*

Her beauty seemed to be having a minimal effect on anyone. It was, after all, Hollywood. Finally one of the henchmen noticed her. "Are you on the list?" he asked, looking her up and down.

"Yes, I'm . . ."

He cut her off with a smart-aleck smirk. "So is everyone else. Get in line."

Mikki's humiliation was so great that she considered trying (in Los Angeles!) to hail a cab and return to her hotel. But oh, what the fuck, she'd been taking people's shit for years, her days of being nobody seemed to be coming to an end. She could swallow a little more for now.

She took her place at the end of the line. A young man in front of her, part of a group of young men who all looked the same (with messy 1960s Beatles hair), turned to her because he had noticed she talked to one of the semi-gods at the front.

"What line is this for?" he asked Mikki.

She had taken a lot of Xanax and was a bit slow in her response. "Christaldi," she managed to blurt.

"The movie wrap party, right?" he asked.

Mikki nodded. "*Shit Floats.*"

"The movie is now called *Mediocrity*," the guy said in a disgusted tone.

"It is?"

"Yeah, man. They changed it from the book." He turned back to his friends, ending the discussion. Obviously Mikki was a nobody, not having the latest info on the film.

Mikki hadn't known that they changed the name of the movie. Why hadn't Jonathan told her? She felt like a geeky outsider trying to crash an exclusive party.

But then the miracle. The henchman, contrite, sweet, apologetic approached her. "Miss Britten? I'm so sorry. You're so much more beautiful in person—I didn't recognize you at first. Please follow me."

As the henchman escorted her past the line, through the entrance, to the penthouse, she noticed the crowd's attitude toward her changed. Now they looked at her with admiration. She was someone awesome. Mikki made sure her expression didn't become haughty or superior. She tried to keep it blank. In her heart, she was still the same nobody.

Walking to the party was stepping onto Mount Olympus. Jonathan was in the center, glowing—*the* god—his silver hair like a plated helmet. He took her by the arm, introducing her around, and she found that she was wrong. No one treated her like a nothing. She was more than Jonathan's trinket. Here her shimmering beauty was recognized and respected. Some remembered her from her fleeting modeling career, and they took her in as one of their own, without viewing her as a joke, as she feared they would. They talked to her intimately, as if they had known her for years. But (and this is no small "but") after Jonathan had introduced her to everyone, he left her on her own for a while as he started a lengthy conversation with an actor. Mikki then ignored the attention he seemed to be lavishing on a very young, dark-haired girl whom she had never seen before but who, Mikki thought, resembled Kate Moss in her Calvin Klein heyday.

Instead Mikki concentrated on meeting the celebrities in the room. She hoped to soon be in their league. Most of the leading ladies Jonathan had worked with in the past were there, and Mikki made it her goal to chat with each one. Celebrities enjoyed her company. She didn't tell detailed stories about her past or upcoming projects. She didn't laugh too hard or too long at a witty remark. She didn't try to be overly clever. Mostly she listened, and when the conversation demanded she say something, her reply was on target. When necessary, her mind could break through the haze of alcohol and tranquilizers she liked to protect herself with and come up with something pithy. They liked her. Julia Roberts, Reese Witherspoon. These were actresses whose acting parts she hoped she'd be offered shortly.

As she turned from a pleasant conversation with Michelle Diamond, she found herself face to face with Chase Bartholomew. She stared at him hard, waiting for him to show some recognition, some feeling of shame for putting his name to a piece of work he had nothing to do with. But of course he had no way of knowing it was Mikki and Mario who wrote it. Carla would have kept that information to herself. And even if he did know, he either didn't care or he had brainwashed himself into believing that he actually did have something to do with the creation of the screenplay.

Her hatred for him had once burned so fiercely she thought she might die from it. Now it died down. She saw the value that was placed on him at this party; stars and directors and producers were fawning over him. Perhaps they would help each other become more famous. *That is Hollywood*, she thought.

After the party Jonathan did not invite Mikki back to his hotel. The following morning, when she was supposed to be flying back to New York with him, he informed her that he needed to stay in Los Angeles another week.

Life has a tendency to send you little clues that you can pick up on when planning your future or, armed with unrealistic dreams, you can totally disregard these tell-tale clues and blithely push forward in a direction that is destined for failure. Mikki was past the point of living in a dream world. She realized she was just biding her time with Jonathan until she was cast by contract in the movie. It was becoming clear he was growing tired of her and would drop her the moment something newer and better came along. He was powerful enough to do that—so powerful that there was always something newer, fresher, and better presenting itself for his amusement. Once she starred in the movie, she'd have power, too. If she could just make the relationship last till then, she'd be safe.

MIKKI FLEW BACK to New York the following day. Jonathan would be busy with last-minute business involving *Mediocrity*, and she knew that he had the perfect excuse not to be in close contact with her. She wanted to view her time in Los Angeles as a conquering success, but she could not.

Back in New York she fought back feelings she called "the dooms." She thought that negative energy would further puncture her relationship with Jonathan. She knew all about the power of positive thinking, a philosophy that she found in most of the religions she studied. But it was hard to remain upbeat. She fought feelings of unworthiness. She thought being too optimistic might jinx her chances, at the same time being too pessimistic would surely ensure failure.

If acquaintances congratulated her on her good fortune of being the lover of Jonathan Christaldi, she simply smiled. Her life had taught her, and she knew well, that good fortune was fragile and one wrong move, one misstated word, could pull it all out from under her.

43.

"DO YOU ACTUALLY think I'm enjoying this," Mikki asked, when I finally reached her on her cell. "I'm just trying to get our movie back."

"But what's he like?" I wanted to know. "What's it like dating him?"

"It's wonderful and horrible," she said. "He's the world's most incredible man . . . so I have to look better than anyone else. I have to worry more. The upkeep is terrible."

"Have you talked to him about our movie? Does he know it's ours? Have you mentioned me at all?"

"Listen, my love. I'm doing the best I can. I'm working on it. I have to go now. He'll be here any minute. I'll call you as soon as I know something definite."

We hung up. I paced around the room. It was a bad month for me. Mikki was always in New York or Los Angeles and not calling me unless I called her first. Not really keeping me abreast of what the hell was going on. I had very little money coming in. My johns were not being complementary or even particularly nice to me. I had one who was obsessed with my pubic hair and was annoyed that it was not clipped enough—and kept talking about the "strays," meaning the stray hairs. "I can't give you a blowjob with all those strays," he said, and I had grabbed my clothes and walked out of the hotel room without being paid. Everything was wrong. All the closet doors in my apartment stuck shut. When I took a shower, the drain backed up and took three hours to go down. The subway system was a nightmare, and I was often stranded on subway stops at two or three in the morning, once for as long as an hour with no announcements, before some disinterested, nonchalant, subway worker came down and informed us that this particular subway was not running that night. There were no explanations or suggestions about what do to. My computer, about four years old at the time, was dying. It would freeze up in the middle of a chat or shut down without warning, or move so incredibly slowly on the Internet that I would start to shake with impatience. Then it would freeze up completely, and I would have to unplug it and start over. Everything was malfunctioning or not working or plotting my destruction.

I decided, *fuck it*. Everyone had used me enough, and I was going to use whatever I had to better my situation in any way I possibly could.

I called the most popular of all the tabloid publications and explained that I was the male prostitute who had the affair with Victoria Sweetzer shortly before she died. "The Viagra-fueled stud," I added in almost a whisper. The editor on the other end said they would expect proof. I explained I could fill in enough details to prove it. He said he would put me through to an editor who would be able to tell if I was real or a fake.

The editor's name was Trent Allen. He explained to me that he had been covering Victoria's Sweetzer's career for over twenty years. He had followed her around the world, photographed her on beaches with telephoto lenses, circled her last wedding in a helicopter, held vigil outside of the Betty Ford Clinic for the entire time she stayed there. He said that her name had sold more copies of the paper in the history of its publication than any other actress's. Then he said, "Prove to me that you were with her."

I said: "Her assistant went by the name 'Cooper.' He called and gave me the time to arrive at the apartment on Sutton Place. The door was opened by a short, Hispanic housekeeper approximately fifty years old. The first time I met Victoria she was propped up in her bed drinking vodka and watching soap operas."

"Describe her bedroom," he demanded.

"It was very hot. Heavily draped. She was sitting up in bed writing on a little table . . . opening mail and autographing fan photos. Oh, and the room was chockful of pictures of her dog. A little, snappy thing. A Chihuahua."

"What was her dog's name?"

I had to think for a moment. The farting little beast. "Helen!" I exclaimed suddenly.

"Okay," he said. "I believe you. What else can you tell me?"

"How much is the story worth," I asked.

There was a pause. "Between five and ten thousand dollars. If it makes the cover, it will be ten. If it is buried somewhere in the back pages, it will be less. It depends on what you tell us."

I could tell he didn't want to talk about money. He assumed I'd be intoxicated by the idea of being in a popular supermarket paper. Giddy with the idea of being a hot item for that week. He suggested I come to the office. I didn't feel like it. The less people involved the better. I invited him to my place instead.

An hour later he showed up with a tape recorder and a camera and a contract. It would have seemed unbelievable, but by now anything seemed possible. I'd killed. But even more unbelievable and unlikely to me, I'd had sex with Victoria Sweetzer. Once you've met someone who was once an untouchable god to you, and you get to know them, with all their weakness and humanity, all their flawed skin, anything seems plausible.

Still, I didn't want to bad-mouth Victoria. The bitch used me. But still. I couldn't forget what she represented. The many moments of joy her movies had given me.

I told him that she was basically a lonely woman who paid me for my time to tell me her stories. "At first she just wanted to talk," I said.

"What did she want to talk about?"

"Love. Her loneliness. How she didn't believe love really existed for more than a moment or two."

"And she paid you?"

"The first few visits she paid me to just listen. But there was an attraction between us and by the third time it became physical. I didn't have to take Viagra in order to have sex with her, like the rumors stated. I'm a male prostitute. I always carry Viagra around with me and take it as a backup. Victoria was still an incredibly beautiful *woman*. When you were in her presence, you understood why she was 'Victoria Sweetzer,' and why she had endured all those decades."

It was obvious he wanted me to say sensationalistic things about her. I said that she had an insatiable sexual appetite. That she was still very much a sexy vixen. It wasn't really the lascivious story he wanted, but it was good enough. He asked if he could take my picture. I didn't want to, but I knew that this would be part of the deal.

"Sure," I said.

He asked me to sit on my bed, which was a tangle of rumpled white sheets and overstuffed pillows. It gave the room the seedy air he wanted. I sat on the bed and waited. "Can you take off your shirt?" he asked.

I was mildly surprised and humiliated in a way that didn't register as a major big deal. My body was meat. It was sold by the pound. It had nothing to do with me, although I longed to connect with it and have someone connect with it in more than a sexual way. I took my shirt off, messing my hair as I did so.

He snapped a couple of photos, but I did not smile. I was not happy about what I was doing. I confronted the glare of each flash stone-faced. Like posing for a mug shot. They backed me up against the wall. All of them. I was doing what I had to do.

44.

ON JONATHAN'S RETURN from L.A. something had changed. Mikki could no longer make excuses. It wasn't subtle. She felt it at once. It was as if he had begun to pick up on her awe of him. And it was beginning to turn him off. That could have been one excuse. The other, more likely reason was that he had started up with someone new out in Hollywood.

Their first night together in his bed, they had sex that wasn't really sex. He rubbed his body up against her but did not penetrate. He did not kiss her. Something was wrong. *He's simply worn out from the trip*, she unsuccessfully tried to assure herself. But that horrible, dead-on intuition she possessed for predicting misery told her it was more than that.

In the morning any warmth he had toward her was completely gone. He had a business meeting, he explained, while rushing around. He handed her a glass of orange juice while she sat on his bed and slipped on her shoes. The kiss he gave was a quick peck on the lips. She took it personally. A horrible thought presented itself: I mean absolutely nothing to him. *Last month's entertainment.*

But she couldn't let it end.

"I'll see you for dinner later on tonight?" she asked quickly.

"Um . . .yeah. But we'll have to make it late. I have a meeting at eight."

She would make it any time. She'd be ready for him. Dressed to the nines. Perfectly made up. Walking around the apartment with vodka on ice, waiting for him to be ready for her.

With Jonathan she was once again the gambler pushing all her newly acquired chips onto the table in a last-ditch effort for a big win.

In the world she'd been living in, there were crowds and delays and disappointments and violence and rude people and inconveniences, and nobody seemed to notice or care. They accepted their terrible fates. And every day things grew a little worse for her. Jonathan represented a different kind of life. And because she felt him slipping, his interest waning, she strangled herself with anxiety to try to make him want her again. She was a beautiful, desirable girl. But she was unable to be herself with him because she felt unworthy. She had to get that screen test before it was too late. Most of her power was already gone. She had to have Jonathan see her on film!

AS THEY SAT at the bar for a drink before dinner, he leaned back serenely, looking at her with his eyes slightly hooded. *Go ahead, entertain me*, his eyes said to her. Or so she thought. She felt pushed up against a wall. What could she possibly say to this man who had seen it all, done it all?

She wanted to bring up the screen test he had promised her, but she dared not. What a spot she was in! If she brought up the test, he would think that she was only with him because she was interested in a role in the film. What should she say? What could she possibly say?

She could feel his eyes drift past her shoulder to some fascinating creature behind her. *Would he be satisfied with the girl behind me?* she wondered. Mikki flirted with the men around her, too. Not because she was interested in anyone else, but to prove that she was a popular item as well. *You see*, her flirting said, *I can flirt, too. It doesn't hurt me when you do it. Am I hurting you?* It just seemed to make him (in her opinion) more impatient with her.

After that night, dinners with him dwindled to once a week. She'd started planning things to talk to him about at the restaurant. She helped herself to her friends' amusing anecdotes, changing them around so that she was the center of the story. Sometimes she'd take notes on things to talk about to Jonathan, a clip from an old movie she wanted to bring up or a passage from a novel. But most of the time, fearing she'd say something stupid, she said nothing at all and let him carry the conversation. He seemed to enjoy hearing himself, so she thought that was okay.

Should I say it? Shouldn't I? Will he think I'm dumb? Oops, too late, I started this date out being quiet and shy, best to finish out the scene that way. Or should I change mid-meal. Can I? I must stop having this conversation with myself and get back to Jonathan . . . but does he want me naive and dizzy, or mature and elegant, or worldly and sexy. Should I be confident or demure and shy? But by the time she said anything, he had lost interest anyway.

WITHIN A FEW weeks, Jonathan and Mikki stopped having sex completely. He continued to invite her over to spend the night on occasion, but it seemed odd, to say the least, that a man who once couldn't keep his body away from her, now never laid a hand on her.

Mikki liked lying next to him, basking in his masculine warmth. But she felt a need. And a definite panic in his lack of desire for her.

She leaned in to kiss him. He allowed one, dry kiss and then turned his face down to the pillow. Every limb in her body screamed with humiliation. But to just turn away now would be to acknowledge rejection. She still wasn't ready to do that. Not to Jonathan nor to herself. She let her hand run up and down his smooth back a few more times. His head remained in the pillow. If she were to give him a massage, he would not protest. He would not move. But he would not initiate sex with her. He would not make a move toward her. So instead she ruffled his hair and turned her back to him. Facing the opposite wall she waited for the sleeping pill to do its number.

IT EMBARRASSED HER to think that he might think she was trying to seduce him with her hideous body. She began wearing undergarments to bed. A bra and panties. Still he never reached for her.

After that she slept with sweats and a T-shirt.

Occasionally, she'd swallow every ounce of pride and make an advance toward him. He'd respond perfunctorily. Going through the motions. Probably planning his next day's strategies.

What he was feeling for her, she had no idea. His touch said absolutely nothing. She felt her own body through his hands, and it felt flabby, loose, not at all desirable (although it certainly was). She hated him touching her now.

In return, she felt his husky but solid body with her own hands, and she could have roused up passion, but she was too busy feeling ashamed.

It seemed like he was waiting for a way to tactfully get rid of her. In the morning when they kissed good-bye now, it was always a dry, quick thing. A brother's kiss. One morning she decided to see what would happen if she gave it more effort. They had their usual dry kiss and then she went in quickly for another. Then another. She decided to keep doing the quick, dry kisses in rapid succession until he stopped. On the fourth kiss he turned away and opened the door.

"He does not want me sexually," she said out loud as she was peeing. She said it while she was walking down the street or alone in her bed. If she said it to herself enough times, maybe she'd get used to the idea and it wouldn't hurt as much.

She dieted. She stopped wearing her hair back in a ponytail in front of him—instead she let it hang freely around her face to her shoulders. She went to bed wearing makeup and perfume.

"Have you been wearing makeup to bed?" he asked.

She thought she had reached a point where nothing would surprise her or further humiliate her, but the question caught her off guard.

"What?" she asked.

"There's makeup on the pillow," he said.

FROM GOSSIP DAILY: What former model is about to be dumped by movie mogul Jonathan Christaldi? Hint, hint: She is blonde and she is gorgeous. And this beauty has never been one to shy away from cameras. So why wasn't the ex-cover girl with Christaldi at the satellite-beamed Golden Globes Awards last week? The gorgeous brunette on Christaldi's arm at that event was hot young actress Jessica Lee Parks, daughter of Oscar-winner Marvin Parks. Jessica was a smash in a small role last year in Christaldi's *Best Kept Secret*, and some say he's looking to star her in his next film. So where was the blonde you ask? Some say at home nursing a broken heart.

45.

EVEN BEFORE I read in the papers that Jonathan Christaldi was dating a rising, dark-haired, heroin-addicted, second-generation starlet, I knew that his relationship with Mikki was almost completely finished. She talked obsessively about it. Mikki felt his restlessness, his absolute boredom, and knew she had to act fast to secure her part in *Fame, Trains and Other Sexual Fantasies*, as the screenplay was once-again titled (though Carla Christaldi was still given coscreenplay credit with Chase Bartholomew). Mikki figured that she could stand losing him as a lover, if she had the starring role in his film—it would soften the blow and lessen recovery time.

But as for me . . . as for me . . . I realized that even with Christaldi out of the way, Mikki and I would never have the kind of relationship I had hoped for. I knew in my heart that we were not good together. We would have been happy together for a few years, but it wouldn't have lasted. In time, when we were both in our mid-thirties, we'd open our eyes and see that everything we shared together was based on desperation and that we had wasted our lives on each other. I should have just fucked her and gotten her out of my wretched system—and then gone back to boys. Maybe then I would have been able to get on with my life, meet someone else, fall in love, feel satisfied. Yes, yes. That was the problem. With Mikki Britten on my mind it was impossible to feel satisfied with anything else. Even with all the sex in my life, I still woke up daily and lay all morning, hungry in bed.

Something was wrong. Killing Carla had not brought Mikki and me closer together. It was a waste. For sure it had done nothing at all to change my life or my luck. And soon even Mikki would be back at zero. Jonathan was getting ready to dump her. Already he wasn't returning her calls. And *Variety* reported that Renée Zellweger was "this close" to signing as the star of *Fame, Trains and Other Sexual Fantasies*. Mikki had not even tested. Well, fuck her. That was her problem.

Several weeks after my interview I finally saw the story about my affair with Victoria. The headline was THE SAD LAST DAYS OF THE LAST MOVIE QUEEN. As I had requested, the paper used only my first name. The piece recounted the story of Victoria's loneliness. She actually didn't come across as being all that pathetic. I was quoted fairly accurately and Victoria was portrayed in a somewhat sympathetic light. *"She had seen it all, done it all,"* Mario explained. *"Now she was tired of being the center of attention, exhausted from living up to the burden of being a goddess. She was a real flesh and blood woman. She had been disappointed in love. She just wanted someone to talk to."*

Identified as her gigolo/lover, the photo of me they chose looked okay. Glowering at the reader. There was the usual mild "buzz"-of-the-day reaction. The day it was published a few tabloid television shows called me. Apparently they had gotten my number from the paper. They asked me if I wanted to be interviewed on their shows. When they informed me it didn't pay, I refused.

A few years earlier, perhaps, I would have considered taping an appearance. I would have thought that maybe some important producer would see me on television, stop dead in his tracks, whip off his glasses, put down his script and say, "That's the guy we've been looking for!" Now I had no intention of throwing my body into the arena of empty-headed fame monsters who would spill details about the wreckage of their mediocre lives, have sex, live in captivity, or eat bugs simply for the sake of being on television. What did it matter? What did they get out of it?

Suddenly, I felt the need to go out. Find my own Jonathan Christaldi. Try for my own life. My own success. But a real success based on work and talent, and not scandal and manipulation. I wanted to do it without Mikki along as excess baggage. It occurred to me suddenly that even if she did marry Jonathan she probably wouldn't help me make it unless it was easy for her to do, without the slightest inconvenience. Like, if it was more than one phone call, forget it, it would be too much trouble. "I tried," she would say. So now that her chances were over, I wanted to give myself one last shot. I'd thumb my nose at her on the way up.

So I gave myself the full glamour treatment—cologne, open shirt to reveal a bit of curly chest hair, slicked-back hair so I might, I kidded myself, really look like Valentino. And I went to my place, my hustling bar.

No matter how bad things got for me, I could always pick myself up, groom to the max, and go pick up a businessman to make myself feel valuable. These men were very educated, made a lot of money, usually loved classical music, and knew what fork to use. All of that couldn't matter less during the course of the night with me. I controlled them in every way possible and, before the orgasm, they would do whatever I asked. I needed to feel power sometimes. Maybe I could get one of these men to love me. I had murdered, so I wasn't so sensitive now, I reasoned, and maybe that would make me more desirable than ever. Maybe the night would be good to me. So I went to The Lion's Den, a bar where I could measure how beautiful I looked on any particular evening by the size of the drinks the bartenders gave me. My first drink, on this night, was a glass of ice with a splattering of scotch.

It wasn't going to be good.

I glanced around the extremely dark room to see if there was something that could hold my interest for more than one second. The first person I spotted was Laird Payne, sitting on an armchair in the corner, wearing horn-rimmed glasses. I noticed he was glaring at me, gripping his drink like a claw, with his legs crossed. We both had things to say to each other, but it became a contest of who would approach whom first.

When I looked away from him and pretended not to recognize him, he jumped up and headed toward me. I hadn't even had a sip of my drink yet.

"I read the tabloids this morning," he said. "I see you made sure you got your share of meat off of Victoria's carcass," he said. "Selling your fairy tale to the tabloids . . . for what? A few grand did it get you?"

He was barking at the wrong dog. I was red hot with fury. "Oh, please!" I said, so loud that everyone, including the bartenders, gawked. "You've been feeding off of her for years. Telling all your little gay friends that you were great friends with Victoria Sweetzer. Writing her biography. Picking up hustlers for her—you fucking pimp!"

He did his fake little laugh.

I did my fake little imitation of his fake little laugh right back in his face.

"You needed publicity so badly that you had to trick me into going to bed with her, you scavenger," I said.

And then he did one of the few things he could do that would reach me. He admitted that he remembered the time, several years before, when I had visited his modeling agency in the hopes of being signed on. All the while I had thought he didn't remember me. Laird must have interviewed hundreds, thousands, of hopefuls since then, but he remembered my interview, my hopes, which he had demolished in minutes, and he used this information against me like a jagged edge. "So you wanted to be a model at one point right, Poet?" he sneered. "Is it that your parents back in the slums told you were so *beautiful*, so *handsome*, that you figured you *had* to be a model—you deserved it? Well, you don't have it, my boy. You never did. Never will. Did anyone ever tell you you're getting older?"

We stared at each other for several seconds. I'm not a fighter, that's for sure. But it took all my might to hold on to myself, not to hit him. You have to be careful as you get older. Youth and beauty add a certain degree of respect to your character no matter what you do. In maturity, dignity comes with behavior. Still, he was making me want to turn myself into a serial killer. But I stopped myself from hitting him with my fist and looked for words that might do the trick.

"Give me a fucking break, Laird," I said at last. "There's no need to be so bitter. You're cock isn't that small. You have money. Go and buy yourself someone else to play with. Someone who doesn't already know how disgusting you really are."

And then, trembling with fury and humiliation and God knows what else, I walked to the backroom bar to see if there was someone, anyone, in this world I actually liked. Sure enough, sitting at the bar in the backroom there was a guy from out of town named Kirk, whom I had spent the night with several months earlier. Maybe things wouldn't be that bad tonight after all. I reached into my wallet and took out a Xanax and confidently plopped it into my mouth, giving the impression I was popping a breath mint. I swallowed it down with a gulp of my drink and waited for it to do the trick.

I liked Kirk. He was handsome but worn, in a Tom Selleck kind of a way. Although he never told me, I knew he was married (one reason being that he didn't give me his home phone number or address—just a P.O. box number, where he asked me to drop him a line from time to time). But there was something about him that was different from the other men who paid me.

After sex the first night we met, he held me gently, his head on my chest, a leg draped over mine. The dawn light streamed in through the partly closed curtains of his hotel room and I heard him mumble into my shoulder, "I love you, too."

I was shocked. I hadn't said anything to him, and we both knew it. His words hung heavily in the air around us. I couldn't just leave them there.

"What did you say?" I asked.

He became flustered, thought for a moment, and then said, "I love your tool." I looked at him curiously in the gloom. "This thing," he said, grabbing my penis. It was a nice try at a cover-up, but I knew what he had really said. I thought about it. He recognized in me, I guess, the fact that I was not hardened. I was not mean. I had some feelings left in me, and I think those feelings drew out of him those words he had been longing to say to another man. Not that I thought he really loved me, but still it was nice to hear.

He held me all morning and called me at home that afternoon. I had confided in him that I was a writer, something I rarely told anyone, and he had gotten us two tickets to see *Lion King*, the kind of big, splashy Broadway musical I detest. But still, I was touched and spent another evening with him.

Now here he was sitting across the bar. He was not Mikki, and I suppose was a poor substitute. I wanted her. And yet, it would be so very nice to spend the night being held by someone who adored me. He saw me, too, and smiled warmly. So what if he didn't call me when he got into town? Maybe he had misplaced my number. Perhaps he had to destroy it to keep it from his wife. In any case, he was here now and that's what mattered.

I was just about to go over and join Kirk when a young boy sat down next to him. This boy was incredibly beautiful and was about seventeen. Blond and blue-eyed—the furthest thing from me. I tried not to let jealousy stab me. But the kid started talking to Kirk, ignoring the fact that Kirk would occasionally glance in my direction and wink or give a half shrug, conveying "be patient."

But the boy knew how to use his considerable beauty, his sensuality, like claws, and Kirk's looks soon stopped coming in my direction as he became more and more absorbed in the conversation with the blond boy-toy. Now, instead of Kirk, it was the boy who sneaked glances at me with a triumphant arch of his eyebrow. He had beaten me at my own game. The desirability game. He knew that he was the most desirable person in the bar and set out to prove it. And he won.

For years I wasn't jealous when I saw a beautiful young boy. For years I was okay about beauty in others because I was young and I could hold my own. I had intelligence and a heart and a soul, too, or so I told myself. And these qualities I thought would make me better than the rest. I thought *that* would matter. But as I got older I began to panic. If you don't have money or desirability, you need something special to make it—to be okay. I needed to become successful so I could reach that place where beauty couldn't hurt me.

But I wasn't successful. And as I saw Kirk and the boy leave together . . . it had a profound affect on me. Even in this buying-and-selling world, a world in which I had always felt safe, I was now defeated. The bar was emptying rapidly. At least Laird was long gone and hadn't witnessed my humiliation. There was some justice. The night was almost over. I became aware that I wasn't going to get lucky. *It's not going to happen*, I said to myself. I had this kind of sensory perception by now and I knew I was wasting my time.

I ordered one more for the road, downed it, and stumbled out into the night. Darkness washed over me. I felt a mood slowly fill up in me, a horrible blackness I was helpless to fight off. *I should have gone to the gay clinic and gotten on Paxil*, I reminded myself. I had been too lazy, plus the last time I was on an antidepressant it made me sick and impotent for over a month. I didn't want to go through that again.

Under the circumstances I thought it was ridiculous to talk to God, but I did anyway. It's never wrong to pray, I reasoned. I turned the corner and crouched in an alleyway on a darkened side street.

"Hold me, Father, I'm lonely," I said.

There was only silence. My insides were quivering like a dying thing left on the side of a road, and my prayers had to reach up over so much noise to the only ears that matter.

"It's just me, God" I said a bit louder to God. "It's just asshole, loser me."

And then an anger that I could no longer keep down took control.

"Yeah, I know other people got it worse, God! But I am me, and I am tired of living in this despair. Do you hear me MOTHERFUCKER?!? And I am not talking like this because I'm drunk, although maybe, yes, scotch does work as a truth serum, and I usually don't have the GUTS to tell you how I really feel! (Whispering now.) You never cared for me, did you, God? You cursed me to a life of expectations and dreams. Cursed me to a life of waiting for subways, of waiting for the next thing—which is nothing. You cursed me, torturer!"

I closed my eyes with shame. I despised myself for talking to my only friend this way. "Disregard what I say tonight, God," I pleaded. "I know not what I do." But then I added: "And yet it's true, isn't it? At least so far."

I got up and started stumbling to the subway station. I wanted to go home. I was crying, but my tears seemed so meaningless to me because in the universe my case was such a small one. At this very moment people were dying, were being mutilated and, murdered; there had been the Holocaust and so many wars. But I couldn't imagine that. I couldn't imagine feeling worse than I did at this moment. *It's okay to feel sorry for yourself*, I reasoned. *There's nobody else around to do the job.*

I'd done enough. I'd seen enough. I'd lived enough. Something in me died that night. My instinct for survival, my desire to be great, had left. I wanted to be in the state I had put Carla in: peaceful, out of the game—free from the struggle, the endless struggle. I looked at the sidewalk and I wanted to become one with it. To be as unfeeling as concrete, to have people walk over me, unnoticed. And I threw myself down. And I threw myself down! And I said, "Please, please, I can't take any more of this," and the sidewalk felt cold, and I longed for nothingness.

46.

MIKKI WASN'T STUPID. She knew that any romantic involvement with Jonathan Christaldi was over, kaput, fini! If she didn't call him, he would never call her, or ever think about her again. But maybe, maybe she had one more chance. If he saw her one more time, and she was exceptionally beautiful, witty, and intelligent, maybe he would recognize that they should at least work together.

Besides, he owed her. He had never again acknowledged his promise to test her for the part in the film, in spite of her hints and outright requests. And it was her film, damn it! How could he have not even had the decency to call her to end the relationship properly? As if she had been a delicious drink on a first-class menu. Time to move on to the main course, dear. He had everything in life. She had nothing. Couldn't he have at least left her with a crumb of dignity? Yes, he owed her, baby. She picked up the phone. He answered on the third ring. She knew he knew it was her from the caller ID.

"I would really like to see you," Mikki said, without saying hello.

She could tell that he was not thrilled to hear from her—but was allowing her a courtesy call. "I was in a conference all day and I'm whipped," he said.

Bullshit, she thought. "It's kind of important to me," she said.

"Where?"

"You pick the place."

So he told her to meet him that night at 9:00 P.M. at a garish, low-key disco/restaurant that was frequented mostly by an affluent, older crowd. The kind of crowd that would least likely make a fuss over him. They didn't follow Hollywood gossip and probably wouldn't recognize a movie director, even a famous one. And if they did, they wouldn't care. On this meeting he didn't want to be seen with her. This wasn't a social encounter. Still she had hopes of pulling some magic tricks out of her hat.

She rushed into the restaurant at 9:20. Flushed. Hurried. Wearing one pink, satin glove. Carrying the other. Late again. Even for him she was late. That was part of her plan. To have him there waiting for her—she'd make some excuse, "I couldn't get a cab," or "The phone rang as I was leaving."

In spite of her air of slight disarray, she was ravishing. Abundant hair brushed through to her shoulders. Tonight her mouth was made up with deepest fuchsia, while her eyes were done up lightly to compensate for the drama of her lips. The effect was innocent and pouty and supersexy.

She was wearing a ridiculously expensive pink beaded minidress, bought earlier that evening for this occasion. The dress was absurd, but Mikki was the type of woman who could pull off this tacky kind of Hollywood outfit. She stood out, but she didn't look vulgar— even though she contrasted starkly with the club's white leather seats. She looked like a glamour-girl movie still from the fifties. She couldn't really afford this outfit, and she'd never be able to wear it again, but it was on her credit card, and if she was extra careful, she could return it as she often did.

Jonathan wasn't there, however, to witness her entrance. To her dismay, he was nowhere in sight. The hostess informed her there was no reservation under the name "Christaldi." Mikki scanned the place again and informed the hostess she'd take a table and wait for her companion.

She chose a booth in the back, away from the dance floor but still with a view of it, and ordered a white wine from a passing waitress. It was 9:30. Maybe he wouldn't show up. He could easily send her a dismissive email tomorrow, inventing some legitimate-sounding pressing business.

She stared at the dance floor where middle-aged women trying to look hip attempted to pick up middle-aged men too rich to care what the hell they looked like. Suddenly she was glad he chose this place. Aside from the waitresses, there was little competition. And there was lots of attention in her direction, which made her feel all the more like the prize catch.

Her wine glass was almost empty. She wanted to order a fresh one so that if Jonathan did arrive, it wouldn't look as if she was waiting a long time. But the waitress seemed to be ignoring her. Mikki caught her eye and pointed at her drink, signaling a refill.

By the time he arrived at 9:55, she was already halfway through her second white wine and seriously doubting he'd show. As she well knew, there was nothing in it for him.

A tear was just beginning to escape her eye when he slid in beside her. Solemn. Not wanting to be there. Making his attempt at being human. Or what he considered human. He ordered a vodka on the rocks. Mikki ordered another glass of wine; after all, he didn't know this would be her third.

For a long time they didn't say anything.

She so wanted to be charming and witty and sexy and fun so he wouldn't pick up on how desperate she was feeling. But she rejected the idea of making fun of the ladies in the place—not that there was any shortage of targets—there were plenty, including a humongous woman wearing a zebra-print pants suit and rhinestone earrings, with silver hair no less. But Mikki felt sorry for them, and besides, she might be one of them some day.

Wordlessly he looked down at his drink, as the waitress placed it down before him.

Mikki was well aware of the fact that she had lost him. Whatever it was that he had originally enjoyed in her had become boring to him now. She wondered if he had ever loved anyone or if it was enough to be able to go through life buying whatever he wanted and owning it until he grew tired.

She stupidly noted how lovely the shade of blue in his shirt looked on him. Not that it was any of her business now. Unfair! Unfair! Jonathan was attractive to other women because of his position and money, while she really loved him. In her imagination she saw him with other girls, going out to dinner, sleeping in his bed (her bed!), being greeted by his doormen (her doormen!), and these images to her were worse than death at the moment.

Mikki was still staring ahead trying to think of a way to start the conversation. She had already rejected the idea of telling him she was pregnant, dismissing that plan as something her Queens neighbors would do. Anyway, all he would do is write out a sizable check for an abortion and move on. He probably had insurance for shit like that. So, for the first time with him, she decided not to act and to just present him with her true self. She let all her guards down, she had nothing to lose at this point, and let her inner vulnerability—uncovered and unadjusted—shine through.

First she brought her hand to his knee, but he did not acknowledge this by stroking it as he had done in the past. It felt foolish now, but she would not allow it to throw her. She looked at him straight on.

"I don't care if you don't love me," she said at last.

He was taken aback by her directness. "Things between us happened too fast," he said. "It was right after my daughter died, and I'm not sure what I was feeling."

Oh, no! She knew the "I'm confused bit" very well. She had used it herself so many times in the past. She wasn't about to let him kiss her off that easily. She leaned her face forward and half closed her beautiful blue eyes, hauling out all the Mikki tricks. She needed them now. *See me! See me!* said her sad eyes.

"I want more time with you," she said. "Maybe if we spent an entire week together—alone—we could sort out our feelings . . ."

He broke in. "I think we need some time away from each other." It was a statement. It was final.

How could she love such a moron, she wondered, still adoring him. Her feelings for him were so strong she felt that they had to reach him, move him, break him. He had to respond to them somehow. She tried again.

"You don't even know me, Jonathan. I haven't been able to be myself around you. You can be an intimidating man. You have to know that about yourself. Sometimes I get flustered. I don't know what to present to you. I lose sight of who I am. Give me another chance. Let me figure out which side of me to show you. I won't disappoint you, Jonathan."

It was, she knew, too honest. She was opening up her heart to him in a way that usually makes men run for the hills. But she realized that if she didn't say everything that she truly felt, while she had him in front of her, she would regret it later when she was reliving the scene in her head, as she was destined to do over and over again.

He was staring at her. She brought her wine glass to her lips, simply to give herself something to do. The wine only touched the tip of her tongue, but the sweet, sickly taste of it made her nauseous at once.

"I want you to be yourself with me, Mikki," he said. "But I'm going through a hard time in my life right now. Professionally. Personally. I just lost my daughter. I'm trying to decide where I'm going in the next phase of my life. And I can't handle being in a serious relationship. Not now."

She could not believe that he was pulling this shit with her. He was a world-famous filmmaker for God's sake! A genius. Couldn't he come up with something better than that? Didn't he at least have the tiniest bit of respect for her? Shit. Suddenly she saw herself clearly through his eyes. Unremarkable. Disposable. Even ridiculous. She felt used and cheap and stupid. She hated herself for kissing up to him and feeding his ego by playing the typical lovesick fool. She hated the idea of all the wasted time and emotions she had already invested in him. Most of all she hated Jonathan himself for seeing her as ordinary and replaceable, and for making her feel that way about herself. She removed her hand from his knee and leaned back in her seat. Her eyes caught fire and blazed ferociously at him. Her Queens accent, always so carefully hidden, came out . . . full force.

"Listen, Jonathan, let me put my cards on the table. I'm trying to be honest with you. Which is more than you could say for yourself. I'm not gonna let you treat me this way. Period. I don't know who the fuck you think you've been dealing with here, but it's not right. And you're not going to get away with it!"

He was so shocked to be spoken to in that tone of voice that for a moment he seemed confused and even frightened. But then his eyes glazed over and he stared at her coldly.

She continued. "You've broken my heart. I'm in pain. Big deal, I'll get over it. Give me six months or less, and I'll wonder how I ever loved you. But the movie, Jonathan. You promised me a chance to test for *Fame*, Jonathan! I wrote most of that screenplay. And I want my chance!"

"I'm afraid that's impossible, Mikki."

"Well, you could make the impossible happen!" she shouted. Then she caught herself and added softly. "Walk on water for me, baby!"

"I'm not going to make a scene with you, Mikki. Just listen to me. Calmly. Renée Zellweger has expressed an interest in that role."

"So? So what? That fucking bitch! Come on, Jonathan! I know you're not a complete asshole. What are you gonna do? Shoot the whole movie with a body double? She won't do the nudity required."

"Renée is a star, Mikki. Her name means something. People want her. People pay money to see her. She's considered the very best there is."

"By whom? A public who could be force-fed into believing anything they're told!"

"By the people who buy the tickets. You want to talk truths, Mikki. You're a nobody. Your name means nothing."

He may as well have been burning her with cigarettes and cutting her with razors, but she knew it was true. Mortally wounded now, the little girl returned, dying and looking for a compassionate soul to save her. "But Jonathan? Jon? This picture will make me a star. Can't you see that? You can create me. You can make me somebody."

"I'm sorry, Mikki, but I don't see it."

She grabbed onto both of his arms with incredible force. Never in her life did she have more at stake. Never had she been more desperate. "Believe in me!" she sobbed. "Believe in me!"

He shook her off. They stared at each other for several horrible seconds. She had bared everything to him now, and she was stripped of every last defense. She sat before him feeling tired and ugly and incredibly naked. She tried to put every last thing she had into her stare, all of her disappointments, all of her longings, all of her pain. She had nothing else to give. Perhaps Meryl Streep would have gotten on her knees.

"Look, Mikki," Jonathan said calmly. Her voice had been at a fever pitch; his voice brought the situation down. "I didn't mean to hurt you. You're a nice girl. I enjoyed you. I hope that you enjoyed me. But I never made you any promises. And it's over. Do you hear me? Whatever we had? It's over."

He leaned over and kissed her on the cheek and then he was gone. The kiss had an affect something like Novocain. Numbness started at the place on her cheek where his lips last touched her, then traveled quickly to quiet the agitated limbs of her body. "I'm numbing myself for protection," she heard herself say out loud. "I don't think that my body can take another rejection at the moment."

She sat there alone. Unable to move. Unable to feel. Hoping that this numb state would last, but knowing all the while that great pain was around the corner, stored in her fingertips and waiting to spread. What then? She probably could live with great pain for few weeks, but she had no more energy, no more drive. Eventually it would kill her. She had explored every avenue she could think of leading to fame, and she had given each one all she had. She felt as though she had been running a marathon and now lay gasping on the side of the road, with the finish nowhere in sight.

Suddenly Carla's ghost walked over and sat in Jonathan's vacated seat. Carla was real, but Mikki was not surprised or frightened in the least. She looked around the club. It was emptying. The hour must be late, she thought. A startled-looking old man was approaching from the bar. He came toward them, unkempt—tie askew, shirt half out of his pants, everything wrinkled. Carla waved him away, he turned around and left, and she leaned forward as if to speak. Mikki met Carla's eyes. "You came from nowhere and that's where you'll fucking die," Carla said quietly, and then she sat back and smiled.

Mikki returned the smile. "Oh, Carla," she said wearily, "you always were a fool. Don't you know anything? You've won. I'm already dead."

47.

THE LAST TIME I really talked to Mikki was the night she unexpectedly dropped by my apartment to give me her diaries and notebooks. I was in no mood for her. Frankly, I was in a lousy mood. I had been sullen and depressed since my argument with God several nights prior.

Just before Mikki had arrived, while furiously staring at myself in my bathroom mirror, I had noticed a piece of hair out of place on the right side of my head. No matter how much I combed or brushed it down, I couldn't get it to look right—the rebel hair kept sticking out. It became an obsession. I took out my hair blower and tried to heat it into submission. Soon my whole head of hair was a mess. I decided I must cut it. I tried to snip off the offending piece that started it all. It was terrible. The scissors I had weren't right for cutting hair, and I really had to fight to cut through the unruly lock. With that piece gone, the left side looked uneven. I snipped. Now the back looked bushy compared to the sides. I found a hand mirror and started snipping at the back. I went berserk. I went into a haircutting frenzy. I must have blacked out for a minute because when I snapped out of it I was standing in a pile of dark hair in front of the mirror. I looked like Sinead O'Connor circa 1987, with sideburns. "I'm ruined!" I screamed out, just as my door buzzer rang.

"Yeah?" I said when I opened the door, without checking who it was first. I was not surprised to see Mikki, since I knew she'd just been dumped.

"Nice haircut. Can I come in?"

"Why not?" I said, stepping aside.

She didn't want a drink. She didn't want coffee. I had nothing to eat, and she rarely ate anymore anyway so I didn't even bother to ask. It was obvious something was on her mind, so I simply sat across from her and waited. I had expected that when I eventually saw her again, as I knew I would, she would be haughty and world-weary because of her affair with Jonathan Christaldi. I thought that she would flaunt the fact that she had, even for a brief time, attracted one of the most famous and desirable men in the world. But what sat before me was a very sad women. Lonely and betrayed. Mikki, my Mikki. She looked older—tired and gaunt and not exactly beautiful. Her voice was flat and void of any inflection or energy.

"Do you believe the balls God has, to pull this shit on me?" she asked.

"I don't think you can really blame God in your situation," I said. "It seems to me it's more Jonathan Christaldi's fault."

"That's who I meant," she said. We were both silent for a moment. It was easy for both of us to take out our frustration on God. He seemed to be working through the people we came in contact with. Then she slid a small stack of leather-bound notebooks, date books, and telephone books across the table toward me. "I want you to have these," she said.

"What is it?" I asked.

"My life," she said. "or what's left of it." She stared at the table and traced patterns on the wood with her finger. "Actually it's just my diaries and things. Ideas I once had and stuff. It might make a good story someday. Maybe . . . after I'm dead. You can write it."

"Give me a break, Mikki. You're not thinking of . . ."

"Killing myself? No. I'm too much of a coward for that. I don't want to end up that much of a cliché. But, then, I don't expect to live very long anyway."

"So, why don't you hold onto them? Wait a year or two, and you can base a screenplay on your earlier life."

She let out a bitter little laugh. "I already wrote it. Renée Zellweger should be excellent in the part."

"It's not definite that he's using her," I said. I had read the day before that there was some kind of several-months delay in production and that Renée probably would no longer be available for the part.

"It doesn't matter. The point is, he's not using me. At least not anymore."

"And what are your plans now?"

"We could kill him," she said simply, and then laughed again with total, tasteless, abandon. She added: "I've done enough. I've seen enough. I've lived enough." And I smiled at her. She had reached the place where I was living.

"But you have to go on."

"Do I?" she asked.

I had no answers. There was a long silence, and then she looked at me and said, "I always thought that if they made a movie out of our lives it would have been a love story."

I felt my body clench. There were tears in my throat. Was it my fault that we never tried to make it together? Had I let opportunities go? Was it my fear, or my knowledge that we would only end up hurting each other?

She grabbed my hand across the table. "So many times," she said softly, "when I'm trying to sleep at night, I grab my pillow and make believe it's you."

I still could not speak. I wanted to tell her how used she always made me feel. How I felt she only turned to me when she was alone. How angry I was when she was sleeping with Justin Landis. How hurt I was when she allowed herself to fall in love with Jonathan Christaldi. But I let it all go. What good would it have done now? We were both defeated. There was no need to kick her now that she was down.

"Marry me, Mario," she said abruptly. And there was a desperation in her voice that I don't think I could have imagined.

There was still a giant lump in my throat and the tears had spread to my eyes. I held her hand and shook my head sadly. I couldn't have her this way. I already felt like a loser. I didn't need her around me forever, reminding me that I was a last resort.

There was another long pause. She let go of my hand and stood up. "Well, we'll always have each other," she said brightly and ruffled the top of my shorn head. "We'll always be friends."

I walked her to the door. She made a motion toward the pile of notebooks she had left. "If anything ever happens to me, do something with them," she said, "that way my name might live on." And then she added, "I'm sorry that I got you involved in all of this mess. There was a time I thought that it would help us."

At last I felt as if I could speak. "It wasn't your fault. I thought it would help, too."

We, of course, were talking about Carla. "I always felt so terrified, no matter what I did. I thought if I did something like that it would make me less afraid."

She opened the door and stood in the hall. We stood there looking at each other for several seconds . . . or was it minutes? She had on a white sheath dress that fit her body closely. It was the same garment that in a few hours would be cut off her body, drenched in blood and mud and semen. She walked down the hall and did not look back at me. If she had turned around, I probably would have told her I loved her. Ran off with her. Gotten married. She didn't turn. I closed the door. I told myself I would call her the next day, and presently opened a bottle of scotch. I would do my drinking alone tonight.

She, however, was on her way to a bar called Walkers and into the annals of history.

48.

SHE WOKE UP lying naked on a filthy bed in a lonely, one-night-stand hotel room. The mattress, where the sheet had been pulled away, was covered with faded yellow stains, their edges rimmed with brown. She traced the patterns with her finger, only vaguely disgusted, but overcome by a welcome numbness. She was trying to think. Trying to think of what to do next. She had not planned on going to bed with him, and now she certainly wished she hadn't. But isn't that always the way? She knew that he thought she was stupid. She also knew that he wasn't a movie producer and probably didn't even work in film development, like he said he did.

"You must be an actress," he had said to her at the bar.

She almost laughed. *This* man thinks that I'm an asshole, she was thinking.

"What makes you say that?" she asked instead.

"I could tell by the way you carry yourself. I'm in the business. I know an actress when I see one."

She had heard lines like that many, many times in the past. Always, they turned out to be just lines. Why was it always so painfully obvious after going to bed with them? By now, she always felt like she was being betrayed. Yes, she knew better. But he'd gotten her at a weak moment. After the past few months, she needed to hear these things. Justifying it to herself later, she would say that there was always the possibility that one night the guy really would turn out to be a somebody. Somebody who would truly see that "certain something" in her. Her specialness. There had to be another Justin Landis. Another Jonathan Christaldi. Just one more. One more chance! She could make it work this time! It wasn't too late.

Anyway, she didn't lose anything by going to bed with him (but uh-oh, she didn't ask him to use a condom, even though she had one in her purse. At the time it seemed awkward, and she didn't want him to think that she was the kind of girl who carried condoms around with her). Shit. Now she had to worry about that for a while. The hell with it. She'd worry about it later when she needed something to think about to make the subway ride home bearable.

Carefully she stepped out of bed. She didn't want to wake him up, but she needed some light to dress by, so she switched on the television set with the sound off and the room was instantly overcome with muted gray and blue shadows. She looked around for her pantyhose and, after a while, found them entwined in the sheets on the floor. They had a huge run in them, but she hated flesh-colored pantyhose anyway, so she decided to leave them. She wondered if he would take them home, hide them from his wife, and use them in sexual fantasies. She smiled. Not slyly. Sadly. She liked the idea. It would mean he found this incident worth remembering. And he'd probably never have another encounter like this one. This was his last call, baby.

She looked at him lying there on the bed, big and stupidly placid, and she could not believe that she had once felt anything for him. One second you're thinking that you can't get enough, the next, after it's finished, you're thinking about the long ride home and how you need a shower. Sex was nothing after it was over.

After they had left the bar together and she saw him in the hotel elevator, it became apparent that bar light had been kind to him. Fluorescent elevator light was not. He had fleshy pouches under his eyes and his complexion was blotchy—ruddy. The kind of skin people sometimes get in middle age after a lifetime of drinking. His hair wasn't as thick as it looked in the dark, and it was combed and sprayed to disguise the fact that it was thinning. But this was part of the reason she was attracted to him in the first place. The turn-on was in the fact that she was the hottest-looking girl he'd had in a long time. The kind of girl he fantasized about while cruising the

Internet looking at porn star Web sites. But here she is. Live and in person. One on one. An incredible star in his life, even for only one night. That's what her passion for him was all about. It was an older man fetish she sometimes indulged.

After Jonathan Christaldi, she felt insecure going to bed with gorgeous specimens, winners with perfect bodies. It was too much of a distraction, wondering if she was living up to expectations. She became aware of her age. She rarely felt that she was beautiful enough, although she was aware that other people found her very beautiful indeed, and she found strength in that.

Catching sight of herself in the mirror, she was taken by surprise. There was something decadently beautiful about the scene. She was fetching, standing there nude, in utter disarray in the bluish half-light. Her dark-blonde hair fell casually down to her shoulders. A few strands were in her mouth. For a moment she felt like what had just happened had not just happened. It was as if she were merely an actress in an art film playing the part of a lonely girl who had just had sex in a sleazy hotel room. She watched herself fasten her bra, and she was not herself but an actress playing a part.

If the snoring man on the bed, whose name he had told her was Larry, had been awake she would have told him her number was in the process of being changed so she couldn't be reached. She would have told him that she had to be up early in the morning for a modeling job. She would have told him that she hoped to get a cab. None of this was true, but that wouldn't have crossed her mind. She had already told him that she was a graduate of The American Academy of Dramatic Arts, that she played small parts on several daytime soaps, that she was twenty-one years old. Lying had become a way of life for her.

She stepped outside the hotel into the night. Several deep breaths brought reality back. This whole incident had left her suddenly feeling empty and nauseous and very weak. She had had a feeling that she would hate herself the moment that he withdrew from her and the act was over, and that turned out to be true. She made a vow that this would never happen again, but this wasn't the first time she'd done that.

The train ride home stretched out endlessly before her. She walked quickly toward the station. Distance was a relief. The farther away she got from the scene of the encounter, the less real it seemed. After she got home, took a shower, brushed her teeth with peroxide and water, and crawled under her covers, she would never have to think about it again. She'd been disgusted with herself so many times before it was something she could brush off fairly easily. And she had buried worse secrets under those covers.

She looked around the city with perfect concentration. At this time of the night she was always at her most sensitive. End of night, just before the sun comes up, still dark. The midtown streets were virtually empty, except for an occasional vagrant. That didn't bother her. She was never afraid to walk down late-night Manhattan sidewalks. At this hour New York seemed a little less cold to her and she felt a little more securely in her heart that one day she would conquer this unconquerable place. She hugged herself tightly and looked up over the buildings. The city seemed to be a gigantic movie set left standing useless and discarded after some multimillion-dollar sci-fi spectacle had finished filming. The sky was a black backdrop.

She couldn't help but wonder what she had done wrong. If she had made different choices, would her life have gone differently and would she be famous by now? She was feeling sorry for herself again. Usually she found comfort in the moon, her only friend during these lonely hours, but tonight she felt judged by it because it had a "here we go again" attitude; cold and humorless and indifferent to her mood. The wind, which felt artificially manufactured, pushed its way between buildings and through her hair, tossing newspapers around in a dreamy slow motion that lent an air of unbelievablity to the scene. It made her feel a little religious. The hurt had arrived.

She closed her eyes and hugged herself tighter in desperation. What can I say, God? It's here—the pain. You commit a murder, you pay the price, right? Please, forgive me, she said. Please. Okay, it was corny and melodramatic, but it seemed like the right line, and the moment was sincere; she was still feeling the last effects of alcohol before the inevitable headache, and as she turned the corner toward the subway that would take her home to Queens, she hoped someone, somewhere heard.

———

SHE SAT ON the subway bench and waited for the train. God, she hoped it wouldn't take long to come. She glanced at the clock. 3:35. Even if it came right now, it would be light out by the time she got home. Every part of her body ached. She could feel her menstrual period just beginning. Oh bed, bed! It seemed so far away. Everything in her life had led to this one moment. It was a destiny she would have never believed. She was still unknown.

"I'm tired," Mikki said, as she sat on the subway platform bench. She hadn't meant to speak out loud.

Down at the other end of the subway platform some mad Brazilian, drinking tequila out of a bottle wrapped in a paper bag, was singing a native song in a contemptible, passionate treble. He was looking around proudly to see if anyone was watching his performance. Grotesque Spanish men, belching, leering, swearing, screaming, passed around beer in plastic cups. Welcome to New York. Welcome to modern times.

———

A GROWING GUST of air signaled that a train was pulling into the station. 3:48. She stepped into the subway car, which at this hour doubled as a welfare shelter for the homeless. Sleeping bums. Sweltering heat. Coughing all around. An incubator for sickness and disease. The subway was her home away from home. A few normal citizens were interspersed, and they made faces, too, from the stench. Someone had vomited. Some of the homeless were mean and angry as a result of life, and there was a constant threat about them that made them dangerous and unpredictable. She took a seat as far away from people as possible. "E to Queens," the conductor's voice boomed.

THE TRAIN TORTURED its way down the subway tracks, crawling, clawing, a dying animal, laboring slowly but steadily for several seconds, then sputtering forward with sudden, spastic jerks. A mournful sigh rose up from her chest, deep and heartfelt. Unbeknownst to her, in a few hours she would be on the front page of every newspaper in the country. But the moment was now. And time dragged on and on and on. And she was getting nowhere. And the stench . . . and the trash all around her . . . and her period ready to begin . . . and what she had done tonight . . .and the mad Brazilian's horrible singing . . . and the past five years . . . and the heat . . . the incredible heat . . . all rushed toward her and hung around her head like a thickening black smog, filling up her nostrils, torturing her, strangling her with the realities of her own failures.

Then the train stopped.

49.

"A RED SIGNAL is holding us up here a few feet away from the station. We will move as soon as we can," the conductor said, finally giving the trapped passengers some explanation for the long delay, overpronouncing each syllable, trying to sound intelligent. But there were strong undercurrents of stupidity in his voice. And the calmness and the slowness of his delivery of this message starkly juxtaposed her broiling emotions.

This was not possible. Not again. Not again. Stuck here? Stuck! With these people! And now she knew, it would always be this way. She bowed her head and felt a moment of pain so sharp and intricate that it reached the extremes of torture. It started up deep inside her, slowly expanding, and this feeling swelled so big and powerful that she wished she could vomit it out of her body. But it was, she knew, part of her now. Unreleasable. And she didn't know where to turn for help.

Everything and everyone before had failed her. She tried to think of a time when life was not a fight or a struggle or an excuse. Her face became so flushed that she could feel the heat exuding from her pores. She opened her compact and studied her reflection as if it were the face of a stranger. She searched hard for signs of age—for lines. She was very tired, and she could just begin to see the places in her face where the wrinkles would start. She could not see how she could go on living like this. So lonely. So very, very lonely. And empty of fight.

GET ME OUT OF HERE!, her mind screamed. And, as if to answer her, a new voice boomed over the intercom system with a brand-new excuse: "Due to mechanical difficulties, we are being held here." Then the voice went on to explain that when the train pulled into the station, they would have to transfer to a different subway line in order to get to Queens. This was important information to anyone who wanted to get home, but the person conveying it could barely speak English.

She buried her face in her hands and stayed that way for quite a long while. Her period, she was certain, would begin any minute. The mad Brazilian started singing again, this time louder than before. The sounds of the other passengers blurred together with the Brazilian's song, then faded to nothingness. She waited and waited. As usual it was the helplessness and hopelessness of it all that caused her anguish.

At last the train started inching slowly toward the next station. But once it arrived there, it simply stopped, with the doors still closed. There were no messages or explanations forthcoming, as was the norm. But surprisingly, she did not feel rage or despair any longer. On the contrary, all the bottled-up emotion left her in one sudden rush, and the hopelessness and absurdity of her life hit her with stunning clarity. That formal feeling after great pain, which Emily Dickinson talks about in one of her poems, took over her, and at last the answer came to her and brought with it great relief. It was finished. Time to give up.

The only thing left to do was to give up the struggle and face reality. Reality. Her eyes opened to the facts for the first time. This is real life. In real life not everybody always gets what she wants. There have probably been thousands of girls, millions, who have wanted fame just as badly as she did. And who worked at it just as hard, or maybe harder. And had just as much talent, or maybe more talent. And they never made it. Millions of women had failed to succeed. Women whom men had told were beautiful. So what did they do? Suicide? Yes, that was an option. She was a loser, so why not take the loser's way out? But some women did survive. Maybe she could, too. She could reevaluate and restructure her plans.

At last the subway doors opened. She wasn't even sure how much time had passed. Vacantly she filed out of the subway car with the rest of the losers.

Okay, to be honest, fame is out of the question (and the thought that she no longer had to fight for it felt like a five-hundred-pound weight lifted from her shoulders). So why bother to stay in New York? Yes, why bother. She didn't have to stay in the game and take it, like some modern-day Christ. New York is only for the very ambitious, the climbers, the backstabbers. Or the very successful. But not for someone who was leaving the game. She could leave. She could leave and find a small town. Maybe she could teach. How about teaching acting to young children in a small town? She imagined herself in a stylish apartment in the Midwest. She'd teach at a local elementary school. The students would call her Miss Britten. Perhaps, eventually, they would grow to love her. Each new season she'd direct a play—*The Wizard of Oz, West Side Story.* They'd all go out for ice cream after the performances. For her there would be no more auditions. No more thumbing through the pages of *Backstage.* No more competing.

Oh, oh! She was getting excited. The lines would come, and her body would spread, and no one would notice. They would love her for her tenderness, her good ideas, her lovely heart. So what if she never became a famous actress? Lots of people live their lives without ever knowing happiness. At least she could bring some to others. At least she would be appreciated.

She walked quickly toward the subway steps. No use waiting now for the next train. Only God knows when it would come. It was better to get a cab. Soon it would be morning. *I want to call Mario and tell him the news,* she thought.

She stepped outside the station into the night air and it all felt pretty damned wonderful. *You see! You see!* her mind reasoned, *it makes much more sense to be sensible. What good does it do being angry all the time?*

The city was eerily deserted. She thought she might be able to get a cab back to Queens on the avenue. She headed down a dark side street, taking rapid steps, her heels clacking noisily, echoing into the blackness. Safety was only minutes away but suddenly she was frightened. The street she found herself on was unusually empty because of ongoing construction. Parts of the street were ripped up and areas of sidewalk were blocked off. It happens that way sometimes. It's one of the fascinating things about the city. The mystery. In Manhattan, still, a bit of bad timing and one wrong turn could get you in trouble, and, unexpectedly, you find yourself in danger. Had she not been drinking, had she not been so tired, she wouldn't have made this mistake.

To distract herself from fear she wondered how Justin would react to her news she was leaving. With relief probably. Lately she couldn't help but feel that Justin, although he had at one point had great faith in her, had not become disappointed in her and her failed career. Now at least she was doing something positive.

She noticed the men, as she passed them, from the corner of her eye, and her heart suddenly pounded wildly. There were three of them, huddled in a storefront doorway—covered in shadows—and they seemed to be smoking something, crack probably. She wasn't up on those kinds of street drugs. Although her mind drank in their images for less than a second, she became aware that her presence had made them instantly alert. She saw that they were young. She saw that they were dangerous. But it was their laughing that bothered her the most: hysterical, inhuman, out of control.

Why didn't the city do something about these fucking monsters? Why were they allowed to roam the streets, destroying the quality of life in their paths? She had seen them everywhere, pissing on corners, spitting on subway tracks, but had never been a victim of them. Until now, perhaps . . . inner alarms were going off. Reality check! How incredibly stupid to be walking down a dark side street in Manhattan at this hour. Certainly she would never do it again. She quickened her stride. But now one of them was beside her, keeping up with her pace. She kept her eyes forward. There was nobody in sight. Her eyes focused on a smoking sewer at the end of the street. If she could make it to the corner, to the avenue, there would be traffic; she'd be all right.

"What are you lookin' at?" the thug asked.

She said nothing, hoping that if she completely ignored the situation it would simply go away.

"I said, what are you lookin' at?"

Better make some sort of reply. "I wasn't looking at you," she said.

"You're lookin' at me now."

It was no use. Something terrible was going to happen. There was only one thing left for her to do. Although she really didn't think that she'd be able to get away (she had on heels), she started to run.

"Get her! Grab her!"

There was an incredible sense of unreality. Where were the cameras? Would the cops from *Cops* appear with a camera crew and throw the culprits up against the car? She started screaming, "Help! Help me!" Even as the words left her lips they sounded absurd. Could this really be happening?

But one of them was on her immediately. His hand clamped around her mouth like a steel claw. He was dragging her back toward the other two. Soon the three of them surrounded her, grabbing her, stroking her, hitting her. The hand was unclamped from her mouth—a knife was instantly produced in its place.

"Please," she whispered, "please," and she did not realize that it was the knife she was addressing, not the person holding it. He cut a slit on her left cheek to prove that he meant business.

Across the street she saw someone passing. She did not stop to think and on reflex she called out, "Help! Please! Call the police! Call the police!" The person across the street started running. She didn't blame him; she would have done the same. Still though, she hoped that when he reached the corner he would at least call the police.

Now fists were being pounded into her face. Everything was

happening so quickly. The hand clamped around her mouth again—she couldn't be trusted—and she was being dragged into a small alcove in a boarded-up storefront. As she was being dragged, they continued to beat her about her head and body. One of them was using a lead pipe. But she was a human being! Besides the pain, the thing that shocked her the most was their capacity for violence without feeling. Her life had been so sad, and yet they thought nothing of destroying her even further.

And they beat her and dragged her and forced their fists into her face. Her lovely face. The only thing she ever had. The only thing that had ever got her anything, which in essence was nothing.

She fought fiercely for her life. She fought with all the bottled-up hate and hostility that had been building up in her for the past ten years. She scratched and tore and lashed with murderous rage—she wanted to leave her mark for the police. Her legs and arms were strong from years of aerobics and dancing, and if it had been only one of them, she was sure she could have gotten away. But the three of them overpowered her. She could feel blood run down her face. She could taste blood in her mouth and feel tiny fragments from a broken back tooth. She wondered how bad the overall damage was. If they killed her, she supposed it wouldn't matter what kind of a ruin was left. So this was the climax to the story—she was to be a *Cold Case File* rather than a *Pretty Woman*.

The alcove was completely dark and drenched in stench. Vomit and urine. Her own probably.

Their voices were a mumble of words: "Bitch . . . tits . . . like a pig . . . blood." Laughter. Mumble, mumble. She couldn't understand them. It made her angry. *Oh, shut up!*

There were certain things she could feel. A knife was cutting off her clothes. She was being held down, and warm blood was pouring down her legs, her arms.

"Don't," she moaned. One of them entered her. It seemed inevitable. For a while she mercifully lost consciousness. But then she heard him speak.

"She ain't so much."

No, she thought. I am not.

Laughter.

"My turn!"

When the second one mounted her, she cried. Her life would probably be made into a Lifetime Television for Women special. Luckily she had left her diaries with Mario, and he could sell the rights. Presently she cried for the actress who would play her, the crew who would be moved by the performance, and the millions of viewers who would see the movie over the years. And somewhere in there she even cried for herself and her own unhappy life.

By the time the third one entered her, she was in and out of consciousness. She was numb. She could feel bits of life escaping from her with each tiny breath. Somewhere in the back of her mind she wanted to live. This wasn't supposed to happen tonight. She wanted to call Justin and tell him her news. She wanted to help children. She wanted to start over. *Oh, irony, leave me alone!*

The third man completed his task and got up off of her. A few quick jabs with the knife to her abdomen to finish the job and the three of them took off. She felt nothing. *It wasn't much longer after you, Carla*, she whispered. *You win again, bitch.* Her head turned to the right. Through the doorway she could see the dawning sky, a muted blue. A bright red light loomed in the distance. *That must be the sun*, she thought. And then she closed her eyes.

FROM *THE NEW YORK DAILY NEWS*: MODEL FOUND BEATEN AND RAPED—A beautiful 20-year-old model was found beaten and raped early this morning in a storefront on West 53rdt Street. Three stab wounds were in her abdomen.

Mikki Britten, once a top model for EYE Model Management, was rushed to the hospital where emergency surgery was performed. Doctors said she was in serious condition.

An early-morning jogger reported that she saw the body in a vacant alcove. Carol Kearns, 31, a legal secretary, said she was jogging down the deserted side street at about 6:30 A.M. when she saw something unusual in a boarded-up storefront.

"I thought it was a mannequin at first," Kearns said. "After I crossed the street, I saw it was a woman. Even in the shadows I could see she was badly beaten. Her dress was torn and soaked with blood. Her breasts and pubic area were exposed. At first I thought she was dead, but then I heard her moan."

So Kearns started running for help. "I would have gotten help sooner, but I didn't have my cell with me and I couldn't find a phone that worked."

Police and medical workers arrived at the scene a few minutes later.

Steven M. Brocco of the Manhattan North Detective Squad said that there were no suspects at this point but that an investigation is under way. "We're waiting until Miss Britten is well enough to speak to us," he said.

Britten has been modeling for the past five years and recently embarked on an acting career.

"Wonderful things were starting to happen to her," said a booking agent for EYE Model Management, who wanted to remain anonymous. "She just recently started moving away from modeling and was heading toward a career in commercials and films. She had a bright future in front of her."

Supermodel Jana Janelow, 23, another model from the agency said she spoke to Miss Britten early yesterday evening. "Mikki was in wonderful spirits," Miss Janelow said. "She told me she was meeting a friend. I warned her to be careful. I always worry about Mikki because she usually takes the subway home late at night from Manhattan."

Britten is a Queens resident. A bartender at Walker's Bar, who knows Britten but asked not to be named, said, "She was in here last night. She stayed for a couple of hours and left with a man she had been talking to. It was about 1:00 A.M."

Police said they are hoping the man, who is described as being dark haired and in his mid to late 40s, will come forward and give any information that may help them with the case.

Ms. Britten, who sustained three stab wounds, lacerations and fractured bones in her face, and bruised ribs, is at Metropolitan Hospital. Doctors said they are optimistic that she will recover.

FROM *THE NEW YORK POST*: CITY PRAYS FOR MODEL—Roses and cards mark the boarded-up storefront where beautiful model Mikki Britten was brutally raped Thursday night.

"We're praying for you, Mikki," was painted on a white cardboard sign surrounded by an arrangement of flowers and cards. Passersby frequently stopped to look at the arrangement and to offer silent prayers. Usually hardened New Yorkers have been touched by her courage and have opened up their hearts and embraced the twenty-two-year-old stunner.

"I feel as if this has happened to one of my own children," said a tearful Rita Perez as she crossed herself and gazed at the makeshift shrine. "She's a lovely girl. God bless her."

FROM *THE NEW YORK DAILY NEWS*: MODEL MAY MODEL AGAIN, DOCS SAY—Stunning top model Mikki Britten may still have a chance to resume her career, said her Manhattan doctor, Martin Pearl. "We have every reason to believe that her facial wounds will not be noticeable. It's the psychological scarring that this crime may leave that will really be the tough obstacle for this courageous young woman to overcome."

Pearl said that only time could tell the true amount of damage she will be left with. "She has some lacerations on her face and a cut on her left cheek that required thirteen stitches. Her nose is fractured and there is a hairline fracture in the upper cheekbone. She also has a mild concussion. But luckily no facial nerves have been damaged."

Although her face is swollen and discolored right now, Doctor Pearl said that, "In my opinion very little or no plastic surgery will be required. Most of the trouble is with bruising and tiny fractures, not to the surface of the face. There will be slight scarring from the gnash on her cheek—all facial wounds leave scars, but if the scar is very deep and noticeable, it can be greatly reduced by sanding."

The 24-year-old ash-blonde beauty was under contract with EYE Modeling Agency and sometimes commanded fees of up to $5,000 a day.

Pearl said, "Of course we'll have to wait and see how her individual healing process works, but she is young and healthy and we do have every hope that there will be a minimum of scarring." Ms. Britten is recovering at Metropolitan Hospital where her condition is said to be improving.

FROM *NEWSWEEK*: MIKKI'S PERSONALITY—MAGIC!—Jana Janelow is one of Mikki Britten's closest friends. They often went on modeling assignments together and hung out in glamorous New York nightclubs. But it's the beauty underneath the glittery surface that Britten's friends talk about more than anything else, Janelow said yesterday.

"Mikki is the girl that everybody falls in love with," Janelow, 23, told reporters. "She has a magic that attracts all people, men, women, grandmothers . . . even animals. Everybody loves Mikki."

"She was on her way to becoming a very big star," said Laird Payne, head of Payne Modeling Agency. "She came up to my agency over a year ago and I wanted to sign her at once, but she ended up going with EYE Management instead. She has a glow that just draws you in, and you want to be around her."

The profession in which Mikki Britten chose to make her mark is a tough one, filled with the world's most ambitious climbers and "the knives come flying from all directions" said one insider. But somehow amongst such hard-edged people Britten was able to retain her original softness and still fight her way to the top.

Dori Isaacs, another model Britten has worked with, said, "It's more than just her face and body that gives Mikki her power over people. Her personality is magnetic and she knows how to work it. She uses the assets that God gave her to mesmerize a lot of successful men. She was always in demand. She's a girl with a lot of facets to her personality."

MIKKI BRITTEN'S COMPOSITE CARD: (As printed in the *New York Post*): HAIR: Ash Blonde. EYES: Blue. HEIGHT: 5'7" WEIGHT: 115. BUST: 35. WAIST: 23. HIPS: 34.

AS THE NEWS headlines continued and the rumors flew, more and more people jumped on the bandwagon hoping to get in on the action. After the image of the poor defenseless woman ceased to thrill, the papers took up more sensational angles. Shadowy friends and boyfriends, whom Mikki had never mentioned and whom are never written about in her diaries, crawled out of the woodwork to give their opinions on her character, or rather the opinions they thought the press wanted to hear. Some people who had been overshadowed by her or slighted, or jealous, used the media as the ultimate revenge and told stories. People who didn't know her at all or who met her once or twice exaggerated their involvement. Everyone wanted a piece of Mikki now.

The woman who was on the mind of every person in the country lay quietly unaware in a hospital bed.

While Mikki lay in the hospital, her scars healing and bruises fading, I figured it was time that I do something to start mending my own battered life. It was very apparent that when she was released from the hospital her life would be very different—at least for a while. I didn't want to find myself in the same situation I had always been in. Time for me to put on a new face, too.

I hadn't been exercising and I'd been eating poorly, and I could feel some fat around my middle. I thought: *I wish I could unwrap myself and reinvent myself over in a new package*. But when I thought of it, what good would it do? Even with my new coating, I'd still have the same amount of money, my same bank account, and the same names in my Rolodex who could help me: no one.

I had to try, at least for a normal life. I mean, find a job, maybe work my way up the ladder to some safe level, save some money. Who knows? Maybe even fall in love some day. With my background it would be difficult to start over, so I had to come up with some ruse. But being a prostitute makes you good at becoming something you're not.

What I did was not exceptionally clever. It was actually out of necessity. I had absolutely no work experience. What could I put on a resumé? So through a little research, I discovered a local entertainment magazine that had recently closed down in Los Angeles. I created a resumé that said I worked in the editorial department of that magazine for five years. Good thinking, right? There was no company to call, no boss to check with. My cover letter began, "I just recently returned to New York after five successful years working in the editorial department at *LA Now*." I went on to talk about how I would be an asset to any publication—that I was sharp, clever, fearless. Just to make it more realistic, I wrote up several movie reviews, restaurant reviews, and I even faked a couple of celebrity profiles. Even though I've never been to the West Coast, I polished these pieces until they gleamed—ready to be published in the glossiest of glossies. Ready to be shown as proof that I indeed had some talent.

I started emailing out my cover letter and resumé to New York publications, PR firms, and advertising agencies. I sent out dozens a day. I was offered less than ten interviews. Small publications would call. I'd get very excited. Here was my chance! The first magazine was a home-decorating publication. A big, expensive, glossy thing that came out every other month. The position called for little more than a receptionist. So what? I was game. I have a good voice. A neat appearance. A pleasant demeanor. I could endear myself to the editorial staff! Eventually get a better position. Everyone has to start somewhere.

I interviewed with a mature and lovely French woman. We seemed to hit it off. Our banter was lively. I thought it was a shoo-in. After all, it was basically answering phones, accepting packages, and maybe a little proofreading here and there. The French woman brought the editor-in-chief into our meeting. She was a plain, plump blonde girl. I say "girl" because she looked to be about twenty-two or twenty-three. Perhaps Daddy had some publishing connections when she graduated from college with a degree in English Literature? Journalism? What difference does it make? She is where she is, and I am where I am. *These are our roles. Accept it! Do your best.*

She was wearing the kind of sweater that used to be called a "twin set," baby pink, embroidered with tulips. She asked me a few questions, but every time I attempted to answer, her face blushed a hot, deep red. What? What was this? What did I say? What was I doing? The girl couldn't look me in the eye. It was as if this Pollyanna could flip through scenes of my life on a whim and was lingering at the most sordid, disgusting things I had ever done. I sat smiling, discombobulated, distracted, ridiculous, as I tried to chat on about my qualifications as a receptionist. Needless to say I never heard from the company. Some other voice is answering their phones. Some other body accepts their packages.

A FEW OTHER job interviews came my way. They all started off with promise. During each, I convinced myself I was doing well and this would be the one I would get.

I would always go through a series of interviews within the company. I'd meet with a low-level employer, charm them, and then I'd be brought over to meet a higher-up. I'd pass that interview, too, and I'd go up and up thinking *Whew, maybe I'm going to make it.* But eventually someone near the very top of the company ladder would recognize that unlikable thing in me. That "thing" I personally was never able to identify, isolate, and quarantine. Usually the higher-up was another gay man in my age range, and he would zero in on the "thing" before the handshake and I suddenly knew it was going to be a "no."

FROM THE *NEW YORK DAILY NEWS*: NEW MOTIVES PROBED IN ATTACK ON MODEL— Possible hostility between model Mikki Britten and a former boyfriend may have led to her assault, investigators said yesterday.

Interviews with acquaintances and co-workers suggest that a spurned lover may have set up the attack.

"She pursues men, and she pursues them persistently and aggressively," a source said yesterday. Britten was recently involved with film director Jonathan Christaldi. "She uses influential men to get ahead and then disposes of them," a redheaded model, who asked not to be named, said. "When you treat people that way, sooner or later you're going to get yourself in trouble."

"Many people in the fashion industry have been coming forward with information about Ms. Britten's social life," a law enforcement source said. "Acquaintances have been talking about the many men in her life. Right now we're following all leads."

"We're looking at this from every angle," said Detective Joseph Campbell. "It's possible that an obsessed boyfriend might have set up the attack."

Close friends and family members describe Mikki Britten as being "vulnerable," "gentle," and "shy." But in other places, particularly in some trendy New York bars and clubs, she's viewed as being "troubled," and even more often, "manipulative."

"She's very insecure," said an unnamed man who claims to be her ex-boyfriend. "I think that's what makes her reach out to a lot of different people. She's trying to fill a lot of different voids. But she doesn't use people. If anything, it's the other way around."

Supermodel Jana Janelow, who calls herself a "close friend" of Britten's, seemed angry and shaken when reporters questioned her about the possible linkage between Britten's social life and the assault. "It's ludicrous to suggest that Mikki in any way was asking for, or deserved, to be raped and beaten. When will the media stop putting women victims on trial and start putting the blame where it belongs—on the people who committed the crime?"

JONATHAN CHRISTALDI (To *Entertainment Weekly*): "That she was uneducated, too sensitive, too eager to please, were all immediately apparent to me. But there was a truthfulness about her that was refreshing and that I haven't seen in anyone before or since."

FROM *PEOPLE* MAGAZINE: WHO IS MIKKI BRITTEN?—Mikki Britten is probably a name that few people remembered or talked about a few weeks ago. True, she had been a successful model a few seasons back and was trying to launch a movie career, having been seen at several functions with movie maverick Jonathan Christaldi, but the honey-haired beauty was hardly a household name. That is until she was viciously raped and beaten by three thugs on a late-night Manhattan street. Suddenly Britten was on the front pages of newspapers around the world. The assault has brought her nationwide attention and a public clamoring for more information on the mysterious 26-year-old blonde. Britten, who will be released from the hospital later this week, has not yet given any interviews, and accounts of her life and just who she is vary widely, depending on who you talk to. She's been portrayed in the tabloids as either an innocent victim of the savage city or as a coldly calculating modern-day vixen who somehow courted tragedy with her sexuality.

Whatever the truth behind the headlines, Mikki Britten seems to have touched many lives. "Everyone is coming forward with a story about Mikki," said one of her boyfriends, a model named simply Fountain. "But it's very unlikely that any of those people know anything about her at all. She was a lot of different things to a lot of different people, but she rarely showed her true self to anyone. She was taking many different roads trying to reach her one goal." Just what was her main goal? "Fame," Fountain says without missing a beat.

No one seems to know what road led Britten to that boarded-up storefront where she was found badly beaten and near death on a warm summer morning, but the media is carefully examining each path. Her modeling photos are greatly in demand, and she's already getting TV and film offers. Her lovers, including tycoon Justin Landis, owner of the prestigious EYE Inc, the agency where Britten was employed, and film director Jonathan Christaldi, are sitting down for lengthy interviews in glossy magazines to discuss her, and the public never seems to stop speculating about her sex life. It looks like the assault will make her more famous than modeling or acting was ever likely to. But just who is Mikki Britten? I guess we'll have to wait until the lady is ready to speak.

50.

I, OF COURSE, could have had a moment in the spotlight. But I decided to keep quiet about Mikki. I knew she would be reading and watching all of these accounts from her hospital bed, where her family allowed no visitors. (Oh yes, in the glare of the media bonanza, the Brittens had materialized.) But I didn't want her to see me as one of the vultures circling her beaten body, even though I was very much aware that every word of it probably thrilled her.

In all likelihood I could have ended up on the front pages of the papers myself and been the star talk-show guest because, as you well know, I had her diaries. I could have made a mint selling them. Mikki was much hotter now than Victoria Sweetzer ever had been in the past twenty years. Especially after the *Post* ran a story that said in part, "A source close to the investigation of the rape and beating of 25-year-old 'it' girl Mikki Britten claims that police are searching for a 'sex diary' Britten kept, detailing her sexual encounters with big names like modeling tycoon Justin Landis and director Jonathan Christaldi."

Just who was the source of this juicy tidbit? I'm not certain—one of her modeling cronies she had drunkenly confided in during one late night shooting, no doubt. They gave comments to the press regularly. I myself remained silent. If I was loyal to her, she would be, I was hopeful, loyal to me.

It was hard. I continued to try to upgrade my life. The job interview that disappointed me the most was for an actual writing position at a Manhattan pop culture magazine. It was the job I was the most "right" for and the one I took the most seriously. I even went out and spent a small fortune on a new outfit. A sports jacket with a flesh-colored silk T-shirt to wear underneath. New shoes. The works. I wanted to look hip but not immature. I wanted to look expensive but not stuffy. The job entailed entertainment journalism, celebrity interviews, personality profiles, lifestyle pieces, reviews . . . that sort of thing.

As I headed midtown, I sat on the subway train thinking good thoughts. I was tired of negativity! I deserved some good things. Sure I did some terrible things in my life. Who hasn't? It's a little late for "what ifs." We are who we are, and we've done what we've done. And I wasn't such a bad guy.

As I was trying to keep my thoughts positive, an odor wafted over to me. The guy next to me had shit himself. He was sleeping, nicely dressed, probably drunk. I've smelled the smell of shit enough times to know he shit in his pants. You know the smell when you step in dog shit? That was it. But there was nothing on anyone's shoes. Oh, to be away from this!

I finally arrived at my destination, a nice building with a doorman staff in midtown Manhattan. As I waited in the reception area, I looked through the glass doors leading to the office space. The employees looked to be around my age. They were dressed in a similar fashion. Hooray! I chose correctly.

I met with an editorial assistant. As a test she asked me to write some snappy, zippy, clever descriptions and reviews of clubs, movies, restaurants, and happenings in New York. This was my territory. This is what I could do. I knew everything about Manhattan and could walk into a place and assess it in a few minutes in two lines. She said to take as long as I liked, writing about the last movie I saw, the last restaurant I ate in, and the last club I danced at. A half hour later I handed in my pieces.

As the editorial assistant read my stuff, I watched as she smiled several times. She looked up at me. She nodded. She acknowledged that I was good. "I want you to meet with our editor-in-chief," she said. She walked me to his office.

I met with a muscled, buzzed, T-shirted man of about forty-five.

He gave me the "once over" three times and sneered. Then there was the limp-fish handshake. Oh, no! He saw the "thing" in me. He glanced at my pieces of writing and put them aside.

He stared at me. Since he said nothing, I guessed he was waiting for me to entertain him. I babbled about the books I had recently read. My favorite magazines. How I could "take on the personality of any publication and add a little vibe of my own." He kept right on staring and I kept right on talking. I was hoping to hit on something, some target, some topic that would penetrate him. That would let him see me as the cool person I was. But he would not allow me in.

Finally, after a long pause, he asked, "If you were in my position, the editor-in-chief of a magazine—what would you do?" Before I could answer, he added: "Who would you hire to work for you."

I didn't think before replying. "I would hire people based entirely on their talent and qualifications. I wouldn't give people jobs solely because they were my friends or because I wanted to go to bed with them. I think recognizing talent is a talent. I feel that most talented people are passed over because of office politics and connections and rivalries and jealousies. I wouldn't let any of those things come into play. I'd only do what's best—what's most interesting and exciting—for the magazine and the company as a whole. That would be my job."

I talked too loudly. Too passionately. I am not a blasé person. That's part of the "thing" that alienates people. Someone who worked outside the office, perhaps an assistant, poked his head in and looked at me. He wanted to see who had made such an asinine speech.

The chief stood up and said, "Thanks for coming in." I walked out of his office feeling as if I've been kicked—and then I wandered around the office space, passing cubicles and conference rooms, until I found the reception area and the elevator leading me out.

"I want to work for you so bad I can taste and smell and feel it." I emailed him the minute I got home. I couldn't give up. I waited for days but there was no response.

Yes, I would have been good for the magazine. But maybe just a little too good. If he didn't hire me, it wasn't a disaster for the magazine. Letting me go wasn't the best choice for the company, but it wasn't his company. And there was someone else waiting for the next interview right at the door—ripe and juicy and bursting with mediocrity, who would fill the job just fine.

I DECIDED TO go to the hospital and wait out front on the day of Mikki's release. I figured the media would be there, but I hadn't been able to contact her and I figured she might want to see a familiar face. Although she was being let out in the early afternoon, I decided to go to a bar near the hospital and wait for the time to come. I felt like drinking but my sour stomach said "no", so I compromised by drinking vodka with Mylanta chasers. It was okay for a while till I cut a fart that smelled like burning poison. My stomach was rotting, I knew.

Although I was tipping more than I could afford, my second martini arrived without olives, and my water glass never got refilled. I was getting drunk. What was I going to do about a job? Sometimes, most of the time, I can't believe that I am a grown man—and almost middle age at that . . . and expected to make decisions regarding my life.

I've played. Badly. I've made stupid decisions and here I am. I don't want to make God angry, but what if I chose death? If life is a game, a wonderful game that people play and win and lose and win again and lose but then revive their strength with a big win, then I wish the players well. I've played, and I've lost, and I've lost, and I've won, and I've lost, and I've won a little bit, and I've lost, lost, lost! I am very tired. If death is sleep, a drowsy feeling of exhaustion— beyond comprehension—that's what I want. Would God forgive me if I chose that? I'm so ready, God. Grateful. No hard feelings. I tried. You helped. But I lost.

I blame no one. The chips were often stacked in my favor. I played unwisely. It's my fault. I accept my exhaustion.

Stop being such a baby, I scolded myself. *This isn't so bad. There's so many more things that could happen in life and will happen. So many experiences. Grow up. Experience it. Take a bit more on. Write a fucking tell-all book about what a bad person you are! It's all the rage! And add in all of Mikki's exploits too. You'd only have to take a very minimal amount of poetic license.*

I downed my third martini and headed to see the new Mikki emerge from the hospital.

51.

SHE HAD BEEN nothing. She didn't exist. Now they wanted her. They wanted to see what she looked like, hear what she had to say.

It must have been adrenalin running through her veins, although it felt more like bubbling volcanic lava. She had already been warned that the hospital's front entrance was jam-packed with reporters. The back door, too. In a very short while, her lifetime fantasy would be turned into reality. A famished, frenzied media would be before her. Starving for her. Ready and eager to record, for all eternity, her every movement, every sound, every expression. They wanted her.

Mikki Britten was front-page news. MY GOD!

What a pity she looked the way she did. She picked up the hand mirror at her side—she'd already grown used to the spectacular purple and black bruises, though now they were changing, starting to fade around the edges into many different lighter colors, predominantly yellow. Luckily her beauty was beginning to peak through again. *What will the reporters think of me*, she wondered to herself. *What will they ask?*

At first the nurses had refused to give her a mirror, but she talked a sympathetic doctor into giving her one, explaining to him that the reality of the damage couldn't be any worse than her fantasy of it.

With her first glance she seemed to be looking into a photograph of a stranger. Perhaps one of those abused and beaten women you see on television sometimes. Eyes swollen shut, the flesh underneath the eyes blown up like plum-colored water balloons. The upper lip exaggerated and comically swollen over the bottom one. The cream of her skin was desecrated with many angry red scratches, bruises, and gory stitches on her left cheek. The screams only started after she realized that she now looked the way she had always felt inside: beaten and ugly. Now everyone would know what she was. She'd been stripped of the only shield she had ever known. The rest became a blur. Screams and screams and screams. Nurses rushing in. A sedative administered.

But later, after she started reading the newspaper accounts of her ordeal and her life, she began to feel a lot better. Although the articles seemed to be about a girl she did not know—they had nothing to do with the real thoughts and feelings and incidents in the life of the real Mikki Britten, and the photos they printed were of her mask, her shield. The beautiful Mikki Britten. The seductive Mikki Britten. Mikki Britten the actress and model. That was the girl the world was reading about. And that was okay.

EVERYWHERE! EVERYWHERE THERE were photographers and reporters. Cameras were clicking, and video equipment was being held high, and people were calling her name. A doctor was at her side; her father, newly appearing in her life was on the other side, plus a barricade of investigators and policeman. Never had she felt so alive. So loved.

She had made it. She had crossed the line.

So I do exist after all, she thought.

52.

I WAS THERE. She spotted me in the crowd. Our eyes met for only an instant. I sort of half smiled, but in that terrifying instant of our locked eyes, I saw that something in hers had changed (what I saw in Madonna's eyes that night I met her years before came back to me). Then she scanned the mob for others. Justin Landis was there. And, surprisingly, Jonathan Christaldi, and almost everybody else she had been in contact with over the past five years, or more. Even high school classmates.

Her heart was beating wildly with excitement and joy, and also with the fear that she might do something wrong, say something stupid, or do something clumsy. The media was frantic, the crowd was pushing and screaming, and for a moment she looked disoriented—surprised at all the attention—confused that she was the center of it, although it had been expected. They were asking what her plans were. How did she feel? She wanted to respond, but it was all so peculiar.

She opened her mouth to say something, but no words came out. She was feeling every possible emotion, all at once so finally the bubbling volcano inside of her erupted. She could not speak. And then she was crying, the tears flowing freely down her face, and even the most hardened reporters were moved. She bowed her head and was whisked into the waiting car.

It was a great moment, wonderfully played. There was not a thing I could think of that she could have done that would have been more perfect.

MIKKI WEEPS the next day's headlines screamed.

I want to be very careful when I talk about this part of Mikki's life. Mikki Britten was brutally attacked and violated. She didn't court it. She didn't ask for it. She didn't deserve it. But it happened to her. And for one brief moment in time, all the eyes of the world were focused on her. And that's something she'd been striving for for a long time. So she had to make a move. I'm not saying that she wasn't wounded. I'm not saying that she treated it lightly. I'm just saying that she had very important decisions to make about how she would present herself, what her next steps would be. She had to tread very, very carefully.

It was only a moment in time, and it would never happen again.

DO YOU REMEMBER the first interview Mikki Britten gave after she left the hospital?

Few people who saw it will ever forget it. It took place at the ABC studios and was conducted by Kelly Blake of *IN FOCUS*, the most popular prime-time newsmagazine show. Mikki's face was still bruised and swollen in places, her hair clipped back simply. The camera pulled in close to be sure to capture every emotion that crossed her face. How fragile she seemed. She talked about how little she remembered of the violent incident. She said, no, she hadn't been reading most of the press coverage, although she had seen some of it. (This was not true; Mikki was fascinated with the stories circulating about her. Even the new, recent rumors that she had been a prostitute.) She said that she was "stunned" by the kindness of the public and thanked them for the thousands of letters, cards, and flowers. One woman had knitted her the sweater she was wearing. She said her doctors predicted that although there would be slight scarring, she would not need plastic surgery.

The TV audience sat riveted as the girl from the papers came vividly to life. Stunning photos from her modeling portfolio flashed across the screen, contrasting harshly with her temporarily ruined face. They tried to imagine her without the bruises. They were touched by her vulnerability, moved to tears by her bravery. But then suddenly the direction of the interview shifted gears when, without warning, Kelly Blake brought up the subject of the publicity she had been receiving. She asked the question very gently and hesitantly that if she felt that—in any way—her lifestyle might have led to the assault.

Pause, pause.

Mikki took a deep breath, looked up to the heavens, and returned her gaze to the woman interviewing her. She leaned back into her seat serenely, folded her arms, and narrowed her eyes.

"I'm trying very hard to think of a way to answer that question without making one of us come across as an asshole."

Kelly Blake, taken aback, looked momentarily nervous but quickly collected herself. "I thought you might want an opportunity to address this. It's what's being said. Here's your chance to clear the air."

She gave the interviewer a lopsided grin to soften the blow of her earlier remark. "I've read some of the things being written about me and it's amazing. I mean, where do they get this stuff from? Some of it is interesting. It makes for good copy. But it's not true . . . and that's what makes it vicious and hurtful."

"But you're an actress," Kelly pointed out. "And a model. When you pursue that kind of a career, you're setting yourself up for that kind of scrutiny. People feel they have a right to know."

"Of course," Mikki said. "I don't care if they write about me. I'm finally being written about—that's what people in show business want, no matter what they say. And if they don't want it, they should get out of the business. Nobody is forcing them to be in the spotlight. But the point is, I wish that they would cover it accurately. I'm very open and honest about myself. Yet everyone forms his or her own opinions of people. I can live with that. But it seems that they take a tiny detail of information and turn it into the most incredible lie."

Here the interview was edited, and the show cut to provocative shots of Mikki on a beach covered in sand, semi-nude, hair in face, orgasmic expression on her face—photographs that were taken, I remembered, for a suntan oil ad the year before. Then they showed clips of headlines about rich lovers and sex diaries, while a voice-over narration hinted at a promiscuous life. They cut back to a close-up of Mikki's face.

"Even if I did live my life that way," she was saying, "and I'm not saying I did, is it anybody's business? Do they have the right to judge? Whose life can stand up to such scrutiny? Can yours?"

They cut to Kelly's blank expression. Then back to Mikki and she said: "Let me say that, first off, I'm not ashamed of anything I've ever done in my life. Secondly, I don't think anyone who's been assaulted should be put in the position to have to defend themselves. There is no excuse for rape and, frankly, I'm shocked at the media for still making a woman's sexuality the issue in this day and age."

Now Kelly knew she was on to something and she pressed on. "Do you think the press is doing that?"

"Yes, I do. There seems to be this attitude that if a woman is sexual she's somehow responsible for being attacked. It's very disturbing—this insinuation that a woman's sexuality is frightening and dangerous. I think that's pretty ridiculous," she smiled crookedly again. "Don't you?"

What she was doing here, and only a trained eye like mine could see it, was pulling out all the Mikki tricks. She had been studying what the papers were saying about her, and in her mind she put all the accounts together and came up with the overall view of what the public expected her to be: a sensitive, vulnerable young lady who, when pushed, became a survivor—very much a woman of her time and place. And she was giving a deft, complex performance as the girl she had been reading about.

She was sharp enough to know that if she wanted her fame to last, she couldn't come out on her first show and play only the helpless, innocent victim. That was too one-dimensional. If she did that, she instinctively knew, the public would listen to her story, feel sympathetic for what she went through, be grateful that she was okay, and dismiss her from their minds. Tomorrow there would be a new tragic case to take her place, researched, written up, filmed, and edited before being served up to a ravenous public.

Don't get me wrong. I'm not saying that what Mikki said on this program wasn't necessarily her opinion, it's just that she knew that she had to present everything as part of an interesting, complex character so that the public would want to see more of her. And saying that a lot of what the press was reporting about her wasn't true, but leaving room for speculation that maybe some of it was, was a nice added touch. Now the public could decide for themselves what about her was true or untrue, allowing them to create even further in their minds their ideal of what they wanted her to be.

The following day Mikki's comments were in the headlines: MODEL VICTIM SEZ: STOP BLAMING WOMEN. Later in the week the papers reported that the *IN FOCUS* show featuring Mikki Britten was the highest-rated show in the program's history.

53.

WHEN *BEAUT* MAGAZINE was preparing its very first issue, the editors approached Mikki Britten about being their lead story. And she chose this magazine as the first publication to do a sit-down, in-depth print interview with because it was the only one that offered to put her fully on the cover. She was most anxious to see her newly-healed, once-again-beautiful face staring back at her from New York newsstands.

On the oversize, glossy cover Mikki, photographed by Steven Meisel, smiled radiantly, her hair long and tousled, glittering jeweled earrings hanging to her bare shoulders. There was no trace of any scars. MIKKI BRITTEN—OUT OF THE ASHES the headline said. Since this magazine was marketing to a young, trendy readership, Mikki did not want to concentrate on the attack. Instead she talked about her struggles before it occurred—mainly her struggles as an actress:

> "I've had years of casting directors not giving me the time of day. They'd cop an attitude like, 'Who do you think you are, you dizzy blonde whore? Go back to Queens and do nails.' That's where the real frustration and hurt comes in. When you're not even given a chance. I vowed to all those people who treated me like a piece of shit: Someday you're gonna want me."

> Mikki broke down and cried when she was asked about her friendship with the late Carla Christaldi: "She was the best friend I ever had. It's one of the biggest regrets of my life that I couldn't help her. I reached out to her, but she couldn't feel my touch. I couldn't reach her . . . I just couldn't reach her."

> In a flip, dismissive way, she talked about her brief affair

with Carla's father, Hollywood playboy Jonathan Christaldi: "He was rich and I was often hungry."

When asked about affairs with other rich men, Mikki gave the oft-quoted remark, "I believe in take, take, take, and give all you got—as long as you've got nothing to give."

MIKKI BRITTEN TURNED down all offers for a movie and a book about her life. She had no intention of capitalizing on the aspect of her life they wanted to focus on—which was the rape. She was putting that behind her and had no desire to see her life turned into a cheap TV movie with a mediocre fill-in-the-blank, tragedy-of-the-week script. Instead she signed with a top talent agency, and she told Liz Smith she was considering film offers. She rejected all the schlock horror films and lurid TV movies that at first came her way. She had waited long enough. She decided she could wait a little bit longer for the right project. The proper vehicle, she was sure, would present itself.

THAT NOVEMBER MIKKI signed her first record contract, a six-figure deal with a major label. She had never even considered a recording career, but why the hell not? Today movie actors make records, and sports stars do television, and writers make movies, and murderers write books. Look at all the markets she could saturate. Car radios, CD players, TV videos, her voice blaring out in club sound systems, her image on the large screen. Also it would be something else to publicize—entertainment talk show appearances, radio programs. *Mustn't let too much time pass,* she thought, *lest they forget me.*

Her first release from the album *Fever 103 Degrees,* went to number one in two weeks. Instinctively she contacted Jonathan

Christaldi to direct the video. Both of them realized the publicity value of working together and he agreed to direct it. What was her concept, he asked. She wanted it, she said, to be talked about. In the video—which was at first banned by MTV (an ingenious, if old-hat, publicity stunt) —Mikki lies on a sweat-soaked bed, her nakedness covered only by a thin white sheet. She writhes about seductively as she sings about the terrible fevers brought on by her lost love. At the end of the video she regally floats up to Paradise, where she tongue kisses another woman dressed in angel garb.

The banning of the video by MTV caused a major controversy and was hotly discussed on top television talk shows and in the newsmagazines. The video and song, Mikki argued, were based on a favorite poem by Sylvia Plath and were, therefore, not obscene, but art. In any case the song and video and Mikki Britten were all anyone talked about. Up-and-coming female singers started copying her look and aping her sexy, husky singing style. Comedians started doing Mikki Britten parodies. Her face and body were marketed on T-shirts.

Fever 103 Degrees was nominated for a Grammy.

JONATHAN CHRISTALDI: (to *Movieline* magazine) *I knew that Mikki Britten was a true star from the fist moment I laid eyes on her. There was something about her that made you take notice. Very few people today have what she's got.*

FROM "COAST TO COAST" COLUMN: Jonathan Christaldi has just signed the sizzling hot, yet very sexy-nasty-cool, Mikki Britten to star in his late daughter's screenplay *Fame, Trains and Other Sexual Fantasies*—originally titled *Mind Trips*. Carla Christaldi, once a close "gal pal" of Mikki's, died tragically last year, by a self-induced bullet to the brain, just before the movie, which she was set to star in, began filming. Since Carla's death Renée Zellweger and Cameron Diaz have been considered for the provocative role. "But Mikki Britten owns the part," Christaldi says. "Only Mikki has the perfect blend of mystery, sex, and vulnerability to make the character real."

Colin Farrell has also been signed to star in the film as a Manhattan hustler who falls in love with the Britten character.

LETTER FROM MARIO DEMARCO TO MIKKI BRITTEN: (This letter was returned to me, unopened, and marked return to sender.) Dear Mikki: It's been a long time since we last spoke. I know the last few months have been amazing for you and you have been incredibly busy, but I've been wondering how you are. I wish you would give me a call. You have nothing to be afraid of. I am, after all, still me. I still have your diaries and letters and stuff, and I've been wondering what the hell I should do with them. Also, while I'm on the subject, I've been thinking, well, how about me writing a book and all? I mean it looks like they're never going to catch those guys who did that terrible thing to you, and I was thinking that we could work on a book together, about your life before it happened. I'm sure the public would be interested. And who knows you better than me? Don't be silly—I know we'd have to leave certain things out. Ha. Do you ever feel guilty, Mikki? I do, but I won't bore you with my dreams and fears. You have to admit, though, it is strange the way that things have worked out. Listen, I read that you will be making our film, and I realize that I can't expect to be in it . . . maybe when it makes a mint, you could take care of me in some way? But I would love to hear from you, old friend. My number is exactly the same.

With genuine love,
Mario.

P.S. No hard feeling about Colin Farrell playing my part in the film. Well, I mean I do have hard feelings for him . . . but you know . . .

54.

MIKKI TOOK HER rightful place on the toilet in the bathroom stall. She had to pee, but the dress was too tight, too complicated to get out of. It involved toupee tape and all sorts of things she didn't want to know about in order to make the garment appear as if it were sprayed onto her body and to keep her boobs from popping out. From her beaded purse she took out an aluminum foil packet of heroin. Maybe she was feeling drained because of the hysteria outside the auditorium upon her arrival. Oh yes, she needed a boost.

This was The New York Film Critics Circle Awards. Very lavish. Before Mikki appeared, Charlize Theron. Renée Zellweger, Jessica Alba, and Scarlett Johansson all glamorously sashayed down the carpet outside the auditorium, causing a minor uproar. The fans cheered and snapped photos and begged for acknowledgment as the famous actresses made their way down the New York sidewalk that had been magically transformed into a thrilling walkway. Each star skillfully posed for the jockeying photographers, gave a few sound bites to the entertainment correspondents' cameras, and scrawled a couple of autographs before slinking into the auditorium, their publicists hot on their tails.

But it was as if the other celebrities' arrivals had all been a build-up for Mikki. When her limousine—twenty-five minutes late—pulled up, the collective tension was at a peak. The car door opened and complete madness broke out in the crowd. Mikki stepped out of the limo, and there was an explosion of flashing lights, while the mob—pushing and shoving and screaming—tried to descend on her like starving wolverines sniffing out fresh blood.

She was wearing a clingy, silvery dress, cut impossibly low in front, barely covering her nipples. Double-sided tape held the neckline in place so nothing slipped out. Police barricades held the frantic crowds at bay, the screaming throngs. "Mikki! Mikki," they chanted. They were clamoring to reach her, touch her, feel her to prove to themselves that she was real.

"Mikki! Mikki!" the paparazzi screamed. "Look here! Look here!" Any photo of Mikki Britten was bread to them. Her image was *that* valuable.

It was a very emotional moment, but her emotions were protected by a numbness brought on by the drugs. *Still*, she thought, *it's pleasant that they want me.*

The scene might have even been frightening, but she was surrounded by bodyguards and publicists and agents and God knows who else. She was gorgeously separate from the pandemonium around her. Fenced off. Protected, she seemed oblivious, in a happy place where she preened and pranced and posed. She seemed unaware of the major accident that occurred between a taxi and a van, as both drivers rubbernecked to get a look at Mikki Britten. Ambulances inched their way through the jam-packed streets, sirens wailing.

Only a few people were allowed to get at Mikki. The hostess for the red carpet segment on the E! Channel was ushered to her. She'd be allowed several seconds with Mikki to be televised to the masses.

"What's in your purse," the feisty, redheaded comedian, who made a living poking fun at celebrities, asked her as she gave her the once-over twice.

"An extra-strength diet pill and a breath mint," Mikki replied.

"Oh, so you packed for the weekend?" the comedian asked, missing not a beat.

In fact, what was in Mikki's purse was a lipstick, face powder, and the stash of heroin she now had in her lap in front of her as she sat in the bathroom stall.

Vaguely she could hear the ceremony going on outside. There would be some speech read off a monitor, a burst of laughter, a winner announced, and then a robust round of applause. It all seemed very far away. Mikki sniffed some heroin. She was nominated for her starring role in the summer's smash-hit film *Fame, Trains and Other Sexual Fantasies.*

In the scheme of things, she knew, this night was meant to be. She was exactly where she belonged, and everything that happened before this moment was out of her control. She was a pawn in life, among many pawns. Her problem had been that she always felt she had the power to move and maneuver the other pawns to help her get to where she was destined. Now she rationalized it was all out of her control.

She thought of Carla. Justin. Maybe even me. But, really, only in the abstract. As a metaphor, we were just deep, inconvenient puddles on a flooded street. She could learn to step over us (in high-heeled shoes) and blithely go on her way to the better things life had to offer. Better bets. More fun! Success! If she thought about anyone else, she'd be held back. "I chose to move on," she declared out loud. "I have no guilt in my heart." But even with her stone-cold rationale, a hint of guilt slipped in. Something was wrong that she should be here. It suddenly seemed selfish. Almost obscene. Unexpectedly, she was crying. She could not believe they had been chanting her name outside. "Mikki! Mikki Britten!"

Suddenly she realized that it was her name being called in the present. Now! She was being summoned to the stage! She had been named best dramatic actress in a motion picture!

She licked some remaining heroin off the package and her fingers, stuffed the package into her purse, and ran out of the bathroom, teetering through the lobby, up the stage stairs to the podium where a bemused Michael Douglas was waiting to hand her the award.

Disheveled. Teary. Out of sorts. She was astonishing and very sexy. "I was in the ladies' room," she purred, her eyes—particularly the right one—half closed. Ah, Mikki Britten. She was *real*. The beautiful mess. In an evening filled with artificial glitz, this was refreshingly unstaged and unrehearsed. The audience roared with genuine laughter for the first time that night. Mikki licked her lips. She giggled. Then she grew serious.

"There are so many stories that led me here," the stunning sociopath began. "I couldn't possibly tell them all. There are so many people responsible for this. But you know who you are. And you know how I feel about you. I thank you. I love you." The orchestra swelled up the music, signaling she was finished, and she began to teeter away. But swiftly she returned to the microphone. "And I have no guilt in my heart," she added breathlessly over the music. Then she was led away to many kisses and hugs administered by the waiting worshippers.

THE AFTER-AWARDS PARTY was not the smashing success she had envisioned. Oh, everyone was there, but she had seen them in action before. She sat at her table with a glazed smile, noticeably subdued. She was no longer having an interesting time. She was not at all moved by the elaborate goings-on—they were staged and phony and financed by the cosmetic company she had recently signed a multimillion-dollar contract with. It was all so ... so ... so temporary. So fake. Collagen-ballooned lips. Implanted breasts—pointing like missiles in every direction. What did she expect?

She should be working the room, chatting up journalists, giving different quotes and different spins on the movie, so that the coverage tomorrow would be lively and favorable. But it didn't matter anyway. Publicists would speak for her, agents would see to it that she came across magnificent, managers would call her with her next deal all wrapped up. Tomorrow she'd read about things that she said which had never left her lips, hear about deals that had been set up for her at this party. She'd go along with it.

For now, she sat at her table like a robot whose batteries were running down. Occasionally she remembered to nibble on something to squelch the rumors she had become anorexic. How cliché!

People continued to approach her, swoon over her, but it all sounded bogus ("You're even more beautiful in person"), and like sentimental dialogue from a Lifetime for Women film ("I'm very touched by your life"). All she ever wanted was to be accepted by these people. Now she was, but she didn't feel a thing. What was wrong with her? She looked into the faces of all the show-business luminaries as they made important business deals over the expensive hors d'oeuvres, and they all seemed to be having moments of uncomplicated happiness. And she felt nothing for them—no love, no admiration, nothing—so she tried an experiment, saying to herself, *God bless them.* But, really, she couldn't care less if He did or He didn't. Where did God fit in? These people seemed to be able to take care of themselves.

And she continued to watch them, drunk with bitterness, because she still did not feel like one of them. She was acidly annoyed when Jonathan Christaldi stood up, wine glass in hand, and said, "Mikki, I know that your winning this award is only the beginning. You're going to have a magnificent career, and I want to be right there beside you every step." It surprised her. She thought of what he felt about her less than a year before. "Thank you, Jonathan," she spat out contemptuously, raising her own champagne flute. "I feel exactly for you, what you feel for me." At the present moment she knew her position with him was safe. There was nothing newer or better than her that could possibly come along. For now she was the most famous woman in the world. There was no one higher.

For most of the rest of the night, she sat discontentedly at the table. She felt she was coming up short, disappointing somehow. Still, she couldn't possibly get bored; it was too much of a spectacle. Every so often she took a stab at making the kind of conversation they'd all understand—with mixed results. Why couldn't she feel like one of them? She needed to be raised to the next plateau.

Somewhere she'd suddenly fit in. But where? Where?

There's always a moment. She's holding up. She's doing well. She's saying hello to people, making small talk. Doing fine. They're glad to see her. And suddenly she runs out of people to say hello to, things to chat about. She locks eyes with a familiar someone, but they look away. They don't want to talk to her. There's always a moment when she runs for shelter in the ladies' room. A locked stall where she can be alone and recuperate.

That's where she snorted more heroin in an attempt to *feel* something—all the while thinking how she had never been older (twenty-eight) and how she had never had more people say that they love her. This award, she had a feeling, probably meant that she would win the Academy Award, *and after that my life will REALLY begin.*

She went back to the table, and she kept on drinking, and she got more and more drunk. She was flying, and she felt a sudden pang, a stab of pain, of undetermined origin. She wanted to go home. But there was no one to call to talk it all over with.

And Jude Law came over to the table to congratulate her, and he told her how much he admired her performance, and the kind of sex appeal he exuded was something she could feel so she lifted her head and smiled and flirted with him while Jonathan Christaldi glared.

Then everyone was up and leaving and saying good-byes and she said to herself, *It's over! It's over! I made it through!*

Minutes later, while they were leaving, Jonathan Christaldi, furious now, raged at her. He had noticed all kinds of gestures and eye contact, all night, between her and Jude Law, and other men, too. It turned into an argument as she tried to convince him that it was all in his imagination. Not that she cared really; she could hardly remember a thing. But he raised his voice and gripped her roughly by the arm, and flashbulbs were popping so she ran away.

She ran down the steps, into the night, into the pouring rain, past the waiting limo. She was four blocks away before she realized how stupid this was. She was blinded by the rain and wearing a tissue-paper-thin silver dress. She tried to get a cab, but they all zoomed past her. She started walking again, slowed by the wind and the incredible rain, and she knew that it was impossible to walk the thirty blocks to her apartment. A cab headed her way, and she ran to the street and raised her hand but it zipped by her, drenching her with a tidal wave of freezing water. She had her purse, but she had forgotten the award. She had left the prize behind. And she leaned against a building and cried. The sky cried too—cold, hysterical tears biting into her face and body.

And when she finally looked up, she saw looming in the not-too-far-away distance two big, round green lights that indicated the subway. Everything in her told her not to do it. But she was ankle deep in water and the only alternative she could think of was to throw herself in the gutter.

So she headed toward the subway.

SHE SAT ON the subway bench and cried. Cold. Wet. Alone, of course. In spite of her gloriously successful night, she allowed herself to feel sorry for herself. Why not? There was no one else to do the job.

Suddenly she became aware of the danger here on the subway. She was nearly naked. Someone might recognize her, and then God knows what would happen. Chaos would ensue. But it was late on a Saturday night. Everyone was drunk. And a lot of people had been out and were dressed up and were soaking wet. She fit in okay.

A man with blue-black skin limped toward her, chewed-up Styrofoam cup outstretched before him. Barefoot. Wearing only dirty tattered shorts and a ski mask pulled down over his face. "Please, folks, I don't steal. I don't rob. All I'm asking for is a dime or a quarter." Impulsively she took off her gaudy diamond earrings, given to her earlier that evening by Jonathan Christaldi, and plopped them into his cup. "Thanks. God bless," he mumbled and continued on his way.

I am rich. I am famous. I have just won an important award for a film in which I am the star.

Two Spanish girls sat down on the bench next to her. Cracking gum. They were actresses. "Did you ever do student films?" one of them was asking the other. " . . . it was a good e'sperience but . . ." And they proceeded to exchange amateur acting stories. She leaned over to look at them. She wanted them to see that she was not like them. *I made it! I made it!* Her wet hair fell in her face. They ignored her. A train's headlights loomed in the distance, the familiar gust of air pushed forward. Everybody stood up and moved forward.

I have my own huge apartment in Manhattan. I am in the process of buying a rambling house in the Hollywood Hills. I am rich. I am famous. I am loved. I am . . .

The Spanish girls cracked their gum and waited. Mikki continued to stare at them. It seemed that in that moment everything was happening exactly as it should. Fast and out of her control. Crack, crack, crack. "I wanna see that new Mikki Britten movie," one of the girls said. The train pulled into the station. Mikki stared at the girls in disbelief. Could it be? *They don't know it's me*, she thought with giddy panic. It didn't seem possible—after all she had been through! After all that had gone into creating herself. All that led to this moment. Don't they read the papers? Surf the Internet. Listen to the radio? Don't they watch TV? She was fucking everywhere!

Carla, she remembered, once quoted Arthur Conan Doyle to her: "Mediocrity knows nothing higher than itself."

And then, suddenly, Mikki was laughing. She couldn't stop herself—it burst out of her. People stopped to stare, pausing in their conversations, looking up from their newspapers or away from the approaching train. It grew wilder, her laughter. *Who cares? What does it matter what they think? They don't know who I am!* Hysterical inhuman, laughter—originating from someplace deep inside of her—growing louder and louder. Uncontrollable! Traveling from one end of the grimy platform to the other. Her body shook with laughter, the subway tunnels echoed with it, the sound bouncing off the filthy tiled walls, throwing it back in her face like an insult, like spit.

Nobody knows who I am!